KAMINORIGA

D.C. FRENCH

MINERVA PRESS
LONDON WASHINGTON MONTREUX

KAMINORIGA

ISBN 1 85863 151 3

First published 1995 by
MINERVA PRESS
1 Cromwell Place
London SW7 2JE

Printed in Great Britain by
Ipswich Book Company Ltd., Ipswich, Suffolk.

KAMINORIGA

FOR IAN CAIRD

FROM THE AUTHOR.

ABOUT THE AUTHOR

David C. French is an engineer who has resided in, and travelled widely throughout Nigeria. He has met many peoples of different tribes in his travels.

He has strived to weave local colour into the events described in this first novel set in Africa.

ACKNOWLEDGEMENTS

I am greatly indebted to the late Sir Alan Burns G.C.M.G., formerly Governor of Nigeria. His detailed history of this former British Colony, has greatly assisted me in the verification of information contained in this story.

DISCLAIMER

Old mariner's saying:

"*Beware, beware the Bight of Benin,*
Where few come out, but many go in."

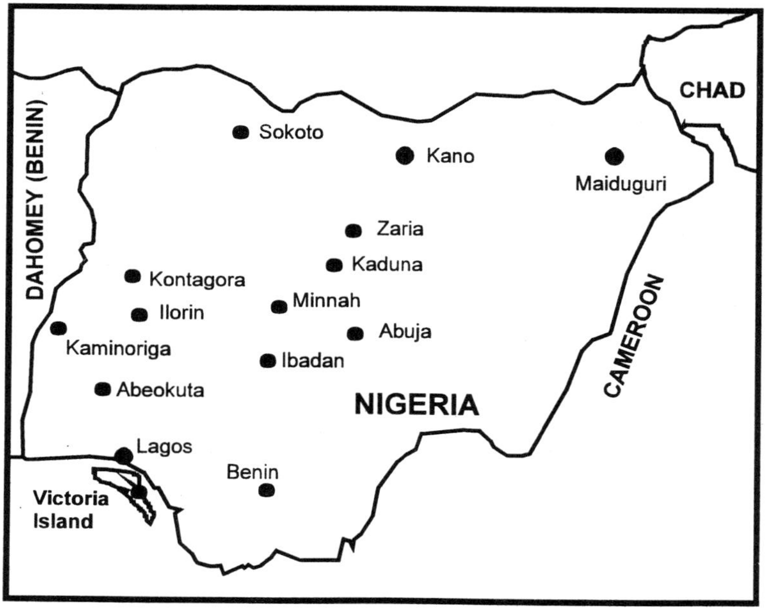

Cities and Towns

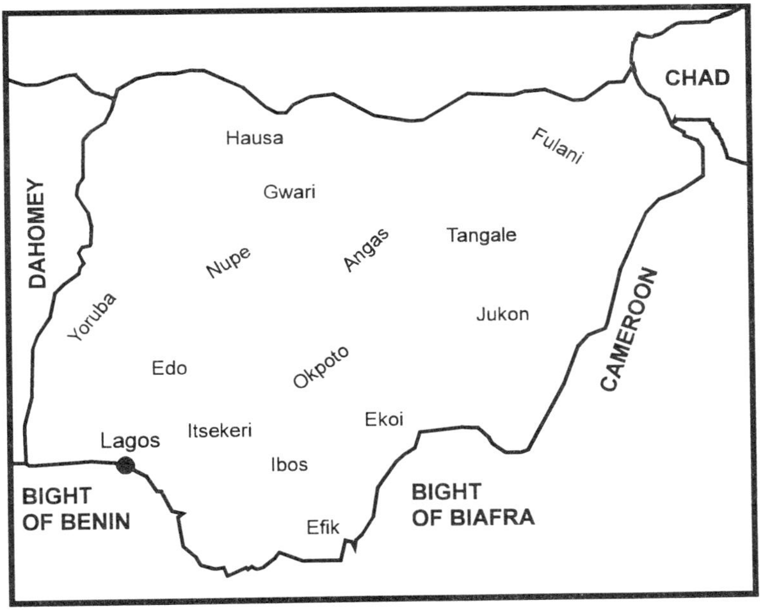

Main Tribal Distribution and Language Origins

Chapter One

At the end of the bar sat two figures. One hunched up on a stool legs tucked inwards, peering occasionally into his pint of lager whilst studying his copy of *The Racing Times*, the other assuming a statuesque appearance, although occasionally one could detect some indication of life, as it appeared to move, albeit slowly, and was engaged in the ritual of slow but methodical meticulous glass polishing, an art perfected over many years. John McDonald sat silently taking an occasional sip from his glass. Tom Fleming, the barman busied himself with nothing in particular. They were usually the only two people in the bar at this early hour of eleven-thirty in the morning.

The telephone rang shrilly, shattering the silence. Tom raised his eyebrows over the edge of the glass he had been polishing and held it against a ray of light that streamed in from a corner window. Putting the glass back alongside its contemporaries, he shuffled slowly down to the opposite end of the bar during which time the impatient apparatus continued its noisy penetration of the silence some five times. He threw his bar towel over his shoulder expertly and picked up the receiver with his right hand.

"Hello! Tom's Bar here, Tom speaking."

There was a slight hesitation at the other end, Tom could hear some paperwork being shuffled then a cultured voice said, "Hello? Do you have a man by the name of John McDonald there?"

Tom turned half to his left and answered, "Yes, he's here. Do you want to speak to him?"

"Yes, please," said the voice, ever so politely.

Tom let the receiver dangle downwards, suspended on its distended cord, and turning further to his left he said quietly, "It's for you, Johnny boy!"

John looked up from his glass which he had been contemplating for some time and shifting his rump from the bar stool, he clambered down and made his way to the end of the bar and the swinging telephone receiver. Tom meanwhile, had padded slowly back to the business end of the bar and had busied himself with the reorganisation of the bottles producing loud clanking noises and the scraping of wooden crates on the floor.

John picked up the receiver and said, "Hello!"

"Is that John McDonald?"

"Ay, it is!" said John guardedly.

"Well, you don't know me," said the voice, continuing, "but my name is Frank Timms of Consolidated Construction of London, and I was informed by a colleague of mine, that I could reach you on this number."

John wondered who this colleague might be, and it occurred to him that no-one really knew where John was located so he was somewhat intrigued by that statement.

"Oh, I see." said John. "What can I do for you, then?"

"I hear that you are currently out of work but available. Am I correct in that assumption?"

"Well aye, you'd be right, so to speak."

"That's just what I'd thought you'd say," said Frank. "I've got a proposition for you which is really too long to go into over the phone, so can I suggest that we meet to discuss it? Say later in the week?"

"Aye, okay then." said John, not indicating any firm commitment.

"Fine," said Frank. "I'd like to meet you, say on Thursday if that's convenient, and I'll send off an air ticket for you in today's post which should get to you tomorrow, Tuesday. Also included will be a map and details of the address and how to get there, etc. Does that sound all right to you?"

John thought for a moment before replying. Must be important if they're willing to fly me down there but what the hell, at least I can go and see what it's all about anyway.

"Yes, that sounds all right to me," he replied, in a typically Scottish brogue.

"Right then," said Frank. "I'll get that off to you immediately and I'll look forward to meeting you on Thursday, say about eleven-thirty in the morning, and by the way, I can assure you that your time won't be wasted at all. Where do you want me to send the ticket?"

John thought for a moment, he could have given Frank the address of his bedsit that he rented cheaply which was about half a mile from Tom's Bar, but then that would mean his landlady knowing his business. As it was painfully obvious that she was of the nosy type, he had strongly suspected that she had steamed open his mail in the past and had perused the contents. He decided that Tom's Bar was the safest place to have it delivered to. Tom was a lifelong friend, companion and confidante all rolled into one, so Tom's Bar was the logical choice.

"You can send it to the bar here," said John, "it'll reach me quicker."

"Just as you wish," Frank replied and noted down the brief address and added, "See you Thursday then, John."

"Well, thanks," replied John, "see you then."

John had not hung up the receiver, he had remained standing there mesmerised, when he heard Tom's voice from the end of the bar saying, "Well, are you in love with that thing, or are you going to hang it up?"

This caused John to return to reality and he quickly hung up the receiver and without comment made his way back down the bar to his vacant stool which was directly opposite Tom and clambered onto it. He shifted his rump into its normal comfortable position, his hand mechanically forming round the glass. He raised it and took a long, slow draught before lowering it to the polished bar top and finally looked at Tom.

"Well, then!" said Tom, in an exasperated tone of voice. "What was that all about?" Tom was anxious to know so he continued looking directly at John's eyes.

John said, "Some bloke from London wants me to see him on Thursday."

"And," said Tom, "are you going then?"

"Yes," replied John, "I'd better really, eh?"

"I'd say you'd better!" exclaimed Tom with a menacing tone in his voice. "It's about time you did something positive with your life, you've been hanging about here for ages now with a face as long as a fiddle, about time you sorted yourself out!"

"Aye, well, I suppose you're right, Tom," said John, again lapsing into thought.

"Bloody right I am!" exclaimed Tom, "and I'll tell you another thing," John looked up, somehow half expecting what he knew would be said next. Tom continued, "If I so much as hear from you that you've turned this, whatever job it is, down, then I'm personally going to kick your arse all the way down the corridor and back again! Is that understood?"

John's expectancy was confirmed, he had no doubt that Tom would carry out his threat if he defaulted so he replied, "You'd really do that to me?"

"You bet I would!" said Tom. "No doubt about it, mate!"

Tom grinned, John grinned, they both instinctively looked at the top shelf of the bar where Tom kept a bottle of finest Scotch Whisky 'for special occasions' and without further ado it was uplifted, dusted off and two large, heavy whisky glasses were placed on top of the bar, while Tom proceeded to fill them up with the amber nectar. Leaving the top off the bottle, a rare occasion for Tom, he passed the glass over to John in silence. Both of them then lifted their glasses to their noses to savour the scent of the highlands, and Tom said, "Right then, John, me boy! Here's to success!"

Where was the photographer John thought to himself. "I'll drink to that!" said John, and they both took a swig, savouring the warm burning feeling as the liquid descended slowly into the depths of the stomach.

Two days later, John was prepared for his trip by air, having dug out what he thought he might need, past references, his curriculum vitae, a résumé, some spare photographs, his battered passport, medical certificates and some other administrative bumph, along with his grey suit.

He arose early on the Thursday morning and he had left early in order that he would arrive at the airport well in advance of his flight, even though the check in time was only twenty minutes before the departure for London.

He purchased a newspaper and mechanically read it as he waited for the flight. The familiar tones sounded on the public address system reminding him of the Avon lady's tones, as the cultured voice announced, "Will all passengers for flight BA5613 for London Heathrow, please proceed through Gate Number Two to the departure lounge." A throng of people mingled around the doorway of Gate Two, forming a ragged bunch, each clutching their boarding cards and tickets and commenced to filter through the restriction and down the short corridor to the lounge. A snake had formed in front of the ultraviolet detector gate, he joined it and waited his turn for the routine procedure of stepping through it, a brief body search by a male person, pity it wasn't a female person, he thought, as he noted a slim but attractive brunette standing to his right. His briefcase disappeared into the tunnel on the conveyor belt and continued its short journey of some eight feet or so, then reappeared at the other side. He collected it and wandered down to the end of the lounge and sat down on one of the stools which were dotted around.

He cast his eyes around and surveyed the scene. There was the usual motley collection of passengers. An old man with a large handlebar moustache wearing a herring bone patterned suit, years out of fashion, and a black Homberg, sitting busily attacking that day's Daily Telegraph crossword. He was deep in thought, statuesque, but sporadically bursting into life with short jabs of his pen as he jotted down a word here and there, at the same time emitting a loud hurrumph. A young woman with a mischievous three-year-old child on her lap was busily attempting to control the child's behaviour with a, "Now darling, don't do that now! Won't you?" to which the ever disobedient child continued her misbehaviour. Two elderly women nearby clucked and tutted in obvious disapproval and cast disapproving glances at the incompetent mother. A clutch of businessmen in identical suits formed a colony of clones, each sporting the inevitable black briefcase, folded up newspaper - *The Times* - and another case of samples and wares. John sat gazing through the soundproofed glass panels as a newly-arrived aircraft taxied to a halt away to his left. He thought, I hope that I don't have to sit next to the now screaming child on the aircraft.

The flight was called, mobilising the semi-inert crowd, who competed with each other to be first to get through the exit gate as if their life depended upon it. He strolled across the apron and joined the short queue waiting to climb the steps. He was greeted with a friendly smile by a fresh-faced stewardess neatly turned out in the company's livery and who conducted him to his seat in Row 10, a window seat. He settled in after placing his briefcase in the overhead locker. Two businessmen approached and sat adjacent to him. He soon became bored with their incessant conversation, long before the aircraft was pushed backwards and taxied to the far end of the runway to its take-off position.

The flight was mainly uneventful; he had breakfast, read the newspaper from front to back and by the time they had arrived in London just over an hour later, he was glad to escape the continuous monotonous flow of facts and figures about profit and loss accounts and forecasts. He exited onto the flexible walkway to a cheery wave from the cabin crew. He joined the sheep as they jostled each other for pole position, as if in a race, and walked steadily following the signs marked 'Arrivals Hall'. He descended the escalator and wandered over to the carousel where he awaited his small overnight bag which he had brought along with him. An interminable wait ensued and eventually his bag appeared, it being one of the last. He picked it up and proceeded towards the rail service exit for the centre of London.

Approximately one hour later he arrived at King's Cross and made his way up the escalators and along numerous corridors amid a throng of cosmopolitan people, each bent on reaching their destination with a sense of urgency and determination. He caught another tube and alighted at a quiet station and proceeded along a busy street until he found the building he was seeking. He ran his finger down the list of companies within. He noted that the building was an imposing structure of glass and steel with a heavily marbled front. He stopped his finger as it reached the wording about two-thirds of the way down the tablet, and read it off. 'Consolidated Construction Limited, fifth floor'. He pushed open the door and proceeded over to the lift and pressed the button. The lift stopped, the door opened and revealed a few office types, a businessman, a man in overalls displaying the words 'Maintenance' and 'Chief Electrician' in large white letters on his back, which he saw in the mirror in the lift. He entered, pressed the button and the lift ascended in total silence. Funny how people in lifts never talk, he thought to himself, as if there were some unspoken rule in effect. After two halts the lift came to a stop at the fifth floor. John alighted into a thickly-carpeted corridor. He followed the sign indicating 'Consolidated' and walked along two right angled corridors until he reached the office door. He pushed it open and stepped into a brightly lit reception area. Behind the desk sat an attractive semi-blonde haired woman whom he estimated to be about forty years of age. She looked up from her typewriter as John approached and said, "Good morning! Can I help you?"

"I'm John McDonald," he said, with an emphasis on the latter word, "I've come to see Frank Timms."

"Oh, yes!" she replied, "he's expecting you." She moved a carefully manicured finger lazily over to the intercom and silently pressed the button.

At the other end a voice responded, "Yes, Susie, what is it?"

"Mr McDonald from Scotland, to see you."

"Ah, good! Show him in, will you, Susie."

Susie fluttered her eyes at John, while he did a quick take of her shapely figure, big bust and the generally well-rounded curves. She arose from her seat and took a few steps towards Frank's door, John's eyes followed the shapely form and took in all the salient details and momentarily savoured the physical attributes before following her, noting the heady scent as they reached the door of Frank's office. Her breasts strained for release but his attention was interrupted by Frank himself, who had got up from behind his busy desk to reach across with outstretched arm and hand to welcome John.

"Come on in, John, and sit down!" John accepted the warm handshake noting its firm grip. How he detested those people whose handshake was akin to a bit of damp lettuce.

"Glad you came, John," said Frank. "Take a seat," indicating a plush leather chair next to John and turning to Susie he said, "Susie, let's have some tea and biscuits, there's a dear."

"Certainly!" said Susie, "just be a few minutes, Frank." A short silence followed during which the two pairs of eyes followed her every movement outwards, and the shapely rear fast disappearing behind the slowly closing door. Some ten or so seconds had passed since the vision had disappeared, during which there had been total silence.

"Nice isn't it?" enquired Frank.

"Certainly is!" said John, "I take it you're not married then?"

"No," said Frank, "always too busy and anyway I never seem to find the time to get involved, one way or another."

John recalled his former marriage which had lasted about eight years and had ended in divorce; a combination of circumstances. He was frequently away from home for long periods and when he was there he rarely saw his wife at all. Inevitably she had gone off with someone else and the resulting long, drawn-out proceedings had left him financially drained and also at a loose end, with no sense of purpose. He returned to the present.

"Maybe just as well," said John in a committed tone of voice, "Methinks you're better off that way!"

"Well," said Frank, "let's get down to business, then."

"Certainly," said John, placing his bag down on the floor. "What is it you have in mind?"

"I've got an interesting position here, John, and I believe that you will definitely be interested in it, and that you are the type of person I am looking for."

"And what sort of person would that be?" asked John, a faint smile upon his face.

"I'll lay my cards on the table, John," continued Frank. "I already know that you are a man of experience in the construction industry and of your achievements in the past, overseas."

"Do you mind if I ask where you got your information from?" asked John.

Frank paused and smiled, "Well, we have our ways as you probably know, John. I make a point of doing my homework thoroughly beforehand so I can assure you that in my opinion you are the right man for the job, so to speak, at least as far as I'm concerned."

John looked briefly at Frank, wondering to himself from what sources Frank had dug up the information. He thought back to numerous firms and agencies he had worked for in the past but could not come up with an answer.

"I see," he said, noncommittally, "let's have it then! What's it all about?"

"First of all," said Frank, "let's have a drink, eh?" And he swivelled round on his leather chair.

"Thanks!" said John, "that would be nice."

Frank retreated to the rear of the office where an expensively made bar occupied the window area. John cast his eyes around the office meanwhile, and noted the plush appearance of its contents; a large, walnut desk with an accompanying smaller desk on which sat a computerised system with visual display units, keyboard and printer, all neatly arranged. Alongside stood a box of discs with various alphabetical and numerical references. Must cost a bomb this lot, thought John to himself. The carpet was deep piled and a lavender shade. A few expensive looking oil paintings were hung professionally around the walls and numerous plants and ferns gave an exotic flavour to it all. The bar which Frank had moved over to and had disappeared behind was well-appointed. Rows of expensive glasses sat alongside an ice bucket.

The sound of bottles clinking together accompanied Frank's reappearance and John noticed that he was carrying a tray upon which a small collection of bottles were perched, and without further comment Frank asked, "What's your poison then, John?"

"Eh, whisky, if you've got it, Frank ..."

"No trouble there," said Frank, "what do you prefer? The Famous Grouse, Bells or The Macallan?"

"I'll have Mr Macallan," said John, pleasantly surprised that his favourite drink was at hand.

"Ice or not?"

"No ice, thanks, just by himself."

"Okay," replied Frank, smiling, "Coming up!"

Frank produced two large glasses and proceeded to pour the whisky for John and a brandy for himself. John noted that no measure was used and quite a few 'fingers' had jugged into the glass before the bottle was raised. There must be about half a pint in that, he thought to himself.

Frank made his way slowly back to his desk and put the glasses down on either side of it. John picked up his, it was heavy and dimpled. He took a whiff of the familiar scent savouring it, before holding it up to the light to appreciate its fine colour and finally taking a sip. The taste and aroma as it passed over his tongue brought an instant warm glow and the accompanying smouldering sensation as it descended towards his stomach heralded the feeling of complete satisfaction. Frank meanwhile, had taken a swig of his brandy and had mulled it around before returning the glass to the top of the desk.

"Well then, John," he went on, "let me fill you in about this position. It's the construction of a dam at a place named Kontagora in Nigeria and it's been in progress for about two years now."

"Must be well on by now then?" commented John.

"Well, not exactly, and that's the problem, John," said Frank. "It's behind schedule so that is why we need you to sort it out for us. We've had to release two of the staff there, the manager, and one of the senior engineers. There's been a bit of trouble as well."

"What sort of trouble?" asked John, raising his eyebrows as he said it.

"Apparently, there's been a problem with the local labour force, some friction caused by the local women and some unexplained disappearances of plant and equipment from various sites."

"Sounds like a real bundle of fun!" John commented.

"Yes, I'd thought I would tell you about that first of all before I said anything else, understood?"

"Perfectly," said John, "sounds as if it's a tall order, then!"

"You could put it that way," added Frank, "but I'd like to know what you think of it so far?"

"Nothing out of the usual for big projects by the sound of it, although I'll need to know some more details. When do you reckon I'd need to start?"

"About three to four weeks from now I'd say, John, but if you are prepared to go I'll have to organise an official invite for you, then a visa and a few other things. What sort of money would you be looking for, John?"

John said nothing, his mind sifting through the information he had had so far, weighing up each piece and evaluating it before trying to reach a decision.

"How about thirty thousand tax free, then?" said Frank, his face completely devoid of any emotion. John still remained silent. John thought to himself, well, not bad, and he was just about to comment when Frank said, "Well all right then, thirty-five thousand!" John was surprised and said quietly to himself, thirty-five eh? Frank met his gaze eye to eye. Neither said anything, and John was just about to accept when Frank again intervened and said, "Well, all right then, I thought that you might not bite, so let's say fifty thousand tax free!" John couldn't believe his ears! Fifty grand was the most he had ever been offered. That would keep him handsomely for quite some time to come but before he could reply, Frank added, "That's for three years with a further optional two year maintenance contract, all tax-free, paid wherever you want it, as far as tax evasion goes!"

John sat dumbfounded, he couldn't believe his luck! It was all too good to be true. Tom would never believe this, he thought to himself.

"Well, what's your opinion so far, John?"

John looked up at one of the oil paintings on the wall depicting a black stallion with a horseman mounted upon it and wielding a curved scimitar.

Into battle, thought John. He looked up at Frank and with a slight smile on his face, said, "Yes, Frank, that sounds interesting enough and acceptable."

"Good! I'd thought you might go for that, we badly need a steadying hand, John, and I couldn't pull the wool over your eyes. I somehow feel that you are the right man for the job, but you may have a tough time of it."

"I'll cross my bridges when I come to them," said John. "I've always found that that is the best way to tackle problems, after many years of expedience!"

"Good!" exclaimed Frank, "I'm glad that's settled then!" At this point they were interrupted by the door quietly swinging open and Susie appeared with the promised tea and a plate of half covered chocolate biscuits. She placed a cup in front of each of them and poured out the tea, leaning slightly forwards as she did so. John's eyes were immediately drawn to her cleavage which presented itself revealing a white lace-trimmed bra descending into a shadowy valley. It was all too much really and he was glad that he didn't have to survey that all day long as it would be too much to contend with, he thought. Susie completed the pouring of the tea and retreated quietly and exited the door, followed by the two pairs of silent eyes. They returned to normality and helped themselves to the tea and biscuits.

Frank pulled a file from a drawer and opened it. "I have here a specimen contract, John, if you want to look at it, perhaps you'd care to read through it?"

John took it from him and glanced through it, making some mental notes as he went along. It was perfectly straightforward, with no traps or other ambiguities and he soon came to the last page of it.

"I'll have Susie fill in the relevant parts for you, John, and you should get it within the next few days or so, will that be all right?"

"Yes. Fine," said John.

Frank leaned over to the intercom. Susie's voice replied.

"Yes, Frank?"

"Ah, Susie, can you come through and collect John's contract, I've pencilled in the relevant parts for you."

"Be right there," she replied and the intercom fell silent. She appeared as if by magic, silently retrieved the multi-paged contract and just as silently she left, her every movement being followed again by the watchful eyes. The door clicked shut and they both returned to the present.

"I'll get that off to you as quickly as possible, I take it that the same address will suffice again?"

"Yes, that'll do fine."

"Good, I can get a flight booked for you, then, and an overnight stop in a hotel, and all the other details will be ready for you before you actually leave."

They continued to talk of other things for some time and managed to quaff their now re-constituted drinks with relative ease.

"I'll give you a ring nearer the date just to make sure that everything is in order and we'll take it from there."

"Yes indeed, that'll be just fine," responded John.

Frank escorted John to the elevator, the two of them having to pass once again, the curvaceous figure of Susie on the way. I don't know how Frank can stand it! John thought to himself as they parted, Susie producing a flashing smile through the part open doorway.

He made his way back to Heathrow, had a cup of tea and a snack in a restaurant and caught his flight northwards. The aircraft was half empty and he had plenty of attention from the cabin crew. He read the London evening paper but did not absorb any of it at all. His mind was taken up with the unbelievable amount of money he had been offered, the problems he would have to face and the general mulling over of the information on hand.

He arrived at his destination and was soon homeward bound in a taxi, first of all making a stop at Tom's Bar. He thrust a ten pound note in the driver's hand as the taxi pulled up and shouted back over his shoulder, "Keep the change, mate!" and burst through the door of the bar. It was quiet within, as usual, a few patrons scattered around but the bar itself vacant save for Tom himself, the only fixture in his normal stance, overseeing his clients and occasionally peering at the television set mounted high up on a shelf in the corner.

"Thought he'd be here about this time," he said aloud, and, turning towards John who by now had slid on to his normal seat at the bar he said, "It'll be the usual then?"

"No it bloody won't!" John said, almost unable to contain himself. "It'll be the whisky! Make it a double and have one yourself!"

"Oh, hoh!" said Tom with raised eyebrows, "a fine kettle of fish this is! The customer telling the barman what he is to drink!"

"Just you get that in the glasses!" John ordered, "and never mind the protocol!"

"Struck gold then, or something?" Tom asked.

"Aye! You could say that in a way!" John replied.

"Well! Just don't stand there like a tailor's dummy! Out with it!"

"You'll never believe me!" said John.

"Try me!" said Tom, "mine ears are for you alone, mein herr!"

"Okay then, Tom, how much for a job in Nigeria for three years then?"

"No idea!" said Tom.

"How about fifty?"

"Quid a day?" asked Tom.

"No, you bloody fool! Fifty thousand a year!"

"You did say thousand, didn't you?"

"Sure did!" replied John, grinning from ear to ear.

Tom looked at him for a moment then said, "You can pay me your bill now then, seventy-four quid it is you're owing me!"

Typical barman, thought John to himself, all he can think about is his profits and the cash in the till!

"Of course! Of course!" said John hurriedly. "I've been waiting for something like this to happen for years!"

"I'm glad it has," said Tom, "now I can get rid of that sour-faced puss that perches on the end of my bar every day, moping around!"

"Who's that then?" asked John, grinning from ear to ear.

"That's the first time I've seen you grin for ages!" said Tom, "must be an all time record!" They had quite a few drinks, both of them now in a jovial mood.

Later on, John made his way back to his bedsit, whistling as he went, and on entering gave a cheery wave to the landlady who was shocked and clearly taken aback, not to mention speechless, at this unusual approach. I bet she's dying to know why I am so cheerful, he thought to himself. Anyway, that would give her something to think about for some time!

The remainder of the week went by at a sedate pace. Three weeks had now passed since his visit to Frank's office, the unforgettable curves of Susie still imprinted on his mind. Each time he thought of the job he had accepted, he thought of Susie.

Frank had forwarded his contract a few days after their meeting and John had read through it carefully, had signed the final page and dated it, and returned a copy to Frank by the same day's post. Shortly afterwards, he had received a registered envelope which contained a cheque for a thousand pounds, marked 'advance of expenses' and accompanied by a brief note from Frank saying that this was to enable him to buy whatever clothes, etceteras, he needed and anything else of relevance that sprang to mind. As long as Frank got receipts back at a later date that would suffice.

John had gone on a shopping spree, buying a few changes of light clothing suitable for tropical climates, a number of pairs of shorts, four pairs of desert boots at a knockdown price of six pounds per pair. He reckoned that four pairs would be enough to last him three years or so, so he chose them in a light beige colour with moulded soles for work and casual wear. He also made a point of buying himself a good quality camera with a telephoto lens, a folding pocket compass and a pair of range-finding binoculars with an infra-red beam. He tested them out on a few prominent landmarks and he was pleased to find that they were indeed accurate to plus or minus one metre, and that they were built to military specifications and coloured jungle green, with a protective case and strap. Meanwhile, he had paid Tom his dues and had some surplus money left to cover his drinks up until the time he was due to leave for Nigeria.

A few days later, Frank called while John was studying *The Racing Times*, perched on his usual bar stool. He had alighted from his stool, picked up the receiver and stuck his head inside the acoustic hood.

"Hello. Is that you John?"

"Yes, this is me, Frank, and by the way, thanks for the expenses you sent me! I thought that it was a bit much though!"

"Not to worry," said Frank, "things cost a lot these days, more than you'd think, just make sure that you have everything you think you will need as I understand that it is difficult to get anything once you are out there, at least where you're going to."

"All right then Frank, have you any more news for me?"

"Yes, I have. I've got your visa in front of me and I've booked a flight down to London for you, that's to Heathrow, for Wednesday of next week, an overnight stay in a hotel and a car the following day back to the airport for the overseas flight on the following morning to Lagos which should get you in to there about five or six in the evening. If there is any last minute changes then of course I'll let you know. I'll send off your ticket first class to you, so you should get that tomorrow morning. I can't think of anything else but if there's anything I can do for you, just give me a ring."

"I don't think there'll be anything, Frank, I'm pretty much all organised now, just killing time until I go."

"Right then, John, I'll contact you later just before you leave."

"By the way, Frank, Tom here says that if you are ever up in this neck of the woods then you've to call in and have a drink on him!"

"Well, thanks! I may just do that one of these days, tell him to make sure he has the brandy in stock, then."

"Okay then, 'bye for now, Frank," and he hung up the phone and walked back to his stool.

He picked up his glass and *The Racing Times* again and studied the nags. His eyes ran down the list of runners for today's race at Sandown Park and Worcester. His eyes came to a halt on three separate horses, all of different mares and all synonymous with Africa. They were, African Venture, Black Gold, and The Jungle Drum. He underlined the names and passed the page over to Tom who was engaged in conversation further along the bar about greenhouses, he signalled his wishes, mouthed some silent words to Tom, and he, being a master of this art, held up a hand in understanding and responded with a thumbs up sign. He held out his left hand outstretched and enquired as to how much John wanted to bet. John indicated fifteen to which Tom raised his eyebrows, momentarily, but without further hesitation, he broke off from his conversation in mid-sentence and shuffled over to the phone, and dialled a number.

"Hello! That you there, Jack?" he queried. A dried up voice replied at the other end giving a brief response. Tom continued, "Treble for you Jack! Fifteen quid on African Venture, Black Gold and Jungle Drum, for you know who!"

"Okay," responded Jack, a man of few words, then he added, "got it. Consider it placed."

"Ta!" said Tom, replaced the receiver and promptly re-engaged his conversation at the point where he had left off and was soon discussing manure and mulches and the like. John accepted that his bet was placed and safely lodged, and returned to sipping his lager slowly and watching the news programme on the television out of the corner of his eye.

Since he had some purpose in life now, he actually found that the days passed quicker, he had taken to going for walks in the neighbourhood, savouring the aroma of plants and trees, and the surroundings about him took on a new interest. His landlady, meanwhile, had kept asking inquisitively where he was going. Knowing what a gossip she was, John confined his replies to "Going away soon!" or "Will be away a long time!" Despite her devious efforts, she was unable to elicit any further information from him.

She was, meanwhile, paid in advance so she had no reason to grumble in any way.

The results of his bet had rewarded him with a handsome return, all horses having come in first, two of them clear winners and the third by a short nose. His fifteen pounds had been well-placed and he had the greatest of pleasure in collecting his winnings from Jack the Bookie who ruefully handed over a bundle of notes, counting out the amount extra carefully, his face stony and not so much as any form of expression was displayed as he placed the last note down on the counter top. John grinned at Jack and winked, and with a backward glance, he commented cheerfully, "Nice one, eh, Jack?"

Jack grimaced but did not respond. That's all he needed, just like a sore head! Jack never could stand smart punters!

The day before his departure, John had made a few final purchases, mostly of toilet articles, some more films for his camera, and had actually, after a long search, come across a road map of Nigeria which was pretty much up to date. Quite a lucky find really, printed by Bartholomew of Edinburgh. He had taken his leave of Tom and the bar, and its surroundings, had warmly shaken hands with him and had promised to call in as soon as he returned to the United Kingdom. He had booked a taxi for ten o'clock the following morning and had gone to bed early for a change and slept like a log.

Chapter Two

The day had dawned early, or so it seemed. He was awake, had risen and gone outside before his landlady was about. As it was a bright day and the sun was shining brightly, he decided to take a walk in the nearby park. He threaded his way along the twisting paths and came upon a dog trotting along, its head downwards and sniffing as it went. John slowed his pace as he approached it and bent down to pat it but was rewarded with a cross between a growl and a snarl as he stretched his hand out in welcome. Unsociable beast! he thought to himself as the dog slunk away, its tail between its legs as it sped up and looked back over its shoulder as it padded off along the path, having resumed its sniffing as if nothing else in the world mattered. Oh well, thought John, you can't win them all. He had done almost a full circle of the park and glanced at his watch. It was almost seven o'clock, so he turned left out of the gate and made his way nonchalantly back towards his digs. As he approached he noted that the landlady was up, her bedroom curtains were already open and a tell tale whiff of steam was escaping from the kitchen window. Probably brewing up, he thought to himself, and more than likely it was last night's tea as well. Actually, the meals there were not too bad, that is if one wasn't too fussy. However, her cooking still left something to be desired and was limited to say the least. John was happy in a way, this would be his last breakfast here in this ancient Victorian house for some time to come. He entered noisily, his landlady almost instantly poking her nose around the doorway to see who it was who dared to enter at this time of the morning. She was surprised to see John and even more surprised when he said, "Good morning," to her in passing, her jaw moving up and down in silence as he passed by the kitchen door and climbed the stairs to his room. She returned to her preparation of the standard bacon and eggs, the bacon cremated, the eggs cardboard, never sunny side up, and an accompanying hard sausage like a brick, the tea was a bit on the stewed side and the toast as hard as nails. He had by now, of course, become accustomed to her standard of fayre, and consumed it without any inkling of relish on his part, and settled down in the dingy lounge to read the morning paper which he had brought back with him.

He awaited the arrival of the taxi he had ordered. It arrived and he took his leave of her, she was paid up to date and he had already been standing outside long before the taxi actually arrived. It headed for the airport and upon arrival he tipped the driver handsomely and walked over to the British Airways desk and checked in his baggage, retaining his black briefcase and the morning paper. He strolled around to the coffee shop, noting that he had just under an hour to wait for his flight and ordered some coffee and sandwiches which would compensate for his meagre breakfast. Even this was streets better than his digs, he thought as he walked over to a vacant table with his tray and sat down. Various people came and went around him but he was oblivious to them all as he tucked into his mini feast and afterwards sat back, stretching his legs and licking his lips like a satisfied cat. He got up and took a wander over to the newsagent-cum-gift shop, bought some Callard and Bowser's treacle toffees and a copy of a raunchy magazine. He paid for it at the till where a middle-aged woman with a severe hairstyle gave him one of those 'you're one of them' looks as she glanced at the glossy magazine cover which depicted a scantily clad female in a suggestive pose. John ignored it, put her instantly into a category of premature senility and old age, he wasn't quite sure which one she fitted best, but either would do to suit her frosty personality and disapproving look. He selected a comfortable seat by a window and read awhile. The Avon tones sounded. Shortly afterwards he joined the crowd of travellers, noting again the large preponderance of businessmen amongst them. He showed his boarding card, passed through the detection machine and took a seat at the side of the departure lounge.

He had time to review his fellow passengers. Some college-type girls with long multi-striped scarves, each carrying a buff folder, stood chattering noisily and animatedly. An old lady in a battered felt hat with a broad black ribbon on it, a bow at the front and pinned to her hair with a large hat pin reminiscent of Grandma in the Giles cartoon, the accompanying black umbrella completed the picture as she stalked up and down the room casting fierce glances at anyone who looked her way. The college girls stopped in mid-sentence as she passed by, and burst out laughing as she crossed the room behind them. A sporty-looking type with a Rudolph Valentino haircut, relaxed against a display cabinet, and a fat man who looked as if he had eaten the world, attempted to place his posterior on a rather narrow chair which looked as if it could not possibly support his weight, by some miracle he sat down on it and it survived the strain.

They'll probably have to give him three seats to himself, he thought, once he gets on the plane. That is if they can get him up the steps in the first place. Would the plane be able to take off? he asked himself. He had visions of the tannoy announcement: "British Airways regret to announce that owing to the fat man in the rear, the flight will be delayed for an unlimited period of time while we find a suitable aircraft to transport the fat man to London!" Two children played hide and seek under the chairs oblivious to all around while their mother walked around the lounge looking for them. It was all part of the game, he decided, and amusing to watch.

The flight was called, all and sundry headed for the exit door including Grandma complete with her national health glasses. John was behind the fat man and, momentarily, the exit was completely blotted out and he had to drop back so that he could see the aircraft, had he not done so he reckoned that the sun would have been blacked out, well, almost. The hulk hauled himself up the steps by some miracle and the steps trembled in sympathy as his large feet propelled him upwards and inwards, and grasping the handrails as if there was no tomorrow. He waddled from side to side to gain access to his seat and managed to manoeuvre his bulk in and out of the rows of seemingly protruding seats and was conducted down to the rear of the aircraft where there were two seats together. Here we go! he thought to himself. After some difficulty he managed to shoehorn himself into them and the stewardess heaved a sigh of relief. John smiled at the pretty hostess as he took his seat near the front of the aircraft, on this occasion he was not bothered by any of the business men or their stereotypes as he reckoned that he had had his fill of them, enough to last a century. Grandma, however, sat nearby, studying the escape procedure in detail as she peered through her glasses.

She'll be okay, John thought to himself, all she needed to do in an emergency was to open up her black umbrella and jump, her long black dress would provide the parachute to descend safely to *terra firma*. His imagination was running riot, but he realised that his sense of humour had returned, it had been missing of late. He donned his seat belt and prepared for take-off. He was glad to notice that the seats on either side of him were vacant.

They were now airborne, the 'fasten seat belt' sign had extinguished so he settled down to a cup of tea and the morning refreshment and, being near the front, he was one of the first to be served for a change. He read the in-flight magazine from front to back including an article on tourism in Italy and Turkey. The flight was slightly bumpy but John hardly noticed, his only attention to that fact was the announcement by the pilot that they were passing through an area of turbulence and the Captain's apologies for that fact. Grandma, meanwhile, was having kittens! Because of the turbulence she had spilt her tea and had almost lost her false teeth in the process as cup and lip met at a pace. She gave a frosty look to all around, muttered something incomprehensible and tried to retain her dignity with all the effort she could muster. The cabin staff, of course, had to go to great pains to conceal their laughter at her antics. All part of the training, thought John. They were soon over London and in a circular holding pattern which was to delay their landing by some fifteen minutes. The aircraft touched down gently, hardly noticeable to anyone on the flight save for Grandma who hung on to her seat belt like grim death with one hand and gripped the edge of the seat with the other one, the whitened knuckles showing. They joined a queue of domestic airliners, almost nose to tail, as they followed one another towards their respective unloading points, the pilots knowing through habit and repetition as to what area they were to proceed. They could have done it blindfolded, John reckoned. He alighted from the fuselage into the brightly lit corridor and walked along and up it at his normal pace while the busy types shoved past and thundered by as if their lives depended upon reaching the exit first.

He eventually arrived at the reclaim area where a large crowd of travellers awaited the arrival of their baggage of many descriptions. Trolleys and their masters rushed to and fro, piled up with hockey sticks, long parcels, cardboard boxes bound with thick string, leather suitcases, cabin trunks and a miscellany of other items all destined for somewhere in the great metropolis. John's baggage arrived in two separate consignments for some strange reason. The indicator above the carousel not complying with the baggage that was arriving and not even with the flight number. Typical! John thought to himself. He retrieved his and placed it on a trolley which by magic had suddenly appeared at his side. He made his way towards the exit door. To his left a sea of faces bulged grotesquely as it surged to and fro, bulging at the seams and bursting out here and there with waving arms in a vain attempt to attract the attention of some long lost relation.

Here, thought John, swayed the whole gamut of society who flowed through the gates of Heathrow daily. He walked outside, pausing to look for some sign of direction. Espying one that said 'Hotel Courtesy Coaches' he made his way across the zebra-crossing noting the restricted parking signs on the road and passed by an eagle-eyed traffic warden in the process, who was waiting patiently for a victim. Numerous buses appeared at random, approaching at breakneck speed, coming to an abrupt halt as someone raised their hand, disgorged their cargo then raced off again to unseen destinations with fresh travellers and luggage in their bowels. A bus marked 'Post House Hotel' approached and John stepped out and flagged it down. He was the only one to go aboard and the bus sped off, and after negotiating the maze of streets, twists and turns, umpteen sets of traffic lights, barriers and mini roundabouts, it eventually settled down to a cruising speed and arrived at the hotel.

The driver disappeared and John alighted only to find that his baggage was already on a trolley and being wheeled inside by a uniformed youth. The bus roared off on its return journey joining the rush of vehicles airport bound. He followed the porter over to the reception desk. A neatly turned out man with silvery grey hair paid him instant attention.

"Good morning, Mr McDonald," he said, smiling, "your room is ready for you." Extracting a key from the shelf behind him, marked 107, he handed it to the bellhop.

John was quite surprised that everything was as smooth as clockwork and was impressed by the slick service he was being subjected to. He followed the bellhop into the lift, then out of it and walked along a corridor to his allocated room. His cases were duly deposited in the room, the operation of the television explained to him, the details of the room service offered and the showing of the luxurious bathroom. He put his hand into his pocket and withdrew a few coins and tipped the youth who responded politely and finished by saying that if there was anything at all that he wanted, he need only call on extension number two and he would immediately be attended to.

He opened his case and hung up a few items so as to let the air circulate and remove the creases even if he wasn't going to wear those clothes straight away. It was before mid-day he noted, so he decided to take a relaxing bath. He ran it, jugging in a generous measure of foam bath and allowing the water to make the bubbles come up to the top of the bath before turning off the taps. He climbed into the hot liquid, slid down the bath and relaxed, closed his eyes and concentrated, feeling completely at ease. The heat of the water seeped through to his bones and pretty soon he was in a trance-like state and dozing off. He reflected upon the information he had of the forthcoming job and slipped gradually into sleep.

He awoke some time later, the water still warm, climbed out and allowed himself to melt into the thick bath towel, towelled himself down and viewed himself in the mirror. He reflected upon the excess weight that he had put on recently which had altered the shape of his midriff and resolved to eliminate that in the near future. He wandered through to the large bed and flopped down on it, allowing his body to sink into its embrace and was soon asleep again. He awoke about an hour later as if abruptly stirred by some unseen hand and reaching over, he switched on the television set. It was on the video channel and was showing a film entitled '*Shall We Tell the President*', he watched it for an hour and a half.

Later on in the afternoon, he dressed casually and descended to the hotel lobby. Locating the bar, he entered and made his way to a vacant stool. In response to the barman's request he ordered a pint of lager and a packet of salted peanuts and munched them leisurely. The bar was fairly busy, even at this time of day with the barman doing a continual to and fro movement from one end to the other. He finished his drink and ordered another. Plenty of time to relax, he thought to himself, before going through to the dining room for dinner.

He sat idly contemplating the task he was about to embark upon, and attempting to come up with some sort of conclusion as to a plan of action. He glanced sideways and noted a young, fresh faced man of about twenty-six years, he reckoned, who sat alone and was drinking a dry Martini. John turned and looked at him to catch his attention and with a friendly smile he said, "Join me in a drink?"

The man swivelled his head to his right, his eyes arresting on John's figure and taking in his meaning.

"Yes," he replied "why not?" and moved over towards John. He introduced himself. "I'm Phil Johnson, a Canadian, staying overnight before travelling overseas," he said. John shook his hand and mentioned that he too was about to travel overseas. This common bond made them instantly attracted to each other, as travellers are.

"I'm going to Nigeria," said John. "Where are you bound for, Phil?"

"Well, that's a coincidence," he replied. "So am I."

"I'm a Construction Engineer, Phil, what line of work are you in then?"

"Not in your line at all, I'm a missionary," he replied.

"Really?" queried John. "I thought that there was no need for them these days!"

"I thought so too at one time, but I discovered that there was an urgent need for them in Africa so I volunteered to go out there and see what I could do."

"Well, I don't envy you at all in your task," said John. "I should imagine that it would be an uphill struggle, as apparently the natives there still believe in magic."

"Yes, so I've been told," said Phil, "but I'm quite prepared for that, it's my job to convince them that this is wrong, that it is not good for them and to win them over to Christianity."

"A tall order indeed," said John. "I hope you succeed then, Phil!"

"Well, we take it as we find it and we build from there, gradually, but of course I don't think it'll be a picnic by any means."

"Are you alone in this venture then?" John asked.

"No, I'm not," continued Phil. "There are about eight of us all told, scattered about, each with an area of responsibility but I don't know exactly where I'm bound for. Someone will meet me there. I'm there for a period of five years anyway so I should manage to achieve something concrete in that time."

John then outlined his task which he reckoned was equally as daunting for different reasons. They conversed for some time before eventually breaking off to go through to the restaurant for dinner. They ate heartily and discussed many subjects and expounded differing opinions about numerous areas of interest. They then returned to the lounge for a night-cap. John discovered that Phil was flying out on an economy ticket and he offered to pay the difference but Phil would have none of it and declined. John, however, would not take no for an answer and after a friendly argument he declared that he was paying the extra for Phil, as he had more than enough in expenses and that in any event he would not be asked to pay it back. Phil was eventually browbeaten into submission, much against his better judgement he thought, but John's persuasive opinion had won through in the end. John then telephoned British Airways and arranged it and promised to pay the difference when they arrived at the airport departure desk. They parted at eleven in the evening and went their separate ways to their rooms having prearranged to meet in the foyer at seven-forty in the morning, as John's transport had been arranged to collect him at that time from the hotel.

John slept soundly, his belly full and he was relaxed and comfortable. He awoke at six-forty-five, showered, shaved and went downstairs for breakfast.

He selected tomato juice, a grapefruit, some bacon and eggs and a large pot of tea. Phil appeared during his meal but only ate a sparse breakfast, explaining that he wasn't up to eating much at that time of day. They finished and each had their baggage taken down to the foyer by the hotel porter. After checking out and settling the bill they sat for a while, awaiting the arrival of John's transport. They did not have long to wait as only a few minutes later a uniformed chauffeur entered the door, dressed in a pale grey suit with a white shirt, grey tie and a peaked hat. He walked directly over to the reception desk and in answer to his query, he was directed by a nod of the head by the clerk towards John. The man approached and coming smartly to attention in front of John, he enquired, "Mr McDonald?"

"Yes, that's me." replied John.

"Good morning, sir! Your transport is waiting outside."

"Fine," said John. "Oh by the way, this chap here will be accompanying me, will that be all right?"

The chauffeur didn't even look at Phil but replied, "Of course, sir, whatever you wish." He immediately walked over to where the luggage was assembled and with clearly practised skill uplifted all the luggage in one move and was soon disappearing out of the doorway. John and Phil followed suit and emerged into the morning sunlight. At the doorway stood a black limousine, its cavernous boot already open while the peaked cap of the chauffeur bobbed up and down as he placed the items strategically inside the compartment and closed it. Phil looked at John quite amazed by it all, while the chauffeur walked around to the rear door and held it open for them to enter, and closed it silently once they were seated. John responded with a raise of the eyebrows. The seats were of leather and the smell of quality exuded throughout. The chauffeur got into the driving seat, opened the glass sliding panel that separated them and said, "Good morning, gentlemen, you'll find the morning papers on the console and if you fancy a drink there is some refreshment in the cabinet." Leaning over to press a hidden switch, the cabinet folded down silently and two glasses and decanters appeared, one of brandy and one of whisky.

They looked at each other. "Shall we?" asked John.

John poured himself a whisky, Phil hesitated but eventually elected to have a brandy, "Just a small one," he said. They sipped their drinks. John read *The Daily Telegraph* while Phil glanced at *The Times*. The journey was silent, the limousine slipping smoothly into the morning traffic and made its way along the M25, commonly known as the world's biggest parking place such was the density of the traffic. They arrived at Gatwick Terminal and emerged through the now open door, the chauffeur having already called for a porter and had loaded the baggage on to the trolley. The porter waited patiently while John and Phil got out.

John moved over to thank the chauffeur for his services. The man came instantly to attention and saluted respectfully and said, "I hope you enjoyed your journey, gentlemen?"

"Yes. Thank you," said John, and fished in his pocket for a tip for him.

"I'm sorry, sir, I'm not permitted to accept remuneration for my services."

"Oh!" said John, "well, thanks very much anyway."

"All part of the service, sir, I hope you enjoy the remainder of your journey." So saying, he entered the vehicle and was soon lost to sight amongst the heavy morning traffic.

Phil said, "Well! Real slick, eh?"

"It certainly is!" exclaimed John, doing a quick impression of Oliver Hardy. They followed the swiftly disappearing trolley and baggage and ascended in the lift to the upper level. They scanned the display boards to ascertain the booking desk. John spotted it nearest to them with only a short queue attending it, while the others all had long queues stretching out from the desks. The nationalities of the people and the variety of the luggage defied description, almost every concoction under the sun. They checked in their baggage and John paid the fare difference for Phil and they collected their boarding cards from the petite girl behind the desk. John was just about to turn round when he heard a familiar voice saying,

"Checked in all right then?"

He turned around to find Frank standing there.

"What are you doing here?" he asked.

"Oh, just making sure that everything is all right, John. I'd hate to think that there were any mistakes."

"No danger of that, Frank! And I was very impressed with the chauffeur service, very professional."

"Good," said Frank, "that's just the way it should have been."

John then introduced Phil.

Frank said, "Well, you'll be company for each other on the journey, I'm sure. By the way, John, the current resident engineer goes by the name of Klaus, he will be meeting you at the other end and will take you to your hotel. It's all been arranged already and he'll be keeping an eye out for you."

"Thanks," said John, "do you know what he looks like?"

"No, I don't," said Frank, "but he'll be there for sure, the normal method, I understand, is that they hold a card up with your name on it. Shouldn't be too difficult to spot!"

"Okay," said John.

They three of them sat awhile and conversed until Frank excused himself to go off to an early morning appointment in the city. John and Phil thanked Frank and shook hands. Frank wished them a safe journey and was soon lost from sight on the down escalator.

They proceeded to the security and customs desks and passed unhindered. A stroll around the newspaper stand and the bookstand passed some of the time and they sat down to await the flight call, noting the many different nationalities of people and their various forms of attire. A short while afterwards they proceeded along the long corridor to the exit gate. They showed their boarding cards again, had the names checked off and took their seats in the final departure lounge. Numerous Nigerians sat around, some with large cardboard boxes displaying the words 'Napisan', 'Deluxe Quilted Bed Cover', 'Kenwood Food Mixer' and numerous other products, all bought especially to take back to their country. A bunch of Rastafarians in dreadlocks and sporting loudly coloured suits, some of garish hues, struggled with enormous ghetto blasters, some of them with multi flashing lights, reminding John of a Christmas tree.

"How on earth are they going to get those on the aircraft as cabin baggage?" thought John to himself.

The chatter of the travellers was interrupted by a clinking noise to which all heads responded and turned towards the direction from which it came. A policeman appeared leading a young black youth in handcuffs. Following him came four others, each with a policeman in attendance.

"What's this all about?" asked Phil of John.

"Oh, I think that they are illegal immigrants or undesirable aliens, or maybe they've just overstayed their welcome. That is to say, that their visas have expired and they are being deported back to their own country."

"Well, I've never seen that before," said Phil taken aback. "Wait until I tell the folks back home about this!"

"Well, it all adds to the excitement of the journey," commented John. They sat for a further ten minutes or so until the policemen got up and escorted the prisoners on to the aircraft and chained them to the seat upright. A few minutes later they joined the few other people travelling first class, passed through the exit and proceeded in the same direction as the now vanished prisoners. They arrived at the door and were immediately conducted to their seats. They sat within a few feet of each other and they noted that there was only about fifteen other passengers in this section. They were handed the dinner menu and sat studying it, meanwhile, the remainder of the passengers, in the cattle or economy class, boarded and filed in and occupied their semi-comfortable seats with the greatly reduced elbow and foot room. The captain welcomed them all aboard and soon the faint whine of the compressors could be heard as the engines sprang into life. The clunk of the doors being closed and locked in position was soon followed by the 'fasten seat belts' sign being illuminated.

A brief demonstration of the safety equipment by the cabin crew followed and then they could detect movement as the huge airliner was pushed backwards by the flat tractor and turned to face the taxi way. The vehicle scurried away to its next waiting aircraft, a journey which it would repeat many times during that day. The aircraft picked up speed and headed for the end of the runway and waited patiently for its take off slot. No sooner had the jumbo jet ahead of them accelerated away than they moved into the take-off position. A few seconds later the engines built up speed to an accompanying crescendo of noise, the aircraft straining against its brakes. They were released and the machine lunged forward in a sharp burst of acceleration as it thundered down the runway, passed the point of no return and with an almost undetectable lift it rose into the air and climbed sharply upwards into the clouds and away southwards on its journey. People and buildings took on a miniature appearance and the only movement visible was of matchbox cars moving along the tiny roads far below.

Lunch was served early and they chose the fish dish, it was excellent and the wine complemented it perfectly. A few free liquors helped to round off the meal and they settled down to watch the film which was just commencing on the screen before them. John fell asleep and awoke some two and a half hours later only to find Phil asleep also. The film had ended, he went to the toilet to wash his hands and face and freshen up and read the newspapers on offer and listened to the programme of music on the personal headphones. John looked out of the window, it was a bright sunny day. It was always sunny up there, however, some thirty thousand feet above the ground. Pity he couldn't live up here above the clouds, thought John, with nothing to obscure the sun's rays. Far below he could make out the contours of some faint rock formations but otherwise most of the ground was featureless. The sands of the Sahara desert came into view, stretching out, it seemed, into infinity.

Some time later, the aircraft started a long, slow descent as it approached Kano and flew along the border for a short period at the northern end of Nigeria, and close to the border of Chad and Niger. It banked right and levelled out as it flew over Kaduna, a city bathed in centuries of trade amongst the Arab races. From then onwards the terrain changed showing up large stretches of jungle greenery and high hills, their surfaces stained by rainwater erosion which had carved out prominent rivulets. The aircraft descended again and slowed, and by this time the light was fading fast and the view took on a misty appearance producing a faint purple hue in the sky. Far below he could see lights dotted about. The 'fasten seat belts' sign illuminated and the tone sounded and the aircraft started its descent into Lagos International, known locally as Murtalla Mohammed.

It landed, braked in reverse thrust and taxied for what seemed to be an eternity and finally came to a halt. The door opened and a hot and stifling rush of air flooded in to fill the compartment. They emerged and proceeded to climb down the steps. John noticed to his left that the prisoners had been unchained and were being led away across the tarmac to a waiting police van which looked more like a bombed out truck with no windows. They were roughly bundled inside by the Nigerian Police and driven off to some unseen fate. Beads of sweat sprung out on their brows and by the time that they had walked about twenty steps their shirts were sticking to the bodies. The heat was stifling. They entered the terminal building and joined the queue at the passport desk. Eventually, they got close to it and handed their passports over the top of the glass partition of non-opaque glass to some unseen person who merely requested the passports with the words, "Give me!" Now and then a black head bobbed up and down, assessing how many people were still left. After an interminable wait the passports reappeared, the unseen person shouting out the name of the owner in an unintelligible voice and when the person took the passport from his hand, the voice said, "Thank you!"

They then proceeded to the carousel, a small one, John noted, that sat motionless as if it was never to move. Many people stood around chattering noisily then suddenly went into an agitated state as the machine jerked into operation once, stopped, started again, stopped again, then finally lurched into life and proceeded to rotate rather jerkily although no baggage had appeared on it. It stopped again and just as abruptly restarted. Finally some items of baggage appeared and all and sundry pressed forwards. The belt continued its jerky movement as more items were placed upon it and it continued its spasmodic operation, stopping unexpectedly whereupon a large pile of baggage fell off onto the floor and remained there for the duration. John wondered why no one bothered to pick them up but the belt continued its rotation anyway. Having retrieved their items, they made their way over to the doorway. Previously this would have been an impossible task as this area was notorious for being frequented by groups of beggars and would-be baggage carriers who fought amongst themselves in order to gain possession of some poor unfortunate's belongings, only to carry them to their waiting transport, then they would demand same outrageous fee for the privilege of doing so. Eventually the airport authorities had quashed this behaviour and movement was now trouble free.

John looked over the heads of those clustered around him but could not see anyone holding up a sign at all, let alone with a name on it. At a further attempt, he spotted it! A piece of yellow card waving about with his name upon it scrawled in large red letters. He waved to the holder of it to acknowledge that he had seen it, and turning to Phil he said, "I can see my lot, but none of yours yet, Phil."

Phil craned his neck above the crowd but was unable to see over the heads of the moving bodies. John got nearer to the door and out of the corner of his eye, he spotted a pious looking figure standing alongside a nun. It wore a very sombre suit and he reckoned by all accounts that this must be Phil's welcoming party.

"Looks like that's your people over there!" he exclaimed, and Phil looked in that direction, craning his neck again, and spotting them he replied, "Yes! That's them."

They eventually managed to squeeze into the outer area and John could now see easily the man by the name of Klaus.

"Hello!" he said, "are you Klaus?"

"Yah! That's me!" he replied, "you are John McDonald?" he queried in a guttural accent.

"Yes, just a minute while I move these bags a bit."

A black face appeared from the rear of the crowd and Klaus said, "This is Samuel, our driver, he will take your cases, John."

John leant forward and shook hands with them both, Samuel lifted up the luggage and disappeared out of the door to the waiting car, parked at some distance away from the doorway.

Phil, meantime, had fought his way over to his people and introduced himself. The answer he received was not from the man but from the fresh-faced nun at his side. "Good evening. I'm Sister Mary."

Well, I'm pleased to meet you," Phil replied. "I wasn't quite sure who was going to be here to meet me."

"We thought," she added, "that we would meet you personally as if you suddenly appeared unannounced at our mission it might cause some hostility, so much easier to take the easy way, don't you think?"

"Quite," said Phil, not quite knowing what to make of that statement, and being the last person to wish hostility on any person of either race, colour or creed. The pious figure approached meekly, and held out a limp hand which Phil warmly shook, noting its flaccidity, and responded, "I'm Phil, your new missionary. What's your name?"

The stony faced priest looked up and replied in a non-committal voice, "Father Williams."

"Okay then, Father Williams," said Phil, attempting to produce some sort of continuity in the conversation. "How goes it with the local people, then?"

Father Williams looked taken aback at this rash question by this young man as he had categorised him. Who dares to question me, of such high authority? Father Williams, Catholic priest to the people, had been in Africa for too long and was long suffering and due for a well earned rest, perhaps early retirement. Soliciting no other response whatsoever, Phil gave the nun a smile and picked up his baggage and moved towards the exit.

The nun interjected with an explanation, "Father Williams has been having a hard time of it lately, you'll have to excuse him, he can be difficult! We rather hoped you could bring a new and fresh approach to our mission. It would be greatly beneficial to our cause."

"Whatever I can do to help!" added Phil.

The conversation ended there, then Father Williams indicated that they should be moving on and they went silently outwards. Sister Mary picked up Phil's baggage and proceeded outwards and over to a Datsun four wheel drive vehicle, placed it aboard and without a word she hitched up her skirt and climbed aboard, considerably non-nun-like, while Father William averted his eyes and looked towards heaven for forgiveness. He got in next to Sister Mary and Phil climbed into the back and made himself comfortable. The station wagon then set off, Father Williams crossed himself twice as if he wasn't going to make it to the end of the journey, gave a short prayer to bless their journey and without further ceremony Sister Mary let out the clutch causing the vehicle to rocket sharply out into the heavy and chaotic evening traffic.

John, meanwhile, had been escorted to the waiting car by Klaus, and Sam joined the traffic flow smoothly and headed off in the direction of the city centre. Amid a cacophony of horn blowing, displays of bad driving, jockeying for position and many spectacles of bravado of the highest order from all the other drivers, they continued their way amid a motley collection of vehicles. The unending streams of traffic all merged, melted and re-emerged into one completely disorganised jam, all hell bent in reaching Lagos in the shortest possible time even if it meant changing lanes a dozen times or more. John was amazed to find a large number of vehicles had only one light or even no lights at all. Some had front lights only while others only rear ones. How they managed to navigate in the total darkness was a mystery. A number of near misses and actual collisions were noted during the journey, notwithstanding the large amount of breakdowns that occurred at monotonous intervals, around which the traffic streams weaved and repositioned themselves. The attendance of numerous peddlers running alongside the cars, selling anything and everything under the sun, at speeds of up to fifteen or twenty miles an hour and managing to keep up with the vehicle until they achieved a sale. Ten out of ten for enterprise, thought John.

As they approached Lagos itself, a huge traffic jam built up, thus providing an excuse for all and sundry to exercise their horns. A frustrated driver hung out of a window and, turning, he shouted to the car behind, "Don' blow yo' hon at me, man!" to which he received the expected reply and response of more horn blowing in earnest. Eventually the mêlée sorted itself out, and the masses resumed their hell for leather impetus for Lagos and its environments. Buses, that is if you could call them buses, lurched or chugged along, their engines straining to keep up with the speed of the traffic flow, their back axles and gearboxes whining and groaning away as if they had no lubrication whatsoever. They were totally swallowed up in a sea of bodies, rows of faces peering out of the windowless windows, a common feature of all buses in Nigeria. Others clung on frantically but with a certain amount of skill to the outsides of the buses with their fingernails, to any part which protruded or offered any hint of an anchorage. The buses rarely stopped or slowed down, most of the passengers jumping off as they approached their stop. The bus still in motion rolled onwards and those that had got up had to be extremely fleet of foot and agile to avoid being run over by the following traffic. So it was not unusual to see some death defying feats, acrobatics and the like, as they avoided the perils of the road. Some, of course, misjudged it and were swept from sight under the wheels but the traffic did not halt and all that remained of some poor unfortunate was a flat mess on the road or a large rolled up piece of meat being deflected here and there by the traffic.

They followed the signs for Victoria Island, picking their way through numerous flyovers and flyunders until they arrived at a relatively quiet road and suddenly they were in a seemingly tranquil neighbourhood. Sam skilfully negotiated a clutch of vendors in the middle of the road and continued along until they came to a sign marked 'To the sea front'. They went round a bend in the road and passed by the area of Lagos which had, in former years, been used as barracoons up until the year 1900 and had been host to the hordes of slaves who had been penned in inhuman conditions in these entrapments prior to being shipped to the West Indies. Only a fraction of them arrived in good condition. Slave traders were of many nationalities. French, Dutch, Portuguese and English were those responsible and reports had been heard of slaves having been chained together and thrown overboard if they showed any sign of sickness. They were then able to claim payment 'for those lost at sea' when they arrived in the West Indies. Many met their fate this way, drowned together. A handsome bounty awaited those that could put their human cargo ashore in a fine 'marketable condition', however unscrupulous the traders and sea captains were. What they lost in trading was more than adequately made up for in 'slaves lost in transit'. Over three-quarters of slaves shipped never even reached their destination on those far shores.

A sudden diversion in the roadway took them along a residential road and a turn to the right took them past some large buildings surrounded by iron spiked fences, walls topped with broken glass and numerous guards on duty outside the gates, their faces illuminated by the car's headlights as they passed by. A sign in black lettering on a white background declared 'Beware of the Dog', and depicted a dog's head with what could only be described as 'happy eyes', as if something sexual had happened to it while its picture was being painted. Another sign further along said again 'Beware of the Dog' and showed a horses head. John looked at it in a questionable manner. Next he spotted an upturned oil drum painted green so that it would show up in the dark. On it was painted in grey, 'Zimbabwe High Commission'. Odd, thought John, strange place to have a Commission in a forty-five gallon drum! On a white wall, daubed carelessly in black paint, was displayed the message, 'DO NOT UNIRATE HERE!' He smiled to himself as he noted the large urine stains on the wall and the mis-spelling of the word. Further along the same wall, another painted message said 'DO NOT UNIRATE HERE AGAIN!' and it had already been partly eroded by the additional urine stains. They re-emerged onto the main road and headed for the hotel, The Eko, where John was to spend his first night in Lagos.

The hotel took its name from the name of the island on which it stood, an island widely known to the old Portuguese and other sea traders who frequented it. At that time it was basically a swampy area populated by acres of mangrove which choked its approaches, rubbing shoulders with large clumps of water hyacinths which impeded the course of shipping. The area had been notorious for the contraction of strange diseases of sickness and eventual sudden death for seafarers. This was known as the 'bad air' disease or 'mal air', a scourge for decades to come, thus giving its better known name of malaria. They passed by numerous rickety side-stalls at every street corner where the local people sold or hawked almost anything beneath dimly-lit paraffin oil lamps until about one in the morning, when they silently disappeared from the scene as if a fairy godmother had spirited them away only to reappear at six in the morning.

They approached the hotel looming out of the darkness. It was only a few hundred yards from the sea front. Sam slowed as the car entered the hotel driveway and John noted that it was now eight in the evening. He negotiated the three sleeping policemen, one after the other, and accepted a check-in token from the casual guard at the gate house. These guards spent all of their day and night issuing these 'important' pieces of paper, while their colleagues stood at the side menacingly wielding a stick with nails protruding from it, and ready to place it under the wheels of any vehicle who attempted to leave without surrendering the piece of paper or stopping at the barrier. Klaus indicated to Sam to carry on and they proceeded up the hill to the hotel entrance and steps. Hands appeared, the door was held open for them and a small army of helpers descended upon them to carry John's bags inside the hotel foyer. Sam, meanwhile, had driven off round the hotel grounds in search of a parking space. John noted the large number of young girls dressed in European styles with very brief miniskirts revealing shapely figures beneath them who hung about. Some stood singly while others were in groups, smoking and in conversation. A middle-aged, well-dressed man, the pimp, directed them towards well-dressed prospective clients as they arrived. Seeing John and Klaus approach, one of them detached herself from them and walked directly over towards John. She took his left arm and applied herself like a leach and said,

"Hello, massah! You want pretty girl tonight. I available, what you say eh?"

Klaus turned on her with venom, "Piss off!" he shouted at her. "He no want you!"

The girl totally unperturbed by this rebuff, continued. "I give you good time, you no want me? I plenty cheap, stay long time."

John extracted himself from her clutches, the girl breaking off with a couldn't care less shrug and wandered back towards her small collection of cronies, and displayed a provocative wiggle of her hips as she went.

"Bloody pests!" exclaimed Klaus. They made their way over to the reception desk behind which three male clerks were attempting to compete with about fifteen gesticulating customers who all demanded one thing or another. Eventually, one of them broke free and spotting the white man, he came towards John and said, "Yes, massah! You is welcome! You wan' room for de night?"

Klaus intervened. "Der ist a room reserved for this man! He is Mr McDonald."

The clerk looked puzzled and sifted through an unruly pile of paperwork on the counter. After a five minute search, he could not find the reservation and he wandered off to the far end of the desk to his right and disappeared through a large door marked 'Front Manager's Office'. A few minutes later he reappeared, saying, "Certainly, massah. We have de room foah you!" and passing a sheet of paper over the counter he added, "please fill in de registration fom." John took the proffered piece of paper and commenced to fill it in. It asked for just about everything apart from the colour of his grandmother's socks in the year 1912. Should I write that down? he thought to himself. Had he done so then it would not have made any difference as the clerk didn't bother to look at what he had written down and was too distracted to read anyway owing to the others at the desk who all shouted for attention. He really needed about six arms, thought John, in order to cope with the crowd. While the clerk busied himself with the document, John had felt another warm body by his side. He glanced to his left, a tall slim girl with modern styled spectacles had attached herself to his person as if greeting a long lost friend.

"Hello Johnny," she said, "you jus' arrivin'? I can come see you later if you like, I give you good time, plenty cheap! What you say, eh?"

Klaus was just about to turn on her when John said, "It's all right, Klaus, I can handle it." He turned towards her, his mind ticking over as to how best to deal with this vulture. "Sure!" he said, "why not?"

"Good," said the girl, now all smiles and moon eyes. "What room you in?"

"Eh, room 368," said John, quickly conjuring up a number in his head.

"Good, I see you in the room in ten minutes, you be ready? We can make sweet music all night long, you not get tired of me, I stay until the morning with you, you have good time!"

"Okay," said John. "Ten minutes then I see you."

She detached herself from him and turned away from John and crossed over to another female friend of hers. He noted that she had given her friend the thumbs up sign, so he interpreted this as meaning that two of them would be proceeding soon to room number 368, but he or she, whoever the occupant was, was in for a big surprise.

"Dat ist gut thinking!" exclaimed Klaus, with a satisfied look on his face. John continued the ritual of booking in, having now joined the queue at the cashier's desk and had paid double the room rate as a deposit of security. This was the norm for all the hotels in Nigeria. He obtained his receipt, exchanged it for an electronic door key and proceeded over to the lift a few yards away which was adjacent to the hotel newsagent and book shop and within easy reach of the gatherings of the ladies of the night.

Klaus had said that he would meet John the next day and conduct him to the Agent's Office. A porter preceded John to the lift door and pressed the 'UP' button. From out of the shade another 'lady of the night' appeared and approached him.

"You go up?" she enquired of John. He turned to view her, about twenty to thirty years of age, he reckoned, but plumpish although dressed stylishly in a black and gold sequinned dress. Klaus had spotted her and had bounded over.

"Bloody night fighters!" he exclaimed, the term colloquially given to the prostitutes. "They're every bloody where! Go away! Or I hand you over to the police and security!" he shouted.

The girl stopped dead and looked at him, then turning to John, she smiled and said, "You have not got a very nice friend, he no like me. Okay, I catch you later. Can give you much hanky panky and plenty jig a jig. You want me, you asks for Lola, okay?" So saying she returned into the shadows, lurking there like a spider awaiting her next victim.

Klaus wandered back to his seat and John and the porter entered the lift and ascended to the tenth floor. His destination was room 610, and he tipped the porter ten niara, this being a small fortune to the man, especially for someone as lowly paid as hotel porters were in Nigeria. The man beamed broadly, and responded, "Thank you massah! God bless you," and after switching on the television for John, he activated the air conditioning and took his leave.

John had arranged to meet Klaus the following morning so he was looking forward to a relaxing evening. He stripped off his clothing which was stuck to his body owing to the high humidity, and stepped into the shower and turned it on. He soaped himself, washed his hair and allowed the water to cascade over his body before stepping out and towelling himself dry. He wandered through the room, pausing to glance at the 'in-house' video showing. It was the inevitable *The Eagle Has Landed*, which he had seen about a dozen times before, then continued out on to the balcony. His view from high up covered quite a vast expanse of Lagos. Even at this time of night the streets were crowded with people. Taxis scurried to and fro, stopping alongside anyone walking along the road and sounding their horns to attract their attention, never giving up on the possibility of attracting an extra fare. At every street corner vendors had set up their stalls and tables, some of them were crude affairs. The smell of roasted corn cobs and goat meat, drifted across on the wind, while a steady consumption of cans and bottles of Fanta and Afri-Cola was taking place.

Down below at the hotel entrance, taxis and private cars came and went unceasingly, the hotel itself being a mecca for the locals. Its Casino, bar and barbecue restaurant, attracting desirables and undesirables alike, such as the hordes of night fighters, all bent on business. There were three restaurants, all in full swing. A Chinese one on the top floor of the hotel, which did a roaring trade and was a meeting point for the night fighters to pick up their clients. The hotel was mainly used by businessmen and tourists and also by the airline staff of the many major airlines which flew in and out of Lagos each and every day. Air crew made night stops here before flying out on the following day to other destinations in Africa and elsewhere. The lights of adjacent buildings shimmered in the heat haze. A pleasant breeze had sprung up, so he dressed and went down in the lift to the ground floor restaurant and ordered a meal. There was no sign of the girls that had previously accosted him, probably hard at work, thought John, earning their crust of bread. The pimp was in evidence, hovering near the door his eyes panning across the room, noting down figures in a book and carefully accruing his ill-gotten gains, and noting the distribution of his collection of girls, most of them very young and in some cases only twelve years of age. If they were big enough he reckoned, they were old enough. John ordered a bowl of soup, consommé, pork chop with all the trimmings, and a fruit salad, followed by a pot of tea which he savoured as he reflected upon past events and what the future held for him.

Tomorrow was going to be a busy day. A meeting with the agent of Consolidated was on the cards at which he hoped to gain more up-to-date information about the current state of the project. He ran through in his mind the questions he wanted to find the answers to and jotted down the major ones in his notebook. The restaurant was busy, a bunch of Germans noisily discussed some subject and occasionally burst into howls of laughter. A young black couple sat alone at a corner table eating Jollife rice and vegetables, while outside, the bar was rapidly filling up. He signed the chit proffered by the waiter, and went out and down a flight of steps to the bar area and took a seat at a vacant table. His attempts at flagging down a passing barman were unsuccessful for quite a period of time but eventually he entrapped one on his return journey, and after a further ten minute wait he was served with an ice cold Star beer and a glass. The barmen often did not give customers a glass unless they specifically asked for one. It went down smoothly and John perused the surroundings. The breeze had stiffened now, blowing in from the seashore. The palm trees and banana trees waved their fronds up and down like giant fans adding to the cooling effect with their movements. Around the tables, a few of the night fighters were conspicuous by their brief attire and their close attention to mainly young single European types. Easy meat the girls called it.

It was almost eleven o'clock so John decided to turn in for the night, although he noted that the foyer of the hotel had become even busier than before, especially during the past half hour, at least as far as the night fighters were concerned. He went to his room and relaxed on the bed and watched the next 'in-house movie', entitled, *The Rise and Fall of Idi Amin*, a violent and grotesquely accurate portrayal of the corrupt General. He was depicted as a tyrant and womaniser to boot, having extremely bloodthirsty lusts for power at any cost, be it murder, extortion or rape. He fell asleep near the end of it so he was uncertain as to how it ended. He awoke at three in the morning and got in between the sheets and slept soundly after his day's travel.

The loud blaring of car horns awakened him rudely at six-thirty. He got up and went over to the veranda window and looked out. He opened the sliding door and went out on to the balcony. Down below in the car park, men were busy filling buckets of water from a tap hidden somewhere in the bushes, then carrying the buckets over to their cars and washing them down with long brushes or, in some cases, just an old rag. Most of the buckets had no handles and they were emptied over the cars in a seemingly never-ending sequence. Numerous cars stood with their bonnets up as if in conversation with each other, and John noted that they were all Peugeot 404's. Black drivers flitted to and fro and tinkered about in the engine compartments, followed by a ritual starting up of the engines.

They then proceeded to rev up the engines to screaming pitch and their peak levels, each trying to out do the next one or anyone nearby. Many had now flocked to this band wagon and a symphony of high revving engines ensued, continuing up to the highest 'C'. Really great for the engines! thought John to himself, must take years off the life of them in one fell swoop. He cast his eyes around. Many people were scurrying along the non-existent pavements on either side of the roadway, taxis hooted their horns to advertise their service and a smattering of the daily beggars had laid siege to the entrance at the hotel gates, some lying down on the road at the gates so that cars would have to stop for them. The car drivers, however, were all mainly locals, and quite accustomed to this ploy, merely negotiating planned detours around them. Some of the beggars were deformed, the most common form of disfigurement being the effects of leprosy.

Most had stunted hands or feet, while others had grotesque distorted limbs with portions of the leg from hip to knee being of mammoth size compared with the rest of their bodies. Glaucoma was common and a large number of them had diseased eyes, some of them totally blind. Destruction of the retina and the resulting blindness was an all too common sight. Any money received was held up close to their eyes for inspection and the bearers moved their heads from side to side in order to identify the coins. If all else failed they would place the coins in their mouths, one by one, judging the weight and texture of them to find out how much they had received. Many were dumb or dumb and blind. Those that were blind usually had a young boy accompanying them positioned at the front, the youngster translating from Hausa or Yoruba into English and vice versa for the benefit of the tourists with plenty of money, hopefully to spare. Some days, they received sufficient money to enable them to buy their daily requisite of food, but as often as not they starved, sleeping rough in the shade or alongside the roads on top of well worn cardboard sheets. Meanwhile, night fighters had descended in the lift and had emerged to make their way homewards, to count their money, grab a few quick hours of sleep, and resume their chore of providing sexual favours for their clients, while at the same time obtaining free food and drinks which was usually the only way they could survive, or whatever else they could obtain from their clients.

He showered and got dressed. The telephone rang so he reached over to it and picked it up.

"Good morning!" said a voice, "have you settled in?"

John could not identify the voice and wondered who it was calling at this early hour of the morning, and assumed that it was a member of the hotel staff, from the reception desk.

"Yes?" he queried.

"That's good! You are welcome, sah!" said the voice, and without hesitating continued, "have you any sterling or dollars you wish to change? I give you very good price! Special for you on de black market, yes?"

John thought for a moment. Sounds like a con man he thought, and besides, what on earth was he calling at this time of day for, so he replied in the negative.

"No I haven't actually, I have neither."

"Oh, well!" said the voice, "but if you have any need of money change, you come an' see me in de foyer, I is always there! I give you good price! You unnerstan'?"

"Yes, well thanks," and he put the phone back down on its cradle. John shook his head at the gall of the man. He thought no more of it and went down in the lift to the ground floor restaurant for breakfast. It was quiet and he elected to have the buffet breakfast, and after indicating that to the waitress he went along the tables and helped himself to the variety of food on offer. He started off with corn flakes and cold tinned milk, fresh milk being unobtainable, followed by fresh pineapple, then cold cooked bacon and equally cold eggs which looked a bit on the anaemic side. He finished off with coffee, black, and some toast. He gazed around. Over at the swimming pool, the attendants had applied a long pole with a net and were busy scooping out insects that had found their way into the pool during the night. They deployed the suction hose and drew off the leaves and other windswept debris that had blown over from the beach not far away. Labourers with brushes, dustpans, mops and buckets went about while others, barefoot, moved to and fro among the many trees and plants with a long hose ensuring a constant supply to each one. A bunch of air hostesses appeared and hurriedly consumed a breakfast before dashing out to the foyer where a minibus awaited them, destined for the airport.

He asked for another cup of coffee and noted that he had yet another half hour to wait until Klaus was due to appear to take him to the agent's house for their meeting. He returned to his room, put on a clean white shirt and a tie as it was a business affair and returned to the lobby in the lift.

As he got into the lift he noted that the girl whom he had met in the foyer who had promised to come to his room, was there. She gave him a very nasty look and said, "So! You are still here? Eh? Why you not come when I say I meet you?"

John thought up a quick excuse. "Had to go to a business meeting," he said with little conviction in his voice.

"Well! You sho' miss a good time, I very good, please men all de time."

"I'm sure you do," he replied.

The girl continued, "Okay, next time I see you again, eh?" By this time the lift had stopped and the doors opened and all exited, going their separate ways. The girl crossed the stone floor her high heels clip-clopping as she went and she was soon out of sight, disappearing down the stone steps of the hotel entrance and onwards down the hill towards the gate.

John took a vacant seat in the foyer and watched some of the hotel's clientele pass by. He noted that many of the night fighters had emerged from the lift doors. It must be chucking out time, he thought. There was no sign of the pimp now, his place having been taken by a youth of about sixteen years selling papers, who called out, "Champion! Telegraph! Concorde!" Numerous people diverted their walk to purchase a few each of the daily rag which were priced at a niara each. Federal Government cars, all Peugeots, appeared and waited briefly at the door, picked up their passengers and sped off into the traffic heading in to the centre of Lagos. Klaus was spotted climbing the steps, so John got up to meet him.

"Gut morning!" he said. "I hope you slept well, John?"

"Yes, thanks," replied John. "Have we far to go?"

"Nein, my friend! It is only a short walk, about five or ten minutes or so, that is all." So saying, he led the way outwards down the hill and out of the hotel gates. They turned right and strolled at a slow pace along the road, passing a bank on the left-hand side and continuing on past an elongated car wash area where lots of young blacks were busily employed in applying their skills to a long line of dusty vehicles. They toiled with few breaks and their bodies glistened with sweat even at this early hour of the morning. However, an instant cure was at hand and without flinching, they poured a bucket of water over themselves providing the cooling necessary to allow them to continue their work. They continued to the bottom of the road, turned left, then right and left again. A brown horse stood in the shade of a tree, head down and looking forlorn. The morning traffic thundered by and the horse took no notice of it. It was a poor specimen, its ribs stuck out through its dull coat looking like it could do with a good feed. They continued along and past the Canadian Embassy and the British Airways building, went on to the end of the road and turned right at the Nigerian Law Commissioners building. They slowed at a residential house set back from the road and waited patiently as the guard inspected them suspiciously through a peephole in the gate, peered at them through a metal grill before disappearing housewards to verify who they were. He returned a few minutes later. There followed a scraping of the gate on the concrete accompanied by the squeaking of a rusty hinge and the gate dragged slowly inwards as it was pulled by the still unseen guard. Klaus stepped over to the door and pressed the bell, and without waiting for a response, he pushed the door open and entered. John followed close on his heels.

They went into a room in which a short nameplate in white plastic with blue lettering stated the occupants of the building. John looked at it, noting that the agent for Consolidated Construction was also the agent for numerous other companies. They passed along a corridor, through a busy office typing pool whose occupants looked up at the intrusion of their privacy, and continued on. The clicking of the typewriter keys resumed its pace accompanied by the rustling of paper and office stationery. They ascended a short cool stairway where an air conditioner clanked merrily away making the corridor much colder than the rest of the building. Proceeding along another corridor of more offices smaller in size, they came to a door marked 'HENDRY J. SIMONS. COMPANIES AGENT'. Klaus walked in unannounced, striding through the doorway with John in tow. A face, middle-aged with greying hair atop, appeared from amongst a heap of paperwork, peering over the top of it as if it were the battlements of a castle.

"Ah! Hello, Klaus," he said. "I see you have Mr McDonald with you, good! Come in!" He rose from his chair and walked around the desk to shake John's hand. "Nice to meet you, John. Would you like a morning cuppa?"

"Yes, I wouldn't mind that at all," replied John. Hendry waved his hand in response and said, "Won't be a minute, I'll just stick the kettle on," and he disappeared into a small room which John took to be the kitchen. There followed a loud clanking noise, the banging of a kettle against something and the sound of rushing water, followed by the marrying of a cup and saucer and the faint rattle of a teaspoon being placed on an earthenware saucer.

Hendry J. returned saying, "Be ready soon," and turning to Klaus he said, "Do you want tea also, Klaus?"

"Nein!" he replied, "eine beer will do instead, or einer whisky?"

Hendry J. threw up his hands in horror. "Sorry Klaus, I'm fresh out of beer, a Fanta perhaps?"

"Mein gott! No!" and before Hendry J. could say anything else, Klaus excused himself and went out of the office door in search of something more in the alcoholic line.

"Won't we be needing him?" asked John

"No. No, not at all, in fact we'll get on a lot faster without him," he added.

"Whatever you say," John commented, and Hendry J. returned to the kitchen area to make the tea while John ran his eye over Hendry J.'s desk. Even from this distance John could see that it was a mess. Total disorganisation was apparent. Sheaves of papers spilled over the desk jostling with others, intermingled with reports, envelopes and official looking documents. They occupied all the available space between two in trays and one out tray. The latter was piled up high and the former could only be described as brimming over with correspondence. Hendry J. returned bearing a tray with two steaming mugs of tea on it, two saucers; a bottle of milk and a box of cubed sugar. A packet of McVitie's biscuits lay alongside a well stained spoon. They each helped themselves to a mug, added the sugar and milk to their personal taste and collected a few biscuits from the tray which, John noted, had seen better days, being almost worn down to the metal in most places.

"Well, then," said Hendry J. "I expect you'll want to get started. There's quite a lot to go over really, so I suggest that first of all I pass you over some files, then you can read through them and if you have any questions, I'll answer them. Then, afterwards I'll give you the company accounts file and some sub-contracts so that you get the picture of what's going on at the moment. How does that sound to you so far?" he said, looking over the top of his spectacles.

"Fine," said John, "that's all right by me."

Hendry J. went over to, or rather steered, a crooked path in between various heaps of paperwork placed randomly about the floor and managed to get himself over to the far right hand corner where two filing cabinets stood. He fished in his pocket and extracted an enormous bunch of keys, more akin to a jailer's, and after a few minutes of searching and cursing, he finally located the correct one. He inserted it into the lock and turned it anti-clockwise. A tortured squeal of metal upon metal resulted and Hendry J. pulled the handle of a drawer towards him sharply, with a loud grating noise the drawer was dragged partially outwards, protesting and squeaking as it opened, and finally came to rest lopsided, giving the impression it had a mind to wrench itself free and crash down on to the floor.

Hendry J. placed the handle of a brush at a strategic point under the drawer, thus attempting to ensure its dubious stability while he busied himself rummaging about inside.

"Ah! Got it!" he exclaimed over his shoulder. "I must really get this office organised one of these days!" he added. "Just never seem to get the time to do it, too busy doing paperwork!" John smiled at the answer. Hendry J. continued unheeded. "Do you know, I moved in here over sixteen years ago, temporary accommodation you understand?" and he looked back over his shoulder as he said it, and raised his eyes roofwards, "and here I am, still here, short of a secretary and not enough hours in the day to cope with all this! Still, I've survived this long so I suppose I'll survive a few more years yet, eh?"

John concurred. He noted a few piles of paperwork bound together with string in bundles, small mountains of files leaning sideways, the overspilling waste basket and a business plan on the wall which had practically no writing space left on it whatsoever.

Leaving the cabinet open, Hendry J. returned and passed a well worn file, bulging at the seams, over the desk top to John.

"You'd better start with this one, I think you will get a better overall picture from its contents," he said thoughtfully. Then realising that John had nothing to put it on he added, "Hang on! I'll get you a desk to put it on." He cast his eyes around the office, followed a second later by John's eyes, but not an empty desk was in sight. They both looked at each other. Hendry J. took a few paces forward and contemplating a small desk amass with box files and miscellaneous items on it, he suddenly swept the lot clear of its surface with a grunt, consigning it directly to the floor level where it arrived with a resounding crash and a cloud of dust. "There!" he said, with a flourish of the arm that had wreaked instant destruction, "been meaning to do that for ages! Much better don't you think?"

John laughed, "Well it certainly got the results!" he commented, as his eyes returned again to the heap on the floor. Hendry J. dragged a chair out from the corner of the room, disturbing more piles of paperwork in the process. John noted that it was a rickety looking item as Hendry J. proffered it to him. John took it from him and checked its stability, it looked safe enough, but to be on the safe side he cautiously applied his weight to it, easing his frame downwards until he was finally seated. He leaned forwards and the chair gave a creak in protest, as if in agony. John looked down at the chair and all around it. It looked as though it would survive. Hendry J. had meantime disappeared inside his sea of paper and was soon heard scribbling away on some hidden notepad and occasionally stopping to mutter to himself before resuming the scribbling.

John busied himself with the files and turned to the first enclosure, it was a preliminary report on the feasibility study and was followed by numerous reports of the original contract to construct the dam. It was relatively straight forward and work seemed to have continued as per schedule for quite some time until suddenly, covering a few months, the reports had become skimpy, vague and clearly indecisive. By this time, the project was behind schedule and a sheaf of paperwork dealing with labour relations spelt out a black catalogue of setbacks. Some workers had mysteriously disappeared, most had left, plant and equipment had gone missing as had a large stock of materials. Further sub-contracts had been negotiated with the suppliers but either the goods had not been delivered, or payment for them had not been made. The net result of it all was that the project had come to a sudden halt. He re-read the enclosures, making notes of the relevant pages for future reference. Having extracted what he wanted to know, he asked Hendry J. for the accounts file. He removed it from another filing cabinet of better quality, it only squeaked once on opening, and Hendry J. passed it over to John. The telephone rang and John looked up. He could hear it but could not see it. Neither could Hendry J. There then ensued a one man pantomime while Hendry J. attempted to discover the source of the noise. After a long search Hendry J. decided to follow the wire from the telephone socket in the wall and like a blind man he felt his way along it, foot by foot, in and out of the piles of paper. It ran under some cardboard boxes and arrived at his desk, then shot off at a tangent only to reappear under another heap of files. The great telephone chase continued whilst the telephone continued its impatient ringing while the intrepid explorer neared his goal.

"Got it!" Hendry cried out in jubilation, as if he'd found the source of the Nile. John noted that he was only two feet away from the desk. John hadn't moved, having remained in his seat watching Hendry's antics with much amusement. A frantic delving exercise then followed amongst the newly consigned heap on the floor which produced the offending but still ringing instrument. Hendry J. grabbed it and plucked the receiver from its nest.

"Good morning! Consolidated Construction. Hendry J. Simons speaking, how can I help you?" he said in his best polished English accent. With all his strength John managed to refrain from bursting out into laughter. Hendry J. noticed this as he spoke and with a smile on his face he waved at John with his free hand. The conversation continued. "Oh! It's you, William!" Hendry stated, "and what can I do for you today?" The voice at the other end made a statement and Hendry J. replied, "What! How? Today? Well, I suppose I'll have to, won't I? Well, all right then, I'll see you shortly." Putting down the receiver, he left the telephone in its new found place so that he knew where to find it the next time it rang and turned towards John.

"Would you believe it?" he asked. "Here I am up to my neck in work and with not a minute to spare, when I've got to go and pick up the stationery I've ordered, as if I haven't enough to do already! Oh, well! I may as well go and get it over with," and turning to John he asked, "Will you be all right while I'm away?"

"Yes I've got quite a lot here to go through yet."

"Right then, I'll be about three-quarters of an hour, if anyone phones I'm out on business at a meeting!" John smiled to himself, but continued reading the company accounts. The sound of clumping feet was heard hurriedly descending the stairs, followed shortly afterwards by the starting up of a car engine, the crashing of gears and a squeal of tyres on the asphalt surface as they bit into the ground produced the noise of a grand prix start for Hendry J.'s station wagon, soon to be lost in the daily flow of traffic heading down town.

John meticulously went through the reports, noting down some relevant details. Once again, they reflected a similar pattern, normality followed by absolute chaos, a sudden loss of monies in notably large amounts at various intervals, a lack of invoices to support transactions and a large amount of petty cash which was unaccounted for. Huge quantities of building materials were also unaccounted for and it was not clear if they had ever been delivered or not. He discovered that it was now two pm in the afternoon and Hendry J. had not returned. Shortly afterwards he heard a car door being slammed outside. That'll be Hendry J. he thought to himself. He had no sooner finished thinking about him when suddenly the door opened and there stood a quivering mountain of stationery, supported by a pair of legs with only Hendry J.'s hands in view and topped by his brow which protruded slightly. The pile moved slowly, he feeling his way with his feet like a man on the edge of a precipice. He stopped, rotated, and spying a small area of unpopulated floor, he made his way gingerly over to it and with a judicious bend of the knees he deposited the stationery whereupon it immediately toppled over to join the rest of the piles on the floor and so add to the confusion. He sat down exhausted, his arms seemingly now two feet longer than they were when he first went out.

"Glad to see you back," John said, "did you have a nice day?"

"Damned stationery!" he said, "just where can I put it all?" and he looked around for inspiration.

John thought for a while, looking around the office but discovered that there was really nowhere for the additional items to rest. He turned to Hendry and said, "How about doing one of your magic acts once again, one of those sudden instant clearances?"

Hendry J. saw the funny side of this and smiled cynically. "Yes! I'll have to do something with it all now!" and having said so, he thought awhile. He didn't know exactly what but he arose and went over to his desk and resumed where he had left off before he went out. "How's the files doing?" he asked from behind the desk.

"Oh, just fine. I've got almost everything I want now, I think. Is there anything else I need to know about?"

"Well, there's ..." and he hesitated, "there's the Juju men and the murders, and the drugs!"

"The what!" John exclaimed sitting up straight in his chair, "I never came across any mention of them in the reports!"

"Quite!" said Hendry, "you wouldn't either as they're not in there! But I'll tell you all about it now, that is," and he paused, "if you're sitting comfortably?"

"Shoot!" said John, his pen poised ready to take notes.

"Well now, where should I begin?" Hendry said, pausing for a few seconds, "all right then, let's go through them as I mentioned. First of all the Juju men. Seems there was some initial hostility among the tribes to the dam being sited on their land. The local chiefs were up in arms about it, and they called upon the local Juju man to perform their rites and to advise the chiefs on the outcome. They carried out these rites which involved the use of a chicken, its bones and feathers, some magic preparations and dust, from which the Juju man can tell the wishes of the gods or something like that. Anyway, the results were in favour of denying the availability of the land for the building of the dam and it took same pretty hard bargaining and a large sum of money changing hands before the chiefs eventually capitulated and the project began coming to fruition. After that, once it was started, a large labour force was assembled, mostly from the local villagers and local tribes, but some also from further afield. They were all good workers and you'll note from the company records that all was going well for quite some time, yes?"

"Yes! I read that."

"Well, you see, the Juju men, or someone, re-instigated the original objections and had spells cast on the local tribes which eventually depleted the number of workers. Some of these who disobeyed the Juju men's calls suddenly disappeared and over a very short period of time, about three weeks, if I remember correctly, some of them were found bound and tied in the bush with their throats torn out as if they'd been attacked by some big wild cat or something of that description. Two of them were found speared to a tree trunk at night and others were found to have some mysterious disease and died soon afterwards. Well! The remainder took fright and ran off. The only ones that remained were those from the outlying tribes and those from far away who did not heed the local Juju man."

"As if that's not bad enough already!" commented John, "Don't tell me! There's more?"

"Yes," said Hendry J., "but let's get on to the next item, the, eh, murders!"

"How many, Hendry, or dare I ask?"

"By all accounts five, again over a period of time and by that I mean a few weeks. You know, of course, that the man who preceded you was sent back?"

"Yes I heard of that, what actually happened then?"

"Well, there was a local conspiracy involving some very shady characters who were supplying drugs to one or two people, the man who proceeded you and the second in charge of the project as well. Anyway, it all got completely out of hand, weapons, that is to say guns, were produced and waved about, all apparently because the drugs had been supplied and no money received. The outcome of it was that two of the workers were found shot dead inside a Land

Rover, both shot through the head. About a week later three locals again involved in this drug running were also found shot dead in the same manner. One of them was the alleged supplier in the first place and it was suspected that the later murders were a tit-for-tat killing and for good measure, they bumped off the biggest fish of all."

"That would explain the missing sums of money, then," commented John, "and the deficiencies on the company accounts. I did make some notes of those items."

"Quite!" said Hendry, "that's how I interpreted it as well."

"Well go on, what's the third one?"

"That was it, the drugs and the murders combined. I'm sure you've got the picture now, John, and I don't think you need any additional worries to contend with."

"Certainly not, are there any others?"

"Not that I know of. Anyway, you've enough on your plate with that lot!"

"That's for certain! Still, it gives me a fairly accurate account of the overall picture so at least I know from where I'm starting."

At this point the office door had opened and Klaus had reappeared, having obviously been frequenting some source of alcohol as he looked slightly inebriated. John continued the conversation with Hendry J., Klaus not having much to contribute, although occasionally he joined in. John thanked Hendry J. for his time and help, and with the additional information he took his leave, wishing Hendry J. a new office of larger proportions with plenty of desks, and finally reminded him as to where the telephone now was. Hendry J., from his point of view, now felt confident that here was a man who would make it all work smoothly again and if he achieved that quickly, it would take an enormous strain off his shoulders. He really had too many companies to look after, that was the problem!

John and Klaus left, retraced their steps to the Eko Hotel, and Klaus informed him that the next day he would collect him from the hotel at eight in the morning and that they would fly up to Abuja. He had already arranged for Sam to drive up and meet them there. They would stay the night there, with Sam picking them up from the new international airport and driving them down to the federal capital of Abuja itself, some twenty-five kilometres away. Abuja only recently had been a small village in the bush and unimportant. However, it had now become the new federal capital and modern society had thrust upon it the new technology and all the trappings that went with that. A new and ever-expanding city had grown up out of the dusty and characteristically red earth. Many new government buildings were in the course of completion. Julius Berger and Co. had, in a surprisingly short period of time, built up a series of motorways and interconnecting roads, flyovers and dual carriageways linking all the areas around Abuja together. The transfer of government departments was imminent from Lagos with their accompanying manpower and resources.

It was now about four in the afternoon and John reclined on his hotel bed.

Outside the hotel, a disturbance was obvious by the noise of running feet, shouts and cries of, "Look! Look!" John went over to the window to see what all the commotion was about. Out in the car park stood an old white painted vehicle. On it, a winch was being operated by a young black youth accompanied by its black driver who was manipulating the controls. Beyond him, crowds had gathered on a nearby road, most of them dressed in brightly coloured clothing, and all pointing skywards. Children ran to and fro excitedly shouting to others. John's eyes followed the direction of the many raised arms and pointing fingers up in to the sky. A large hot air balloon with a wicker basket was drifting slowly over towards the hotel. In it, a man stood waving to the crowds below. It was a publicity stunt and John could read quite plainly the wording on the sides of the balloon which were emblazoned in large red lettering stating that the advertising was for the Coca-Cola company. Three cars had crashed into each other as the drivers attempted to watch the balloon's descent while they drove along. They were embroiled in a heated argument about whose fault it was, gesticulating wildly and pointing up into the sky at the same time. It all seemed so comical to John. At the petrol station just opposite the hotel, those waiting in the long queue for petrol, had abandoned their vehicles to move over to a better vantage point so that they could see the balloon more clearly. Now it was slowly descending and drawing nearer to the ground as the cable winched it in. Some of the locals fled in fright as it came closer to the ground. Tribes still had superstitions about things from the sky and this may have been a bad omen. Others remained, entranced by this strange apparition which by now was rapidly approaching the ground. As the occupant let the air escape by pulling on the balloon's cord, it fell sharply and landed with a thump in the middle of the car park, narrowly missing some parked cars. Taxi drivers who had been washing their cars fled into the nearby bushes at breakneck speed and crowds quickly gathered around the man who had stepped out of the basket on to the tarmac. The three of them then proceeded to fold up the balloon neatly, stow it inside the basket and secure it inside the vehicle. Those around gaped in wonder at this man from the sky. Some crossed themselves twice, and pairs of eyes with only the whites showing could be seen through the branches of the nearby trees.

The man disappeared into the hotel entrance and John, inquisitive to see who it was and where he had gone, went downstairs to the hotel bar where he found the man sitting quietly enjoying a drink of cold beer. He walked over to him and introduced himself. "Hello! I'm John McDonald."

The man looked up, rose from his seat and replied, "I'm Harry Johnson!"

"Quite a display out there, Harry!" he commented.

"Yes, I suppose it was, it must seem strange indeed to these people."

"Is this your hobby, then?" John asked.

"No," then he added, "well I suppose you could say it was really, as I do it for a living mainly now, would you believe? I used to be a salesman for the company and I went off ballooning at weekends. One of the managers at the plant thought that it would be a great publicity stunt and asked me to do it so now I do it full time and, naturally enough, I enjoy it. It advertises the product very effectively and I get paid handsomely for it to boot!"

"Do you just do this in Africa, then?" John asked.

"No, I've been to South America, Australia, and next I'm off to China. That should be very interesting, I think!"

"Yes, well it certainly was spectacular, Harry! Certainly got the crowds flocking to you from the surrounding area."

John and Harry remained in the bar for some time and consumed quite a few beers in the process before John took his leave from him and went upstairs to his room. He felt as though he had had a long day, maybe it was all the files he'd had to read or the copious notes he'd taken. Hendry J. had promised to keep in touch with him and went so far as to say that he might eventually manage to tear himself away from his office and get out to see things for himself for a change. John doubted that, as he could quite easily see him still behind his desk in another sixteen years time and still amid the mountains of paperwork and still hunting for the ringing telephone.

If he did ever get a secretary, which was extremely doubtful, he or she would need to have an extremely firm constitution to cope with that lot! He had said that he would see Klaus in the morning so he had plenty of time to relax until then.

The hotel as usual was very busy, a constant stream of people coming out and going in, the reception desk a sea of bodies, a pushing heaving mass, as they all manoeuvred to claim recognition and the attendance of the meagrely distributed desk clerks. In his room, he switched on the air conditioner to 'FAST COOL' and 'HIGH' and stood for a while looking out below from his veranda. Nothing seemed to change down there no matter what time of day it was. Day and night the procession of people moving to and fro was repetitive. The vehicles came and went continuously, and the only time that there seemed to be a lull in the proceedings was between the hours of two and four in the morning when it diminished but only slightly. John went indoors and had a shower and, feeling refreshed, he lay down on the bed and switched on the television. An interesting film was showing, *The American Ninja*, which was a bit far fetched he reckoned. His mind wandered, he went back over the files he had read in the office, and thought about it all. Hopefully, all the previous events were things of the past, but he had a sneaking suspicion that he hadn't heard the last of it at all. The telephone rang, he picked it up. It was the money man, again! Did he have any dollars to sell, yet? He declined the offer and hung up. How come he had called at this time? John wondered. He decided that there must be a system whereby the hotel desk gave the money man the nod whenever anyone came in. It sounded logical enough anyway.

It was still quite hot with only a gentle breeze blowing. He dressed casually and went down to the bar by the swimming pool and ordered a beer. It came chilled and he savoured its taste. It slid down, depositing itself with a nice cooling sensation as it reached his stomach. The bar tables were sparsely occupied. Mainly European types with briefcases ajar as they read over the day's business deals, some with calculators at the ready, noting down sales figures. One sat writing furiously, glancing down now and then at a busy notepad. A number of day fighters flitted around, flaunting themselves at every man in sight.

One of them, accompanied by his wife looked longingly at the classily-dressed females as they moved about and paraded by but quickly averted his gaze when he noticed out of the corner of his eye that his wife was watching him at the same time. She gave the day fighter a look that would kill, as if two cannons were about to fire a blast in her direction. The girl retreated and went off in the opposite direction where she hesitated to pose on the steps for the benefit of any who just might be watching. She spotted a friendly face, an elderly looking man in expensive clothes, who patted the seat next to him and waited patiently for her to come over. The girl signalled her willingness, sat by him and ordered a drink. The waiter, unspoken, noted her request and reached under the bar and produced a Coca-Cola and a small glass. The two engaged in conversation. Obviously known to each other, he thought, perhaps she's his regular bit. The bar was now filling up and there were few vacant seats as it was almost seven-thirty in the evening. At an adjacent table sat two men, one of them obviously English and the other who John took to be an American by his style of clothes. They hailed him and invited him over. John had looked behind him, thinking that they were gesturing to some other person but then realised that it was himself they were referring to. He arose and stepped around the table. The Englishman got up and offered John a drink and a handshake, and introduced himself as Dave and his companion as Walter. Dave said he was in sales and that Walter was a farmer from Oklahoma.

"What brings you here then?" he asked of Walter.

"I'm on the exchange programme," he said. "I work for the United Nations so we're over here studying the African farming methods and all that sort of thing. I've found out so far that they're quite different to what I'm normally used to."

Dave joined in, "Yes, it will be Walter. I've been here for a few years now selling pesticides but as fast as we introduce them and they start to take effect, the insects develop an immunity to them so we have to modify them quite a bit. It's not easy, I can tell you! What line are you in then, John?"

"Construction," he replied.

"Is that hotels then?" queried Walter.

"No, I'm involved in a dam project which needs a shot in the arm, so to speak."

"That means a fairly long time here, then?" he queried.

"Yes, about four years, I reckon, but it's a play it by ear situation, it may take longer, it may take less. I'll see how it goes but it could turn out to be difficult."

"I think you'll find lots of things out here difficult," said Dave, "there always seems to be a hold up in one way or the other in what should be a relatively simple task."

"I've noticed that as well," commented Walter, "but you just have to bend with the breeze as we say and adapt to their system. I find it gets results quicker if you do it that way. One thing for sure, you certainly have to reduce your standards by a large amount!"

They continued their conversation, each finding that they had a lot in common in addressing the local problems and having a good laugh together while at the same time consuming a number of bottles of cool beer which helped to make the conversation more fluid and animated. Meanwhile, night fighters had taken over, singly and in pairs, on their beat looking for a nightly catch. They were ruminating about things to do in the evening, or rather places to go, when Dave suggested they go to KoKo's.

"What's that?" asked Walter.

"Well, it's the local dive bar down by the waterfront where almost everybody goes for a few beers and a laugh, and it's also noted for its female presence!"

"You mean the ladies of the night?" said John, taking another swig of his beer.

"Yes! That's it," said Dave, "fancy it then?"

"Well! I'm game," stated Walter, nodding his head at the same time.

"Me too!" said John. They finished up their beers, and called for a taxi after paying for the bill with some well worn niara notes, and made their way out of the hotel.

"How are we getting there?" asked Walter.

"In the taxi, of course, it's not far, about five minutes ride, that's all." He hailed the short queue of waiting yellow and blue coloured taxis. The drivers were sitting talking. An instant scramble ensued during which a lot of pushing and shoving occurred. First into his car for a standing start, was the driver of number two car who succeeded in getting into it, started it up and with the door swinging open, he pulled out from the queue, revving his engine up highly he advanced quickly and screeched to an abrupt halt alongside the three prospective customers. Meanwhile numerous cat calls and impolite phrases were uttered by the driver's compatriots who were not amused at all by his antics. The driver shouted back at the rude faces behind him, "Yo' all too late, too late!" and added, "De early bird, he catch de worm!" then, "Okay massahs, where we go?"

"Do you know KoKo's?" asked Dave.

"Do I know KoKo's?" said the driver, "Sho' I knows it! Is very nice place!" and he grinned, "Deh is plenty beer, plenty wumman, good time place, was once called Julie's Bar. Okay! We go!"

They roared off down the slope and out of the gates not slowing at all for the three sleeping policemen which resulted in the occupants being catapulted up into the air, and the gate guards were not amused either as he roared past flinging his gate pass at them through the window as he went.

"Sorry, massahs!" he shouted, grinning widely. "Dey is only small bumps!"

He continued grinning as they all laughed in unison. The car turned left out of the gates, then right along Bar Beach Road, and they were soon lost in the local streets of Victoria Island. The driver took a few short cuts down some side alleys and came out alongside the waterfront and passed under the bridge that spanned the waterway. A few minutes later the cab slowed almost to a halt, turned sharply to the right and drove into a car park in pitch darkness into the only vacant space by the entrance. The car park, they noticed, was absolutely jam packed full of cars. They clambered out and gave the driver his fare and a generous tip to go with it, following his pointing finger they picked their way in the darkness over to the entrance of the bar. It was dimly-lit inside and they passed along a short concrete walkway that sloped downwards sharply. On either side, rows of wood carvings were just visible in the darkness but it was difficult to focus in the amount of light present there. They moved a few more steps forward and emerged into an area where white painted tables were pushed together and placed over planking which straddled the actual river itself.

Few tables were vacant, most having been taken up by Europeans and a groups of young black girls, who talked incessantly with them.

Trays of bottled beer passed to and fro and it was obvious that business was brisk. A few girls immediately broke off from the group as they entered and came towards them as they sat down.

"Hello boys!" followed by, "You are welcome!", they all repeated this individually and deposited themselves professionally amongst the three of them. They lost no time in engaging in conversation with them. Walter thought the whole thing was incredibly funny and they had a good time while they looked about them and took in their surroundings. As soon as someone new arrived, the girls would break off and move over to them, like moths to a flame they flitted to and fro until they were offered a drink by the customers. Those that were unsuccessful quickly went back to their former customers or hung about the entrance to waylay new visitors. Some of the girls were young and attractive, while others were obviously older and had seen a few wrinkles. John guessed those to be about fifty years old, but in fact they were only about twenty-five. Life expectancy here in Nigeria was low, averaging about forty-five years, although quite a few old people did survive into their eighties before departing for the next life. One girl, he reckoned, was about fifteen years of age but had legs like match sticks and a figure to match. She had a very outgoing personality and she moved to the music well and was indeed friendly. She was immediately given the nick-name of the 'stick insect', which suited her perfectly. Another, with well rounded curves and an attractive hair style, sported a tight fitting pair of leather trousers in black complete with metal studs and an imitation holster around her hips. Most were dressed in European fashion, some spoke little English, but most were quite adept at it and, of course, at other things. The girls were all out for one thing and, of course, as many free drinks and meals as they could get out of it in the process.

Each turned out to be expensive, but sex was the most expensive of the three. Fifty to one hundred niara plus a taxi fare of about ten niara was the norm. However, the owner of the bar slapped a two hundred niara a month fee, for 'registration', so all was not pure profit. Nevertheless, it was a decent living as far as they were concerned. Numerous men of differing nationalities left at various times with the odd girl or two, language being unimportant as far as sex was concerned. Names like Lola, Yvonne, Patience, Mercy, Mary and Julie were commonplace, some girls changing their names nightly to confuse the clients. They all knew each other and a sort of camaraderie existed between them. However, they did not support each other if they were arrested and locked up by the police for soliciting. If that occurred then they suddenly became individuals. Dave, Walter and John had a good night out and they were merrily inebriated, everything was a huge joke and a laugh, and even the offer of some of the company of the girls was laughed off. The girls volunteered to accompany them to the hotel but they managed to execute some skilful ploys to avoid capture and to hail a taxi to returned to the hotel completely unscathed. Aids was prevalent in Lagos, being a common disease amongst at least fifty percent of the prostitutes. So much so that companies operating out of Lagos provided their employees with free condoms without limit in green, yellow or pink, this being a sensible address to the problem. After all, treatment was very expensive in Nigeria, and rare.

They spilled out of the taxi at the hotel entrance, laughing and talking loudly, and went their way to their respective rooms after running the gauntlet of the clutch of night fighters gathered in the foyer, agreeing that they should meet at some future date for a rerun of the night's outing.

John awoke the following day early and looked around. He tried to get out of bed but could not, his head was swimming. He tried to focus his eyes on some point around the room but it was all in vain. He closed his eyes and the room swam. He fell asleep, awoke again some fifteen minutes later but now he was able to take in his surroundings. Struggling up into a semi-standing position, he held his hands to his head and the room slowly came into view. He peered at his watch and noted that it was six-thirty in the morning. He tried to recollect last night's events but his memory was cloudy. He recalled something about having a few drinks at the bar and going out somewhere but after that it was all lost from memory. He staggered to the bathroom and rested his hands on the edges of the sink, then raised his head slowly to the level of the mirror. He didn't like what he saw. He appeared to be completely washed out. He stuck out his tongue and noticed that it was a horrible white and yellow colour. A grope for the toothbrush and paste, followed by a hasty scrub around the inside of the mouth made him feel a lot better. He climbed into the shower, turned on the water and stood beneath it for some time until he felt better, then clambered out and sat down on the edge of the bed on the towel and slowly towelled himself dry. Once again he went out on to the balcony and gazed downwards. Little caught his attention, not even a large crowd assembled on the roadway where two taxis had met nose to tail and were locked together, the drivers in an argument while the crowd increased in size. He dressed and packed his bags, recalling the meeting with Klaus and the trip to Abuja that morning. He went down for breakfast but could not stand the sight of the fried eggs, sausage and fried bread on offer, instead he had a large glass of fresh orange juice, some cold sliced pineapple and about five cups of coffee. By seven-fifteen he felt human again. Neither Walter or Dave had appeared for breakfast, probably hung-over in their rooms, he thought. He returned to his room, collected his bags and made his way down to the reception desk.

It was, as usual, busy. Numerous businessmen were checking out while behind them a small collection of drivers waited patiently talking among themselves, each having been allocated to the individual businessmen for that day. He managed to catch the attention of a passing clerk and got across to him by hand signals that he wanted to check out. The clerk rummaged about in a busy overspilling folder, produced John's bill and laboriously pored over it, totalling up various amounts on a calculator, writing it on a piece of paper, totalling it up again, then repeating the exercise all over again, and finally cross checked it against the original calculation. With a puzzled look on his face, he passed it over to John for his signature. John ran his eye down it carefully, noting the entries and the respective charges. Near the bottom he noticed an entry marked, 'telephone calls, six niara'. Not recalling having made any telephone calls he called the clerk over and asked, "What's this six niara telephone bill?"

The clerk looked uncomfortable and then replied, "It is de telephone bill, massah."

"But I didn't make any telephone calls," he said angrily, then added, "Tell me then, what number did I call?"

The clerk looked at him, then referred to a sheet of paper on his desk. Passing it over to John, he indicated an entry marked 'Currency service, six niara'.

"What currency service?" he asked.

"Is for money change, massah!" the man replied. "You make de changes, yes?"

"No! I certainly did not!" he replied. All of a sudden he recalled the man on the phone offering to buy dollars and sterling. Of all the cheek! he thought to himself, the so and so had added the charge to his bill!

"Well! You can take that off straight away!" he said, glaring at the clerk, then added, "Get me the manager!"

The clerk looked perplexed and consulted with an associate who nodded silently towards John, then indicated to him that the clerk should go into the front office manager's room and speak to him. The clerk disappeared for a few moments, then returned and without any further comment, he erased the entry from the bill, passed it back over to John to sign. He glanced at it, noting the deletion, counted up the bill and when he was satisfied, he signed it and passed it back to the clerk. He passed it into the cashier's office and John joined the short queue which waited impatiently for their respective rebates. The girl behind the desk, chewed gum lazily, consulted a few well-worn pages of a book and looked at John's bill, made out a receipt for the refund of his balance after having deducted the hotel charges. She slowly counted out the notes, all grubby ones, John noted, and passed them through the access hole in the window. John counted them carefully. A common trick was to pass them over in a heap and short of the amount hoping that the customer would not notice the deficiency. He pocketed the notes and left the desk. He took a seat in the foyer, noting the ebb and flow of the night and day fighters as they changed over.

It was now seven-fifty. The morning was bright and cheerful and he noted, to his great relief, that his hangover had almost entirely disappeared. Shortly afterwards, Klaus appeared beside him and asked if he had a good night. John briefly described the evening's outing, or what he could remember of it.

"Ah! KoKo's!" said Klaus, smiling a knowing smile, "you went there, eh? Plenty women and plenty beer!"

"Yes! Something like that!" John replied.

"Okay then, ve vill go now, I haf the taxi waiting!"

Without further delay they crossed the flagstones to it, a more decent looking one John noticed, as the driver eagerly put their bags into the boot, finally slamming down the lid twice for greater impression on the travellers. They climbed aboard and Klaus said something in the local language in which the word airport was included and the driver set off, looking briefly in the mirror at the passengers and then at his watch. They were soon engulfed in the morning traffic jam of jockeying cars, screeching tyres, blaring horns and the countless police roadblocks along the roads which occurred at monotonous intervals, the police apparently looking for stolen vehicles. A few judicious swerves by the driver avoided numerous collisions as they made their way along the road and over a bridge heading out of town. Some frequent diversions and the changing of lanes was obvious as the driver expertly picked his way through the mêlée, and they turned off this road onto another dual carriageway only to join another horn blowing throng. He spotted a dilapidated sign ahead which indicated on it, in some faded painting, a crude arrow and the words 'to the airport' in an uneducated hand, the lettering all higgledy-piggledy. As they approached the domestic airport of Lagos, they passed on the left-hand side a huge sculptured figure, about eight or nine feet high, mounted on a large stone plinth. It was of a native warrior beating on a drum. It must have been frightening, John thought, to those who infiltrated into this country in the early eighteenth century, a ferocious looking figure indeed!

They arrived at the airport, unloaded their baggage and made their way to the ticket desk. After paying for their tickets, they entered the scruffy-looking departure lounge in which many locals huddled together, shoulder to shoulder, while they awaited the various flights outward from Lagos. The seating was old and worn out, having seen better days, and not too clean either. Not a vacant seat was in sight so they walked over to the refreshments bar and ordered two cold bottles of Coke. The girl behind the counter had a washed-out appearance and sullenly went off through to the back room with a shuffling of the feet which she employed both leaving and re-entering the room. She returned with the two bottles which did not display any indication of coolness. John placed his hand around one of them and sensed that they were more hot than cold, although the outside of the bottles were in fact wet.

"Don't you have any cold ones?" he asked.

"No, massah," the girl replied, "these is de only coldest ones I is got!" John and Klaus looked at each other in despair.

"All right then, we'll have them," and they paid for the drinks and asked for a tumblerful of ice. The girl went away again with more shuffling of the feet and returned with two glasses half filled with ice and passed them silently over to them. They poured the Coke over the ice and took slow sips of the refreshment. The flight was scheduled to leave at ten-thirty in the morning. A sudden, continually echoing announcement on the public address system informed all that owing to an engineering difficulty the flight would be delayed by one hour. Someone quipped in English but with an Australian accent, "What they mean is that the bloody plane's broken down again!" Quite a few people laughed at this knowing it to be nearer the truth. Eventually, after about forty minutes of frustration, the flight was called. The usual jostling of bodies at the exit ensued, people spilling over onto part of the concrete apron while a female ticket collector in the drab airport uniform tried to control the unruly pushing mass of bodies.

After the crowd had milled around for some time someone from the aircraft signalled that they were ready for the passengers to board, and the crowd instantly rushed forwards. The race was on! They sprinted across the apron hell for leather to see who could reach the aircraft first, while John and Klaus took a leisurely stroll along behind them, as if following the charge of the Light Brigade, and joined the still bustling throng as they stumbled in their eagerness to climb the steps of the gangway. They eventually gained access to the interior of the aircraft. The tickets were marked with the seat numbers but there was obviously no control over who sat where and most sat in any convenient or inconvenient seat that presented itself to them. The aircraft suddenly became full up, and brief but noisy arguments broke out at the doorway and at the foot of the steps with the passengers and the cabin staff. All of the cabin staff were big butch women with billiard table legs and they forcefully pushed the remainder of the passengers back down the steps with no form of ceremony, employing the skills of a disco bouncer. These unfortunate people were now arguing amongst themselves and shouting obscenities at the Nigerian Airways staff, and were hurriedly shepherded away across the apron to the terminal building to await the next aircraft, whenever that was supposed to be. The outer door was shut and the engine started and revved up. A crackling noise sounded and the cabin address system mushroomed into operation.

"Hello! Dis am yo Captain speakin', I is de Captain Sambo! And today we is flying to Abuja and de flight will take us one owa! I hope you all enjoy de flight!" The system crackled a few times then fell silent. The aircraft took off normally and was soon on its route for Abuja. One of the cabin crew struggled to dish out the in-flight refreshments, but when she arrived at John and Klaus's row they discovered that the refreshments consisted of a polystyrene cup with cold water and some not too fresh Rich Tea biscuits. They declined this generous offer and the mountain of flesh bearing it moved on to the next row. Halfway down the aircraft the refreshments ran out, only to be greeted by impolite remarks from those intelligent enough to realise that no further refreshments would be forthcoming.

Before they realised it, the aircraft started its descent and maintained it until it was over the airport. John was able to look out of the side window over the shoulder of a big fat man who, by himself, blocked out most of the window. There was no sign of life down below, in fact, nothing to suggest there was an international airport there at all. It settled down into its approach run some eight miles out and continued descending slightly as it progressed along the flight path. A sudden gust of wind caused it to slew to the left and the pilot countered it, albeit slowly, the wheels were heard to go down and the turbulence caused by them slowed the aircraft even more. Flying low over sparsely-populated ground the aircraft dropped and with a bounce it landed on the runway about one-third of the way along it and continued taxiing all the way to the end before turning and taxiing halfway up the runway again, to turn off to the right towards a wide open pan where only one other aircraft sat. The aircraft halted abruptly, coming to rest with a jerking motion as the brakes bit and the aircraft rocked back and forth on its undercarriage. Five or so minutes later, which seemed like an eternity, the outer door was finally opened and through the doorway John could see a set of steps being manhandled out of a shaded area and being pushed ever so slowly over to the aircraft itself. Eventually it arrived and the masses struggled to be the first out of the plane and pushed and shoved as they descended the gangway. John and Klaus followed after the rush was over, stepping into the bright sunlight as the sweat sprang out on their brows like a racehorse suddenly released from a starting gate.

They walked across the tarmac and arrived at the terminal building. A faint breeze had sprung up as two men appeared pushing two trolleys on which to transfer the baggage. After a long wait, the trolleys appeared with the baggage all piled up in an unruly heap. When the trolleys halted most of the items on the top fell off onto the ground, much to the chagrin of some passengers while others merely treated it as a normal event. Two sweating figures in airport uniforms dumped the items unceremoniously on the ground and a scrabble ensued amongst the people as they retrieved their individual items.

The two porters then returned to the aircraft for a second load and John and Klaus waited patiently for their items to arrive. Five minutes later, it appeared and another minor mêlée ensued leaving only their baggage on the ground. They strolled over and picked up the bags and looked around for Sam. He was there standing at the doorway where a hot wind provided a minimal amount of cooling. He moved over and took the bags from them, and said, "Welcome, sirs! I have a taxi ready for you."

"Why a taxi?" queried Klaus, "where is the car?"

"Car break down boss! Has gone to the repair shop, be back tonight 'bout six!"

"Vat happened to it!" demanded Klaus, "it was all right the day before!" he added, sounding more German than ever.

"I don't know, boss, the clutch he give out and no go, so I take it to de repairer, must have new clutch I think."

"Das ist all I need!" exclaimed Klaus, "How much vill it cost?"

"Maybe one thousand niara, boss!" he said looking slightly hurt by the query.

"What!" then thinking for a moment he added, "all right then, we will pay it, but just make sure it is ready for the morning, eh?"

"Okay, boss! I make sure it is there, no problem, I understand."

So saying, Samuel conducted his charges to the taxi which had the engine running and they set off, speeding through the airport gate, the barrier being up, fortunately. Near it, a group of people hung about eagerly trying to flag down any passing vehicle in the hope of a lift into town. They continued along the road which was about two and a half miles long to the junction where it joined the road to the federal capital, along the way were native women bearing a load of firewood on their heads. Some of them were old, their customary form of dress was a cloth around their waists and they were bare from there upwards. Their elongated breasts swung to and fro as they plodded along. The custom of suckling their young into their second or third year, common throughout most of Africa, resulted in the breast tissue not being able to recover and the muscles becoming weak and flaccid with the inevitable drooping. Their faces appeared strained as they bore their loads, backs bent under the strain, but with a short and quick gait they continued along the roadside for miles at a time until they reached their local area and turned off into the bush and onto some unseen path leading to their village.

Piles of yams were built up along the roadside, seemingly unattended, but religiously guarded by unseen eyes. They hoped for a sale and good profit from their customers who stopped at will to haggle for the produce and to reach the best price as far as the customer was concerned. They passed, on the left-hand side, an old post box marked clearly with the letters 'VR'. Passing local villages, some women emerged from the bush bearing large water containers made of earthenware or clay balanced expertly on their heads, and were returning from some nearby spring or source of water. Again, bowed down with the heavy weight, their shoulders and heads were bent towards the ground and they made their way along the roadside oblivious to the traffic that passed them by. A few young children were amongst them, John reckoned them to be only about three years old, but yet they walked with perfectly straight backs in order to support their burdens.

Twice on their journey, they had to stop for a herd of bush cows (mostly white with the odd black or brown one amongst them) as they lazily crossed the road, pausing at will to munch at the surrounding greenery which presented itself for attention. Their herders, mainly older men and a woman swathed in a long dress of a yellow hue, each bore the customary wooden staff and kept station as their charges plodded on steadily through the bush. The oldest man sported a long white cloak which draped from the shoulders to the knee and almost to calf length at the back. He had thin limbs and upon his feet were a well-worn pair of sandals made of leather which had obviously seen many miles of usage. In his right hand he held vertically a long pole about two feet taller than himself which he occasionally applied to the rump of some errant cow who had strayed away from the normal line of advance. Upon his head sat a large conical hat with a wide brim thus masking his features, but it could be seen that his skin was wizened by age but he possessed incredibly sharp eyesight. These people had a good sense of humour but a harsh life. They wandered continuously across the country as they manipulated their herds to and fro at will. They always acknowledged those motorists who stopped to allow the safe transit of their cattle but cast glances of hate at those local ones who did not heed their movement and who made no attempt at all to slow down.

A few miles further on a procession of women travelled along, again in single file, bearing huge bunches of elephant grass tied around with a few strands to prevent the separation of the grasses, later to be woven into mats, dyed in pits in the ground into various hues and later sold along the roadside.

They continued their journey. Large vultures soared and wheeled above them, their sharp eyes keeping watch for some likely prey down below. They passed by flags of many nations supported by huge cylindrical blocks of concrete at their bases. These flags were reputed to represent the many countries who had embassies in the country. Approaching the capital they emerged through large blackened trees onto a modern road system where dual carriageway had been laid by Julius Berger and had carved out of the red ochred earth new roads which interconnected many areas of Abuja, some of it still in its early construction stages. This company was notorious for its reputation in providing the finished article with an amazing efficiency, working seven days a week in the heat. Their efforts continued unabated and the work was always ahead of schedule. By this method they secured lucrative contracts for further roads, bridges, flyovers and hospitals, all to a modern design and high standards of quality. In the distance they could see the new Islamic mosque which had been built for the faithful, the huge dome and minarets in the process of gilding were prominent against the skyline. Their taxi continued into the city, now busy with new buildings in various stages of completion, then turned left at a petrol station and right onto a road marked 'Festival Way'. A large hotel, The Agura, stood back from the road amid attractive gardens and the taxi turned into the entrance, pausing at the gate to obtain a pass. They proceeded through the trees and gardens with many flowers and drew up alongside the entrance portico. A young smiling African in black trousers, a military-styled tunic of red and black and a peaked hat appeared as their car drew to a halt and in Sergeant-Major fashion he called out, "Welcome, massahs!" and gave a crisp salute as the car's occupants stepped into the shaded entrance. Porters in wine-coloured suits sprang into action, their luggage was unloaded and Sam paid the driver from a huge wad of notes that he carried in a briefcase.

"You stay here tonight, bosses! Very nice hotel, I come and see you later in the evening."

"Thanks!" said John, looking around the entrance hall, noting the cleanliness of everything in sight. The interior conveyed the appearance of tranquillity, yet with efficiency. They crossed to the reception desk passing on the left an old traditional carved African chest. At the desk, two young attractive girls with wine-coloured hats and skirts and white blouses stood ready to attend to the guests. They both welcomed John and Klaus by saying, "Good morning, masters, you are welcome!" They produced the registration forms and a pen and asked them to complete them. This done, the two of them paid the customary deposit, being twice the amount of the daily tariff of two hundred and fifty niara. Their keys were issued and they were taken to their rooms up on the first floor by the attendant porters. John was pleased to note that the room was large, airy and cool, and that the air conditioning worked efficiently. Two large double beds stood side by side, a colour television and a well-appointed bathroom completed the picture. He tipped the porter and opened the curtains, the swimming pool and pool bar-restaurant came into view, unpopulated at the moment but tastefully surrounded by gardens, white tables and chairs and sun parasols. Adjacent stood a tennis court on which two figures energetically pursued the ball. He disrobed and had a shower, changed his clothes and rang for room service and asked for the express laundry.

He went downstairs and into the bar where the barman, Augustine, a small man neatly turned out, had already served Klaus and asked what he would like to drink. John thought for a moment and decided on a Star beer. Augustine bent low inside a fridge and produced a glass professionally, as most barmen do, and slowly poured out his drink for him. A dish of roasted peanuts sat atop the bar. John and Klaus decided to take their drinks out on to the patio next to the swimming pool and Augustine efficiently ferried their drinks out there for them. They sat down at a vacant pool-side table and sun umbrella which rotated slowly in the breeze and sipped their refreshing drinks.

For the first time since they'd met they actually found time to discuss the project together. John had formed the opinion that Klaus was a sort of a good for nothing but in the course of the conversation, it emerged that he was in fact quite concerned about the past events as a whole and eager to apply himself to the restitution of the workforce and the project's future advance. John was glad to hear this and they discussed a plan of action. Firstly, they agreed that they would need to take on extra hands to cope with the work involved. Then they would have to meet with the local contractors and re-negotiate supply details and deliveries. The administration was sadly lacking and they were short-handed on the management side. Klaus had a number of good engineers that could oversee the work. They consumed a few drinks in the course of their discussion and it was nigh on five in the evening although it was still sunny and the pool itself still busy. A sudden influx of guests, who arrived in two Range Rovers, turned out to be agronomists, horticulturists, and a few other 'ists which were unpronounceable. They were all employees of Nigerian Breweries, working some distance away, on a well-earned break from their labours, complete with their families. The Agura had an excellent reputation for being refreshingly spic and span with a constant supply of cold water, a feature much desired by other hotels but always maintained by this hotel. It also sported the most comfortable beds, even surpassing the nearby Hilton Hotel in this respect. The ever friendly staff was another plus being usually in conversation with the hotel guests and could remember most of them by name, even if they were only infrequent visitors. It was a long standing tradition with the hotel staff and it was a marked and appreciated form of service.

They formulated a plan of action to be executed once they had reassessed, on site, the situation in general. Klaus had pledged his wholehearted support and John was glad of that as he formed the opinion that he was going to be fighting a one man struggle against tall odds. By now, the time had drifted on to almost six-thirty and they adjourned their conversation until later in the evening. Having had a look at the menu for the restaurant they elected to go over to the Hilton for their evening meal which promised to offer more variety albeit slightly more expensive. They left at eight-twenty and had a drink in the bar before entering the restaurant. They then proceeded to the Bouka Restaurant, here the evening speciality was the 'German Night', and on offer before they actually went in was a selection of German wines and fayre. A wide selection of food was on offer and they spent about half an hour sampling the various wines and chatting to the two staff who were administering them. Finally they entered the restaurant itself and were conducted to a vacant table. The display of food was sumptuous to say the least, and they had a difficult choice to select their preference. The meal was of the buffet type and they wandered up and down along the lines of trays of food and selected what they wanted.

During the meal they outlined their previous plans again and devised alternatives should anything go wrong with the original. They followed their meal with a few cups of the excellent coffee and then relaxed before paying their bill and taking a casual stroll along the marble corridors of the hotel and having a brief visit to the hotel souvenir shop which had a wide variety of traditional African goods on sale and numerous original paintings. Shortly afterwards they went outside and got into one of the waiting taxis to return to the Agura Hotel. They turned right out of the gate and along past the Islamic mosque, now floodlit and prominent. They continued along the numerous sections of motorway that were not officially in use yet and arrived at their hotel, alighted from the taxi and went indoors. The Moonlight Bar was quite busy so they entered and ordered a beer and were served by Judith, one of the bar staff. At the bar were the men who had arrived late in the afternoon and they became engaged in conversation with them on the subjects of growing maize and the brewing of the local beers.

They retired to bed shortly afterwards and John switched on the television. There was the local programme, the 'in-house movie' or the Sky channel. He opted for the latter as it gave excellent coverage of an athletics meeting.

He fell asleep at about one-thirty in the morning and awoke, still fully dressed, at six-thirty. He sat up and noticed that the sunlight was beaming in through the window. He went over to the it and looked out. The hotel staff were busy tidying up in the grounds. He showered and changed and went down to the coffee bar for breakfast at seven-fifteen. There were only a few customers around and Andrew, one of the waiters, welcomed him smiling, and took his order. He did not have long to wait and the first course arrived, a plate of steaming porridge with a jug of hot milk placed before him by another waiter whose name he noted from his badge, was 'Booker T'. He followed this up with bacon and eggs and while he was starting to eat this, Klaus arrived, but declined to have breakfast and instead opted for a cup of coffee only. They chatted briefly, signed the chit for their breakfast, and went upstairs to collect their baggage and then down again to check out at the reception desk. They completed this simple computerised process and sat down on the circular seating arrangement in the centre of the foyer to await the arrival of Sam. John studied the old wooden chest, noting that on it were depicted scenes of various tribal events.

Sam appeared shortly afterwards, dressed in a freshly pressed safari suit. He walked over to them and said, "Good morning, bosses!" then followed this with, "The car is ready!"

"Is it fixed now, Sam?" asked Klaus.

"Yes, sah! It is okay now, and he drive very well, yes, very well," and he indicated the car standing at the doorway.

"Gut! Let's get started then, as it will take us a few hours to get there and we best get on the road before it gets too hot."

"Okay boss! I ready!" and he picked up the bags and loaded them in to the car. The doorman in the red tunic saluted smartly again as they set off towards the gate.

John sat in the front with Klaus in the back. They handed in the pass at the gatepost and turned left, left again and along past the municipal housing scheme, past the local indoor market which was in full swing even at this early hour of the morning and carried on up to the next road junction, passing the rows of newsboys who waved the newspapers at them and hawked a multitude of wares at each and every car that passed by. They stopped at the junction where a policewoman controlled the traffic in her bright orange blouse and gave them some vague signals to proceed. As they turned right a long line of men, women and children waved and gesticulated at them as they passed by, each hoping for the offer of a lift to some unknown destination. Some had huge sacks of gari stacked up awaiting transfer and they eagerly awaited a communal taxi to came along or an old Peugeot 404 truck to stop which could carry quite a load. They continued on and headed out towards the airport and on to Suleja. They passed by local villagers walking along the road, barefoot, carrying a mixture of items. There was the short right-angled spade used for digging the soil, bundles of grasses and home-made baskets all balanced on their heads. The young children, too, shared in the burdens, the younger ones maintained the delicate balance with a hand as they moved along. A tall thin man wearing a ragged pair of shorts and devoid of any cover whatsoever on his buttocks, carried a car wheel on his head perched vertically in perfect balance. Women trudged along with heavy loads, their eyes fixed on the pathway. It was the woman's responsibility to do all the work for their family. Old crones headed the columns with the younger ones following on behind, their ages diminishing as the line reached the rearmost, save for one more elderly person to supervise them. A band of hunters, two old men and two young men, were armed with a rifle, obviously one handed down through the generations over the years, with the younger ones carrying spears and a large carved wooden club. They turned off the road into the bush and soon disappeared along a track and vanished from sight. They drove on passing a bridge over a stream where a huge colony of bats with wingspans of about four feet or so soared in the early morning ritual flight around the tops of the trees before resting for the day in some shaded area.

They stopped a number of times to allow the herds of bush cows to cross the road, their drovers carrying their long poles horizontally across their shoulders with their hands draped over the poles as they walked along. Some of them carried a bag which resembled a satchel with a long shoulder strap which went around the neck.

"Who are these people?" asked John of Sam.

"They Bororoje," he replied, "they are cattle people, wander all over the country, not stay long anywhere, just buy and sell cattle and move on."

"Don't they have any homes then?" he asked.

"No boss, no home, just wanderers, used to belong to Fulani tribe from the north and north-east."

The cattle looked anaemic, some with protruding ribs, the bulls with large curved horns. They were attended by flocks of small white egrets who went along for the ride on the cattle's backs or strutted around busily in amongst the cattle's legs to pounce on disturbed insects, mostly grasshoppers, which was their staple diet. The Bororoje gave them a friendly wave as they passed by, quickly turning their attention back to the cattle and the shepherding of them. A local bus passed by on the opposite side of the road, fully loaded with people and freight, sagging low on its suspension and axles as it crabbed along on its twisted chassis, a sea of faces peered outward at the Ebos as it trundled on down the road. The hot air rushed past. All the car's windows were fully wound down thus allowing the maximum flow of air and at least keeping the temperature down. Roadside piles of yams attracted the attention of travellers, who stopped to bargain for them and who eventually left with a huge amount after much argument and gesticulation. They passed the turn off for the International airport and again the old post-box which still received the customary coat of red paint. John wondered if anyone actually put mail in to it, it being a reminder of the days not so very long ago when Nigeria used to be a British Colony. The road was mainly straight with a few gradual undulations and bordered on both sides by a variety of greenery and small villages scattered throughout them, amid which smoke could be seen drifting slowly skywards.

They continued on to the end of the road and turned right towards Suleja. The road here was much busier with a heavy flow of traffic, it being the main route to many other towns in the area. Descending a long hill they came into sight of the Zuma rock, an enormous, roughly conical-shaped rock, sheer on all sides, which could be seen for miles around and in same cases obvious from about twenty miles away. On the side nearest the road it had the appearance of a grotesque face of some description, although stained and blackened. Local folklore suggested it had some magical properties or figured in ancient tribal superstitions. Its imposing appearance hinted at its constitution. It appeared to be of sandstone but it bore the signs of having been formed from something more substantial and denser, perhaps granite. Its blackened surface and weathered coating prevented identification. A partly finished luxury hotel stood adjacent to it, having been abandoned by its builders through lack of finance, a common occurrence throughout the country as a whole. They noted an asphalt production centre on their left as they passed by the rock, with a stream of large trucks awaiting loading with the material bound for the multitude of road programmes which were in existence in the area. The road was potholed in many places, the traffic having to weave in and out of them as they progressed along the road and having to swerve quite regularly to avoid the holes. It was obvious that many burst tyres had occurred, broken axles were commonplace and for those that did not heed the potholes, the resulting loud thumping noise as the chassis hit the ground and the wheel dropped into these chasms usually resulting in the cars having to be abandoned by the roadside. Numerous vehicles had met their fate this way and they had been abandoned on the road, not by the wayside but left where the event occurred, the remainder of the traffic merely streaming around them and proceeding onwards as if nothing had happened. Eventually, these broken down obstacles would be shunted off the road as they were struck by other passing vehicles, especially during the hours of darkness when numerous cars travelled the route without lights.

Ahead on the road was a dead bush dog, freshly killed by some unseen speeding vehicle. Cars manoeuvred around it. It would not be long before some locals appeared out of the bush and removed it as it was, after all, fresh meat and that was always at a premium in any area of Nigeria. They passed many groups of women and children, all frantically attempting to wave down the passing vehicles for a free ride onwards. They passed through Suleja, a bustling city, densely populated and busy with the daily trading and movement of a seemingly unending stream of people. They stopped briefly at a service station by the roadside to haggle and pay for some bottles of ice-cold cokes from a young girl who was hawking her wares with an earnest expression on her face. Women of varying ages also approached them selling hot roasted sweetcorn cobs, plantain and boiled eggs, carefully displayed on huge trays which they carried on their heads, skilfully balanced as they walked along.

Sam followed the sign for Lokaja, although they were soon to leave that road and strike off towards Minnah, Klaus having previously agreed with Sam that they could detour via there so that Sam could visit his family as he hadn't seen them for some ten years now. It would not inconvenience them at all, and as there was no real rush to get to the site John had been in agreement. The road now had become more potholed and hazardous and had slowed the traffic down to a crawl in places while the vehicles snaked their way around the obstacles or drew to a halt at the numerous narrow bridges which forded small streams which always seemed to be at a much lower level than the roads. These bridges were only just wide enough for one vehicle at a time and at either side of the bridges the roads had been washed away by frequent rainfall which made navigation all the more hazardous. Passing through Kwakuti, a small village, the traffic was stopped as a duck and a following line of ducklings casually waddled across the road totally oblivious to the cars, the blaring of horns and the loud shouting of the drivers. The motorised machines set off again northwards, passing small villages at which young girls pounded yams in their deep wooden containers, raising their long wooden poles up and bringing them down again with force to squash and crush the yams into a pulp suitable for baking. They worked non-stop, only occasionally breaking off from their task to attend to a naked child who squatted nearby playing in the dust while chickens strutted around pecking at anything that looked as though it might be edible. Ahead, a few vultures circled low above a clearing where something dead awaited their attention and their deliberations. They were clearly visible, their sharp curved beaks prominent as they lost height, rapidly descending towards their prey. Close by, a few white-necked crows also circled, waiting to see what was in the offing after the vultures had had their fill. A short procession of native women wound their way down from a small hill on a bush path to the roadside each bearing conical containers of cooled goat's milk. One or two of them had infants strapped to their backs with the legs protruding at either side of their waists and the infants tied firmly to their backs with long strips of cloth. Most of these infants were asleep in the heat of the day and their heads flopped to and fro as their parents walked along. Like rag dolls, thought John to himself as the women reached the roadside. His eyes wandered to and fro taking in much of the detail of the passing countryside while at the same time becoming educated in the local customs as Sam turned out to be a mine of information in all things local.

They passed a sign on their right-hand side which stated that they were soon to be passing the Minnah Marble Quarries which were located in a tree-screened depression in the bush. The road turned and twisted monotonously as they progressed. They passed through Makutu and Paiko, an area where many were busily engaged in experimental farming and the education of children. This was being carried out by the Voluntary Services Overseas who dedicated themselves to their tasks for a mere pittance in living expenses, in return for the rewarding experience of making the villagers life more meaningful in culture and education. A sign crudely hewn out of a piece of wood stood crookedly facing them as they passed by. It had written upon it the name 'JIMMY STITCHES', and underneath it in larger print, 'TAILOR'. This brought a smile to John's face as his eye caught it in passing. He had seen quite a few of these signs en route, one declared, 'THE TWO BROTHERS...MOTOR MECHANIC', another, 'JOSHUA ODINONEWE - TRADITIONAL MEDICINE', and immediately alongside another one 'SONS OF SAMUEL - JUJU MEDICINE'. There seemed to be no end to the ingenuity of most of the locals, motor mechanics were in abundance although John noted that not a car was in sight. A 'punctah repah man' sat engrossed in his trade by the roadside, a small but hot fire was kindled with a foot bellows while the man extracted hot stones from the fire and laid out a large india rubber tube from a truck on the ground. He applied the hot stones to melt the rubber and picked up a huge pair of ancient scissors, proceeded to cut off strips and applied them to the damaged area and again applied the hot stones, thus vulcanising the rubber on to the damaged area. He applied pressure and after inspection with his diseased eyes, he extracted more hot stones from the fire and repeated the exercise on the edges of the patched area and kneaded by hand the patch accurately into position. He then held it up again to the jaundiced eyes and, being satisfied with it, hung it up on the branch of a nearby tree with a long pole to dry in the sunlight. Quite ingenious, thought John as their car passed slowly by, vulcanising at its simplest.

Next they came across the wreckage of a vehicle which had run off a bend, obviously overloaded, and which had toppled and become mangled in a tree, the cab embedded in the trunk. Its cargo lay scattered along the roadside and into the bush, which by now had almost engulfed it, such was the pace of the fast growing vegetation. A kilometre marker indicated that it was now only thirteen kilometres to Minnah. By this time the car occupants were slightly saddle sore after the bumpy journey and they were looking forward to stopping there for a rest and to stretch their legs. In the distance the tall marble gates of the city of Minnah were visible, which were still in the stages of construction and from which a new modern dual carriageway with fluorescent lighting stretched away into the distance. They turned left after they had negotiated the array of potholes which preceded the gates of the city through which every vehicle had to manoeuvre to get there, and followed the busy road leading away from the city and along to the site of the new airport.

After driving for a few minutes they arrived at the gates of the Shiroro Hotel where they were to stay for the night. They halted at the gate where a small collection of security men had assembled around a table. They interrupted their conversation and card game, and one of the men broke off and made his way over to them. He extracted an entry token from a wooden box and raised the entrance barrier and passed the token over to Sam who drove through and up to the hotel entrance and parked at the door. They climbed out and stretched their legs as Sam got out the baggage and went inside to the reception desk. They followed and walked along the long hallway which had obvious signs of dilapidation. Although once a plush decor it had faded considerably and was now only a fraction of its original splendour and a slightly damp smell was apparent throughout. A desk clerk passed them the registration forms and after a delay of about fifteen minutes or so, they eventually secured their room keys and proceeded up the lightly sloping corridors to the top floor wing. The corridors were shaded and cool, and as they went along they passed by many varieties of sleeping moths that were dotted around the walls almost everywhere they looked. They turned into an even dingier corridor and arrived at their rooms which were clean but only just, they too had a slightly musty smell to them. The porter switched on the air conditioning and a clanking noise ensued as the machine struggled to burst into life and continued making weird noises until it finally, with great difficulty, produced some cold air. In the bathroom, a black plastic jerry can stood beside a well-worn plastic bucket in the bath. The porter explained that the water was only switched on between six-thirty in the evening and six-thirty in the morning. John sighed, noting the poor overall standard but decided to accept it as Sam had said that this was the only decent hotel in this area, and the only hotel for miles around worth frequenting. God knows what the rest of them were like then, John thought.

Sam had parked the car in the car park next to the entrance and taking his leave, he had gone over to the gateway and had waited for a passing taxi and had flagged it down, saying that he would be back at eight-thirty in the morning to collect them. Klaus and John dumped their baggage and drifted down the corridors where a few lizards scuttled quickly out of sight as they approached, and made their way over to the bar. Lunch time had passed so they had no option but to settle for a cold beer. The barman disappeared out the rear of the bar and, following a clanking of bottles, he returned with some cold beers and poured them out for his customers. It was two-thirty in the afternoon so they took their beers out on to the patio area and terraced bar where some sturdy steel tables and chairs were scattered around beneath some straw covered sunshades. It was hot; a hot breeze accompanied the intense sunshine. Other guests sat around but most of them were locals and no Europeans were amongst them. John and Klaus discussed their plans and decided on some minor changes, but in any event they were prepared to amend them to cater for any situation. As if by magic, a replacement round of beers had appeared on their table, ghosted in while they were talking by the unseen barman who was obviously well-trained in the art of keeping the customer satisfied. They continued drinking and the beer had loosened their tongues and they signalled through the window for some more, but the barman had already made his way across to them with the replenishment.

About four-thirty in the afternoon they espied, through the same window, some Europeans and called over to them to join them. These did not hesitate and were soon seated next to them and engaged in conversation, the barman, meanwhile, again ghosted over with a fresh tray full of drinks. They introduced themselves as employees of a pharmaceutical company who worked at a nearby factory producing sterile products for a new hospital. They were based in Havant in the south of England, and had been working in Nigeria for a few years. The elder of the two, a happy, rumbustious character went by the name of Peter and introduced himself, then his friend. They sat in the comfortable chairs and a refreshing conversation sprung up, each, it seemed, acting as a foil for the others and they were soon laughing loudly, even Klaus, who had only laughed and smiled a few times since John had first met him. Experiences were related amid howls of laughter and some common ground was discovered in the course of their conversation. Peter started to tell them of an Irish priest he knew who apparently liked to have a drink now and then. His name was Father Cann, and he related his exploits at which they laughed at uproariously for some time. No sooner had they passed on to another subject than who should appear but Father Cann himself, complete with his African driver. The chairs were hurriedly shuffled about and space made for them, and the waiter appeared again with yet another round of drinks for all of them, and the conversation continued where it had left off.

Father Cann was from County Cork, he said, and he had just been to a local wedding nearby where he had been officiating, and had already been plied with a fair amount of palm wine and he had just popped in to the hotel, he said, for a 'quickie' as he put it. He was, they noted, well oiled and they had a great time in their animated and hilarious talk. Before they knew it, it was time for Father Cann to leave, at least so said his driver and the good Father, pillar of the church, got unsteadily to his feet, swayed a bit and with the help of his driver and a little help of the divine kind, they just managed to steer a zigzag path out to his car. The driver poured him in and they were soon lost in a cloud of dust. Those remaining, however, thought this was the funniest thing that had occurred for such a long time and it was ages before they stopped laughing.

By this time none of them could actually stand up straight. The drink had been flowing well and a quick sortie across the floor by one of them to read the evening's menu revealed that nothing exciting was on, so they all decided to go down town to a well known restaurant. They went to their respective rooms and got ready to go out and met shortly afterwards in the hotel foyer, went outside and climbed into Peter's wagon and set off for town. They drove along in the pitch blackness for some time before emerging into the lit up area of town and along the dual carriageway, which was well-known to the locals for being extremely brightly lit, and for some distance, across a small roundabout and finally arrived at a dimly-lit bar set back off the road. They pulled up and spilled out onto the compacted earth and made for the entrance. Peter told the guard to keep a close watch on his vehicle and left instructions that it was not to be stolen.

They entered the bar, it was dimly-lit and at first it was difficult to see but then their eyes got used to the darkness. A few coloured lights were draped around the bar and around a small square of concrete in the centre. A few tables, scattered at will, were attended by a few young persons, but the bar itself was packed to overflowing with scantily clad girls, fifteen to eighteen years of age each wearing brightly coloured tops and modern miniskirts which accentuated their ebony limbs. Some of them stopped talking as they entered and after giving them the once over, they resumed their talk and turned back to face the bar. The owner appeared from inside the restaurant, beamed a wide grin to welcome them and quickly organised a table and a few chairs for them, welcoming Peter especially as he was a well-known patron there. They each ordered their drinks, two Stars and two Rocks. A few other Europeans sat around in the dim light and were in conversation with these other ladies of the night before setting off with them to unknown destinations. Apparently, this place was the common meeting point for them and they all congregated there before setting out on their nightly trading. They ordered their meal from a well-thumbed menu and they did not have long to wait for it. The restaurant owner called them indoors to the seated area and they found themselves in a private secluded area with bright orange tablecloths on the tables. A waiter appeared and efficiently placed their meals down before them. They ate heartily, their hunger appeased, and they followed the main course with ice cream. The bill, they noted, only came to about ten niara each and on the whole it was exceptionally good value for money as Peter had accurately forecast. They emerged again into the darkened area and ordered some more beer. Most of the girls by now had disappeared to earn their crust, usually it only met their food and lodgings but as long as they achieved that they were quite happy.

The four of them eventually decided to go back to the hotel and went outside but when they got to their wagon, they discovered that it had a punctured rear tyre. The guard when questioned just shrugged his shoulders casually but did not make any comment. Peter went to change the tyre but discovered that he did not have a wheel brace and he cursed again. He called to the hotel proprietor who got out his own wagon and agreed to run them back to the hotel.

As John looked out of the window of the wagon, he noticed a puncture repair business just opposite the restaurant. Klaus also noticed and leaning over towards Peter, he said, "No puncture, my friend," and he nodded towards the business, "maybe just a shortage of trade, eh?" They all looked out of the window and laughed when they realised they had been set up. The repair man, seeing them looking at him gave them a toothless smile.

"Quite a normal occurrence here," Klaus commented. The wagon had now come to a halt and the door opened. In piled all the girls that had been at the bar.

"Where's this lot going?" asked John.

"Oh! They're all going to our hotel," commented Peter, "a sort of taxi service, you see."

"That means that their normal beat is our hotel as well then?" queried John

"Yes. That's about the size of it," added Peter.

They all laughed again and the wagon set off along the brightly lit road and soon they arrived at the hotel whereupon the girls spilled out quickly and disappeared inside. Peter and company went to the bar and ordered more drinks while girls positioned themselves around all those present and attempted to chat them up. They decided to call it a night shortly afterwards and went off up to their rooms. There were only a few lamps lit in the dim corridors and the moths flitted about, hell bent on destruction as they attacked the lights. Black crickets crawled up the walls while a preying mantis sat still on a leafy plant, surveying the insect life around it. A variety of frogs ranging from about one inch long to about six inches leapt about in the corridor and a few toads hopped up and down and went off to shady corners to avoid detection. John leant down and caught one and picked it up, but promptly dropped it when he felt something burning his hands.

Peter laughed, and said, "That'll teach you! They do that on purpose, piss on your hand. The strong acid content in their urine burns the skin and makes you drop them. It's a defence mechanism."

John looked at his hand, there was no obvious damage but it hurt. Peter told him to make sure that he washed his hands anyway.

Steering their way around various coloured lizards, they eventually got to their rooms while a few of the toads hopped up and down along the corridors outside the room doors where they would stay all night, and probably still be there in the morning, if only asleep. John closed the door of his room, remembering about the six-thirty rule he decided to have a shower. He stripped off and stood in the bath and by using the plastic bucket, he emptied the water over himself. Although it was cold, the flow of cold water from head to foot made him feel a lot better. He switched on the air conditioner which again fought its way into life and barely managed to produce some coolish air and loud clanking noises with the occasional squeal. He lay down on the bed, but had to get up again almost immediately as a cricket chirped loudly from under the bed. He fished it out and driving it over to the corner of the wall he picked up his shoe and gave it a polite tap on the head which silenced it forever. Outside, a cacophony of frog noises and the inevitable crickets continued their calls non-stop and he fell asleep to the sounds of them.

Next morning he awoke early, it was almost daylight. During the night the mosquitoes had had a feast of his ankles and he had to do a bit of furious scratching while he fished in his bag for the tube of Savlon antiseptic cream which brought about instant relief. At seven-fifteen, he made his way down to the restaurant, along the sloping corridor where most of the insect life had now disappeared but a few lingered on, now asleep. Quite a few lay dead after their night's outing while others made the most of it, namely the toads who gobbled up everything in sight.

He crossed the dark red wrinkled carpet adjacent to the bar and went over to the restaurant. A few waiters hung lethargically around and one of them ambled slowly over to him. Although wearing the hotel uniform of the red top and black trousers, his feet were bare save for a pair of well-worn leather sandals. He proffered the menu and John looked at it. John ran his eye down the meagre choice of items and selected the porridge, followed by the two boiled eggs, tea and toast and waited patiently for it to arrive. He had also asked for orange juice but got tomato juice instead. The eggs did not appear, so he waved the waiter over. The man stopped alongside the table.

"Yes, massah?" he said

"I asked for two boiled eggs, are they coming?"

"I'se sorry, massah. De man who do de eggs, he not heah today, so no eggs, yes?"

John laughed at the explanation. "All right," he said, "forget the eggs."

"Yes, massah, I understand, no eggs today," and he went back to join the other waiters in the corner of the room. At that point, Peter and his friend, and Klaus appeared and joined him at the table, but they only had a light breakfast.

"Well," said Peter, "I suppose I won't see you two again but if you're ever down this way again, just drop in. We will no doubt be here. We tend to be permanent fixtures in this hotel, part of the furniture, I guess."

Klaus and John thanked them for the night out, their friendship, and said farewell. Peter went off to get a taxi at the bar to take him to his wagon and see to the fictitious puncture. Klaus and John checked out of the hotel, collected their deposit minus the charges and sat in the foyer to await the arrival of Sam. A blast on the horn signalled his readiness and he appeared through the door smiling and saying, "Good morning, bosses! It is the lovely day!" and without further ado he picked up their cases and preceded them through the doorway to their car outside. A few hotel employees toiled with watering cans outside while others swept the dust with home-made brooms of twigs and attempted to make the dingy entrance more attractive. They climbed aboard and set off out of the hotel gates, turning left and went along to the main road where they joined the daily throng of taxis, overloaded buses and donkey-powered carts, all jostling for position as the incoming and outgoing throngs of traffic met at the city gates in opposite directions, each trying to out manoeuvre the other. Tempers were raised and rude suggestions could be heard being bandied about. The flow of traffic weaved its way along the rutted road; part tarmac, part dust and part holes. Soon they reached a better part of the road, the traffic sorted itself out into a more coherent stream and they were able to proceed at a more decent speed towards Baji and Zungeru. Recent rains had washed away much of the surface and numerous landslips had occurred making the early part of the journey a jolting experience. At some parts of the road, small gangs of boys aged between five and twelve years, shuffled busily with rough implements to fill in the holes with the red earth and purposely standing in the path of the cars so that they would have to stop. When they did so, they cheekily asked for money for the road repairs. Surprisingly enough, quite a few cars stopped and they were making a steady income, John thought. As their car approached they shouted out, "Hello Ebo! You dash me niara? Yes?"

John asked Sam to stop and he dug in his pocket and handed a five niara now out through the window. Seeing the note the boy took it slowly from his hand, stood open-mouthed as his friends stopped their digging and gathered around him in awe. An older boy, at the rear called out, "God bless you, massah!" and in a sudden rush they were gone into the bush abandoning their implements on the road and were soon lost from sight, no doubt carrying their prize off to their village. They continued their journey westwards.

"Tell me Sam, what's this 'dash' they all ask for?"

Sam turned his head and said, "Well, boss, goes back a long, long time! When Nigeria used to be British Colony," and then he hesitated, "no! Before that! Was when Nigeria was being visited by traders back in the time of 'bout 1712 to get de slaves for de colonies. They has to give a gift to the local chief so that they can get de trade, sometimes goods, sometimes slaves. The chiefs demand the dashes, or you say bribes, before de trade takes place, so now, to get the service or trade you have to give de 'dash'. You understand?"

"Yes," said John, "sounds like a good money making system, eh?"

"Yah," added Klaus, "but not good to dash them too much, only a little."

"Okay," replied John, "I get the message!" and he smiled as they journeyed on. After a few minutes, John asked Sam if he had seen his family.

"Yes, boss, see them! My father he is very old, and my mother too, they live in the village and they are the only old people there! Rest all young, many children and de village it now very big, many huts!"

"Did you see your wife, too, then?"

"I has no wife boss, she dead long time back."

"What did she die of, then?" asked John.

"Well, she die of de guinea worm from de unclean water, is disease from de dirty stream she got when she was very young, was twenty years old, only."

"Sorry to hear that, Sam," John said.

"No need to be sorry, boss, many peoples here die of this disease, is very common. I lucky! I come from de other village, few miles away, not drink de same water!" He then shrugged his shoulders and added, "Is life! Some live, some die. Is no problem."

A philosophical outlook, thought John. "So you have not got a wife, then?"

"No boss, but maybe next time I find me a nice wife," and he grinned, then said, "I still looking! You see one, a good one? You tell me! Okay?" They all grinned at this statement. They were now approaching Zungeru, which was originally a garrisoned town and was the military Headquarters of Northern Nigeria in 1902. The road twisted right and left for a few miles before straightening out and they were able to pass a long string of lorries, all heavy articulated and straining with their heavy loads, most of them overloaded and they belched out black smoke from their exhausts as they proceeded along. Frequently they passed by piles of locally made pots of various shapes and sizes, all being offered for sale to the passing travellers, a useful commodity and always much in demand.

They passed through the town and, as it was market day, the crowds of people in multi-coloured garb were attended by naked children, and they clamoured around the numerous stalls laden with fresh fruit and produce. Purchases were wrapped in cloths and slung across their shoulders or balanced on their heads. Huge mounds of fresh grapefruit and oranges shone brightly in the sunshine alongside a variety of green produce. A few partly butchered goats hung up on meat hooks, showing meagre portions of meat on which clouds of flies flitted to and fro attracted by the odour of the meat dispersed by the breeze. Row upon row of yams, some about two feet in length attracted many people and a steady trade was maintained in this alone. Boys with wheelbarrows which had seen better days, wheeled them to and fro, ferrying the purchases to waiting trucks, buses or donkeys, the latter standing sleeping and laden down heavily with long saddle bags. Two of the wheelbarrows stood at the side of the pile of yams in which two boys lay, one in each, sound asleep as the crowds milled to and fro. A tall man, aged and wizened, inspected a rat trap for sale on one of the stalls which was a roughly hewn plank of wood, and while investigating its operation he accidentally set it off and the metal bar sprung sharply back to trap his fingers in it. A sudden look of surprise came over his face but he did not yell out at all, merely summoning up as much dignity as possible he extracted the trap from his now bruised and smarting fingers while a group of girls nearby were in stitches laughing at the incident. A huge mountain of red tomatoes was being steadily eroded as trade built-up and a constant flow of customers came and went, each bargaining for the lowest price. Those buying were often pernickety in their choice and arguments often broke out between them. Alongside the road leaving town they passed inbound villagers with elephant grass mats, goat's milk and a variety of other products, all piled up on their heads, they would remain there until every last item was sold before returning to their villages in the evening. John noted that under the eaves of many of the huts that they passed there hung huge bunches of tobacco leaves, drying in the air. Most would be eventually sold but the owners always retained some for their own use. Many of the older men spent their days under shaded trees, sitting on an old wooden chair, smoking peacefully and lost in some unknown twilight world of their own.

Quite often many of the villagers and those from out of the bush would appear as they crossed over the roads, only being visible for a few seconds or so before disappearing again into the bush on the opposite side. Once in amongst the tall elephant grass no trace of them could be seen and only the tops of it swayed gently in the breeze.

Sam pointed out items of interest as they travelled along. John was taking in a huge amount of information which was adding to his education about Nigeria itself. However, he felt that he had much more to learn yet before he could form a complete picture. They slowed to a halt as they came across a sudden road block which consisted of some old rusty oil drums with a plank of wood on top of them. Two scruffy looking policemen, one of them armed with a wooden club and the other with an old rifle, stopped and searched the local people and most of the cars for suspected stolen goods. As they halted at the barrier, the man with the rifle stuck his head in through the window and in an uncivil manner he said something unintelligible to Sam. He, quick as a flash, replied in an equally insulting manner. The man withdrew his head, glowered at Sam taking in his neat safari suit, and with a reluctant scowl he signalled to the other man who lifted the barrier and allowed them to pass through

"What was that all about, Sam?" asked John.

"Oh, no problem, boss, he want dash to let us pass. I tell him you big friend of President Babingida! He not like that because he not get any money and so he has to let us pass."

"How many times do we have to pay dash, Sam?"

"Oh, quite often, is very common, we pay de dash for lots of things, you will see!"

John turned to Klaus and said, "How much do we pay out on dash, then, Klaus, in the course of a year?"

Klaus, thought for a moment, then replied, "Vell, I think maybe about four thousand niara a year."

"What!" said John, "that much?"

"Yah, meine friend, a lot really but it is necessary," and he shrugged his shoulders and added, "it is a necessary evil, we haf to pay."

"Well, we must see if we can reduce that, Klaus," John commented.

Klaus shrugged his shoulders and said, "Difficult to do, only way is to offer goods for money."

Sam chimed in, "That right, boss! Is the only way I think!"

"Hmm," John said, thinking to himself there must be a solution to that somewhere. He dismissed this from his mind as they came up behind a heavily laden lorry weighed down on its rear axle which protested loudly, squealing and grinding as the lorry went along. On the rear of it daubed in paint was the saying, 'NO SINGING, NO DANCING!'. A row of faces was evident above the load looking backwards at them and all appeared to comply with the sign, each possessing a look of abject boredom. However, as they overtook the lorry they all smiled and waved at them and shouted at John, "Hello Ebo!"

"Why do they say that, Sam?" asked John.

"They call you Ebo 'cos you is white, boss! Is de people of the Ebo tribe who live in de south-east of de country and have very light skin, almost white, and dey is usually de most intelligent, all from de Ebo tribe, so they look up to you."

John raised his eyebrows and commented, "I see."

They travelled on closing their eyes momentarily as they drove through a whirlwind which had suddenly appeared from out of the bush, darted across the road and had engulfed everything in its path before cutting a swathe through the grass on the opposite side of the road and sped away on its journey. The trees were grouped together tighter now, rich in foliage and much greener, long sloping hills now prominent as they progressed upwards into the higher lands and interspersed with swathes of granite strewn boulders in indiscriminate clusters, completely bare and crudely presented, forming ugly blots on the landscape. They pulled in at a lonely petrol station, with Sam having to awaken the sleeping attendant by sounding his horn at the man who had been stretched out in the shade of the canopy alongside the petrol pumps. John wondered how on earth he didn't get run over by the cars and trucks that pulled in at the station, his clothing being oil stained and his body difficult to see when he was lying down on the ground and almost the same colour as the ground around the petrol pumps themselves. The man disappeared inside the kiosk and returned with three Pepsi-Colas and a church key. Sam took them from him and passed them around and paid for the drinks. They all got out of the car and stretched their legs and wolfed down the cool drinks, taking a few wild swipes at some unruly flies which went around and around in circles above their heads. After a few minutes rest, they got back inside. The attendant had by now already gone back to sleep in the shade, so they set off again. A motor cyclist, conspicuous by his agaba billowing and flapping in the wind, rode unsteadily along amidst a cloud of white exhaust smoke produced by an obviously incorrect mixture and giving him the appearance of a ghostly apparition, his features completely hidden in the cloud.

Perhaps he could be consigned to heaven, thought John, no preparation would be needed!

They passed a semi-erect sign stating that Katunka was ahead. A herd of bush cows had just passed in front of them, leaving on the road indiscriminate piles of black dung through which Sam carefully steered. They waved to the herders and they in turn waved back, one of them waving his stick at them in response before returning it to his shoulders. A young boy by the roadside held up what looked like a furry animal suspended from a pole and tied to its tail.

"What's that he's holding, Sam?" asked John, innocently.

From the rear, Klaus replied, "Das ist bush meat, John."

"What is bush meat, then?" he countered.

"Bush meat is any kind of game you catch and kill in de bush boss," said Sam. "This one de boy has is porcupine, keep long time if you smoke it, yes, very long time, but very smelly!"

John laughed at the statement. "What else do they sell then, Sam?"

"Anything! Sometimes rabbit, rat, monkey, or bat is very sweet meat, or lizard, crocodile, fish, anything they can catch or spear."

"Why don't they eat it themselves, then?" asked John.

"Sometimes eaten, but usually sold, boss, get more money that way."

"I should have known that," said John.

Sam smiled and returned his gaze to the road. More lorries were passed with different sayings on the rear of them, one declared 'He who endures will win'.

That's a good one, thought John, I must make a mental note of that. Another said, 'Beware! Many have gone before!' and shortly afterwards another stated 'More time, more hope!'. As they passed the one at the front, piled high with mattresses perched precariously on top of each other and tied with a flimsy rope, the saying, 'Man who is always right is in danger' was visible on the rear. John smiled at all of these philosophical sayings.

Passing through the village of Akerri, they passed over a small stream where the village women were washing clothes in a muddy stream while a collection of naked youngsters splashed around in a nearby pool. Some fish were hung up on poles and a small fire had been started to commence the smoking process. They continued on through the village of Kutiwanji on the way to Bokani, where the surface had been repaired and they were able to make up some lost time, although they were still not in any hurry to reach their destination. They halted by the roadside to buy some fresh oranges and bargained for about ten minutes before leaving with a sackful of them.

"Plenty oranges here, boss," said Sam, "no shortage of de fruit in dis country."

"So I've noticed," added John, "so how come so many of the children are undernourished then?"

"Is old story, boss, is easier to sell de fruit and have money to get other things, so not so much is eaten. There is saying, 'Is better to have modern things than to hoard fruit'!"

John didn't answer that but thought about it for some time. It really was appalling that so many of the young suffered from malnutrition when there was ample fruit and vegetables available. Perhaps it was a lack of education, he thought, and decided on reflection that must be the reason for it. Out of the corner of his eye, he spotted some containers tied up at the top of a tree, just under the foliage and close to the trunk.

"What's that for Sam?" he asked.

"Is cut in de bark of de tree, boss, they gather the juice of the tree in a calabash and use it for many things, boss."

"What sort of things, Sam?"

"Well," he said, "they use it for de lamps. Day get de palm oil and dey put it in de lamp, is like paraffin, yes? And then it burns for a very long time. Is also used for cooking, and we mix it with other oil and make de perfume, and sometimes!" and he smiled as he said it, "we make de palm wine, very strong! Get drunk quick! Is good, you mus' try it sometime, eh?"

"Yes, I'll make a note of that," said John.

"I know, boss, I get drunk many times on it, yes, many times!" and he smiled. Klaus had been silent for some time now so John had a look at him only to find that he was asleep and totally oblivious to the occasional jolting of the car on the bumpy surface, the potholes appearing at random. A bunch of children played in the dust with a gird[1] and a stick, noisily and excitedly running about, going round and round in circles. As they passed by they stopped the gird when one of them noticed John and they chorused, "Hello Ebo!"

John and Sam both waved to them. Funny, thought John to himself, all the children greet you even if they've never seen you before. The gird and hoop bought back memories of a form of play in John's younger years when almost all the young children in Scotland played in this way.

Sam stopped the car and got out and pointed to a hill and turning to John he said, "See that hill, boss? The village on the hill?"

John looked up, squinting against the light and he shaded his eyes, he said, "Yes, what about it?"

"Is where I was born, boss, is old now, no people live there any more."

"Not at all?" John asked.

"No. I leave there when I was ten years, now is bad place!"

"Why is that then?" John asked.

"Is haunted by the bad spirits! Our village medicine man try to drive them out but he could not do so. Try many spells but we all have to leave for another place." He continued, "Even today, in this time, no-one will go there, is still bad!" and turning to John, he said, "You understand?"

John answered him by saying, "I see that the people still believe in the evil spirits then?"

"Yes, suh! Dey never go there again."

"What sort of evil is it, then?" asked John, determined to find an answer.

"All of de women in de village dey all fall ill and catch a disease, then de crops all fail for no reason, den some of de men who is out hunting, dey not return and the village head man he die suddenly, all in two months. Bad magic at work! So all of de people leave, we walked for twenty-six miles over there!" and he pointed in the direction and indicated a hill on the side of the valley. "We go there

---

1 A 'gird' is the scottish name for a hoop, a toy struck with a stick to induce movement, and guided in motion by this stick. As Nigeria was a British colony, a large number of Scots were in residence. This toy was adopted by local tribes and in some areas is still known as a gird! (From girdle, girded and other words of similar derivative.)

and build new village, now have no trouble, all is well and we have a good life."

"I see," said John, not really seeing but amazed that some of this type of magic still existed to which the local tribes still adhered and were definitely respectful of it. They climbed back into the car and drove on. The landscape became increasingly hilly and dense with trees. Many brightly coloured birds and butterflies flew about and the area seemed pleasant and inviting. At the roadside some hunters displayed their catch, a squirrel and a large rabbit.

"Ah! Fresh meat!" declared Sam, and he stopped the car and got out and walked over to them. He engaged in a sing-song type of conversation with them, interspersed with much laughter. John, meanwhile, alighted and stood close by taking it all in.

Sam noticed him, called him over and introduced him to the hunters. Surprisingly, one of the men, unshaven and whom John took to be about fifty years old, shook John's hand and said in perfect English, "Welcome, mastah! You come to work in our country? You new mastah for Girma dutse? Yes?"

"What's Girma dutse?" John asked.

"It is the big rocks, he means the dam."

"Yes!" replied John "how do you know that?"

The man smiled a toothless smile, and with a twinkle in his eye, he continued, "Many people know of your coming, you will be here long, but you will have success, it is seen!" and with that he lapsed into an unknown dialect and returned to speak with Sam for a short while. Sam paid the men for the meat and took from him the large rabbit.

They both thanked them and got back into the car. As they drove off, the man who had spoken to John in English, raised his spear up in salute to John who waved in response, and then the two hunters disappeared into the bush as if by magic. John looked back at the spot, not sure if he had actually met them or not, but the rabbit was certain evidence of it.

"How did he know I was coming here, Sam?" he asked.

Sam looked sideways at John, not taking any real notice of what he said, and without taking his eyes off the road he said, "He knows. Many people know, that's all."

"Yes, Sam. But we are miles away from the site!"

"Yes, boss, but they know for sure!"

John felt a cold sort of chill fall over him. How very odd that this knowledge had become known. Perhaps some hidden form of communication was at work. His mind went back to stories of the jungle drums but, try as he might to find an explanation, he could not fathom it out. He set it aside but determined to probe Sam at a later date for the information and to obtain a satisfactory explanation.

They had passed through Bokani and had joined the main road for Mokwa and Kanji. Sam interrupted his train of thought by saying, "Away to left, boss, is Jabbeh Dam on the river Niger, is built many years now near the Naja hill, we maybe visit it sometime, the big man there, he is also English."

John made a mental note of that, if ever the opportunity to visit it arose he would. A larger than normal sign came into view which picturesquely advertised that Lake Kanji Wildlife Park was twenty-seven kilometres away. They descended a hill and entered the narrow road through Zugerma and as they went along it, John asked Sam if there was wildlife there in the park.

"Sure, boss," he replied, "there is much wildlife there, but only a few places left in Nigeria now where it is protected. Most of them now all killed by de poachers. Plenty elephant there. You must go and visit sometime, is big for de tourists! I have a cousin, he work there in Fashe village, he is game warden. I can see him, any time you want to go, you tell me, I arrange it for you, boss!"

"Good! That would be fine, I'd like to have a good look round it, maybe in a few month's time when we get the job sorted out, eh?"

"Sure, boss! Is no problem, dat will be fine."

A Peugeot 404 estate car, slightly the worse for wear, sat by the roadside the driver absent. On the rear door the saying, 'BE CAREFUL - NO KISSING' was evident. John, smiled again, there seemed to be no end to these sayings, and every now and then one could come across some new and amusing sayings in the most unlikely places. As they got closer to the National Park, the road got busier and many buses were in evidence, the abundance of tourist stalls did a steady trade. The road started to wind in and out of the hilly country amid the varying tracts of different types of foliage and the numerous changes in the species of trees. Villages were grouped more closely together and smoke from their fires drifted up vertically to be dispersed quickly by some breeze. The park was way off to the right hand side and at this moment, Klaus had awoken with a grunt but was not fully awake, however, he realised roughly where they were by the surroundings, and said in a sleepy voice, "About fifteen miles ahead of here is the village of Katsatshi where we turn off and go up the banks of the Kontagora river. Your residence is alongside it," and added, "I'm sure that you will like the setting, John."

"Well, I'm not too worried about the setting as long as it's adequate for my needs."

They entered Katsatshi itself, most of the villagers raising their hands to wave in recognition of the vehicle that Sam was driving, although perhaps not aware of the white man in the front seat next to him.

Immediately on leaving the village they turned off on to a rough track and bumped along it until it met a dirt road, and after a mile or two they drove through some elephant grass and back on to a narrow tarmac road which closely followed the river below, hugging the winding course as they progressed along it. They passed through a settlement of about a dozen huts, the occupants busy with the daily chores. The young girls stood in circles around the tall wooden containers, naked to the waist and sang as they pounded the yams. There were five of them grouped together and they each sang in turn as they commenced the downward stroke of their outstretched arms. A huge cooking pot sat astride a fire on a triangular support surrounded by a circle of stones. Nearby, bread was being baked and fed into a large circular oven by an old woman in an orange garment who expertly handled a long spade and pushed the bread deep into the depths of the oven.

The incline of the road, now mainly dirt track, rose in sympathy with the contours of the land, turning alternatively left and right as they proceeded along it. They moved slowly up an incline and round a sharp left-hand bend, the right-hand side of it being densely wooded but offering, now and then, a view of the river far below. At the top of a hill, the road turned sharply to the right and a man-made clearing came into view. In this clearing stood a strange looking house, a mixture of traditional and semi-European design, appearing as if they had hurriedly been married together to produce an overall large structure. It faced immediately onto the roadside, while the road itself bent around it almost at right angles. The area had been cleared of trees, but a screen of them had been left at the rear of the house to provide sufficient shade. As the leaves moved in the gentle breeze, they scattered the sunlight indiscriminately on the house giving it a dappled appearance. Sam pulled up alongside the entrance and switched off the engine, giving it a well-earned rest. Klaus and John stepped out and stretched themselves.

Sam said, "This is it, boss! Big house, very nice, very cool and not far from de site."

John stretched his frame as he walked over to have a closer look at it, being very stiff after the journey on the bumpy roads. He surveyed it and noted that it was certainly large, the upper story having a traditional thatched roof whilst the overhanging storey had the distinct character of an added-on extension. He crossed to the door and entered. The door swung silently open and he appreciated the coolness of the interior. It was dark and it took him a while to get his eyes accustomed to the dim light. It was comfortably furnished with quite modern furniture, and had large rooms, an air conditioner - which worked very efficiently to his surprise - and large wooden slatted shutters on the windows. The kitchen lay off to the side of the large dining room and it was well appointed.

Sam preceded him and called back, "Out here, boss!" and led the way out of the kitchen door, "is de servant's quarters!" and so saying, he called out in a loud voice, "Chop, chop! De boss come!"

A hurried scuffling of feet was heard and the scraping of chair legs on a concrete surface, then two men appeared, one tall, and one small.

Sam introduced them to John. "This one," and he indicated the smaller of the two, "is de chief cook and his name is Nathaniel."

The man stepped forwards and said, "You are welcome, massah! You will like it here, of that I am sure."

John shook the outstretched hand in welcome, noting its firm grip, and replied, "I'm sure I will."

"And this one," and John turned to the taller of the two, "is Ebenezer de chief servant!"

John shook his hand also and Ebenezer grinned widely and said, "Welcome! Welcome!"

John noted that Ebenezer was about six feet tall and that Nathaniel was small and rotund.

"How long have you been here?" he asked.

"Oh, long time!" answered Nathaniel almost instantly, "I work here for many years, know everything, is very nice here, no trouble, plenty food here all de time."

"Good," said John, "I'm glad to hear it. What about you, Ebenezer?"

"I been here for four years, massah," he replied, "but before, I came from the north, many miles away, but I like it here, is nice area."

"Well, that's a comfort," said John turning to Klaus, who had been standing behind him.

Nathaniel asked John, "Does the mastah want refreshment, cold? I have it ready!"

"Yes, thanks, that would be very nice," and without further ado, Nathaniel disappeared into the kitchen and busied himself with his duties. Ebenezer quickly scuttled around and manoeuvred three easy chairs around a small glass topped table and invited the three of them to sit down.

"No! Not me!" said Sam.

"Yes, of course!" commented John, "you too!"

"But I only servant, boss! Is not my place!"

"Sam!" said John "you will sit, I insist!"

Sam looked at Klaus, then back at John, and then said, "Yes, boss, I sit."

John then said for the benefit of all, "Anyone who visits my house, is welcome to sit! And that goes for any visitor! Okay?"

"Yes, massah!" replied Ebenezer, "anything you wish."

"Okay, then," continued John, "why are you two still standing?"

Nathaniel and Ebenezer looked at each other and without further ado they sat.

John turned to Klaus and said, "I take it, then, that there is some sort of discrimination here against the servants and the employees, Klaus, is that so?"

Klaus looked at John, hesitated for a few seconds and answered, "It is not the custom, John, we do not encourage it! It will not go down well."

"That remains to be seen, Klaus! Anyway, that is my wish. Do I have your support?"

Klaus hesitated, then said, "Yah, you have my support."

"Right then, that's got that out of the way, now let's have this nice cool drink!" After this brief historic statement, Sam, Nathaniel and Ebenezer had said nothing but had cast surprised glances between themselves, not quite believing what they had heard. Sam smiled. Wait until the workers hear about this! he thought to himself. It'll be dynamite! Nathaniel had already decided to go down to the local village to tell them about it as many of the workers lived nearby. Ebenezer had many acquaintances up at the site of the dam who lived in the local shanty town, they too would be surprised at this. Nathaniel disappeared into the kitchen, and reappeared quickly with the tray of cold drinks, the glasses topped with slices of melon and he placed them down in front of each person. There were only two glasses and John turned to Nathaniel and said, "Have you got any more of this?"

"Yes massah!"

"Then please go and get the glasses for Sam and yourselves."

Nathaniel scuttled dutifully away to do what he was bidden and returned shortly afterwards with the other glasses.

"Now, then! We can all sit down and enjoy it," said John, "can't we?"

They all smiled, except Klaus, and bent to the task. There then followed a very relaxed discussion between all five of them which lasted for almost an hour. Klaus and Sam said they'd have to be leaving as they had to go up to the site and they got up and went outside. The sound of the engine starting up and the noise of the engaging gears confirmed their departure. John remained speaking to the two of them and during the ensuing conversation he managed to winkle out other details of present and past events and made mental notes of them. He found out that Nathaniel had five children of varying ages, four of them still at school and one of them only three years old. Ebenezer, apparently, was a widower of some years. He also obtained some very useful information about the local populace and the work-force which served to confirm some of his preconceptions and suspicions. Eventually, he decided that he had as much information as he could get for the moment so he got up, Nathaniel and Ebenezer doing likewise. Ebenezer showed him to his room where all the necessary things were, and pointed out the shaded area in the garden at the rear with a table and sunshade. He opened the shutters in the bedroom to allow John to savour the view up the valley, took him on a mini-guided tour of the library, and the laundry and ended by saying that he was always available at any time if the massah wanted anything. John thanked him and shook his hand warmly and went into the bedroom.

Ebenezer had already unpacked his bags for him, had hung up his clothes, and had put his other things in a drawer, and had left his personal items out on top of the bed. He thinks of everything, thought John to himself, smiling. After his shower in the hot water he felt completely relaxed. He dressed casually and went downstairs to the lounge. Ebenezer stood by the door.

"Dinner is ready, massah, any time you want it!"

"Thank you, Ebenezer," he replied, "say in about fifteen minutes?"

"Yes, mastah, fifteen minutes is fine," and he went off into the kitchen.

John crossed over to the library and looked along the rows of books. He noted quite a few classics, some reference books on aspects of construction, and numerous paperbacks. He selected a few from the construction section. Some of them were very old and outdated but basically were still relevant in some areas. Only two of them were published recently, however, he didn't really expect to find anything modern or up to date in amongst them. He heard Ebenezer call from the dining room, "Dinner up, mastah!"

"All right! Coming!" and he put the books back on the shelves and went through to the dining room. The table was expertly set. There had been prepared a fish starter which was very tasty.

"What kind of fish is this, Ebenezer?" he asked

"Anything wrong?" queried Ebenezer.

"No! Nothing at all, it's very nice and tasty but what is it?"

Ebenezer smiled, and replied, "Is catfish, mastah. You like?"

"Yes! Very nice," John replied.

Ebenezer heaved a sigh of relief, and picking up the empty plate he went off into the kitchen again and returned with the main course which was a vegetable stew with an abundance of carrots, numerous greens and large sliced tomatoes. Finally, to finish off with, he brought in a large, sliced, chilled pineapple on an oval platter. John had thoroughly enjoyed his meal and said so.

"Thank you, mastah!" he replied, "I will tell de cook."

Shortly afterwards, the cook stuck his head round the corner of the door.

"Tell me, Nathaniel! Where did you learn to cook?"

"Oh! Many years ago, I was cook to de Embassy of your country for fourteen years!"

"Were you indeed!" commented John, somewhat surprised, then added, "well you certainly know your stuff," he said.

"Thank you, massah! Does the massah want coffee?"

"Yes, please," said John, "black, no sugar."

"Certainly, ready in one minute," and he vanished into the kitchen.

John arose and went over to the stereo player and rummaged around in a box of tapes and selected one marked 'Reggae mixture'. He put it on in the slot, switched on the set and turned the volume up to a comfortable level. Ebenezer appeared with the coffee, and placed it down on the table and commenced to clear the rest of it. As the music played John noticed that Nathaniel was sort of half-walking, half-dancing as he went in and out of the doors. Ebenezer came out to adjust the air conditioning as the temperature had dropped slightly now. He was smiling to himself.

"What are you smiling at?" asked John.

"Have not seen Nathaniel so happy for a very long time!" and with that comment he disappeared back into the kitchen. John surmised, that this was perhaps a portent of things to come. He wandered outdoors into the hot, still air and looked out and over to the river below. It was a very tranquil scene. A faint breeze stirred the leaves on the trees and the crickets had started their calls, frogs tried to outbid each other with their croaks, clicks and rumbles which started off very low and grew in volume at an increasing rate until they reached a certain level then fell suddenly silent, but not for long as they soon resumed the calling. This was to become a familiar sound for many nights to come. Bats swooping over the house in search of a tasty morsel of flying insects, their faint shapes barely visible in the gloom but the flapping of their long wings and the high pitched squeaks made them conspicuous as John watched them fly to and fro.

A knocking noise sounded at the door of the veranda, not the inside door but the outside one. John went over to it and opened the fly screen then the outer door. He looked around. There was no one in sight. He looked around again and then downwards. A large toad stood near his feet, nonchalantly surveying the scene then resumed its jumping up and down against the door in order to catch the flies and mosquitoes that were attracted by the outside light. The crickets flew about with their whirring wings, some of them making a rasping noise as they passed by. The light had attracted a host of insects, large delta-winged moths with sharp angular patterns of white, black and brown, perfect camouflage for the woodland around. Other moths, like Kamikaze fighters, fiercely attacked the light only to fall stunned to the ground but reaffirming their mission as soon as their strength returned. Numerous coloured lizards darted in and out of the shadows to quickly grab the insects that fell to the ground within easy reach.

The evening drifted slowly on, its sounds continued unceasingly, while the smell of wood smoke greeted his nostrils coming from some unseen fire in a nearby village. Amid it all, the cry of a night bird shattered the frequent periods of silence.

Chapter Three

The herald of the day was a cloudless, clear blue sky as the morning dawned. The crickets having long given up their leg rubbing to be replaced by the noisy squawking of parakeets and the pleasant chirping of small birds, the only sounds to break the silence. John awoke to their music and peered out of the window. It was still and cool outside as he looked at his watch. It was only five in the morning. He arose, showered and dressed in a short-sleeved, loose shirt, shorts and a pair of ankle socks and donned one of his pairs of bondu boots. He looked down at his legs and noted that they appeared as two shining white pillars. It won't be long before they change colour, he thought, once the big old sun got at them they'd soon be cured. He went outside, a few morning flies were about and circulated around this new odour causing him to take a few futile swipes at them. He descended the steps at the front of the house and stepped on to the road, crossed it and walked part of the way along it to a point where he could see through the bush, out over the river bed, from the rocky escarpment and also up the valley. Far below in a shallow pool, he could see some women washing clothes, bashing them on the large stones, a traditional way of extracting the dirt, then rubbing and rinsing them in the water, eventually stretching them out on the stones to dry. Upstream some younger women were busy filling the large water pots from a pool of clear water before hoisting them up on to their heads, achieving the balance and walking off, backs completely straight, and following the track back to their village. A sudden rustling of the leaves at his feet caused him to look downwards. A snake slid by, almost indistinguishable from the green and brown foliage around, and not paying the slightest bit of attention to the human close to it. He made his way back to the house. A large spider's web glistened in the sunlight, suspended across the branches of a bush, and the big hairy insect was engrossed in rolling up the night's catch into a ball for later consumption.

As he came abreast of the house Ebenezer was in evidence, and espying him he called out, "Hello Massah! Good mornin' to you!"

"Morning, Ebenezer!" he replied, and went inside to find the breakfast table already laid and Nathaniel ready to serve his breakfast.

"You must be up early, Nathaniel?" he asked.

"Yes, mastah. I rise early, see you go out. Where you go to?"

"Oh! Just for a short walk."

"Ah! You like the morning air, mastah, is very fresh and quiet, is it not so?"

"Yes, it is, Nathaniel, I'm going to enjoy the early mornings, I think!"

"Is good time for thinkin' too, mastah! You have clear head in the mornings, can see all things clearly!"

"Yes! I suppose you're right there," he replied. He breakfasted on fruit juice, bacon and eggs, and toast and tea. He went upstairs, collected a file and his notes which he had prepared the previous day following the meeting with Hendry J. in Lagos, and briefly read over them, refreshing his memory on some of the points. He took out his binoculars, put the notes into his briefcase and made ready for Sam whenever he appeared. He stepped outside and sat down on a chair overlooking the road. It would be almost a full hour before he arrived. He called to Ebenezer, who appeared promptly.

"Yes massah?" he queried.

"Ah, Ebenezer! Come and sit!"

"Yes, massah! I comes!" and he appeared and pulled up a chair and sat down next to John, resting his hands on his knees.

Without looking at him, John said, "Well, Ebenezer! You must know something of what happened in the past, eh?"

He shuffled his feet a while before answering then said, "Well, massah, all I know is that in de past it is all bad magic!"

"And you believe in this magic?"

Ebenezer looked in the trees over at the far side of the road, then said, "Yes and no, mastah. I believe in de magic but now is not same. I not believe but many people," and he hesitated, "they believe!" and he waved his hand all around. "Witch doctor tell them!"

"Are there many witch doctors, then?"

"No! Not many, long time before one to each tribe or village, now only a few, but still there are some!"

"So, do you think that they had anything to do with the troubles then?"

"Mus' be, massah! Workers very good, work long hours, but now many have gone back to de village because of de black magic."

John decided not to press Ebenezer too much on this subject for now and said, "All right, Ebenezer, thank you."

"You welcome, massah," he replied, then asked, "You go to work today at dam?"

"Yes, Ebenezer, today I start, but first of all I see the men and talk to them."

Ebenezer nodded his head as he moved away without comment. By now it was six-fifteen and the sun had climbed higher and a warmth filled the air. The trees around now hosted a wide variety of birds, all chirping noisily as if in conversation. The smell of wood smoke greeted his nostrils from somewhere down the river. There must be a village nearby, he thought to himself.

"Where is the nearest village?" he called out to Ebenezer.

Ebenezer pointed to the west saying, "Not far up de road, two kilometres, is very small, only four families live there but many children."

"Do they go to school?" asked John.

"No massah! No school here! Only school many miles away at de mission! Too far to journey!"

"I see," said John, "so how many children of the men at the dam go to school then?"

"Some but not many. De chillun they work for de village, is our way."

"Yes, I understand," said John.

The wood smoke hung in the air in faint layers just above some trees which skirted the rocky area.

"Where do you come from then?" asked John of Ebenezer.

"From de far north, massah. I is from Hausa tribe, village name of Nguru."

"So when did you last visit your people then?"

He thought for a moment before replying. "Two years gone. I go for three weeks, see my old father, he very sick, very old, can no longer walk."

"And your mother?"

"Oh! Is dead massah, long time ago!"

"Are you married, then, Ebenezer?"

"No, massah, I just by myself."

"Well, maybe it's better that way."

"Yes, I think so, massah," and he smiled.

Their conversation was interrupted by the sound of an engine being revved. The sound cut through the clear air but no vehicle was yet in sight. The sound got louder as John watched the road for some evidence of it. Soon afterwards through the trees he spotted it, a white Land Rover descending slowly negotiating the hairpin bends. A few minutes later it appeared in sight now on the open road with Sam expertly steering to follow the bends in the road and to avoid the numerous potholes. As he approached the house he sounded his horn twice to signal his arrival. John and Ebenezer got up from the seats and Ebenezer went off to his duties. Nathaniel appeared at the door to see who it was blowing the horn. Sam pulled up sharply with a squeal of the brakes and came to an abrupt halt. He climbed down from behind the wheel and leaving the door swinging open he walked over towards John.

"Good morning, Massah!" he called, "I see you are ready to go!"

"Yes, Sam. It is a good morning as you say, so I'se ready."

Sam grinned, noting the mimicry of his speech, and replied, "Okay! We go then!"

John turned to Nathaniel and said, "I don't know what time I will be back, evening time anyway, so no hurry to prepare anything."

"Yes, massah!" he replied, "I wait until you come, is no problem!"

John waved to Ebenezer and walked over to the Land Rover. They climbed aboard and Sam started up the engine.

"Okay, massah! We go to de site but I take you to de top of de hill first, so you can see all over de site, is better for you."

"That'll be fine," he replied, "let's go, then."

Sam selected a gear and after doing a one hundred and eighty degree turn which stirred up a cloud of dust, they set off uphill, avoiding the potholes as they went.

"Road not good here, many holes, but soon gets better," he commented as they proceeded. The road climbed steeply, swinging left and right through the trees. They climbed higher and higher, now above the lower tree level and the banks of the river.

The ascent continued steeply at each turn and soon they emerged at the top of the rocky scree, the remnants of long forgotten upheaval.

They halted, got out and walked over to the edge which protruded over the valley. Away to the right, just visible, was a naturally shaped bowl, deep and looking as if it was carved out of the rock especially for them. Geologically, it was well suited for the site of the dam. The river had been diverted successfully, the coffer dams had steered the downflow to the sides without any loss of access to the villagers below. Out of the sides of the valley rough roads had been constructed and a temporary surface laid by hard packing the red soil, ferried in by large trucks from some distant source.

The south side of the existing river bank for some miles was considerably higher than the north side, and although some wooded area could be seen along it, it was relatively free from growth and was mainly short grasses with a few stunted bushes. Alongside this bank a new tarmac road had been laid and along it the bulk of the construction material was shuttled to and fro, then across a temporary bridge to the opposite bank and conveyed downwards from there to the work level. John could see from here that the excavation of the bowl had been completed and that stage two, the base section, had been laid out and buttressed fully, forming a wedge on the downside of the dam base to counteract the eventual downward pressure. Now stage three was in progress, the vertical curved wall of the dam, starting to rise up in a tapered manner which would withstand the total force of the wall of water which would form behind it. He took out his range finding binoculars, took a sighting and marked it down in his notebook.

Straightening up he turned to Sam and said, "Let's go then Sam, back to the site!"

"Yes, massah! Okay," and they both climbed back into the vehicle and commenced the descent. On the way down, Sam pointed out a few abandoned vehicles, mostly burnt out, which he indicated were casualties of recent problems.

"These trucks burnt by people wanting to stop de work, massah, four months ago. De drivers shot and de cargo stolen."

"Who did this, Sam?" John asked.

"Not sure, boss, men who did it, they villagers, all of dem workers, paid to do de sabotage, boss," then continued, "they paid by the men for de drugs, I think you have heard of them, yes?"

"That's right, Sam, I had read about that when I was in Lagos. Did Klaus know about this, Sam?"

"Yes, boss! He knows, he was very angry, he fire many of de workers who took part, was not popular but necessary."

"Yes. I'm sure it was," he added.

The Land Rover continued its descent, the gearbox being subjected to a fair amount of torture as it was exercised fully due to the sudden differences in the surface. The road eventually levelled out, still high up above the bowl but much closer now and John was able to see out over the area, the layout of the construction site and its associated buildings. They drove alongside the dam and along a boulder strewn path. John peered out at the various stages of progress. The Land Rover slowed as it approached a collection of temporary Portakabins which formed a letter 'L' in a carved out compound. As they approached some of the workers raised their arms in salute as the vehicle passed them by. John acknowledged their signs with a cheerful wave of his arm as he passed by. Sam pulled up outside the larger of the Portakabins, which bore the sign 'CHIEF ENGINEER', the words painted clearly black on white. John got out as the vehicle drew to a halt and looked around. All seemed to be fairly well organised. He scanned the remainder of the huts, noting the sign posting as to where they were in relation to his. He entered the Chief Engineer's cabin. It was functional and neatly laid out. One wall area was covered with plans of the dam and diagrams, each depicting various stages of it. On the wall a frame hung, the notice saying, 'Definition of a Nigerian road: A series of holes, joined together by strips of tarmac'. John laughed at this and thought to himself, how accurate indeed! The sound of footsteps at the door heralded the arrival of Klaus, who came in and said, "Gut morning, John, how goes it today?"

"Oh! Just fine," he replied, "just having a look around to start off with."

"Have you seen the dam site yet?"

"Yes, I have. I'll have a look through the paperwork, though, before I start."

"Gut!" said Klaus, "I vill be in the next hut if you need me." and he left.

John sat down, getting the feel of the chair and the desk. His immediate reaction was that he could not see out of the window of his cabin, so he spent about half an hour moving the furniture around so that he had a direct view out of the window and on his right he could view the plans without having to move his head or get up from behind his desk. He rummaged through the desk drawers, rearranged some items to his satisfaction and taking out a large notepad, he made a note of his immediate priorities. First of all, he went outside and had a look around, then he went over to Klaus's cabin and asked him to come over to his own. Klaus followed him indoors and John invited him to sit down.

"First of all Klaus, I want to know how many workers we have here."

Klaus dug a battered notebook out of his rear trouser pocket and consulted it. "Ve haf now two hundred nineteen workers, John."

"For a project of this size?" queried John, "That's not much!"

"Yah! Ve used to haf many more but as you know many left. It was about fife hundred of them."

"Well, Klaus, we certainly need a lot more than we have at present if we are going to show a profit, so can we recruit more of them?"

"Yah, ich denke!" he replied, "but it vill take time."

"Do you know of a man who can do this for us, then?"

"Yah!"

"Right then, I want to see him, and I also notice that no one is wearing any safety helmets or boots here, why is that?"

Klaus looked partially surprised, then replied, "Yah, that is right, but all local men do not wear boots, only work in bare feet! That is their tradition."

"Well! From now on, all men will wear safety equipment. Do we have any of it in stock?"

"No! Ve haf not," replied Klaus.

"Then we will have to get some then, how long will it take?"

"Oh, 'bout four days, to get it all."

"Do you know where from as well?"

"Yah!"

"Okay, see to it then Klaus, and do we have a list of our workers?"

"No list, John," he replied.

"Then, how do we know who gets paid?"

"Before, we call each man out and he maked his mark for his pay."

"Not a very good system, Klaus."

"Agreed, but that is the one that was used."

"Who is head man of the workers then?"

"We haven't got one now."

"Well! We'll have to find one, is there anyone you know who fits the bill?"

"Yah. There is one man who has the respect of the others."

"Who is he then?"

"He is called Football Boot!"

"What?"

"Yah! That is right, John. His name is Football Boot."

"All right, then, I want to see him straight away."

"We can see him from here," Klaus added, and he asked him to go outside. They walked over to the edge of the road and looked down at where the workers toiled. Cupping his hands to his mouth, Klaus bellowed, "Football Boot!" with the emphasis on the latter part of the name. Allowing time for the sound to carry down to them, Klaus waited. Sure enough, a large heavily built man stopped shovelling and looked generally upwards. He swivelled his head around and espying Klaus at the top of the hill, he waved. He parked his shovel and started the long climb up the winding pathway to the top. After about five minutes or so, he came into sight and approached on the now shallower stepped levels. John noticed that although he had been climbing upwards for some time he was not out of breath. Must be very fit, John thought to himself. He came to a halt in front of them and Klaus said to him, "This is the new boss. He wants to talk to you."

"Yus, sah!" said Football Boot.

Klaus suggested that they return to John's cabin and the three of them walked on over to it and climbed the steps.

Inside John turned to Klaus and said, "Why is he called Football Boot, then?"

Klaus replied by saying, "He got his name because he is boss of the working men, they do as he says, he is the only one who can keep order amongst them."

John then asked, "Yes, but why Football Boot?"

At this point Football himself answered. "Is because I can kick many asses, massah. You wan' anything done I organise it."

It took John all of his self control to prevent him from laughing out loud at the response. "All right then, Mr Football Boot! How do we know how many men we have?"

"Ovah two hundred foah suah, boss!" he replied.

"So how much do we pay them a month then, Klaus?"

Klaus shifted uncomfortably, then answered, "We pay about one hundred niara a month," then added, "but some get paid in cowrie shells," and before John could ask what they were, he continued, "is the old method of payment."

John did a quick calculation, then said, "But that's only about ten English pounds! That really is pathetic, Klaus! Who authorised that?"

"It was the last man who was here." Klaus replied.

"Christ!" exclaimed John, "No wonder we have problems! What sort of organisation is that? That's bloody awful!" He sat down and looking at the table top he said, "Right then! There is going to be a change. I want a list of every man's name by tomorrow morning. You can get Football Boot here to do it for you. I want the name of his village and his age. We will cease the payment of cowries. I want to know how long each man has been working here and from now on the payment will be in cash only. Is that understood?"

"Yas, suh!" exclaimed Football Boot and he looked sideways at Klaus who appeared none too happy.

"I kick de asses! I have it for tomorrow, boss! They not call me Football Boot for nuthin'." So saying, he left immediately and the sound of his big feet on the cabin steps was heard and then silence.

John continued with Klaus and said, "Tomorrow, I want all the men assembled here outside the cabin at eight in the morning without fail! Will you please see to it, Klaus?"

"Yah! I vill haf them here for you."

"In the meantime I am going to have a personal look around the site myself so that I can see how things are progressing and also to see if there are any other anomalies that need redressing. Have you got a helmet I can wear?"

"No."

"What? No helmets!"

"No!"

"Not at all?"

"No, we have none!" then Klaus added, "It wasn't my decision."

John looked at the roof and said exasperatedly, "All right then, Klaus," and walked over to the door. Before leaving, he took out his small black notebook and made a few notes in it, namely the items that needed urgent attention. Men, pay, names, languages, safety equipment, then folded it up and put it in the rear pocket of his shorts and set off on his task. He walked over to the edge of the roadside in the brilliant sunshine and the warm air. On reflection, it all looked a bit on the spartan side for a big project, not much plant and equipment in evidence and everything had a certain 'Sunday afternoon appearance' about it. Instinct told him that work was proceeding at a snail's pace, if not slower. He lifted up his binoculars and trained them on the site far below. Few men toiled in earnest and he noted some bad practices and some very time consuming methods in use which would have to be improved upon. Football Boot was in evidence actually doing some of the work himself as well as moving about in a supervisory category. He was quite pleased with him so far, the obvious choice for a leader of the men and he would make a good site foreman. He descended the sloping zigzag path down the side of the site, stopping every now and then to cast his eyes about and to make some more notes. He looked back up the valley to where the river had been diverted.

In the old river bed the bushes and grasses had sprung up to fill the gap left by the river. A gradual winding path led up the far bank to the top of the escarpment. This must have been the route down to the river bed perhaps to a crossing point, he thought, although there was no evidence of one in existence. Further back, a rickety structure of wooden poles was in view, spanning a narrow part of the valley. He decided to go and have a look at it but on reflection he thought that he would be better having Football Boot along. He descended lower until he reached the level where he had last seen him. The concrete base was stretched out before him, its down side sloping away to his left. He walked along it, taking a few sightings with his range finder and noting them down again in his book. He saw Football Boot moving and hailed him, his voice echoing off the sides of the valley. Football Boot heard the call and raised his hand to signify that he had seen him and started to make his way across to meet him. A few minutes later they met and Football spoke first.

"Yes, boss! You wants something?"

"I want to have a look up there," and he indicated further up the valley.

Football replied, "Yes, boss, okay, we go up. I gets de wagon, is quicker."

"Okay, Football," and they both walked over to where a dusty Land Rover stood. They started the long climb up the winding road to the top.

"How many men did we have when this job started, Football?"

"Long time back, boss! We has 'bout," and he took his hands off the steering wheel while he did a quick calculation on his fingers, then with a smile he slowly returned his hands to the wheel and said, "was five hundred, massah!"

"So, now we have only about half of that?"

Football did not answer.

"Why they leave, Football?"

"All went back to de villages after de trouble, were frightened away by de spirits, some go one day, but all go in de same month."

"I see," said John, "do you think that we can get them back then?"

Football Boot looked across the valley and said, "Not suah, massah, maybe, but many now is far away, would take long time to get message to them."

"Well, we'll have to try," said John, "we definitely need them and many more as well. What areas are they from?"

"Many areas, massah, we has men from all over!" and he waved his arm in a big circle.

"Tell me then, Football, I want to know where we can get them."

Football looked down at the ground and then started to reel off the areas where the men could be recruited.

"We have some from de north, Hausa people from Sokoto and Kano, Fulani from Katsina, and de Kanuri, they is from Maidugerie and Yola in de north-east; Shuwa from neah to Cameroon and also other mens from there, but they go back, is very long way. Then we has de Ebos from de south-east and also de Ekoi. Den der is from de south Ijaws, but mostly they is Tiv or Nupe or Yoruba. Yes, massah we have many peoples you see from all over de place."

"Which are the best workers, then?"

"Oh, many massah, but de Ijaws, they greedy and make much trouble, lazy worker. Not good! All others good, but de best they come from de north, they come a long way, they not come for nothin' or no reason."

"I'll remember that," said John.

They reached the top of the embankment, stopped and started again, and proceeded along a track for about a mile. They stopped again and Football got out and said, "We walk from here now, massah, is not far."

They passed through a low bushy area, disturbing the dust as they went along, then crested a rise in the ground. Below them lay the full view of the dam and all of the valley around it. John took a sighting here and made a note of it. Immediately in front of them stood the rickety structure. On closer inspection, it appeared to be quite solid in its construction being braced at regular intervals by cross struts and some other complicated stressing, faintly reminiscent of the Forth Road Bridge, he thought to himself.

"How long was this in use for?" he asked Football.

"Long time back was only bridge across de valley, only way for de wagons to get to other side."

John peered down into the depth of the valley and pointing, he said, "Is that trucks I see down there, Football?"

Football followed his gaze while John raised his binoculars to focus on the area.

"Is water tankers, massah. Fell over de side, de drivers they killed, long time back. Is long way down to de bottom, yes?"

John inspected them through his binoculars. Their outlines were clearly visible and he could identify them clearly as being Leyland trucks of a military design despite their crumpled appearance, both of them lying close together, their white paint work now stained a brownish colour with the dust which had settled on their surfaces. Further off, the river flowed downwards, its surface glinting in the sunlight until it reached the diversion point where it welled up slightly before splitting and disappearing into the coffer dams.

"Who is de other boss man here, Football?"

"We has de Massah Tony! He de rock man."

"You mean the geologist?"

"Yes, massah! Dat is him, de stone man, and den we has de other man with de foah eye, he look after de store."

"What's foah eye, Football?"

"Is man with," and he hesitated, then indicated circles round his eyes. John laughed when he realised what he meant.

"Oh, you mean glasses?"

Football grinned, "Yes massah, he has dem! De glass on de eye."

They stood for quite a while surveying the scene, John asking a question now and then. His list of notes now was considerably longer and the mental picture was now much clearer. They walked back to the Land Rover and drove slowly back down to the site, John still asking questions as they went. Football obviously knew a great deal so it was fitting that he made him supervisor officially. It was now ten-thirty in the morning, so he asked Football to take him to the 'foah eye building', and Football smiled at the request. Dis man, he thought to himself, he good man, will get on well with de workers foah suah.

"You know where the storeman is?"

"Yes massah! I knows wheah he is," and he turned off the road and down a broad track. Part of the way along it, they came across a newish looking Land Rover with no wheels.

"Stop here!" John said as they came alongside it. "Why is this here with no wheels?"

"Stolen massah, only two weeks ago! In de night."

"Don't we have any spare wheels, then?"

"Yes suh! I think so, but you have to ask foah eye, he tell you de answer."

They continued down the track past piles of bedrock, smaller stones, sand, rolls of wire, cement, steel poles, power tools and rows of excavating vehicles. Further on stood many other miscellaneous items, all fenced off. They turned right into the main compound, and moved over towards a large corrugated building which stood three storeys high with a door at the bottom of it which bore the sign 'MATERIALS'. Adjacent to it was another sign which warned all and sundry that all materials were to be signed for at the control office. This office was in an adjacent Portakabin, and they pulled up alongside it. An engraved plate on the door notified the occupant, 'David Hostelthwaite - Chief Storeman'. An awkward name to get one's tongue around, he thought to himself, no wonder the workers called him 'foah eyes' it would be very difficult for an African to pronounce that name.

He turned the handle of the door and entered with Football Boot in tow. The office was laid out tidily with two desks, numerous charts on the wall showing the current stock levels, a list of sub-contractors which caught John's eye immediately, and over on the far right hand wall were maps of the dam project, one of them an aerial view and the other a projected view of the finished article made up by a draughtsman, whose signature appeared in the bottom right hand corner in black ink. An assistant, a local man, wearing a faded shirt and baggy trousers got up hastily from his desk as he saw John enter.

"This is Joshua," said Football indicating the man, "he is the assistant storeman, he know where everything is, massah."

John shook him by the hand, and he replied, "Lo, massah! You de new boss! Yes?"

"Yes! I'se de new boss man," said John imitating the local tongue. Joshua smiled widely, and grinned as did Football Boot.

"A man with a sense of humour is good!" commented Joshua, "I is pleased to meet you boss! You want tea? I have it always ready."

John was surprised at this and said, "Yes, please! A cup of tea will go down well."

Without further ado, Joshua busied himself in the corner of the room with the makings while John took a closer look at the list of sub-contractors on the wall, which was of great interest to him.

"Is this the only list we have, Joshua?" he asked

Joshua broke off from the tea making and said, "Wait boss! I get the boss man here." So saying he opened the door and in a loud voice he called out, "Lo, boss! Is you there? We have visitors."

His voice echoed around the corrugated building and it was some seconds before a voice was faintly heard replying. Shortly afterwards a head appeared round the door, complete with the 'foah eyes', and the man entered.

"He comes!" Joshua said to confirm the reply to his shout, and returned to pouring out the tea, now making it four cups instead of three. He continued, "I pour out my boss's tea, he always likes it at this time."

John smiled to himself. Obviously an ordered regime here. Joshua placed the four cups on a plank of wood and did a skilful balancing act as he crossed the floor and laid the plank down on top of the table and returned for the teapot. The door creaked as Dave entered and did a quick one take of those in the office and walking over to John, he reached out his hand and introduced himself. John shook the hand and Dave said, "Sorry not to be here when you came, I was down checking the stock in the shed, we have to keep everything well screwed down. It pays to keep on top of the situation, so many items in and out daily, but we keep tabs on it and we have it down to a fine art. Joshua here keeps a regular update so we don't have any problems. He knows as much as I do."

"Yes! Quite impressive, Dave, I never doubted it for one minute. How about the back-up stocks?"

"Well!" said Dave taking a mouthful of tea and reaching over to a clip file hung up on the wall, "Here is the current stock levels," and he passed it over to John. "The projected six month level and the assessed annual level. We always keep a years stock in hand, that way we don't run into shortages."

"Have we had any shortages at all, then?"

"Occasionally. Some of the suppliers are very slow to deliver so we have to drive down to their premises and give them a gee up to ensure delivery."

"And does any of the equipment we order go missing at all?"

"Yes! Frequently it just doesn't arrive at all."

"You mean it gets stolen?"

"Yes! That's about the size of it," replied Dave, "without an armed guard on it, it is open to theft. It's quite common here, you see."

"Does it all come by road, then?"

"Normally, but sometimes it comes through the bush or through what they call the jungle roads. There is a system here where a few of the robbers dig a hole in the road so that the vehicle is obliged to stop and when the driver gets out to see how bad the hole is, they jump him from the cover of the bushes, steal the load and disappear back into the jungle again. In fact, there's been one or two occasions when I've suspected that the replacement consignment we receive is the same one that we originally ordered so we end up paying twice for the same amount of goods."

"Do we still buy from these suppliers, then?"

"No," replied Dave, referring to the stock book at the side of his desk. "We change suppliers but it is difficult to locate alternative sources. Sometimes, I suspect that all these suppliers are in cahoots with each other."

"That wouldn't surprise me," commented John, and turning to Joshua he said, "Who are these robbers then, Joshua?"

"Is villagers, but not from this area, they travel many miles to get here, steal the goods and travel back again and sell it to the other tribes, very clever man, eh? Not easy to trace then, you see."

"Do you think then that we need armed escorts, Dave?"

Dave thought for a while, then said, "No, I don't. But perhaps a show of force and a few rounds fired off might make them think again, it would certainly scare them off but how long for, I don't know."

"What do you think, Football?" he asked turning to him.

"I don' know boss, maybe."

"Well, I'll think about it," said John.

They continued their talk for a while on different subjects related to the supplies then returned to John's cabin. John asked Football where the geologist was.

"He down bottom, boss!"

"Okay then, will you go down and find him? Tell him I would like to see him please? And you come back with him too, but there is no hurry, just tell him to come when he is finished whatever he is doing, all right?"

"Yes, massah, I go find him," and he went out of the door and headed for the winding path at the side of the valley. John realised that he had forgotten to ask Dave about the radios, so he quickly jumped into his Land Rover and headed off down the hill. He arrived and entered the door as before.

Joshua looked up from his typewriter and said, "You back again boss! If you wants de big boss, he is down in de big store," and he indicated where it was with a pointing finger.

"Thanks," said John, opened the door and went in to the storage area and down a set of metal steps and called out. "You there, Dave?"

A few moments later the reply came back; "Yes! Up here!"

John followed the sound of his voice and after scanning the rows of racks he spotted him three levels up.

"Hang on! I'll come down!"

John walked over to row 5F where Dave was perched aloft.

"Don't bother Dave! It's just something I forgot to ask you about."

"What's that then, John?"

"Its about radios, do we have any?"

"No! Not now, we used to have a few but they were all stolen over a period of time, but we could certainly do with some, John."

"Right than I'll see to that," said John, "see you later, Dave," and he walked back to the stairs and climbed upwards. John waved to

Joshua as he left and climbed into the Land Rover and drove back uphill to his office. Football was still on his way down the path, now only a small figure below as he descended. John made some more notes in his book and noted down a few items that were urgent and went next door to find Klaus who was busy studying an overlay sheet of one of the elevations.

"Ah, Klaus," he said on entering, "about the safety helmets, how many of them do we have on the site?"

"We have only now about eighteen, most of them lost, damaged or stolen."

"Yes, I thought so, all right, thanks for now and by the way, I've sent Football down to get the geologist so can you come in next door, say in half an hour's time so that we can a have a discussion with him?"

"Okay John, I will be there."

John went next door and wrote some items on his pad for discussion. He got out the big desk diary from his bottom drawer and pencilled in some planned dates for other events. He decided to contact Hendry J. the next day. He would have to send Dave down to do it for him to make sure the message would get through to him. The most recent report he had on the construction was about four months old and he needed to know the current status locally. Shortly afterwards he spied Football and Tony reaching the road level and starting to cross the crushed rock and sand at the entrance to the compound, making their way over to his cabin. He got up from his desk and went out to meet them. Approaching Tony, he held out his hand and Tony did likewise, they introduced themselves and walked over to the office and climbed the steps. John turned to Football and said, "Can you go and get de massah in de store, Football, and ask him to come up to my office?"

"Yes boss! I go get him!" and he quickly set off down the hill. Football smiled to himself as he went noting again the use of the common language by John and the accurate pronunciation.

"I hear that you have got on well so far, John!" Tony commented.

"Really?" said John, "well that's good to hear! I always say that when in Rome, do as the Romans do. Don't you agree?"

"Exactly!" said Tony, "I do the same, that way the labourers can identify with us. If you come down to their level then you don't have any problem with them, but on the other hand, if you try to talk down to them, they resent it."

"What sort of work-force have we got then, Tony?"

"Oh, quite a good one really, that is, those that are left. A good core of hard workers with some right characters amongst them, but we get on well, all things considered."

"I'm glad to hear that," said John. "I haven't had a chance to meet them yet but I've arranged that for tomorrow morning with Football Boot. By the way, what's he like?"

"Well, he's quite switched on really, the men look up to him as a sort of spokesman, he's good at organising things and best of all he can get them to do almost anything he asks."

"Do we have a foreman as such? I mean of the workers themselves?"

"No! We used to have one but he was one of the ones who did not return from his village when we had the previous troubles, why he didn't come I don't know, but Football would have the answer to that."

"Yes, I was thinking of making him officially the foreman, what do you think of that, Tony?"

"I think it's a good choice John, he also speaks about five of the dialects so he can converse easily with the men. Yes! I agree with that."

"Good! I'll tell him when he returns then, I just wanted your opinion first of all and that confirms my feelings as well."

At this moment Dave and Football had appeared and almost simultaneously Klaus could be seen approaching the cabin. "That's good, we're all here at the same time," said John, as they all entered.

"Right then, we can get started." He waited until they were all inside and they each took a seat.

"You too, Football. Sit down."

"Yes, boss!" he said and hastily moved a chair over to the desk and sat down casting an unsure glance at Klaus and adding "Me, massah?"

"Yes! You! We all sit in this office for de meetings."

"Yus, sah!" he replied. He had never been asked to sit down before.

"Right," said John, "now that we're all here, we are going to have a general discussion about our work here. Now, I know a bit about the rough background to the project and the recent events, so I don't want to waste time on those. However, what I want to know is how things are at the moment and I suggest that we go around us all in turn and if you want to comment on anything, then we will all benefit from that, is that agreeable?"

A general agreement was made on this, and turning to Klaus, he said, "You first then, Klaus! What's the current situation?"

Klaus got out his notebook and started. "Vell! Now we are at the start of the phase three, which is the upper part of the dam," and walking over to the diagram on the wall, he indicated the area on it which was marked 'Phase 3'. "This will take quite a long time to construct as we have to go up four hundred feet vertically and then across the curvature about two thousand feet or so from side to side."

"And how long will that take, Klaus?"

"Is about three to four years, but with the number of men that we have it will take longer."

"How many at the moment then, Klaus?"

"Two hundert and seven, altogether." He turned to Football and said, "That right?"

Football, looked down at the floor obviously counting, and after a short pause he replied, "Yes, boss! That be right!" Then after a moment he spoke again, "But today two more men go, so now we two less." Klaus took his word for that and made a note in his book.

"Not very good, eh? We need to recruit a lot more."

At this point they were all deep in thought.

"Well then? How many do we need?"

Tony spoke first, "At least three hundred more, maybe even four hundred."

"Depends if we can find that many," commented Dave. Klaus looked at Football who had now realised that all eyes had turned to him.

"Is verrah difficult to finds foah hundred mens, massah, I can gets two hundred, but foah?" and he shook his head, "is verrah difficult," and he looked doubtful.

"What about the villages in the north, Football?" asked Dave.

Football replied, "Is long way to go, is possible! I can go but be away for long time may be many weeks befoah I'se back."

Klaus said, "Vell! Ve have to have them so I think we should go as far as we need to go to get the men."

"I agree," said Tony.

"Well, it's no problem, I have sufficient funding to cover that," then added, "how about raising the pay?"

They all looked at each other and no one said a thing.

"You told me, Klaus, that the men were paid one hundred niara a month before, didn't you?"

"Yah, that is so."

"Well for that money we will not get anybody," and he leaned forwards and did some quick calculations on his notepad.

"We will make it," and he hesitated, "five hundred niara each man, then!" He laid his pen on the paper and looked up at them.

Footballs eyes rolled and he looked at John as he said, "Five hundred, massah?"

"Why? Isn't that enough?"

"Yes, massah," he said breaking into a big smile which revealed two shiny rows of teeth and pink gums.

Dave commented, "That'll bring them in for sure, they won't be able to refuse that offer."

"Any comments, anybody?" asked John. They were all in agreement. Klaus thought that it was a very bold move but Tony was enthusiastic about it. "I'll tell the men tomorrow morning when I meet them, Football. So no mention of it at the moment."

"Yes massah, you tell dem in the morning."

"Who is going to go and find the men, then?"

"It's got to be Football," said John, "he's the only one that knows where to go! Tomorrow then, Football, after I address the men, you can organise with Dave here to get two of the large trucks with the trailers and rations, better take four drivers as well and Dave will give you money for living expenses and I will give you money to give out as an inducement to those that you recruit, that will get us the men we want."

"Yes suh! I get de men, you not worry."

"Well, if we get all the men we want we will revise the schedules, and that will change the time scale and all the other schedules."

"Okay! Dave, have you any comment?"

"No problem, I will project the figures and order accordingly. There will be, of course, a lot more foodstuffs, we will need another mess and accommodation, beds and the like, but I will see to that."

"Make a list then, Dave, say for six hundred and add to it any other things you may need and let me have it by tomorrow as I'll need to pass it on to Hendry J. in Lagos. Do you have a note of the telephone number as well?"

"Yes, I have it," and he wrote it down and passed it over to John.

"Tony! What about you?"

"All is going well as far as we can see, last week Klaus and I went to check on phase one and two to ensure that the next phase acted as a caisson. We have almost finished the dynamitable plug location and we have checked on the preparation of the access tunnel.

This week we have to check the stress factors and compare the figures. We will make up a report for you, John. The drains have been prepared and are half way through construction."

"That sounds good, then," commented John, "who is going to supervise that?"

"I will," said Klaus, "but I will allow the four good men we have to keep an eye on it as well, I can leave much of the work to them entirely but I will double check it, too."

"Good!" declared John.

"So far, the workers have done everything correctly, John," said Tony, "we haven't had any mistakes on the construction side, I can tell by the figures I keep myself."

"That's what I like to hear," said John, "us all keeping tabs on each other."

"Yes! We are very organised," added Tony.

"How about the turbines?" asked John. "I know it is early yet, but do we know what make and type we are to be installing?"

Klaus raised his hand, and flicking through his notes he quoted, "Ve are having either a Frances rotating water wheel, or the alternative is a Kaplen propeller and the appropriate engineering, but we are still awaiting the design engineer's recommendation which we expect to receive very soon."

"Fine," said John. "Well folks, everything seems to be going all right for the moment so if we all keep our minds on what we are engaged upon that seems to be about all for now, so this meeting is now closed."

So saying, they all got up amidst the scraping of the chairs on the floor and some shuffling of paperwork. They went outside, but John shouted Football back in.

"Remember Football! Nothing about de pay until tomorrow!"

"Yes boss, I knows!" and he went off down the path to the valley whistling to himself as he went, with the odd skip in his step thrown in for good measure. John decided to go down in the afternoon and have a look around the base and see the progress for himself. Not that he had any doubts but he liked to verify the facts. He took a stroll over to the edge of the road and studied one or two areas through his binoculars.

He went back over to his office, took his notepad and went off downhill. The day was pleasant, hot and sunny but with a slight breeze blowing from the east, and any noise from down below was diminished by the time it reached the top of the valley and just sometimes one could think that the work was being carried out in silence. He made his way downwards, admiring the greenery of the trees as he went along, stopping occasionally to investigate a rustling in the bushes, lizards darting into hiding as the human form approached them, disappearing quickly underneath the nearest stone. Mostly they stretched out on the stones to absorb the sun's rays to maintain their body temperature. Some were green and yellow speckled, others brown, and a larger variety were pink with bold splashes of black and brilliant red on their bodies. Dave's storage area came into sight through the undergrowth as he rounded the bend in the road. A couple of dumper trucks were busy ferrying materials over to flat beds on which workers manhandled the items for transfer to the site and another temporary storage area. Joshua was in evidence walking around, checking on the quantities being loaded and crossing them off a list he held on a clipboard. He spied John from a distance and raising an arm he called out, "Hello, big boss!"

John replied with a wave of his arm but didn't bother to shout back to him. He continued over to Dave's office and entered. Dave, as usual, was deep in the bowels of the racks and it took him a full five minutes to locate him, being guided by the sound of the electric motor of a large forklift truck that Dave was skilfully manoeuvring in and out of the narrow corridors between them. On seeing him, Dave killed the motor and climbed down and walked over to him.

"I've got that list for you, Dave! Do you want it now?"

"Yes! Why not, let's go up to the office," and they went over to the stairway, climbed up it and reached the office door. They sat down and John passed the long list over to Dave, who ran his eyes down it.

"Quite a lot of money's worth here, John," he commented.

"Yes, but as I said earlier, there is no limit to our funding at the moment, so just indent for it and tell Hendry J. that we want it pronto pronto, if not sooner. I'll leave it up to him to arrange the transportation to the site, he's normally quite efficient I understand in getting that organised."

"Yes, no trouble there, we'll get it quick enough."

Dave looked again at the items. Safety helmets, 500 white, 100 yellow, 50 red, 50 blue all with inners. Safety boots of various sizes, fluorescent orange and yellow jackets and waistcoats, 500 camp beds, goggles, ear defenders, gloves, a large quantity of spades, picks and shovels and wheelbarrows. There were medical supplies, rubber boots, portable radios with batteries and a few charging units, holsters and a large quantity of miscellaneous items including ten bicycles.

"He'll need an army to get that lot ready," he said, "but knowing Hendry J. he'll know where to get one. If I asked him for a slice of the moon he'd get it to me, sooner or later!"

"As long as he can find the telephone when it rings," said John, recalling Hendry J.'s office, "and providing he can find the list again once he's noted it down." John remained chatting with Dave for a while before taking his leave and wandering slowly back up the hill. As he left, he noted that all the piles of construction materials were tidy with no spillage or disorder. A tidy mind, a tidy job! the old adage went. Yes, what they said about a storeman was true. A good storeman's worth his weight in gold! Dave certainly was one of those. A truck passed him by, the driver changing down a gear as the incline increased.

John arrived back at his office. Viewing it from the road, he decided that he couldn't see much at all from his office window. He walked over to the opposite side of the compound and looked back. If his cabin was re-sited, he would be able to see the road and part of the way downhill for some distance, and also the top part of the latest phase of the construction, just above the baseline. He went over to Klaus's cabin and asked him to organise a big forklift to move their offices over to the other side of the compound and to raise them up as well. Klaus said he'd get that seen to straight away and left in his Land Rover.

He was gone about half an hour, before he returned, and shortly afterwards, John heard the sound of a powerful diesel approaching, and a giant forklift driven by a heavily built black swung into view, the forks raised up high above it. It rocked back and forwards as it approached in the bumpy road and then swung into the compound. It came to a halt and the driver climbed down. He wore only a pair of ragged shorts, heavily encrusted with dust, his body being marked with rivulets of sweat which had carved indiscriminate patterns on his torso. His short curly hair and broad nose and mouth gave him a sort of powerful look. He approached John and said, "How do, massah! My name's Ise."

"Hello, Ise, can you move these cabins for me?"

Ise looked at them, then over to the other side of the compound where John had indicated, and said, "Suah! No problem, I go down for de big frames from Massah Dave, I be back five minutes."

He climbed back into the cab, and gunned the engine into life and disappeared in a cloud of dust which hung suspended in the air for a while after he had left. Ten minutes later he returned, stopped the truck, got out and walked over to where the cabins were required. He climbed up onto a rock and after a few quick glances around he crossed back to the truck, agilely climbed in and raised the forks up high. He tooted his horn and John looked out of the window. Seeing the vehicle approach, he came out as Ise came abreast of him and as the truck drew level he allowed the forks to drop down and in one smooth movement, he slid them under the cabin and picked it up, and with a gradual turning movement he swivelled it around and took it over to the other side and deposited it on the ground. Meanwhile a panic had ensued amongst the groups of lizards that had been using the cabin as a shade and they scuttled off in all directions. He returned for the large rectangular frame he had brought with him, raised it up and positioned it adjacent to the cabin, then lifted the cabin on the top of it and returned to do a repeat performance on Klaus's cabin. Picking up the two sets of steps he had brought up from Dave's compound he laid them down at the doors of the cabins and nudged them into place with the point of the forks. It all looked so easy and John was amazed at how fast he had achieved the whole operation. Giving John a wave, he set off down the hill in another cloud of dust.

John climbed the wooden steps and stood looking out of his cabin from the doorway. Now he could see exactly what he wanted. Ise had made an excellent job of his positioning. About three-quarters of the base area was now in view. It was now two in the afternoon. He remembered that he had told Football of his visit to the site and calling on Klaus, he climbed into one of the Land Rovers and drove off down the hill, pushing the windscreen wide open to get the benefit of the maximum airflow. On his way, he passed two women with water jars on their heads on their way down to the river bed. They both gave him a wave as he passed by and the younger of the two smiled at him. The decline was quite sharp and he had to concentrate on the bends as he descended. Near the bottom, the road levelled off slightly but the decline continued and he turned off to the right onto a well-flattened road which had been covered to a good depth with crushed rock and red earth. He continued along this for about half a kilometre before turning another right-hand bend and coming into view of the site and the base of the dam itself.

The sides of the valley rose sharply upwards and tapered inwards as they did so giving the appearance of enclosing the dam in their embrace. He noted this feature and made a mental note of it as it would cause extra work when it came to the time for forming the curvature of the arch and the buttresses. He took a few sightings with his binoculars and made a rough sketch of the general layout of the area. He got out of the cab and walked around for a while, looking closely at the workers and their methods, paying particular attention to detail. No-one stopped work as he looked about but as he passed by the eyes of the workers exchanged glances along their line in an unspoken sentence that said 'here was the new boss having a good look around'. Some of the men were clad only in shorts or had a loin cloth and some wore no clothes at all, their complete bodies stained with the grey dust, making them seem like ghosts with only the whites of their eyes moving now and then. They were sure footed but wore no shoes, their bare feet being hard and callused. Around their waists they had suspended on a string a calabash of water which hung in the area of their genitals. Some had a leather thong which went around the waist and held a stiletto type of dagger used for some unknown purpose. One or two of them wore sweat-stained shirts. Two men were busy manhandling a huge boulder and were having difficulty levering it sideways. John moved over to where they were and taking up an iron bar that lay on the ground, he wedged it underneath and with the concentrated efforts of all three of them they succeeded in moving it out of the way. He shook hands with them both on completion of this task and their faces showed an element of surprise, even after John had moved away over to where another group were shovelling stones and cement together into a wooden frame. He looked up to where others were suspended on crudely fashioned rope chairs, who were dressing down the recently grouted areas. The men were stretched out along the width of the base, most them on the downflow side. The base section was one hundred feet thick and was reinforced by a large angled buttress which rose at an angle of twenty degrees and continued until it met the base section. In the previously filled river bed, now empty, fresh growth had occurred and numerous bushes had secured a foothold in the stony ground.

Temporary channels, dug on either side of the river bank conveyed the diverted flow from the coffer dams and carried the water further down the valley where the villagers were still able to fish and obtain drinking water. A faint echo could be heard as the items of huge machinery were moved to and fro and the noise of excavating vehicles was borne on the breeze and echoing off the sides of the valley at irregular intervals. Overhead a vulture soared, its head bent downwards with a keen eye on all that moved. By now, he had crossed to the far side but had not seen Football anywhere. He called out, "Football! Where are you?"

His voice answered, echoing off the buttress, but he could not determine where it had come from. A movement amongst the men revealed his presence and, on seeing John, he commenced his descent from a point up above where John was standing, and in agile leaps and jumps he soon came down to John's level and approached him.

"Hello massah! I not see you come."

"That's all right, Football, I came up from the floor. I see that the men are all busy."

"Yes, massah John, all busy, we has finishing to do first, then tomorrow we do de drain installations foh de uplift pressure."

"I see you know quite a bit about it then, Football."

He grinned and beckoned John over to the drain holes which gaped open at the base, alongside which sat reinforcing panels and piping, still in their wooden packing crates.

"We seem to have quite a good group of workers here, Football, do any of them leave for any reason?"

"No, suh! Only men dat are away is them who is sick, normally dey are heah every day."

"All right then, Football, let's go along this way, I want to speak to some of the men," and he led off, Football falling in alongside him and matching him stride for stride. They stopped at a small group who were setting explosive charges higher up in preparation for the hammerheads.

"Who is in charge of them?" he asked, looking upwards.

Football looked around, and seeing the man he indicated a small wiry figure with his outstretched hand and replied, "Dat is him, massah."

"Okay, Football, call him over and ask him where he gets the dynamite from."

Football called to him in some unknown dialect and he came down to stand beside John. Pointing, the man indicated the building further along the site. Turning to John, Football said, "He say, massah, that he get de charge from Massah Dave, he axes him foah it, an' each time he needs one, he go the day befoah an' axes him, an' den he makes his mark an' signs foah it."

"Makes his mark?"

"Yes, massah, he no write, so makes de mark of his name," and he indicated it in the dust with a stick. John nodded in understanding.

"Okay, Football, let's move on," and he thanked the man who dutifully returned to the laying of the charges. As he walked along he came across Tony, bent low amidst the rocks at the base where it met the old river bed. He was taking rock samples and also noting strain gauge readings which, he explained, he regularly took so that he could detect any movement of the sub-base and would compare them with previous readings and with the natural elastic properties of the rock bed.

"How many measurements do you take, Tony?"

"Oh, about six each side of the base every three or four days, that way I can draw up a graph and if there is any change with the normal elastic properties then we can spot it instantly and take any remedial action. It's a good policy to follow, rather than taking things for granted."

"Yes. Good idea, Tony! I'll have a look at your graphs later this week, if I may?"

"Certainly, any time, you just give me a shout and I'll bring them over, but they are pinned up on the wall in the office of the endmost cabin so you can see them any time you want."

"Thanks," replied John, and he and Football carried on with their informal walkabout. "How about meals, Football? When do the men eat?"

"Usually in de mornin', 'bout seven, and den in de evenin' after de work finish, we eat in de canteen at de livin' place."

"Food, okay?"

"Is good, massah, but not much to eat."

"How about water?"

"Some men, dey carry de water," and he pointed to one of them and the calabash around his waist on its cord, "some men have de water but others, no water."

"Well, I'll get that seen to and the food as well."

Football smiled, his massah, he suah is good, is good foah de men also.

They stopped now and then to look at this and that, John making copious notes as he went along. He observed the condition of the equipment being used, the state of the vehicles and the lack of lighting which would be necessary in the evenings.

"What time do we stop work, Football?"

"Jus' befoah de darkness fall, massah, de men dey knows when is time."

John made a note of that in his book and, thanking Football, he returned to his Land Rover. John drove downstream along the river bed, noting its previous course until he reached the point where it resumed its normal route and continued its flow down the valley.

He stopped there, backtracked to the access road and commenced the ascent back up to the office site. On the way up, he stopped at Dave's office. He was busy writing at his desk.

"Be right with you!" he called out, "just got to enter a few figures on this sheet and then I'm all yours." John waved his hand in an understanding and shortly afterwards, Dave put his pen down and said, "Now then, John, what can I do for you?"

"It's the food supplies, Dave, who issues them?"

"Well, I do. The cooks tell me what they need and I order it. We send a truck once a week to collect it, they issue it out as required, usually a day in advance. Why? Is there any problems with that?"

"No! Just not enough food, Dave, it's more variety and quality we need, so can you add that to your list as well?"

"Yes, no problem. I'll do that straight away."

"Who does the cooking for the men?"

"They have four or five local cooks; they are all women from the village downstream and they do all the cooking for the workers."

"And do they get paid?"

"Well, now that you come to mention it, no. They get paid in kind, if you see what I mean?"

"You mean that they take food away with them?"

"Yes, that's the way it has been for a long time now. They don't overdo it and it's the accepted thing and there's no problem with the system." John made a few notes in his book and rising up he thanked Dave for the information. Just as he was leaving he asked where the living quarters were and the mess hall.

"You go downhill, past three bends, then turn off the road through some tall trees. It has a green corrugated roof, you can't miss it! The man who runs it, that is the chief cook, his name is Bombay," and he smiled as he said it.

John thanked him again and returned to his Land Rover. He drove downhill and followed Dave's instructions, passing two bends and then another while his eyes scanned the trees, and in a small break he spotted the green roof of the building which was of a different hue to that of the trees around it. He drove on following the tyre tracks in the earth, came across the entrance path and turned onto it. It followed an arc, almost reaching back to the roadside, alongside which stood a long, low building open on all sides, more like a shelter with poles, in the shade of a tree and near another shaded area. Inside, an almost continuous line of messing tables was laid out with frequent gaps, the benches crudely fashioned out of wood and unshaped inasmuch as the edges of the tops were uneven. Nearby stood some smaller shelters, obviously the cooking areas in which the ashes of a large fire were evident. Mud ovens were placed against a large rock with the vent at the top and an access flap at the side, and long handled shovels stood on end as though they were patiently waiting for the next load of baking. Traditional red mud bricked buildings were scattered around and John noted that the site was quiet. John climbed down from his seat, and called out, "Hello! Anybody there?"

A few seconds later a head appeared from the bushes, followed by the rest of the body. Wielding a long machete, it looked around until it saw John, then emerged and walked towards him.

"Hello Massah! You is de boss?" it asked without expression, more of a statement than a query.

"Yes!" John replied, "That's me, you is de cook?"

The face broke into a smile, revealing a large mouthful of teeth which glinted in the sunlight.

"Yas suh! Sho' is! I am de cook! You wants to eat?"

"No," said John, "I just came for a look around. What's for eating tonight then, Bombay?"

"Tonight we is having de water melon," and he pointed to a heap of them lying on the ground, all ripe, which he had been in the process of slicing when John appeared, "then we has de goat meat stew with potato and befoah that we has de egusi soup. You want to try? You come here tonight and you can taste! Is verrah good, massah."

"Yes, I'm sure it is! And it sounds fine, but do we get enough meat, Bombay?"

"We has enough foah now, massah."

"But if we get more men?"

"Den I needs more. If I gets de meat I cooks it, is no problem."

"Right then Bombay, thanks for the information," and he walked back past the huts to his Land Rover.

As he went, Bombay called out, "See you, massah!" and he returned to his execution of the melons.

John drove back along the arc and uphill again.

The sun was now falling in the sky, causing him to look at his watch and he noted that the shadows had lengthened slightly. More women were now evident, engaged in the transporting of firewood and water to their villages. Piles of leaves which draped down around them gave the impression of a moving bunch with no obvious means of propulsion. Those with basins in which were containers of cooled goats milk, balanced them expertly as they went along, very few of them suffered from sore backs in this country, as they had been trained from a very early age to carry their loads correctly. A point worthy of note, thought John as he drove on, waving to them as he went. He changed down a gear, negotiated the last bend before the road levelled out just prior to his compound and steered around the corner over to his cabin. Entering, he sat down and compiled a list of items that he had seen and observed and upon reflection decided that he had done enough for today. He got up and walked over to Klaus's cabin where he found him also writing.

"Well Klaus! I'm quite pleased with what I've seen today, it is all much better than I expected. How about a drink tonight at my place?"

Klaus looked up from his desk and said, "Yah! Das ist eine gut idea, vill I ask Dave and Tony as well?" and before John could answer, he added, "Yes, why not!" and that was that.

John concurred and added, "Then we will make it a no work evening, no talk of work at all!"

"Stimmt!" replied Klaus, "ve vill come at nine."

"Yes! Nine will be fine," and after saying it he thought, a rhyming line indeed. He crossed back to his cabin and tidied up his desk for the day, locking some of his paperwork in the top drawer. He went out, pulled the door to and descended the steps. Before he drove off he decided to have a last look at the site and crossed over to the roadside and peered down, noting that the workers showed no sign of stopping, even though the light was falling fast, the shadows were now much more prominent and the air had cooled rapidly. He drove off down the road waving to Dave as he went, noting that Dave was standing at a heap of sand with Joshua in attendance. Winding his way downhill he found that he had memorised all the bends already and he looked about him as he drove on. A herd of bush cows passed ahead of him and he slowed to allow them to pass while the bushman waved to him and he continued on until he turned the last bend and came in sight of his residence.

Ebenezer was sweeping up outside as John approached and stopped in mid-sweep as the vehicle came into view and called out to Nathaniel, "Massah comes! Massah comes!"

Nathaniel who had been dozing in a chair in the kitchen corner, came to abruptly and made a start to the preparation of the evening meal.

Ebenezer raised his hand once John had come within hailing distance and called out, "Good evening, massah!"

John pulled up alongside the front of the house and got down from the driving seat. He went over to the chair on the veranda, sat down on it and stretched himself as he relaxed. He cast his eyes around taking in the stillness around him. It was all peace and tranquillity. It was now almost dark and the crickets had started up the nightly ritual. A sudden breeze sprang up and rustled the leaves in the trees, causing a miniature vortex as it caught the few leaves about, holding them in suspension in the air for a moment before quickly dying out and allowing them to fall quickly to the ground again. Ebenezer appeared bearing a tray with a jug of iced water and a tall glass into which he poured some lime and topped it up with water for John and proffered it to him.

"Thanks, Ebenezer," said John gratefully. He sipped the drink, then took a long draught, noting how refreshing it was. Ebenezer moved up to the end of the house and lit a lantern and hung it outside at the far end of the veranda. In the fading light it cast a homely hue over its range of luminance.

Ebenezer said, "I put de light away from you, boss, it will make the moths and insects stay away," and indicated the instant cloud that had already formed around it. John watched as he spoke and noted the numerous insects that were rapidly approaching it. Ebenezer went inside, leaving John alone.

He allowed his thoughts and the things he had seen to trickle over in his mind. Altogether it had been a good day and he hoped that there would be many others like it. He had spent quite some time outdoors so he got up, taking his drink with him and went upstairs for a shower. Afterwards, he changed into a pair of tropical overalls, all in one piece with wide, short sleeves and sat down at his desk and wrote up the report for that day. He crossed over to the drinks cabinet and poured himself a whisky and soda and sat sipping it, then walked back over to the veranda and went outside again. The light still attracted the cloud of insects, now thick around it and the noise of the crickets rubbing their legs together had risen almost to a crescendo and echoed off the upright surfaces around. Another outside light had attracted some lizards who had discovered this source of heat and had congregated closely around it. They vied for pole position, but each in turn vacated it as tasty morsels in the form of night insects flew directly into their striking range. Some large cockroaches had also appeared and had settled on the wall adjacent to the light. John hated these, they were absolutely anathema to him, as long as they stayed outdoors and away from him he was quite happy. A sharp piercing whistle sounded from out of the trees, some night bird calling, but he was unable to locate the source of it. Every now and then the crickets fell silent, as was their habit, and so quiet was the silence that he reckoned he could hear a pin drop.

Nathaniel was putting the finishing touches to the meal and had come out into the dining room and laid the table. He placed the cutlery and a napkin on a side plate, got out the salt and pepper and the jug of cold squash and then returned to the kitchen. A voice called, "Dinner is served for de massah!"

John waited for a moment, then went over to the dining room. Ebenezer was standing by the table, towel draped over his arm, waiting patiently for the massah. As John approached, he moved the chair out and pushed it in gently as John sat down. Silently he disappeared and returned shortly with the plate of hot soup which he placed in front of John and passed the basket of freshly cut bread over to him. John was quite surprised to see that it was a plate of Scotch broth. He tasted it, just like his mother used to make and he bent forwards to do it justice and finishing it, he asked Ebenezer to bring him another plate. After he had licked his lips, Ebenezer appeared with the 'dish de jour', as he put it, which turned out to be shepherd's pie. It, too, was excellent and he soon polished that off, but this time he only had one helping. Coffee, strong and black followed, with biscuits and cheese. John surmised that he was on to a good thing here, good food and great cooking. He arose from the table and went outside and pulled up the chair on the veranda and sat down while Ebenezer cleared away. A few minutes later, Ebenezer reappeared with the pot of coffee and a tray with a cup, sugar and milk on it, and placed it down beside him, saying, "For de massah," and before John could say thanks, he disappeared inside quietly again.

The night sounds were in force now and John looked at his watch, noting that it would not be long before his visitors arrived. He got up and went indoors and into the kitchen, where Ebenezer and Nathaniel were busy washing up. One washed while the other dried.

"By the way Nathaniel, that was an excellent meal tonight, you are a very good cook!"

Nathaniel smiled, and said, "Thank you, massah!"

"Ebenezer! Can you put a table and four chairs outside for me?"

"Yes suh, I do it for you now," and went off into the study to find a suitable table.

"There's no hurry, Ebenezer, just when you're finished what you're doing"

"Yes massah!" he replied and slowed down a bit.

John went through to the lounge and took the bottles out of the drinks cabinet, collected an ice bucket and some glasses and placed them out on the veranda, that would save Ebenezer some work at least. In the darkness, he could just see the glimmer of the fires from the native village downstream, away to his left Ebenezer appeared with the table, then the chairs and arranged them, also the glasses, and filled the ice bucket and returned and placed it on the floor adjacent to the table.

"By the way Ebenezer, I don't need you and Nathaniel tonight, so you can take the rest of the night off, okay?"

"Not want us tonight?" then looking at John sideways, he added, "you sure, massah?"

"Yes I'm sure, you both take the evening off. I'm sure that I can manage by myself."

"Yes sah, massah!" and he went off hurriedly into the kitchen to give the news to Nathaniel, pausing to look back at John as he went, not sure if he had heard correctly or not.

Nathaniel was busy putting food back in the freezer when Ebenezer entered, and looked up. "What's up?" he queried, seeing the expression on Ebenezer's face.

"Boss man says we can go! He no need us tonight!"

Nathaniel looked at him for a moment, then said, "You sure he say dat?"

"Yes! He say we go home!"

They looked at each other, and deciding that they'd better go in case the massah changed his mind, they hurried up and switching off the lights, they locked up the kitchen door, put out the lights, went out of the side door of the house and went around to the front of the house.

"We off then, boss!" they chorused, and waved to John.

"Yes! All right! See you in de mornin'!" and he waved to them as they disappeared into the bush track at the side of the house. "See you in de mornin' foah de breakfast!" he called out after them and almost immediately the reply came back more faintly,

"Yas massah, we be there!"

Silence fell and only the sounds of the night were heard. John looked at his watch, and pulling up one of the chairs, he put up his feet and dozed off, casting a quick glance at his watch as he closed his eyes and noting that it was seven-forty-five.

The sound of an approaching vehicle awoke him abruptly and he focused his eyes on the beam of the headlights that stabbed the darkness as they picked their way around the bends in the road. The sound of the engine was now audible and it changed pitch as it came around the last bend. The horn honked and the driver slid to a halt on the tarmac in front of the house, the brakes squealing as he applied them, and some shadowy forms got out.

"You round here somewhere, John?" Tony's voice enquired.

John responded, "Yes. Over here! By the door."

Tony hesitated for a moment, so that he could locate the voice and spotting John, he replied, "Got you!" and they made their way over to him. They appeared out of the darkness, Dave bringing up the rear, crossed over to where John stood awaiting them. They each drew up a chair and sat down.

"Help yourselves!" John said, and waved his hand over the bottles assembled in front of them, "I expect it's whisky for you, Klaus?"

"Yah! Das ist richtig! I see you remember, John."

"Yes, I remember. What's your poison Dave?"

"It's whisky for me also," and he rattled some of the ice cubes into his glass. Tony, however, reached for the gin and poured out a measure while the others were getting theirs organised.

When they were all set, John raised his glass and said, "Prost!" and they all drank as one.

"Well! What do you reckon on the plan for tomorrow then?"

Dave intervened. "Hang on! You said there was going to be no mention of work! Is that not so, Klaus?"

"Yah! He promised!" and they all scowled at John.

"It's all right!" John said. "I was only pulling your leg, just testing!"

"So!" said Klaus, "Then it's prost! Again!" and they all raised their glasses again and took a swig.

"Any more excuses for another prost?" queried Dave, and they all laughed out loud. The winding down then commenced and they discussed women, politics, beer, places they had been to, and the conversation wore on for a couple of hours while the contents of the bottles decreased sharply. A brief interruption for a quick visit to the kitchen for more ice and another bottle of whisky were the only interruptions in the proceedings and the continuance of the jovial conversation. By now, the tongues were loosened, the voices raised and the laughter became more raucous, and soon afterwards they broke into song. So the night progressed and it was almost two in the morning when they decided to call a halt and broke up. Dave and Tony propelled Klaus, or rather poured Klaus into the back of the Land Rover, feet first, causing him to come to a sudden halt with a bang as his head hit the tailgate. Tony climbed into the driver's seat and Dave just managed to haul himself into the other seat. The Land Rover started up and proceeded uphill disappearing amongst the trees to the strains of 'The Farmers in the Dell', and the revving of the engine as it was swallowed up into the right. John had a good laugh to himself, as the nonsensicality of it all struck him. The Land Rover had now disappeared from sight, only the mixed up choruses of Tony and Dave could now be heard, dying away as the vehicle climbed higher and higher towards their respective houses.

Chapter Four

Both Ebenezer and Nathaniel were in early, in fact earlier than usual. The fact that they had been given the evening off by the massah was a rare event in itself, so as a matter of respect they had come in early, got the breakfast ready and waited patiently for the massah to appear to show their efficiency. Not that John had any doubts about that, they seemed to do everything perfectly. Ebenezer decided to take a tray of tea up to John, so he assembled the items on it, and went upstairs knocking on the door gently. He received no response so he opened the door carefully and peered into the room. John appeared to be asleep, so he placed the tray down on the table at the side of the bed. John stirred slightly and opened his eyes.

Ebenezer said, "Good mornin', massah!" while John struggled into an upright position and just managed to get the face of Ebenezer into focus, glancing at the tray as he did so.

"Thank you, Ebenezer!" he said thickly, and pulled himself up into a semi-prone position.

Meanwhile, Ebenezer crossed over to the laundry basket, collected up John's soiled clothes and silently went out of the room and back downstairs, calling back to John as he went, "Is nice day, massah, today will be good for you I think."

John reached out and poured a cup of tea and added the sugar and tinned milk and took a brief sip.

"Ah!" he exclaimed. It was amazing what a sip of tea could do to refresh one, he thought. He had slept like a log after the consumption of quite a lot of alcohol, and he had been oblivious to the sound of the generator at the back of the house which powered the air conditioning. He arose, opened the window and looked out at the quiet scene in front of him. Nothing moved, not even the trees and no-one was in sight, not even the villagers who normally passed at this time on their way for water. He padded over to the shower and turned the water on and stepped into it. He turned the cold tap full on which produced just the right temperature, the water being heated even at this time of the morning by the sun as it beamed down directly onto the water tank at the rear of the house. He recalled a joke by a music hall artist which ended with the saying, 'the water was only lukewarm, although it looked warm', and he smiled as he soaped himself and let the water cascade down his body for quite a while. He wrapped a towel round his waist and went over to the sink, had a shave, cleaned his teeth and combed his hair. He wondered if Dave, Klaus and Tony would be feeling fresh this morning as they each had consumed as much as he had as he dressed in a pair of blue shorts, a short-sleeved shirt, a pair of blue ankle socks and the inevitable bondu boots. He went downstairs to the dining room where Ebenezer and Nathaniel stood side by side next to the table.

"Good mornin', massah," they chorused.

"Mornin' all!" he responded and sat down as Ebenezer held the chair for him.

Nathaniel disappeared into the kitchen and returned with a large jug of pure grapefruit juice, handed it to Ebenezer who poured out a glassful for John. He sipped it, it was certainly refreshing and placing the glass down on the table he said, "By the way, we left a bit of a mess outside last night."

"Is okay, massah, I already clear it up! Is no problem," replied Ebenezer. Nathaniel stuck his head around the corner of the door and beckoned to Ebenezer, who promptly disappeared into the kitchen and returned with a plate of steaming porridge and bowl of tinned milk. John got stuck into it and Ebenezer was soon back at his side with the bacon and two fried eggs. John looked at the eggs and decided he could just about manage them, and before he could finish Ebenezer was back again with the tea and toast. They're certainly making sure I have enough to eat, thought John, before I go off to work. The breakfast would certainly set him up for the day, if not longer. He looked at his watch and noted that it was six-fifty, so he crossed to the radio, switched it on and tuned it to the World Service, awaiting the hourly news service which followed the traditional regimental marching music, renowned throughout the world. He sat listening to it for fifteen minutes while Ebenezer cleared away and Nathaniel could be heard washing the dishes, then he went upstairs and collected up his notebook and the clipboard and reviewed the list of items that he was to speak about to those who would be assembled before him this morning. Everybody would be there and he intended to outline his plans to the work-force. He read over it and made a few minor alterations.

It was twenty-five past seven when he descended the stairs and went outside into the sunshine. He walked around the corner of the house and over to the Land Rover and checked the fuel, oil and water, and the operation of the lights. He cleaned the windscreen and the mirrors and then climbed aboard. The engine started easily and ran smoothly and he hoped the day would go as smoothly for him. The driver's seat was sunken so he swapped the cushions around and tested with his hand before wiggling into the driving position making sure his buttocks were firmly placed.

"That's better!" he said to himself, engaged first gear and drove off round the first bend in the road. Ebenezer waved as he went about his normal daily tasks just as John disappeared from sight. The road was empty as he climbed up the hill, taking the time to enjoy the fresh morning air as he went. The early morning bats still flitted about and wheeled on their last sojourn before retiring to a shaded area to hang suspended by their legs, their bellies full of insects caught on the wing during their night flights. A snake hurriedly slid off the road as the wheels rushed by it. John passed a long line of women of varying ages heading downhill to the river bed for the first collection of water of the day. Among them were a few young girls aged about eight or nine years, who flashed smiles at him and waved enthusiastically as he drove by. John waved back to them as he passed and gave them a friendly smile. A lone hunter crossed the road in front of him, off on his task of providing the meat for his family for that day, his long barrelled shotgun slung across his shoulders. As he climbed higher, the dam base came into view below and to his left. All appeared still and quiet with no sign of life about. The road inclined sharply now as he passed the storage compound, then levelled out as he continued up to the office sites. He arrived to find that he was the only one present, got out of the Land Rover and went over to the steps to his office and climbed them.

A mist had formed now over the lower part of the valley leaving just the top of the most recent section visible. It hung like some large spider's web as it draped almost everything around it, as though it was unattached at either end.

A few moments later the sound of another vehicle approaching heralded the arrival of Tony and he swung into the compound and drew to a halt. He sounded his horn and climbing out, he called, "Morning, John!"

"Any sign of Klaus or Dave?"

Tony laughed and said, "Yes, they'll be here soon, I just passed Dave coming out of his compound, he'll be here in few seconds, although I don't think Klaus will be here as quickly, he's not feeling too well this morning, I hear. Apparently he banged his head getting into the vehicle last night when we left your place but I can't recall that, so he may be suffering from a loss of memory today methinks."

John laughed, recalling the incident, and replied, "Well, we'll wait and see if he appears or not!"

Dave and Joshua arrived at that point and the four of them went over and into John's office where he had already put the coffee on for them and they each poured out a cup. Shortly afterwards the grating and crunching of gears was heard and this announced the arrival of Klaus. Everyone, including Joshua, got up and peered out of the doorway. Klaus managed to steer over to the other parked vehicles, coming to a sudden halt at an angle and got out amid curses and oaths. Scowling he made a weaving track over to John's cabin and just managed to climb the steps. He emerged at the top of them and was confronted by the beaming faces. He stopped and got them into view as Dave called out,

"Nice day, Klaus!" and grinned at Klaus.

"I'll blotty nice day you!" he replied ruefully. "I haf eine sore head! Must be the alcohol, ich denke!" They all laughed and pulled him indoors and sat him down, he was looking exceedingly fragile to say the least.

"You mean to say," Tony said, "that you can't remember what happened last night?"

"Last night? What happened? We had a drink, it was late, that's all I can recall."

"Yes! But you can't remember testing the tailgate of the Land Rover then, with your head?"

"Ah so! Then that is why I have this sore head!" and he put his hand up to the top of his head and rubbed it. They all laughed and thrust a cup of steaming coffee into his hand. They conversed whilst Klaus peered into the cup and took large mouthfuls of the coffee and rested his head against the wall behind him. Joshua sat and listened to the events of the previous evening and his sides were sore laughing at the narration of it. Their talk was interrupted by the sound of a powerful diesel engine as the first of the long trucks arrived on the site and pulled up in the centre of it. Behind it came four others and

Football was in evidence shouting out orders and making the men form up in large groups on three sides, as if forming a parade, and when he had them assembled he came over to John's office, bounded up the steps and on entering said, "De men is all here, boss! Dey is ready foah you."

John noted that today Football had smartened himself up and was wearing a red tee shirt and clean shorts.

"Thanks, Football," John replied, and stepping towards the door, he picked up his clipboard and said to the others, "Let's go then, and get this out of the way." They all followed him out and down the steps on to the hard earth in front of the office.

"Football! Get me something to stand on, will you?" He went off to the side of the compound and returned with an empty forty-five gallon oil drum, rolling it over he upturned it and John went over and climbed up on to it. "Can you bring the men in closer Football? It will save me from shouting." Football spoke in some other tongue to them all and they all merged into one great mass in a rough semi-circle.

"That's better, thanks, Football," and he called for silence. He looked around, surveying the sea of black faces before him. A motley crew he thought to himself as his eyes finished their scanning of the far edges of the crowd. There existed here just about every description of person on this earth, he thought. Tall men, short men, fat and thin, most of them young and fit, but there was also a smattering of wizened ones, some old, some deformed and a few with obvious stunted growth. A few looked as though they had suffered from leprosy at some stage of their life, and these were intermingled amongst the throng.

"Are all these men fit?" he asked Football.

"Yes, massah! All de men is fit, can do all de work every day!"

"Hmm! Well all right, Football, I'll address them then, but I'll need you to translate for me."

"Yes, boss! But some of de men dey speak yoah language so I only need to speak de other languages for some of dem."

At this point, Tony interjected by saying, "You'll have to stop every now and then, John, to allow Football to speak in the other languages."

"Yes. Thanks, Tony."

"He'll have to translate into Yoruba, Hausa, and a few others as well, but the men will translate themselves anyway."

"Right! I'll do that then, Tony," and he turned towards the men and started.

"Good morning!" he called out and quickly came back the reply in chorus,

"Good mornin', massah!" followed by, "Salou ta zuna!"

"What's that?" he asked, turning to Football.

"They are saying, massah, that you are welcome."

"I see!" said John, and continued, "I am de new boss heah, and I'm going to improve the conditions you are working under," and he hesitated as Football carried out the translation. A few murmurs broke out in the crowd. John continued, "It is good to see you all here, and in return for these improved conditions I want to see an improvement in the work." A discussion broke out amongst them and then they fell silent again. "We are going to get this project finished on time." Football translated again and John waited patiently while he did so. As there had been no adverse comments so far, John thought, it's going well, he half expected some discontent but there was no evidence of it. He continued, "In the past, you were not paid very much," and at this point the crowd was immediately silent, listening intently now to what was to be said next.

"From now on, and that means from today, you will all be paid in money! No cowries! And the pay for each man will be five hundred niara a month." Football translated this for the benefit of the others and instantly a noisy chatter broke out amongst them and an excited buzz went around. They all responded almost instantly with a loud cheer which was accompanied with smiles and large grins. "In addition to this you will all be issued with new work clothes, shirt and shorts, socks and safety boots, helmets like this one!" and he took off his and held it up so the men could see it, "and other safety equipment such as glasses and ear defenders!" He waited patiently again as Football carried out the translation. "Your food will also be improved. That is to say there will be more variety and more of it, and we are going to have a doctor here to attend to any of your ills. If you wish to use your own doctor, a witch doctor, then you must tell Football here who will in turn tell me."

John waited again while Football carried out the translation. He certainly had his work cut out for him and it was quite some time before Football carried out the individual translations in the various languages, however, he got the message over to them all, and turning back to John he said, "Okay, continue massah."

"So you see that in return I want a good day's work, is that agreed?" He waited until that had filtered through. The discussion broke out again amongst the men and after a few moments a spokesman stepped forward, having been hastily elected, and said something to Football.

"What do they say, Football?"

"Dey say dey will do that, massah."

"Good!" exclaimed John, "tell them, Football, that they won't get the new clothing for a few days yet but when it comes they will draw it from Massah Dave!" and he indicated Dave standing next to him. Football translated this again to the men and again the response was that they understood, their eyes moving to look at Dave then back again towards John.

"In addition, the work hours will be seven in the morning until half an hour before sunset and there will be two breaks during the day of half of an hour." Football translated again.

"If there are any problems, then you will tell Football, or de Massah Tony, or de Massah Klaus, or myself. Is that understood?" He waited for Football.

"Yes, boss, dey get de message."

John continued, "Shortly, we will have an alarm system installed. If there is any danger at all the alarm will sound, and if that happens you must leave the site at once to a safe place which Massah Klaus will arrange for you!" Football took longer to get this over to them as it took a bit of explaining to some of them. Eventually they nodded in understanding and John continued.

"That is all I have to say. But before you go away I want Football here to get all your names, what village you come from and how long you have been working here at this site for."

Football called out the instruction in the differing tongues and when he had received the reply from a spokesman that they understood, he turned to John and said, "Okay massah! They all understand." This was followed by a loud shout from them all.

"What was that, Football?" asked John, looking a bit worried.

"Dey say dat you is good man, massah!" and picking up a thick notebook and a pencil, he walked down to a point in front of them and proceeded to take down the information that John required. Each would be given a number which would ease their identity as many had the same or similar names.

"Well, that seems to have gone down all right," he said, climbing down from the top of the oil drum.

"Yes, especially the bit about the pay, that'll certainly fire them up! I'm sure that you'll find the work rate improving from now on."

"Yes. It should do! I want Football to get up a team and go out and recruit the extra workers we require. He knows where to go so I'll get him organised and he can go off to the towns and villages and see just how many men he can come up with. I've said a figure of around five hundred."

"Yes. Five hundred would be ideal, but I don't think he will find that many, John."

"Yah! About three hundred, I'd say," added Klaus.

Joshua, who had remained silent all this time then spoke, "If he go to the north and the east, that is the north-east, he will get all the men he needs, this I know! Although it will take many days to find them."

"Well, it'll take as long as it takes, so the saying goes," said John. "I'll send Football out this week, the money for the inducement should take care of that. By the way, that means that although the workers pay is to go up, then so will the pay of you three as well, is that all right?"

"Thank you, massah!" Joshua replied immediately, while the others nodded in understanding.

John went down to the table where Football was sitting on a folding wooden chair, busy writing as John approached him. John shook hands with some of the men and they each replied by saying, "God bless you massah," or "Thank you, massah!" or the equivalent of this in their own language or special dialect.

He stood at the table and as the men approached, he asked them his name. The first man he asked replied, "I, Ignatius, massah!" Football noted it down, then his family name and the village of Zente. The process continued, with Football calling for the next man in turn. The names varied widely with the occasional repetition. John looked down the list and noted them as Football wrote. They read Femi, Sunny, Ode, Ogo, Ile, Andrew, Aje, Oluwa Sunday, Akinbile, Isliaku, Nidabo, Ajimabwe, Odigwe, Odindonkwe, and a host of other unpronounceable names which John could not get his tongue around.

It reminded him of Dave's name on his office door. He looked at the list with interest and commented,

"Quite a variety, Football. Everybody except Jesus! Eh?"

"No! I is Jesus!" a voice called from the line of men. All eyes turned to the man, who revealed himself to be a small, wizened, sinewy character who flashed a toothless smile at John, and waved his arm to him. They all laughed simultaneously.

"Okay! I see you, Jesus!" John called out.

"I see you too!" Jesus replied, "I has de good eyesight!" and they all laughed again. John stood smiling and shook his head. He might have known. Still, the men were all in a happy frame of mind so he remained standing behind Football as the list got longer and longer. He looked over his shoulder again at the names. There were Pius, Jim Jim, Rupert who looked nothing like a bear, Jaguar, Ebenezer, William, David, Alfred, Billy, Sammy, Nick Dick, Claude, Obinike, Two Brother, Simon, Tuesday, Olo and Ake. As the list increased, he looked at it again as Football wrote down the next name, Tin Can Billy.

"Why do they call him that name then, Football?"

"Is because he always carry de tin can for de water, massah!" said Football innocently. John smiled again to himself, obvious when he thought about it!

Quite a number of the names conjured up instant pictures in his mind, but some defied description, such as Big Smoking Joe, Long William and Monday Friday, and the names bore no relevance to their appearance.

"Does each man understand the number he has been given Football?"

"Yes, massah! Dey do. An' I tells them when they come for de pay dey speak de number and we check de name, right?"

"Yes. That's right Football."

"How many to go before you finish the list?"

Football looked along the line and back, " 'Bout one truck load, massah, den dey can go back to work."

"Good! Let's get them finished with then and get them there."

"Yes, massah! I gets them back to work plenty quick, they don' call me Football Boot for nuthin'!"

John smiled to himself again and left, saying as he went, "I'll leave it up to you then, Football," and he went off over to the office.

In the office, Tony and Klaus were discussing a large stubborn rock that was causing a problem, and they had decided that it would require blasting to remove it. As John approached them through the doorway, Tony said to him, "I've a feeling that today marks a turning point, John, you should reap the benefits soon, I reckon."

"Yes, I hope so! I'm looking forward to some good progress now."

Klaus and Tony departed with Dave and Joshua for the storage compound to draw out the explosives, and John went to review the next few stages of their work. By now the men had all remounted the trucks and to the signal of a blaring air horn they all set off out of the compound in a huge cloud of swirling dust and proceeded back down the hill to the dam site itself. The sun was up, the day hot with no breeze and the birds were singing loudly. John went over to the roadside and studied the base with his binoculars. Down below the trucks occasionally came into view as they swept around the bends in the road, disappearing and reappearing momentarily from view, then they were lost from sight in the trees. He studied the faces of the valley and the areas where the hammerheads were to be situated, made some notes and went off into the office to look at the diagrams. He made a note about his requirement for a doctor, he would have to see to that today.

He had planned to send someone to the telephone today to call Hendry J., he had all the contacts and would know where to obtain the services of one on a long term basis. Down at the base the trucks had arrived, the men spilled out on to the ground and made their way to their accommodation, collected up what they needed for work and soon they were at the work face and happily going about their tasks. This new boss, he certainly was one to sort things out, many smiles could be seen on the faces of the men, their talk was lively and animated now and they were in a buoyant mood. Some of them reflected upon how rich they would become, and how pleased their families would be when they returned to them with all this money. A fortune indeed for a common black worker. Football directed them to their areas of work but they were mainly self-governing and he did not have to exercise too much authority to get the work organised or done. The promise of the extra pay had put new impetus in their efforts. About two hours of the working day had been lost through the meeting, but he reckoned that by the end of the day, that would be made up quite easily. The breaks were to be at midday and at four in the afternoon.

Meanwhile, Klaus and Tony had drawn their charges and had set out for the hammerhead site which was far up on the right-hand side of the valley. A team of six men had dug out the holes for the charges and were standing by. Tony planted the charges, packing them in tightly to ensure that the shock waves would travel inwards and dislodge the rock face sufficiently to enable them to have access to the area for the hammerhead foundation. The men climbed back into Tony's truck and drove back down a makeshift road which was coated in loose rock and shale, warning those below to prepare for the blast and the danger of falling rock. They arrived there and Tony sought out Football and indicated where the rock might fall and had him clear away the workers from that area. Football in turn, sent one of the men over to the other side and alerted the men there to the imminent danger. The men retreated and Tony signalled to Klaus, who had the plunger already connected and raised his arm to signify that all was clear below.

Klaus saw the signal and waved in response and having a last look around to make sure that all was clear, he bent down and pushed home the plunger. The charges went off simultaneously, showing small puffs of dust as they exploded. There followed a two second interval before the sound was heard and then it echoed along the valley walls in each direction before dying out. Tony and Klaus watched the rock face for signs of the fractures but they had to wait for what seemed to be an eternity, actually it was only a few seconds. Then a vertical crack appeared in the rock some ten feet away from the marked line and rapidly spread down downwards, then upwards. Then, in what seemed like slow motion, the cracks widened and the gap opened, followed by the falling away of a huge shard of rock which broke loose from the face and crashed downwards, bringing with it a shower of boulders and fragments as it slid and toppled into the void below. It rushed downwards and struck the valley floor with a tremendous force, the rock shattering as it did so and the vibrations were felt all around. Far off, the booming noise echoed off the valley walls. Once the dust had settled Tony gave the all clear signal and the men resumed their positions and carried on working. Tony asked Football to organise a clearance party, and he and Klaus climbed into a Land Rover and set of up the side of the valley to the point where they had blown the rock face away. John was alerted by the explosion and had watched through his binoculars at the activity below, noting that all was well in hand he returned to the office desk. Shortly afterwards, he went over to his vehicle, climbed in, dusted off the seat and drove off down to Dave's 'empire', as he called it. He entered the compound gates and passed Joshua driving a fork lift with a large wooden crate. He waved to John, and indicated that Dave was over at the back behind the storage sheds. John raised his thumb to indicate that he understood and drove over to the rear of the compound, stopped and climbed down while the associated cloud of dust settled itself. He walked through the shade offered by the high corrugated sides of the building and after a brief search, he spotted Dave checking off a list of goods next to a row of steel-banded crates at the fence.

Dave saw John approach and walked over to meet him.

"I was just checking what little we had of the safety equipment left, John, but there's not much, we'll have to wait until we get the shipment from Hendry J."

"That's fine, Dave. Can I get you and Football to go down to the nearest Nitel office and get that long order through to Hendry J., as soon as possible?"

"Yes. I'll get hold of him and we can go and do it shortly."

"How long will it be before we actually get it then, Dave?"

"Oh! Well, knowing Hendry J. I'd say about a week or thereabouts, but he's usually on the button so it may be sooner."

"Fine. We'll just wait for it then, but while you're on the phone, remember to tell him of our requirement for a doctor, full time."

"Yes. All right then. I'll mention it first of all so that I don't forget it."

"Is there any accommodation for him at all?"

"Yes, there's a house half way down the hill, perhaps you've seen it."

"No, not that I can remember but if it's in good condition, it will do him fine, whoever it may be."

"It's got all the facilities John, not as big as your house but perfectly adequate, but maybe you can ask your Ebenezer to get a cook and a servant for him whenever he comes?"

"That won't be a problem, I'm sure that Ebenezer will be able to find them."

"I'll go off about eleven or so with Football, then."

"Let me know when we can expect him when you return."

"Will do."

Dave and Football returned later that day, their task completed.

"Did Hendry J. say when we were likely to get it all?"

"Yes. He said that most of it was available in Lagos, it was just a case of getting it released from warehouses and shipped up to here, but the radio equipment and the electrical equipment you asked for, he'll have to get from the United Kingdom and have it flown out, I expect that will take about two weeks longer."

"Good! As long as it's not delayed too long, I want to get all this organised."

"I'm going off down to see Football, so that's where I'll be if anybody's looking for me."

"Right. See you!" and they parted.

On the way out of the compound he sounded his horn as he passed by Joshua, who looked up and gave him a departing wave. John followed the road to the bottom, crossed over to the dried up river bed and drove up towards the rock face. In the mirror of his vehicle he could see the local women busy with the washing in one of the pools not far away. They were busy rubbing the clothes with stones to remove the dirt, while another group rinsed the clothes in a clear pool and stretched them out to dry on the largest rock at the side of the river bed.

Football was still in evidence clearing away the rockfall with the group of men. He was directing a large truck which was being used as a bulldozer to manoeuvre a large piece of rock away to one side. Trucks were already in evidence carrying away some of the pieces to a dump further downstream and were fully laden. He got out and watched the proceedings. He noted the sharp incline of the valley wall here, different from that higher up on the east topped by a row of trees but only remnants of rock and scrub on the west where the charges had brought about the change in the contour of the edge of the ridge. On seeing John, Football had handed over to one of the men and had joined John as he walked along.

"I was looking for the supervisor, Football, have you seen him?"

"You means Massah Klaus? He up top."

"No! He's down here, I think!"

"No massah, you wrong, he up top!"

"No, Football, I is standin' looking at him!"

"No, I is not de supervisor, is Massah Klaus."

"Well, Massah Football, from now on you is de supervisor of de men! All right! So whens I'se axes foh de supervisor, I expects to see dis man here, you got de message?"

Football looked at him in silence for a moment, then silently he pointed to himself and said, "You means, I is de supervisor now?"

"Yes, Football. You."

"But when I become supervisor, boss?"

"Now. And when I wants report on de mens, I axes you! Okay?"

"Yes, massah!" and he grinned widely. "Thank you, massah, thank you!"

They continued walking along, still talking, when all of a sudden, John stopped short in his tracks and said, "What's that!" and pointed to a huge cloud of dust that had suddenly appeared in front of them, hanging suspended in the air. Football looked at the cloud which had now dispersed slightly, and a herd of bush cows came into view. He estimated the herd to be of about seven hundred in all, as more came into view around a bend in the river bed. The lead animal, an older cow approached and John could clearly see its long curved horns.

"Is only de bush cows, massah," he said.

"I know that Football, but what are they doing here in the middle of our site?"

"Dey pass heah verrah often, massah, on de way to de valley below."

"Yes, but they can't just come in here at any time, Football, they might get injured or cause an accident. Go and see the herdsman, and ask him why he's here."

Football looked at John, unsure for a moment what he was to say to the herdsman, and went over to the other side, as the herd approached he intercepted the leading cow and the attendant herdsman. They greeted each other and with an expert move of his stick, the herdsman halted the lead animal and shortly afterwards the whole herd drew to a slow halt, seizing the opportunity to munch at anything green which was about. Others milled around and sought out new areas of foliage and that too was soon cropped out of existence.

The herdsman sat down, so did Football and they remained in conversation for quite some time. John, eager to find out what was happening, went over to them and sat down next to them in the dust. The herdsman raised his hand in recognition of his presence.

"What does he say then, Football?"

"He say, massah, that they are the Fulani and they have right of way here."

"What? Here in this valley?"

"Yes, massah, for many years now. He say not do any damage, not stay long, only passing through."

"Yes. I understand that, but you must explain to him that I can't be responsible for any accidents that occur if they are on the site or passing through."

Football translated this to the man, and they continued in their conversation for quite a while, finally the herdsman nodded in agreement and Football turned back towards John.

"He says he understand but they come often from de north to de south and that there are many herds who will come this way, and he asks that you respect their custom to graze and pass through dis place."

John, thought for a moment, then said, "Well, all right then, as long as they're careful when they come and tell them to watch out for any of the big heavy vehicles that move about here, I don't want any accidents on this site at all!"

Football launched into another lengthy conversation with the man, and after about five minutes or so they both got up. The herdsman shook John's hand and said something to him.

"What did he say, Football?"

"He say, massah, they will respect your wishes and asks that you do not interrupt their movements. If you not want dem to cross any part den you fence it off, or de lead cow will go and de rest follow."

"All right then, tell him I understand that and I will agree to it."

Football spoke again with the herdsman who raised his stick above his head parallel with the ground, and the whole herd in understanding started to move off, following the lead animal. They passed by slowly, a large part of the herd being cows with young calves. Behind them the accompanying flock of egrets kept pace, strutting along, some of them diving on the grasshoppers that had been disturbed by the hooves of the cattle while others sat atop the cattle themselves, pecking at the flies that were attracted to their rumps. Some of them used the cattle as vantage points and as soon as they saw any insects, they swooped down on them, returning to their backs again. They would stay with the herd forever as it was a constant source of food. The herd passed by crossing from one side of the valley to the other in a diagonal movement, then pausing to drink at a pool before moving off in response to the indication of the herdsman, and continuing their journey. Once they had passed by John noted that much of the growth that had appeared in the dried up bed, had now disappeared completely.

He and Football continued their walk along and John stated that the clearance of the rockfall would take a few days but would not affect the remainder of the work in hand.

"By the way, Football, I want you to select four of your men and go off on this recruiting trip up country. You'd better take men who can speak the dialects and I want you to get as many man as you can find."

Football thought for a while then said, "Who take over heah, massah, when I is away?"

"Is there a man who can do this?"

"Yes, massah, there is a man."

"Okay then, you tell Massah Klaus who it is and you go the day after tomorrow. You come to de office tomorrow morning and we will look at the map together. You know where you can get the men?"

"Yes massah, I knows, but I needs de trucks as well."

"You just tell Massah Klaus and Massah Dave what you want, they will arrange it for you."

"No problem, massah. I get de men, plenty of dem, foh suah!"

"Good," said John, "just do the best you can, Football."

"Okay, boss! I get!"

John left shortly afterwards and walked along the river bed and to his Land Rover and set off back to his office. On the way back he passed a bunch of youths excitedly chasing a wild pig through the undergrowth, rushing here and there in their attempts to catch it, the pig squealing loudly as it made its escape into the bush hotly pursued by the youths. On the way up he passed Dave on his way down and as they approached each other, they slowed up and stopped to speak. Dave was on his way down to Shagwa to the Nitel office but if he could not find a phone that was working there he would go on to

Ouna. John arrived back at his cabin where Tony and Klaus were present making notes about the hammerhead preparation.

"Some nice geological specimens here, John!" exclaimed Tony, fishing about in the bag of samples he had taken from the rockfalls after the explosion. "Very interesting, too!" and he took out a largish rock from the sack which had been split evenly in two by the blast.

"Look at this!" He held up the rock with its flat face towards John and said, "See this? Agate here! Perfect!" He held up the two halves for comparison, the tones of which were clearly evident. The grey, white and brown of the stone was formed in a beautiful pattern.

"I'll grind this down and split it up, it'll make some fine ornaments or even jewellery," he said with an air of satisfaction. Klaus had marked up the diagrams to show the changes of the rock face and they were busy estimating the volume of rock that had been removed. John mentioned the Fulani and the bush cows.

"Oh, them," said Klaus, "they come often but you've no worries there, John, they move on quite quickly and the good thing about them is that they help to keep the flies down, and the mosquitoes too!"

"Yes! And the undergrowth too!"

"They have their uses, we often trade them for cattle so we can get fresh meat, but we don't make a habit of it."

They continued discussing the rock fall and they were engrossed in that when John interrupted them and said, "What's that sound?"

They all stopped speaking and listened, but they couldn't hear anything, and they continued the conversation. John heard the sound again and breaking off from them he went outside on to the steps and listened again. Klaus and Tony joined him.

"It sounds like singing," said Klaus.

"Yes! It is singing!" and he laughed and said, "Well I haven't heard that for same time now. It's the men down below! It's coming up from the valley floor." They listened and sure enough they could now hear the singing clearly, the walls of the valley acting like a funnel as the sound drifted up.

"They're probably singing because they're happy, John, it's probably the pay increase that has brought this on."

John sighed with relief, "Oh well, that's a good sign indeed."

They then went over John's plan for Football to go out and do the recruiting and Tony suggested that they leave it all up to him, he knew the areas and they felt sure he would get what he said he would get, he was that type of person. The local tribes would listen to him, that they were sure of, and John felt relieved at this confirmation.

"We will have to start on the new accommodation immediately then, Klaus."

"That will be done, John. I will see Dave about the materials, there is plenty of room down at the site below and there is also plenty of room for the new messing area we will also need to build. The workers don't want anything too fancy, but we will make sure that we build it to be adequate for their needs."

"Can I leave it up to you, then, Klaus?"

Tony went off with his bag of rock samples to go over them and to catalogue his finds, while Klaus returned to his office to catch up on his paperwork and organise the construction of the messing facilities.

Two hours later Dave returned, calling in on John before he went to his own site.

"Hello Dave," said John, looking up from his desk, "were you successful then?"

"Yes!" he replied, "I got through right away to Hendry J., and we spoke for quite a while. He said to tell you that it's all in hand and he will get it up as soon as he can. Most of it will be coming up next Tuesday, it will be in two trucks and he will send it with experienced drivers so that there won't be any chance of it going astray at all. As far as the request for the doctor, he says that it might be a while before he can locate one but he has been on to the embassies and he is hopeful. He said that he can't get an English one but he will try the French, Canadian and German embassies as well. He reckons that they have one from the French embassy but he will not be available for a few weeks yet, as he is away on leave but it could be a Doctor...," and he fished in his pocket for his notebook, "...a Doctor Dupeppe. I have to phone him again in two days time to find out for sure."

"Well, that sounds just grand! Tell me Dave, did we have one here before?"

"No, we had a local medicine man but his remedies didn't seem to be all that effective and besides, some of the men didn't trust him as he was from an unknown tribe and you know how partisan these tribal people can be? There was a lot of bad feeling about so he had to go in any case."

"Well, I hope it all works out well, anyway," commented John, and they parted, each to his own tasks for the day.

It was soon early evening and the sun had dipped in the sky, the men, however, were still working and singing and it was almost pitch dark by the time that they stopped and climbed into the wagons and left for the accommodation site. John closed up his office and, waving to Klaus, he went off down hill. He arrived at his house, which he had nicknamed 'EL GRANDE', and went indoors. Ebenezer greeted him as he stepped through the door and John said he was off for a shower. While he was doing that Nathaniel put on the kettle for the tea which he served as soon as de boss came home, and Ebenezer had taken a bottle of whisky from the drinks cabinet and as soon as John appeared from his shower, he poured the tea and added a measure of whisky to it.

Ebenezer turned down the air conditioning as sometimes it was over efficient, and when that happened the temperature dropped sharply. Shortly afterwards he announced that dinner was ready and signalled to Nathaniel in the kitchen, who could be heard rattling the pots and pans around.

John ate mechanically, his mind on future plans. Having now got the bit firmly between his teeth he knew exactly how he was going to go about the fast progress that he had planned. Little could be done until the extra men arrived but once they were here his plans would bear fruition. The evening passed quietly and John allowed the two of them to knock off early again as soon as they had washed up. He crossed off a number of things from his list of 'things to do' and added a few more that had sprung to mind. He relaxed on the veranda outside his bedroom window and listened to some music that he had selected from the box of tapes which he had rummaged through. During the course of the evening, two vehicles had passed by the house, one an old Ford Cortina sounding more sick than well as it struggled up the hill, and the other was a Peugeot 404 station wagon loaded up with yams on its way down to the residential compound of the workers. No doubt Bombay would soon be engrossed in some hard bargaining there. It reappeared some two hours later but now empty, and moving at a greatly increased speed as it rounded the bends in the road and was soon lost from sight up the hillside. The nightly crescendo of the crickets and the frogs was evident and the bats squeaked loudly as they wheeled through the trees on the nightly forage towards a grove of fruit trees that grew nearby. The silence, when it occurred, was deafening. Just the ideal place to relax, thought John. Out here on the veranda it was just high enough to catch any slight breeze that sprang up which made the heat of the night bearable. Following Ebenezer's advice, he had set the oil lamp at the far end of the veranda and sat at the other end where it was insect free.

The following day broke, summoned by the crow of a far away cock from the village just up the hill which, in the still air of the morning, carried far. John got up and went down to the kitchen. Ebenezer and Nathaniel were not yet in so he rooted around, discovering the makings for the tea and made himself a cup, and returned to the veranda.

Shortly afterwards Ebenezer appeared below with a bush brush and commenced to sweep around the outside of the house, skilfully applying the fanned out end of it to the leaves and dead insects, he soon had the area all ship shape and bristol fashion. Some of the small clouds of dust that he had raised in the process hung in the air before settling down on the ground. He spotted John on the veranda and looking up, he called out, "Mornin' massah! You have a good sleep?"

"Yes, fine!" replied John.

Ebenezer signalled that he had got the reply by raising his hand and continued his sweeping without further comment. Looking up again, he called out, "De massah want tea?"

"No! I already have it!" and he held up the cup for Ebenezer to see.

"Okay, massah!" he replied and returned to his duties.

John showered and dressed and went down to the kitchen with the empty cup. Nathaniel was washing dishes as he entered, and seeing him, he spoke. "Good mornin', massah!"

"Morning, Nathaniel!" he replied.

"You wants de bacon an' eggs for de breakfast today?" he asked.

"Yes. That will do fine. Do we have bacon?"

"Yes boss! We has!" then added, "Well, sometimes," and he grinned at John.

"If we pay de money we get de bacon," and he rubbed his thumb and fingers together.

"And the eggs?"

"Is no problem, many egg! My sister, she have many hen, so we has many eggs every day, foh suah," and he grinned again. Nathaniel started to cook the breakfast and John called to Ebenezer that he was going out for a short stroll and would be about ten minutes or so.

"Okay, massah! I tells de cook! I tell him not to burn de bacon."

John smiled to himself as he descended the steps at the front of the house. He walked around to the back of the house and made his way up the steep path which led to the top of the hill and emerged at a large black rock. From there he could just see over the tops of the trees when the wind moved them aside and could see the top of the base section of the dam. When the dam was fully constructed it would tower high above the point where he stood.

He viewed it through his binoculars and took a range bearing, noting it down for future reference and at the same time he scanned the panorama, familiarising himself with it and its layout from this vantage point.

He commenced his return and Ebenezer having seen him descend the path called out to Nathaniel, "De massah comes!". Nathaniel recommenced the grilling of the bacon and reached out for the eggs and the pan. While John seated himself, Ebenezer brought out the pot of tea and promptly disappeared back into the kitchen again. He reappeared shortly afterwards with a huge plate of bacon and eggs, all done sunny side up and placed it down in front of John, followed by a rack of toast and some chilled butter.

John looked at it and thought that he would not be able to eat all of it, but nevertheless he did it justice and poured himself out another cup of tea. He looked at his watch and noted that it was only six-thirty in the morning. He decided to go up to the site early, called out to Ebenezer that he was leaving early and set off up the hill. Ahead of him, as he wound his way upwards, he spotted Dave and followed him up to the compound, pulling up just as Dave was getting out of his vehicle, "You're up early today, Dave.

"You too, John. Well, once I'm awake, I have to get up so I may as well come to work as do anything else. I can't stand hanging about waiting for the appointed hour to come. Besides, if you start the day with a clear head, it bodes well for the rest of the day."

"By the way, Dave, do we have enough in hand to buy our usual food supplies?"

"Yes, but sometimes I'm convinced that the bills and the goods do not always match up."

"How do you mean, Dave?"

"Well, I order the food, give Joshua the list and the money, and he and one of the drivers go down with a truck and buy it at the local market."

"What's the problem then?"

"They get the food but they always use all of the money, or often they say they have to pay more the next time they go as they're owing from the time before."

"So! There's a fiddle going on, then?"

"Yes, I know that for sure but I can't prove it, they always say the prices have gone up but when I ask Joshua about it he just shrugs his shoulders and says that it is common here, that is the corruption."

"Yes! I've heard that but I'd like you to keep tabs on that, Dave."

"I already do! It's all in a book here!" and he tapped a drawer in his desk with his knuckles. "You'll find that the same goes on at your house, John they're all at it! Not an honest one amongst them!"

"As long as I know about it, we can keep an eye on it and take action if necessary."

"Sure," said Dave "that's no problem, but before you came out it was really laughable, there was a lot of it going on then but I didn't have control of the money at that time, or the control of the food. That was one of the reasons why those that were sacked were sent back to their countries."

"Who passed the control of it on, then?"

"Klaus decided to do that, he was getting fed up with it all and in the end he was going to take control of it himself anyway."

"Just as well he did, then, Dave!"

"Don't worry, I'll keep a sharp eye out for any fiddling! There's been a lull in it lately but I'll let you know as soon as it occurs again."

"Okay. You do that, Dave, and I'll be grateful."

John left and went on up to his office. Even Klaus was in early today and had already left on his morning tour of inspection of all the workings around the site. He had left a note on the top of John's desk to that effect. John went over to the roadside and trained his binoculars on the area below, after a brief search he located a movement far below and focused on it. He followed Klaus in the eyepieces, he went around stopping here and there to make notes on his clipboard. Klaus inspected everything, climbing up and down amongst the sections, taking measurements every now and then.

John reflected that Klaus was a good, conscientious man and always seemed to be on top of things. Initially he had had his doubts about him but up to now the evidence was that he was on top of the job and knew it inside out. John returned to his office and sat down to read some old reports that were in the drawer. Shortly afterwards he heard the singing again as it wafted up on the breeze. It was the workers who had just disembarked from the trucks and were commencing the daily tasks. John smiled and congratulated himself on this early evidence of success. Tony called in and said that he would be 'down town' as he called it for a few hours and left immediately. John reviewed the up to date report that he was about to send off to Hendry J., and completed the pages of the Sitrep. As he put it down on the desk, he heard a vehicle pulling up sharply outside and the thumping of feet as the driver bounded up the steps of his cabin. In burst Football, his eyes wide and excitedly saying,

"Massah! You come quick!" and beckoned with his arm.

John got up from his desk and said, "What's up, Football? Has there been an accident or something?"

"No! No accident, massah! But you betta come quick!" and so saying, he leapt down the steps and headed for the Land Rover. John was just one step behind him, climbed in as the engine burst into life and the vehicle shot forwards, made a one hundred and eighty degree turn in the dust and headed off at high speed.

"What's the panic then, Football?"

Football turned towards him and said, still wide-eyed, "Is gold, massah!"

"What? Gold? Don't be bloody silly, Football! There's no gold around here, we haven't got the right type of rock for that!"

"I knows gold whens I see it, massah!"

"Okay then! Let's go an see this 'gold'."

They sped downhill, the bends being taken at a high speed as they flew around the corners. It was too fast, for John's liking, and he said, "Football! Slow down or else we won't get there in one piece!"

"Yes, massah!" he replied and took his foot off the accelerator pedal and reduced the speed of the vehicle to a fraction less than breakneck speed. They rattled along the dirt road on the valley floor, and as they approached the work face they could see the men crowding around the point where they had been clearing the rockfall from the previous day's explosion. Tony was in the middle of it and trying to force his way through the throng with little success, but after much shouting, his voice lost in the babble that had ensued, he managed to instil some sort of order in the men and gradually forced his way to the front where the men were excitedly jabbering and pointing at the heap of stones. Football pulled up to a sudden halt and leapt outwards. John got down from the cloud engulfed Land Rover and started to make his way through the tightly packed crowd, gradually he reached the front.

"What's going on, Tony?"

"Someone said there's gold here, but there's been that much pushing and shoving that I've been unable to see what's happening!" So saying, he elbowed some of the men out of the way and came to a tightly formed group who were pointing at the stones at their feet. Tony went in amongst them and reached for the stones and inspected them while John had just managed to reach him and came abreast of the still milling crowd.

"Football tells me that it's gold, we'd better have a look."

Tony was examining closely the stones and had out his magnifying glass as he held them up to the light and pored over the structure of the own he held in his hand. All now had become suddenly quiet while they awaited the expert opinion of Massah Tony, he would know for sure.

Meanwhile, John had asked Football to find the man who had come across this supposed gold.

"Okay, boss! I finds him!" and he looked around for a moment, before he spotted him. "He is deah, massah! Is Abraham!"

"Right then! Let's have him over here!" and pointed to a spot next to him. A small man emerged from the crowd and made his way towards them while many eyes followed his movement. He stopped next to John and he waited until the noise had reduced sufficiently so that the man could be heard.

"Tell de massah what you is findin', Abraham!" Football said in his best supervisory voice.

"Massah! I is movin' de rock ova heah," and he indicated the pile of fragments, "an' I is lift up dese pieces," and he indicated those that Tony was still examining, "an' I see de gold! Is shinin' like de mornin' sun!"

"And you think that it is gold you have seen?"

"Yes, massah! Is gold! I not stupid! I knows gold if I sees it!" Abraham looked around him for support and many heads nodded in confirmation.

John then said, "But I've already said that the rock here is not likely to have any gold in it! But we will see what Massah Tony says!" and he called out to Tony who was now down on his knees and inspecting the pieces closely. "What is it then, Tony?"

Tony turned about and said, "Come over here, Abraham!" He made his way through the crowd and emerged next to Tony. "Show me, Abraham!"

Abraham bent low and moved to his left and after a moment or so, picked up the pieces he had seen and passed them over to Tony. He inspected them for a few seconds, then the other pieces that Abraham had picked up and he took from him one of the larger pieces that he held in the crook of his arm. Now, utter silence reigned and they all leaned forwards, watching Tony's face for the slightest hint of confirmation. Tony, without comment, passed the pieces over to John, who in turn examined them. Amid the darker fragments there was, sure enough, a brassy-coloured line. John passed it to Football who looked at it closely. No-one spoke in the expectant silence. Football passed it back to Tony, he realised that all and sundry were waiting for a statement, and said, "Well! For my money, it's gold, certainly!"

A huge cheer rang out, all of a sudden the men were all whooping and shouting excitedly, gesticulating at the pile of rock and slapping each other on the back in a form of congratulation. John looked at Abraham who was now grinning widely, as was Football. Amid the now raucous noise, Klaus approached elbowing his way to the front.

"What goes on here?" he demanded as he got closer to the front.

"It's all right, Klaus!" replied John, "we've got the situation in hand now."

Tony passed the pieces over to Klaus without a word and also handed him the magnifying glass. He looked at it for a brief moment, then said, "Gold?"

"Yes, Klaus! It's gold for sure, although how much of it there is here I can't say. That means that we will have to recover all that which we have already moved and inspect it piece by piece, only then can we assess how much there is."

"Yah! That vill take some time, eh Football? You get the men organised then! Get all de rock back here and Massah Tony will examine it."

"Yas sah," he replied grinning, and started to call out to the men who eagerly volunteered to assist in this wonderful experience.

The men all started to chant, "Gold! Gold! We has de gold!" and there was little they could do to stop it.

John spoke up and said, "We'd better assemble all the men then and inform them of this discovery, it's the only thing we can do in the circumstances, agreed Tony?"

"Yes! But you're the boss so you tell them."

John called to Football, he broke off from his current task and sent men off to assemble all the others in front of him. About ten minutes later they were all there. Of course, by now the news had spread like wildfire and most knew of it, however just to keep the record straight John addressed them, the crowd fell silent as he spoke.

"We have found some traces of gold!"

A loud cheering broke out and a buzz went around those assembled.

"Abraham here," and he pointed to him, "has discovered it. It may not be much but Massah Tony will examine all the rock and he will tell us just how much there is." The buzz continued and much discussion followed that. "It is my intention that we will share it out amongst all the workers." The noisy discussion broke out again and John had to call for silence so that he could continue.

"I have also decided that the massahs will not share in it, it will all go to you, the workers!" The cheering broke out again and John had to wait until it diminished before he could end this short address.

"Now, I want to see you all back at work right away."

The men broke up and slowly they all went off back to their tasks, now smiling broadly. The recent pay rise and the finding of the gold on top of it would make them rich men in their eyes, they were unable to take it all in really and it took some convincing by some of the others before the less intelligent of them understood it. Football translated into the dialects for them, and he commented to John that all the men were extremely happy with the decision.

"Good! Football, let's get it all separated out then and we can see just what we've got in the way of gold."

Klaus, Tony and John all met by the side of a vehicle and discussed this most recent event.

"We'll have to keep this to ourselves here and tell the men not to spread it around or else we'll have every Tom, Dick and Harry up here looking for gold."

"Yes, agreed," said Klaus, "I'll pass the word around, especially amongst the servants and the cooks and these others that deal with us but it will be difficult, John, to suppress it entirely."

"Yes, I know, we'll just have to hope that all goes well, that's all we can do."

Tony commented, "I'm going to be busy for quite a while, I can see!"

"What do you reckon to the quality, Tony?"

"I'd say medium to low grade, must have formed here thousands of years ago as the samples I looked at here show that it was formed very early in the geological structure."

"Well, let me know when you can make an accurate assessment, Tony, then we'll see what we can do about getting it valued."

"Will do!" Tony replied, and they broke up.

"Now, we can get to a normal day's work then," commented John as he and Klaus got into Klaus's vehicle together and set off back to the offices up top. The remainder of the day continued at its normal pace and came to an end on this high note. The workers sang all the way back to their compound and John could hear their voices clearly on the wind.

Football Boot appeared just as John was about to depart for his house, and said, "De men say to tell you that you bring them good luck, massah."

"Oh do they now? Well, thank them for that then, Football. I'm sure that all will be fine from now on, eh?"

"Yes, massah! It will be, this I know!" and he grinned as he departed, the sound of the old Land Rover that he used dying away as he went downhill.

The sun plummeted to the horizon and by the time that John had locked up and left it was dark, the moths were visible in the headlights as he drove at a steady pace downhill and pulled up at the front of the house.

Next day, John asked Football to call on him with the names of the men who he was to take with him on the recruiting drive. Football arrived about midday and knocked on the door of John's office as he entered.

"Ah! Come in, Football! Take a seat!" and he indicated the chair at the side of his desk.

"Thank you, massah," Football replied.

"Well then, Football, how long do you reckon you will need to get de men?"

"I think I go for one week, massah, with de wagons, then when I come back, I go again for one more week. Maybe have to go four times to get all de mens we need, 'cos I go to de north and west, and maybe all over," and he waved his hand around.

"I'll leave it up to you, Football, go and see Massahs Dave and Klaus, they will see that you get all you need, de trucks, provisions, and de money."

"Yes, massah," he replied obediently.

"And also I want you to give each man who wants to come and work for us an inducement in their hand of fifty niara."

"What is inducement, massah?" he asked, having difficulty in pronouncing the word.

"Is the same as dash, Football."

He smiled and said, "Yes massah! I understand."

"But that will be taken off his first months pay, you'd better make that clear."

"Yes massah! I understand."

"Okay, then, Football, off you go and see what you can do for us, eh?"

"Thank you, massah," he replied, and got up from the chair and went out and down the steps.

Later on, John met Dave and asked him if Football had been in to see him.

"Yes, I've given him what he needs and he will be leaving first thing in the morning. I've a feeling that he may be able to get back most of the men we had before as they were good workers."

"I hope so, Dave. It would certainly help but we'll wait and see what he comes back with."

"By the way the new quarters are well under way, and the messing area, the next time you're down that way you should have a look in, we have got a lot of good, willing workers who can turn their hand to the joinery here as well."

The remainder of the day passed quickly and it was soon time to finish up again for the night. Ebenezer was waiting for him as he approached the house with the jug of cold squash in one hand and a glass in the other and poured one out for him which he drank with relish. He sat reading while the evening meal was being prepared and sat down at the table when Ebenezer signalled to him that it was ready. Ebenezer was in chatty mood.

"I hear that you are needing de cooks, massah," he said sounding as though it was a matter of fact.

"Yes," replied John, "how did you know that?"

"I knows!" said Ebenezer, "I have two sisters, very good cooks, dey live nearby, you can have if you want," then added, "and Nathaniel, he has some, too!"

John smiled at the comment and the audacity of it, enterprising they were indeed, it would save him having to get someone to look for them. He hesitated before replying, then said, "Tell them to see Massah Klaus at the site, say that I sent them, they should get the jobs."

"Thank you, massah," said Ebenezer mechanically, as though he knew all along that John would say that anyway. "I tell them tonight," he said and went off into the kitchen.

When he returned, John asked him, "How did you know we need the extra cooks, Ebenezer?"

"Is bush telegraph, massah!" and he smiled broadly, "not much de bush telegraph not tell."

"I see," said John frowning, and thought, I'd better watch what I'm saying up at the site. He wondered how long it would be before the news of the gold got out, that was if it wasn't out already. However, there was no mention of it for the remainder of the evening, so he dismissed it from his mind.

Next day, Football and his team of men set off on the trucks, two of them pulling trailers, they headed for Kubli and Karengi, and the numerous villages on the way to Benin, which were mostly Hausa people, but he would also be calling on the villages of the tribes of the Borgu and Borgawa, Ghonna, Nupe and Zamfara as well. John wished him luck as he set off and the trucks disappeared in a cloud of dust. The sound of the powerful diesels could be heard as they descended the hill and continued on to the main road which was ten miles ahead.

Chapter Five

A week had passed by, quickly it seemed. Football had returned with a wagon load of men, and amongst them John could see quite a number of very tall men, in fact about six feet he reckoned. Apparently he had little difficulty in finding these and the fifty niara sweetener was sufficient to entice many, notwithstanding the now high level of pay that they were to receive. These men had integrated well with those that were here already with no problems whatsoever, a few of them being those that had absconded previously. Football stayed for a day only and then set off again with the trucks and team of men, this time driving over to Sokoto, and the Gwari and Anga peoples. This time however, it was a full ten days before he returned but with only fifty-two men. Apparently the availability of able men was a bit on the thin side there. So far he had managed to recruit one hundred and fifty-seven men. Two days later he departed again, this time to the south and on to the south-east. He said that he would be going to the villages of the Tiv, Okpotos, Jukon, and the Ebos. After that he intended to return via a circuitous route and see what he could obtain from the region where the Ibibos, Ekoi and Efiks were. His return was a success and he arrived with the trucks spilling over with men, and dropping them off as fast as he could be refuelled and set off again back to the area he had just come from to pick up the rest that he had left behind. Two days later he returned and Klaus was surprised to see that he had in fact amassed a total of five hundred and thirty-nine all told. So much so that a further accommodation hut had to be built and also an extension to the new messing area to cope with this sudden influx of humans. John was taken aback at the speed of this sudden influx of bodies but he was, of course, more than pleased at the response. John was now on a new high, he had more than adequate manpower to do all the work involved on the construction and he had to sit down and calculate the shifts in order to give himself the greatest flexibility.

Dave and Joshua had to take on two extra hands to cope with it all and they had a busy time of it. Dave's normally full racks in the store were now almost empty following the frantic issuing of every description of items that he held in store. He spent a whole evening making out fresh requisitions to send to Hendry J. for replenishment, and had added to the list more racking and some extra wheelbarrows and trolleys to aid the men. The road to and from the site was now busy most of the time, and whereas before the odd cloud of dust could be seen as the vehicles went back and forth, it had now grown in size and a constant flow surged to and fro for many days afterwards.

Hendry J. for his part, had pulled out all the stops and there arrived regularly for a few days a constant flow of delivery trucks. The compound which Dave had had neatly arranged now took on the appearance of supplying the world and little space could be found in which to move around. Dave had arranged for a team of men to extend the compound and it had almost trebled in size, occupying the length of two football pitches. Amongst it all, there were only a few minor hiccups and all went smoothly throughout the exercise.

Football now had a gargantuan task of getting all the names down in his book, and the list of villages occupied about four pages in itself. At about the same time the trucks bearing the items of safety clothing had also arrived and John was thankful for that, it was issued as quickly as possible. John could see in advance that there would be some problems in explaining to some of the men as to how it was to be used, but that was inevitable anyway and he would pass the orders on to Football who would see to it in any event. Each man was issued his personal items of a bed, blankets, eating utensils and other items.

John and Klaus had Football assemble the new men, this time down at the accommodation site, had addressed them as before and finally asked Football to demonstrate the proper way to wear the safety clothing that they had been issued with.

"Football," John said, "tell the men that the safety clothing and equipment that they have been issued with is to be worn at all times when they are working on the site. Any man who reports for pay and is found not to be wearing it will receive no pay at all." Football called out to the men and also translated this edict, and after having to repeat it a few times, he turned to John and said that they understood.

"Tell them also, Football, that their number will be marked on the front of everybody's helmet. The only time they are to take the helmets off is when they are travelling to and from the site and when they are off work or on their break periods."

"Okay, massah, I tell!" and he did so.

Then John had a thought and said, "You'd better remind them that the helmets are not for carrying water in, or urinating in, or doing anything else in! Anyone who breaks or loses their helmet is to tell their supervisor who in turn will tell Football here, and we will have a new one issued to them." Football called out the message and the men understood although there was much merriment at the comment on the use of the helmets and its other uses, but they understood perfectly.

"Now! Tell them about the boots, Football! Everyone is entitled to two pairs of boots. Anyone who cannot wear them is to tell the supervisor! There will be no work carried out in bare feet!" Football meantime, held up a pair of the boots so that they all could see them, they were black and had quick fastening buckles with steel toecaps. Football then modelled the bright yellow and orange safety waistcoats which provided the men with more merriment. Supervisors, who would be responsible to Football, would be issued with bright green waistcoats. The workers were to wear the red helmets and the supervisors the blue ones, the white helmets would be worn by the bosses. All men were to be given a whistle on a cord which they would use at any time if there was an accident or some other danger when they would stop work immediately. This took a bit of explaining but Football got it over to them at the second attempt.

"Tell them also, Football, that we are having an alarm system installed. I will brief the supervisors on how it will work, and they will be responsible for passing the information on to the men." Football conveyed this to them in his oratory voice that he had now cultivated in keeping with his new authoritative position as supervisor over this mass of workers. He had also taken to growing a moustache which was black and wiry and filled the large gap between his upper lip and his nose, although the lips protruded out below it anyway. With his short wiry hair receding at the temples, he looked the part and John allowed himself a small smile as he noted it while Football gave the oration to the men.

"Is that too much information to give them all at one time, Football?" he asked.

"No massah! I tells them again tomorrow, dat is foh de benefit of de thick ones!"

John and Klaus burst out laughing at this comment and Football allowed himself a wide grin at the same time. John said that that was all for the moment, Football dismissed the men and they returned to their huts.

"Have we decided who are to be the supervisors, Klaus?"

"Yes. I have had Football pick them out, some of them were here before and we have organised them into one supervisor for each fifty men, it works out better that way. If any of them turn out to be no good then we will appoint new ones."

"That sounds all right to me, Klaus. I'll leave you to it but let me have a list of them when it's finally decided and make sure, Klaus, that the supervisors know that they will get slightly more pay than the workers, it will give them added incentive."

"Okay, John! See you later," and Klaus got into his vehicle and drove off up the valley.

John called on Tony to see how he was getting on with the assessment of the gold and found him in his hut that he had down on the valley floor which was convenient for his frequent forays out in amongst the rocks

"Any news yet?" he called out as he entered.

"Hello, John. I've had the fragments separated now into a pile and I've looked at them through the microscope and it's gold all right. About twenty carats I'd say but we will have to send for an assayer to come up and confirm it and do a valuation as well."

John whistled in surprise, "Well, that's a turn up for the book!"

"Yes, I thought so too. I've had a look at the point where it came from, I reckon most of it has fallen away. I've scanned the face with my field glasses, getting as close as I could but I can't see any more of it. However, we'll have to leave that up to the assayer when he comes. Most of it was in the middle of the rock," and he went over to a diagram of the rock face and indicated it with a pencil outline, and shaded in the area where the gold came from. "By the way, when it is valued, John, we'll have to be careful transporting it out of here as there are quite a few bands of robbers around these parts and some of the information is bound to have leaked out by now."

"Yes, Tony, I'm aware of that. I'll get on to Hendry J. and see if he can provide some sort of vehicle which will be able to transport it safely."

"Anyway, John, I have enjoyed this investigation of the gold find, it certainly makes a change from the humdrum everyday life."

"Okay then, Tony, store it away in a secure place when you've finished, and see Dave, maybe he can find a good secure location for it in his building, it'll be safer there, I think."

"Will do, John," he said and gave John a wave as he went off up the hill to visit Dave's compound. John arrived there amid the incessant activity that now was the norm but Dave being a professional storeman had taken it all in his stride. He sought him out, he was busy in the yard overseeing the movement of some large heavy crates.

"How are things going, Dave?" he said as he approached.

"Just fine, John. I've just got a bit more to do than usual now."

"Do we have adequate stock of the safety equipment to issue?"

"Yes, no problem, I'll get it moved down to the site at the bottom shortly. Joshua will be in charge of seeing to it and I'll leave it all up to him. We've had all the helmets marked with the numbers according to Football's list, so as long as Football oversees it there shouldn't be any problem."

"Good! I'll probably call by the site then if I've time. How are the assistants doing that you have got?"

"Great. At least Joshua thinks they are, it has taken a load of work off him and he has them doing almost all his work now, he has made one of them his personal assistant, so you see, all is in order."

"Good to hear that, Dave, I'll leave it all up to your lot then," and he went back over to his vehicle and drove off up the hill, calling back to Dave to tell him to call by in the evening.

"I'll be working until about seven-thirty John, so it will be about nine in the evening before I get to your place."

"That'll do fine," John had replied.

Later in the day, John watched the men through his binoculars from the roadside. Football, being prominent, constantly on the move and ranging back and forwards as he directed the new labour force. John likened him to one of the cattle herdsmen. As sunset arrived, the work ceased and the smoke from the cooking fires hung in the air, the crickets chirped, the moon was up above the tree line and the early evening bats were out on their first sortie of the night. He drove to the house where Nathaniel and Ebenezer were sitting on the veranda steps awaiting his arrival, who sprang into action as they saw the Land Rover pull up at the front of the house.

"Good evening, massah!" they chorused, as John approached.

"Evening!" John replied and made his way slowly over to the steps. "What's for dinner this evening?"

"Tonight, we has soup, massah! Then we has rice with meat and de fresh fruit."

"Have you got enough for two?"

"Yes, massah."

"Good then, can you prepare it and leave it out, I will dish it up."

"You means we go early again tonight?"

"Yes. You is correct!" and he smiled.

"Yes, massah."

Nathaniel went off into the kitchen to see to it and leave it all prepared. While Ebenezer laid the table for two, then brought a pot of tea out to John who was sitting on the veranda savouring the calm of the evening.

"Thanks, Eb!" he said as Ebenezer laid it down on the small table outdoors. John had decided that he would shorten their names to Nat and Eb and they were in agreement. The two of them took their leave and went off up the path at the side of the house towards the village only a few kilometres away. John waited until about eight-thirty in the evening and went into the house, as he did so he heard a Land Rover descending the hill and pull up at the front of the house. He looked out and saw that it was Dave, he was early but that suited him. He took the dishes of food out of the kitchen and placed them on the table with the jug of ice cola squash and the glasses.

"Have you had supper yet?" he asked.

"No, not yet."

"Good! Well, I have plenty here for both of us so if you'll be seated, I'll do the honours. Help yourself to a drink, Dave, you know where it is."

"Thanks!" he replied, and made his way over to the drinks cabinet, "How about you, John?"

John stuck his head around the corner of the kitchen door and said, "Whisky for me, Dave, and it'll be the same for you, I know."

Dave went out on to the veranda and picked up John's glass and sniffed it. Whisky, he mused, and returned indoors, sloshed another measure into it and poured himself one as well.

John returned from the kitchen and said, "Just be five minutes or so, Dave, it's meat with rice, probably goat meat I should think, that okay?"

"Yes, fine by me, I'm accustomed to goat meat, it's about all I get from my cook, although recently there's been a variation, I'm glad to say."

"There's plenty of pig around, Dave, so why don't they have it more often? I've often thought about that."

"Sure, there is plenty of it but they don't seem to be very keen on meat from the pig, probably a hangover from the days when the Islamic religion was in the forefront, I should imagine."

"Don't you fancy any of the monkey or porcupine then?"

"No! That doesn't turn me on at all."

"Ah! But you wouldn't know what it was unless they told you, eh?"

"No, I suppose not, but I'd still be wary of it, John. I'd rather stick with the goat meat for now, even if I turn into a goat one of these days."

"How about bat, then?"

Dave thought for a moment before replying, then said, "Well, they say it is very sweet but I think you'd have to get quite a lot of bats together to get enough meat to make a meal of it."

"Mind you, Dave, the ones that fly around here are huge, they must have a fair bit of meat in them."

"I'm sure they would, John," and gave a shudder, "but I'll still stick with the goat meat. What's all this about the porcupine, then, John?"

"Well the locals reckon it is a delicacy around here, supposed to be on the strong side, apparently, but they smoke it which takes away the strong taste, and it's supposed to be good for their sex lives, too, I hear."

"Judging by the amount of kids I've seen around here, I shouldn't wonder, there are plenty of them, sure enough!"

Dave changed the topic of conversation, said, "Cheers!" and raised his glass, and they each took a swig of their drinks. John returned to the kitchen and brought out the meat on a big tray, with the rice on a separate one. They dished it up and set to the task of demolishing it. They chatted amiably throughout the meal, then John went through to the kitchen again and returned with the fresh fruit. Having eaten their fill they retired to the veranda where the night air was cooler now, and still sipping their drinks they turned to discussing other things.

"Right then, Dave! Tell me about the events that led to the dismissal of the people here before."

"I wondered how long it would be before you asked me that, John, but anyway, I'll give you the gen. It was a long time ago, or so it seems," and he thought for a few moments. "Let's go back to say, about a year and a month ago. It was last summer, very hot and dusty if I remember correctly, and everything was going along just fine. One day, it was a Wednesday and I remember that as I usually do the stock checks on a Wednesday, and some of the men didn't turn up for work, I think it was about seven or eight or whatever, John. They were missing from two of the squads we had excavating the foundations. When we asked where they were no-one knew at all. We suspected that their workmates knew but no-one would say anything, so to find out if they were really missing we organised a search party. First we went to the accommodation huts, there was no sign of them there and no-one had seen them since after the evening meal the day before. Well, we searched all the likely places all day long, and even the local villagers who knew them hadn't seen them, either. By nightfall we got some torches and set off again this time in a wider sweep of up to about three miles radius, that is taking in the dam site as well. After about two hours they were found by a group of the workers. They were all tied to individual trees with a rope, two had been beheaded with a machete, we reckoned, and the remainder were mutilated and then disembowelled.

"I didn't see it, John, but apparently it was quite revolting, even the men themselves were horrified by it. It was claimed that it was the work of some tribal magic ritual of some sort but others claimed it was Juju magic. Anyway, that put the wind up them and all the other workers too.

"Then I had a heap of trouble with some of the stores going missing. They were stock-piled in the open air but in a locked compound and they had been checked by Joshua just before he finished up for the night, but by morning when I arrived there was a big hole in the fence and, you've probably guessed it, the stores had gone."

"What type of stores, Dave?"

"Bags of cement, sand, shovels, spades, metal stakes, foodstuffs, tools, you name it, it disappeared. I reported it to Klaus who did the same to your predecessor, who, incidentally was named George

Chalmers, he was Scots as well. But there it stopped, there were no investigations, but Klaus tried to find out for himself, he got no co-operation at all and any questions he asked were met with a wall of silence. In fact, on a few occasions, he was told to shut up and go away."

"Really?" stated John.

"Yes. You ask him, he'll tell you, the problems got worse. We sometimes sold off excess stock, that is to say, stock that we didn't have any use for, to the local villagers but strangely enough, no money was ever received for it at all."

"None?"

"No, not a kobo!"

"What happened to it then, you reckon?"

"Went into someone's pocket obviously, I suspected it was into George's but I couldn't prove it."

"How much?"

"Difficult to say. A few thousand pounds worth in all by the time that he left. I can look it up in the books and let you know for sure how much it was."

"No, that doesn't matter, anyway carry on Dave."

"Well, he, that is George, handled a few of the transactions himself, and I was frequently told to put the amounts down as expendable items as there was no need for invoices for these. Then, one night, a break-in occurred at my office, the door lock was forced and the petty cash box was taken although there was little in it, it was someone's gain. Then the troubles stopped, as though someone was controlling it and I thought that I'd heard the last of it as life returned to normal again.

Later, one weekend, on a Sunday, a man who had earlier reported a theft was found pinned to a tree with a spear through him. The result of that was that over a period of a few months, three other men were murdered by persons unknown, one shot in the back, one stabbed with a knife and the last of them was garrotted! All in the night and all were found in areas where you would not expect to find a missing person. Later, we found out that this George was dealing in drugs and supplying them to the workers who were prepared to kill to get them. At first, I didn't believe any of it but gradually the story all fell into place, and therefore it was no surprise when suddenly he was given the order of the boot, and not before time either, in my opinion."

"What was Klaus's part in all of this?"

"None at all! He knew it was going on, how much he actually knew I don't know, but he was told as before to shut up and say nothing, he told me that himself."

"Well Dave, that bears out what I read in the company reports in Lagos, so I'm not entirely surprised at what you have told me. I've always had doubts as to what was fact and fiction in those reports I read."

"Do you think that we've seen the last of these events, then?"

"Perhaps."

"Well, John, with this extra amount of men we have now there will be a lot of new blood, so to speak, and I hope all will go well but I've noticed that there are quite a lot of different tribes here and that may prove to be a problem later on, but then again maybe not."

"I'll keep an eye on that then, Dave, thanks for warning me of it."

"Yes, I'll ask Joshua to keep an eye out as well, he would sense anything if there was any trouble, and Football too."

"Well, I think we've exhausted that subject so let's talk about something else," and they did so. Eventually, it was late and they decided to retire for the night, Dave took his leave with a 'see you in the morning' as he climbed into his wagon, and drove off to his residence.

Next day the safety equipment was issued, and Football had all the men lined up, an elongated snake filled all the available space, and he called them forward according to their number. They were then handed their safety boots, the numbered waistcoats, orange and green, the ear defenders, safety glasses, earplugs and military style water bottles. Football insisted on demonstrating the use of each item and went amongst them to ensure that they were clear as how to use the items. After that, he called out to them, "Remember! No wear! No pay!" The men understood and they noisily discussed the use of the items as they went about the daily tasks. Once back at work, the men could now be clearly seen against the pale grey of the cement foundations, their fluorescent jackets reflecting the sun's rays as they moved around. The helmets went down well and everybody was happy to wear them, some even wearing them when they slept at night, Klaus had reported, laughing as he said it. John was pleased that there were no problems with the equipment and that work was now proceeding at a fast rate, but he was also aware that if it continued at this speed they would get quantity but not quality, and that he would have to change it to a more manageable system.

He called on all of his team to discuss it and they assembled in his office, Football now sitting down first of all without any prompting from anyone. After a brief discussion, it was agreed that they would change to a system of twenty-four-hour shifts, that way they could best use the work-force to their advantage. It would ease the pressure in the feeding of this mass of bodies and would normalise many other aspects as well.

At present Football seemed to spend all his time rushing about controlling the work. They agreed on which supervisors were to be allocated for each shift and they would take over on the following day. The next day the changes were implemented and the work-force was split up into their new shifts, which was to be three shifts of eight hours each duration, and a back-up shift to cope with any additional work that occurred at any time of the twenty-four period. These new supervisors were given their change of hats, and John only needed to cast a casual glance around to find out where they were on the site. Football oversaw all the day work and he had allocated a man to do the same for the night work with the proviso that he was to be called upon if anything warranted his attention and presence. Tony and Klaus had monitored the changeover and had reported that all was going well, only a minor hiccup occurred the first day with a mix-up between truck drivers, but that was quickly seen to.

Next afternoon, John went down to see Dave. "What's the latest word on the doctor, Dave?"

"He should arrive any day now, Hendry J. assures me that he is on his way."

A day later, he arrived, a youngish man with a dark moustache. He introduced himself to John and made his apologies for arriving late as he had taken a wrong turning on his drive to the site and had to stop at a village and ask directions, causing him to have to backtrack for about thirty miles or so. He was Marcel Dupeppe, and he was an expert in tropical medicine which John took to be a bonus, he also spoke good English although with the traditional French flavour to it.

"There's not much work for you at the moment, Marcel, but we always have some injuries to attend to, and with this amount of men we need to keep a close eye on their health, too."

"I have a good supply of drugs which I have brought with me, and later there will be some of my medical equipment arriving as well."

"Right! We'll get you fixed up with a Portakabin then, Marcel, and if you need anything else, tell me and we will see to it straight away."

He asked Dave to come up and when he had arrived he introduced him to Marcel, and said, "Dave here, has got a house all organised for you, Marcel, and he will arrange for some of the joiners to alter anything you need in the way of a surgery or clinic or whatever you need. Meantime, I'll leave you to get settled in to your accommodation and I'll see you later."

"Merci," said Marcel, and he and Dave went over to the Land Rover, Dave asking him to follow him downhill and they set off.

"Tony! Have we got a mechanical engineer amongst the men?"

"Used to have, John, but I'll ask Football to see if he can find one. However, I'd much prefer we got a proper one as those that say they are mechanics leave a lot to be desired."

"Yes, my opinion as well, and we could do with an electrician too, there's quite a bit of work that I want done on that front."

He went over to Klaus's office and found him busy at his desk. He discussed the need for these two people at length, and after about twenty minutes they came to an agreement to obtain them both, John saying that he would see to it on the following day. Football however, dug around in his large work-force and came up with one and three others who were of sufficient experience to carry out the servicing and repairs. He organised them into a team, had the joiners knock up a garage and gave the orders for them to order any parts they needed through Massah Dave. Next day he and Dave, went down to the nearest Nitel office but found that when they got there the phone was out of order, a common occurrence Dave commented, and they had to go a further ten miles to the next one. After an hour's wait, they eventually got through to Hendry J.

"Hello, Hendry! John here, how are you?"

"Oh! Normal, and by the way, before you say anything, I know where the phone is now! I've rearranged the desk, would you believe?"

"I'll believe that when I see it, Hendry! Hendry, I need an electrician, can you find one for me?"

"I'll have a dig around, I assume that you want a European?"

"Yes, if you can find one but it doesn't have to be. Just whatever you can provide."

"All right, give me a few days, I'll get on to the embassy and see who they can recommend."

"As long as he speaks English and knows his job, that's all we need."

"By the way, John, anything you're still waiting for should be with you today or the day after. It left yesterday by road at midday and you'll recognise the trucks easily enough as they're painted red."

"Fine," replied John and Dave nodded in understanding.

"Bye, Hendry!" he called, "keep taking the pills!"

"Yes, all right! Bye!"

They paid the clerk behind the desk and left to make their way back to the site. They stopped on the way at one of the village markets and bought some fresh grapefruit and melons, and a large bag of oranges, all of which they haggled for and secured a bargain.

Marcel was settled in, he had allocated a secure area for his drugs and medicines and had a Portakabin transferred up to the site offices and placed on the opposite side of the compound from John's office. He had the joiner erect a sign in English and Hausa saying 'MEDICAL CLINIC', and he had asked Football to tell all the supervisors who would in turn inform the men as to where it was located. He got organised quickly and had already treated a few patients in the first few days, had organised a system of record cards and the accompanying filing system. He had also arranged for a first-aid post down at the work face where he could attend to injuries initially, and transfer them up to the clinic if need be. Next day John went in to see him in his new clinic.

"Morning, Marcel!" he called out as he entered, noting how clean it seemed and with that normal clinical aroma that one associated with the medical world.

"Et bonjour, John," Marcel replied, getting up from his seat behind his desk.

"How are you getting on then? I hear that you are well organised already."

"Mais oui! It is different from a normal practice, but I like the open air and the challenge too! I think I will enjoy my time here. I do not like to be shut up indoors all the time."

"Good, I'm glad to hear it. Any problems so far then?"

"No, but I've seen one or two of your men who have the Aids disease."

"Really!" John exclaimed, "are you sure?"

"No! But I will have them up here and take some blood samples and let you know."

"Will it affect the work then, Marcel?"

"No it will not, but we will have to be careful where there are injuries where is blood lost, and I have asked Mr Football Boot to tell me of them." John smiled as he heard the words 'Mr Football Boot', it sounded so proper and out of place, not exactly in keeping with his image which was, at best, a bit on the scruffy side.

"Yes. All right then, any others?"

"Only minor ones, a few cases of malaria which is normal, I have given them tablets to take which will take care of that. I've only seen a few of the men but I will need each man to have a medical examination, and I intend to check each man individually over a period of time, it will take some weeks to get through them all. Does that sound all right to you?"

"Yes. Why not! A good idea, Marcel, I'll get Football to arrange it in rotation with the shifts."

"Tres jolie!" replied Marcel enthusiastically. "And I will be giving you a full medical as well and all the other staff too, I will do this as soon as possible," and leaning over his desk he looked at his appointment book and said, "tomorrow or the day after, but not any longer, agreed?"

"Yes! I'm in agreement with that, I don't think that any of us here has had a medical for some time! I'll tell them that you are to do this, Marcel."

"Excellent!" said Marcel, "now if you'll excuse me, I have quite a lot to get through today."

"Au revoir, then Marcel," said John, and left him to his administration. He went over to Klaus's office, and before he opened the door he could the hear the sounds of something being struck. He opened the door gently and put his head around it. Klaus was leaping about with a fly swatter in his hand, one of the cheap plastic varieties, and performing leaps and bounds to be envied by any self-respecting ballet dancer.

John surveyed this ridiculous scene for a moment, then said, "I'm glad to see that you are fit, Klaus!"

He stopped the furious swiping in mid-flight at the sound of John's voice and dropped to the floor but still keeping his eye on the offending insect, as a spider would its prey.

"Yah!" he replied, "you haf to be to kill these damn flies!" and he took another lunge towards it and reduced the insect to a bloody pulp on the wall. "Got you!" he stated in triumph, then sat down on his chair.

"You will find out tomorrow, Klaus, if you are fit or not, as you're having a medical."

"Vat? Mich!" exclaimed Klaus, "but I am not sick!"

"It's Marcel, Klaus, everyone has to have one so you and I are down for it tomorrow, like it or not, meine freunde."

"Yah! Das ist gut, then I vill go! No problem, und what time?"

"Oh! I don't know, Marcel will come and drag you over to the magic cave once he has sharpened his dissecting scissors!"

"Very funny! So you think I am past it, eh? Vell! I tell you I vill pass with flying colours, as you say."

"Yes, Klaus, anything you say!" and John left him scouring the office for more of the offending insects. John made a note in his diary, medicals for all starting Tuesday.

Next day, Marcel started with John early in the morning and he waved him in as he saw him cross over the compound, "First, the usual," he said, "come into my parlour, said the spider to the fly, and let me have a look at you."

He checked his general appearance, his height, weight, did a sight test, took a blood sample, checked his reflexes, and asked for a urine sample.

"Now strip off," John obeyed and Marcel viewed him from all angles. "No ruptures, varicose veins or bleeding from the bowels?"

"No."

After another customary look all around him, he said, "Okay, get dressed," and left John to it while he disappeared into a room and did the necessary tests on the blood and urine samples. He returned and sat down at the desk and made some notes in his files.

"What's the verdict then, Doc?"

"Well!" said Marcel, not looking up from his writing, "you are overweight! Lots of flabby muscles and you need to watch your diet. You need to get more exercise! I suggest you stop driving everywhere, walk instead as you must get some exercise, you have not had any of that for a long time I can tell!"

"Yes, I suppose you're right," said John.

"I know I am right, John! Also your eyesight is poor in one eye, the left one, you had difficulty in reading the smaller letters! You agree?"

"Yes."

"If you were in the city, I'd tell you to go and get some glasses but being as you're out here, is better that you get them as soon as is practical, Mr John! Do you get headaches?"

"No, not at all."

"Well! You will if you don't get the glasses, that I can assure you."

"How about the rest of me, then?" he asked, hoping that there was no further bad news to come.

"All normal for your age, in general you pass, and I will not need to cut you up yet for specimens!" and he smiled as he said it.

"Thanks," said John, "that's a relief."

"Okay, John, you can go now," and he continued his writing.

John got up from the chair, went out and over to his office, thinking about what Marcel had said, musing over it. Yes, more walking was called for.

Marcel finished writing up John's notes, then went over to Klaus's office, and seeing that he was not there left him a note to call in at the medical clinic as soon as possible.

It was about an hour later when Tony and Klaus returned from down below, and on entering Klaus's office, Tony picked up the note and said, "Klaus!" in his best German accent, "this says you haf to go and be turned into horse meat!"

"Very funny, Tony! You wait my friend, you'll see! I'm in very good condition." So saying, he exited the office and made his way over to the clinic.

Tony called after him, "Fresh meat in the kitchens tonight!"

Klaus responded with a scowl and the internationally recognised two finger salute, as he climbed the steps and entered the door of Marcel's clinic.

A voice from within, on hearing the footsteps, called out, "Ah, Klaus! Come in! Let me give you the treatment!" and he indicated the seat by the table and Klaus sat down.

"Tony said I am fit for horse meat," he said smiling.

"Well then, we will see just what kind of meat you are, Klaus," and stood up and commenced his examination. He went through the motions and paid particular attention to Klaus's lungs. Afterwards he said, "Well, Klaus, you have had asthma for some time, yes?"

"Yah! When I was kinder but now I'm okay, yes?"

"A bit on the wheezy side, but I don't think it's anything to worry about. I see that you're losing your hair," he commented raising his eyes up from the desk to view Klaus's receding hairline.

"Yah! Meine vater, he was balt, when he was my age."

"Family trait then, Klaus, well, not to worry about it, it will no doubt be some years before you reach that stage. Okay! You can go."

"Danke," replied Klaus, and as he went through the door he turned and said, "What do I tell Tony?"

"You tell him that I said you are top quality horse meat!"

Klaus laughed and grinned as he descended the steps, and when he was half way across the compound, he called out, "Tony! Where are you?"

"In here!" he replied and stuck his head out of Klaus's office door, "Well? What time do I haf to take you out and shoot you?" he asked, grinning.

"Blotty cheek!" replied Klaus, "Marcel says to tell you that I am top quality horse meat!"

"Did he now?" and he stuck his tongue in his cheek and then said, "I'd say more like top quality corned beef!"

"You wait until you go for your medical! I expect he vill give you the big stone cross, my friend!" he commented ruefully, and gave Tony a friendly nudge as he went through the doorway.

Next day, it was Tony and Dave's turn. Tony was in first and came out soon after but with a slightly tarnished image as Marcel told him he had what the English called, 'a wonky knee'.

"You must have damaged the cartilage," Marcel commented.

"Yes? Well, I do a lot of climbing about in my job, that's to be expected I suppose."

Marcel listened to it through his stethoscope, straightened up and said, "Keep an eye on that, then. If you get any trouble whatsoever with it, come and see me!"

"Yes," replied Tony, "am I fit otherwise?"

"Yes, everything else is fine, you can go!"

"Before I go, what do I tell Klaus?"

Marcel cottoned on to this sort of running joke and said, swinging his stethoscope round in a circle, "Tell him that you are so fit that you are to be made the head killer in the abattoir of old German horses!"

"Great!" replied Tony, and went quickly down the steps, and called out "Klaus! Where are you?" He was at the far end of the compound, and as Tony got closer, he called out "Hey! Horse meat! Are you there?"

Klaus looked up at this, and waited until Tony had come abreast of him and said, "So! My friend! Just how sick are you, then?"

"Me? I'm perfect, Klaus, Marcel says that I have to open up an abattoir for old German horses like you!"

"What! You wait until I see him! I'll old German horse him!" and he continued muttering to himself as he worked. Dave then took his turn after having made a wager with Klaus, John and Tony that he would be the fittest of all. They all took him up on it, at stake was a bottle of whisky and they waited patiently for his return.

Dave had spent longer in the clinic than the rest of them and they waited expectantly for his return. After the wait, during which time they all speculated on his state of health, particularly Klaus, Dave returned and Tony called out, "Well then! What's the verdict?"

Dave didn't answer, but just grinned.

"Who has won the whisky?" Klaus called out in exasperation.

Dave turned to Klaus, and said with a big smile on his face, "Me!"

"What was that?" said Klaus, not quite believing what he had heard.

"Yes! It's me! I am the fittest of you all, you are all old goats, so it stands to reason that I would win anyway!"

"If there's one thing I can't stand," said Tony, "it's these perfectly healthy people! Never mind, Dave, we will help you to drink it in case it damages your health."

"Yes! I may even give Klaus a sniff from the top of the bottle!" and, smiling, he crossed to his Land Rover and drove off downhill, singing as he went. John and Tony had a good laugh about it, eventually Klaus joined in and they parted in a jovial mood to continue their work.

Over the following three weeks, Marcel saw all the workers, made out medical cards for them all, planned the treatment for those in need of it and carried out quite a large number of injections for various ills. John had a meeting with him later on and they discussed what the current state was.

"What manner of diseases have we got then, 'o witch doctor'?"

"Well, I'll go through them for you. As I said earlier there are those that have Aids, about thirty percent of them, but none seriously, then I have," he looked at his pocket notebook, "about a dozen or so with Guinea Worm, that's with drinking unclean water, not here of course, but probably in the villages, those that have it are all amongst the new men we took on, so I'll pass that information on to the World Health Organisation who are looking into this sort of disease at the moment here in Nigeria."

"Can it be treated successfully, then?" asked John.

"Yes! Quite successfully in these modern times, John. It takes a long time however, and may be up to a year before they recover completely."

"What else then, Marcel?"

"We have dysentery which is common; a few cases of leprosy and the normal preponderance of glaucoma, that's the eye infection which often leads to blindness, you have perhaps seen it often here, it's very common. Then we have one with typhoid, and two with symptoms of yellow fever, they feel very cold and shivery even though they are quite hot to the touch. These I have placed in isolation in the clinic but with the right treatment, they will recover and be back to work in a few weeks time. The one with the typhoid, well he is too far gone and all I can do for him is to reduce his suffering with drugs but I expect him to die within a week. It sounds bad but not from my point of view, I've come across it before in this country."

"Hmm! Not so good, then. I'll get Football to find out where these men came from, that will help as well, Marcel, and you can add that to the information that you send to the health people."

"Certainement! But there are very few doctors here, only the ones that liaise with the missionaries."

"Yes, I thought that was the case, but we'll do what we can anyway."

"I'll let you know about the three in isolation, but in the meantime I will go and find Football and see if can get more information about them."

"Right then, Marcel, I'll leave it to you for the moment," as he exited the office and went back across the compound in the dust to his clinic.

The new shift work had taken effect and the men had taken to it willingly, so far the results of it were excellent. The electrician that Hendry J. had promised, materialised, one by the name of Matthew Johnson, who had arrived and started work immediately. He initially withdrew a large amount of stock from Dave, all in the electrical line, and had set to rigging up the lighting that John wanted down at the site, this had greatly enhanced the night work.

The mechanics that Football had found from amongst the work force turned out to be good at their job and were great at improvising, they had greatly reduced the mechanical failures to an absolute minimum, so all in all John was a very happy man. By now the team under John had grown considerably since he had arrived. Dave had overcome difficulties with his suppliers, and Tony had found, quite by chance, a man working with the Voluntary Services Overseas, a geologist working as a teacher and had 'claimed him' as he put it, and had made him his assistant and that aided him in his work also. He was named Simon Wilson and the workers quickly christened him Simon Rock, and so the name stuck.

Marcel's patient with the typhoid died as expected, and Marcel was cautious as he had expected an outbreak of the disease, but by some miracle it did not materialise. How no-one had spotted it earlier defied credibility, he had said, but on investigation it had become apparent that from the time that he was recruited the man had, as the workers said 'been asleep' for most of the time, even when he climbed slowly on board the truck. Football was able to recall the village from where he had obtained him, it was in a remote area. Another who came from the same village, showed signs of having the disease also, and Marcel had placed him in isolation as a precaution but so far he seemed to be quite normal.

John sent a messenger down to the nearest mission and a priest duly appeared, as the man had no family where he had come from he was buried higher up in the valley in a hastily dug grave in the red earth. The priest stayed for the night at John's invitation and it was a refreshing change to have a difference in the conversation of the evening. He was English, Norman Phillips by name, and he had been travelling throughout the country officiating at the numerous villages throughout the bush in weddings, marriages and births, liaising with the farm projects and numerous other related problems. He said that he hadn't a minute to spare and was glad of the short break to have a rest for a change. John then asked if he had come across the man he had met earlier, Phil the Canadian.

"Not that I know of," said Norman, "but I'll ask around. The problem is that there are quite a number of us here in this country, all of different religions, so it is a bit like ships in the night, John, we rarely see each other and if we do happen to meet up with another priest, it would be purely by chance! However, if I come across him, I'll certainly tell him where you are located."

"Fine!" replied John, "I'd like to meet him again, anyway. How goes your struggle here, then?"

"Struggle is the word! You see, we're up against centuries of superstition here, not to mention the local tribal customs, black and white magic, as well as the Juju men!"

"The Juju men?"

"Yes! They're a pain really, get the people all wound up about the same nonsense, as usual over nothing of any consequence, feed them with rubbish beliefs, tell the villagers that we are the evil ones, and if they adopt our religion, they will all die! Can you honestly believe that? Fortunately, we've managed to convert quite a few of the people to a Christian religion, but in the remote villages the black magic and the Juju man still holds the power, even above that of the tribal chiefs. Still, we don't give up that easily and we will win through in the end, once we get one or two converted, then the rest follow soon afterwards, the remainder get curious and then we can gradually erode these old, stupid beliefs, and with a bit of luck from him up there," and he looked skywards, "we can win them over and succeed. So you see John, a priest's life out here is not an easy one at all."

"Well! I never thought that it would be that difficult," said John.

"Yes, it is."

"How long, then, have you to do out here?"

"Initially we came for three or four years, but once you get involved in it all and you get a foothold, you're bitten by the bug, as they say, so you finish up staying here forever perhaps."

With that sobering thought, they relaxed and gazed at the evening swaying of the branches in the trees.

"'Do you know, I went to a village last week and the last time there was a missionary there, was the year nineteen eleven!? Quite amazing really and they even had the Bible that was given to them then!" They continued to talk of many other things late into the night before retiring to bed.

In the morning after breakfast, Norman took his leave and took with him a message from Ebenezer to a relative of his who lived near one of the villages that he called upon frequently. Norman thanked the three of them for their hospitality and drove off down the road, pausing to wave to some of the native girls on their way for water.

John went down to the valley floor first and spent about three-quarters of an hour walking around and talking with the men on duty. He was greeted often by salutations of 'Good mornin' massah', or 'Hello massah! God bless you', to which he responded and stopped to speak to all of those who had addressed him in this manner. He came across Klaus coming the opposite way and he asked him how things were going.

"Guten tag, John! Yah! Alles gut! They are all in competition with each other now, Football tells me that they have to see which shift is the best which is gut! But I have to keep an eye open, as you would say, that they don't go too fast."

John smiled at this and said, "Yes, that wouldn't do at all if they rushed things," and they walked along together and met up with Tony's new assistant who, for some obscure reason, had now had his nickname changed from Simon Rock to Fred Flintstone. John thought this was hilarious and laughed for quite a while after he had heard of it. Thinking of the name he agreed that the name would not be forgotten easily and so it stuck in the minds of all. Football had cottoned on to the funny side of it and even if he passed by Simon at any distance, he would call out, "Hello, Fred Flintstone!" to which of course, he always got a huge grin back from Simon. This also went down well with the other workers. John asked Fred if the assayer had been yet.

"No. Tony is still waiting for him to come, and by the way, he has had another look at the remains of the rock face above and he confirms that there are no traces of the gold in it."

"I'm glad to hear that," said Klaus, "we don't want too much excitement to interrupt our routine."

They broke up then and went their separate ways, Football and Fred went off over to the far side, Klaus went over to a team pouring concrete, and John went uphill and called in by Marcel's clinic.

"And how is life in the butcher's shop today, Marcel?" the cold air of the air-conditioning system flowing around him as he entered from the heat outdoors.

"Business is good!" replied Marcel, as if he were a shopkeeper, "today, I have one man with a cut leg, one with a sprained foot and pulled muscle, and finally, the pièce de résistance: a hernia, for which I prescribe light duties only! C'est tout, et vous?"

"Oh, everything is normal, no problems, Marcel, so I'll leave you and get on with my work," and he went back out into the baking heat and the dust.

Later in the day Marcel went down to his first-aid hut on the floor of the dam to re-organise it with some extra equipment, a cot, a table and chairs and a large medicine cabinet. Finally he was satisfied that he had here a rudimentary treatment centre. There he would attend daily from now on for about two hours in the morning if he wasn't required up top at the clinic.

Dave extricated himself from his writing and went uphill to see John. He entered his office and John looked up and said, "Hello. What brings you up here then at this time of morning?"

"You remember that radio equipment that you asked for?"

"Yes."

"Well, it's arrived at long last, only about half an hour ago and I've brought it up with me in a box, so where do you want it?"

"Best leave it by Klaus's cabin, I'll get him on to it soon and we'll get it issued. The base unit will be in my office and the aerial can go up there," and he pointed to a largish hole in the roof where the sun shone through, "and there is a convenient rock behind it to mount the aerial tripod on, that way we will have the maximum height so we should get good communication with the floor below."

"Fine, I've got quite a heap of it, I've checked the frequencies and that all the radios are crystallised on the same channels so there won't be any confusion when we come to use them. We'll have a discussion no doubt as to who is to have them?"

"Yes, I'll get that organised."

"Okay John, I'll place them inside Klaus's office, he should be here any minute as I saw him coming up the hill as I left."

"Thanks, Dave."

Klaus arrived shortly afterwards and called for Matthew to come up top. He arrived and set about installing the base station and the aerial, and after about an hour's work it was ready to use. He also had a walkabout with the hand portables so that he could discover any blind spots and noted where they were, although there were not many of them, but he marked them on the map of the area and the site and shaded them in for clarity. He took a radio down to the floor, which they had now decided to call 'down town', a name that everybody would recognise and explained to Football how to use it. He was a bit reluctant at first but when he realised that his voice would fly like magic through the air, he was enthusiastic about its use, although Matthew had a hard job in explaining its use to him. Eventually he was satisfied that he had got the message across to him and returned to the site up top. Klaus went down town later and sought out Football and informed him that each supervisor was to have one of them as well, and asked if he thought they would be able to use them.

"Yes, massah, they all Ebos, de intelligent ones," and he smiled, "theys able to use them, no problem."

"All right then, Football, Massah Dave will give them batteries for the radios as well, and tell them that they must put in a fresh battery each time they come on shift, understood?"

"Yes, massah, I tells them!"

Football went off to the other side to give the supervisor on shift his radio and Klaus walked along to a point where he was obscured from the site up top and tried a test call to John.

"Klaus to John! Do you read?"

A short delay followed, then the radio burst into action. "Hello, Klaus, sorry for the delay, couldn't find the transmit button."

"Okay John, you're loud and clear down here, I'm on the east side, I'll go over to the west side and give you a call from there."

"Roger."

Klaus walked for about four hundred yards across to the other side and called again. "Klaus to John, do you read?"

"John to Klaus, yes, loud and clear also, that sounds good to me, we shouldn't have any problems, then, Klaus."

"Roger! Coming back up top now!" and the radio lapsed into silence.

When Klaus was making his way back, John took a fresh sheet of paper from his desk drawer and started to make out a list of the users and their names, devising relative call-signs that would be necessary. After a bit of thought he finally arrived at a conclusion, rewrote the list on a fresh sheet and read it over again. He also allocated the remainder of the base stations, and after re-examination he concluded that he had covered every aspect of the workplace and their usage of the radios. Klaus arrived and he called for the remainder of the team to came up top. They had a short discussion about the radio equipment, then all being in agreement, they each went off to their work with their personal radio, and John pinned the list up on the wall of the call-signs. He had some copies made and distributed also, so that all knew who everyone else was on the radio net, and with a feeling of satisfaction, he sat down and reached for an ice cold can of Afri-cola from the small fridge next to his desk. He ran his eye down the list again, it read: John - Kingpin; Klaus - Chief; Dave - Boxer; Tony - Rock; Fred - Flintstone; Marcel - Doc; Matthew - Sparks; Football - the same; and the Supervisors as One, Two, Three and Four.

The arrival of the radio equipment had increased their efficiency and had already proved to be invaluable, even at this early stage. He could now quickly access all of those that he needed to and it saved on the countless number of times that they had to journey up and down to the floor to pass on messages. At this point John asked himself how they had managed without them previously.

A few days later John remarked to Klaus that things were running very smoothly now.

"Yah! But it is too smooth for my liking!"

"Oh! Why is that then, Klaus?"

"I don't know, just a feeling I have, too smooth to be true, John."

"You're just looking on the black side, Klaus," he commented, pointing to the progress chart on the wall. "See! All is ahead of schedule now!"

"Sure! That is good, but it is not that I am worried about."

"Well, what is it then, Klaus? Stop being an old woman and tell me what's bugging you."

"Well, it's just that I've never come across such a large amount of men getting on so well with each other."

"And what's wrong with that then, Klaus?"

"Nothing, John. Just a feeling I have."

"Well, stop worrying, Klaus. To ease your mind, I've decided to have a social evening at my house tonight. So you can stop worrying. I will have all the team members up and that includes Football as well, so it will be a good night, I can assure you. And by the way, we don't expect you to do your party trick of heading the Land Rover tailgate!"

Klaus laughed at this, and said, "Okay, John, tonight it is then," and went off to see Tony, and called back over his shoulder, "Just make sure you have enough whisky for this old piece of German horse meat!"

John smiled back at him, and resumed his work.

Night fell, and it was soon time for all of them to assemble at the residence. They arrived in dribs and drabs, and although Nat and Eb had cooked all the food and had placed everything out on the tables, he had asked them to stay and take part in the gathering to balance it up. After they had partaken in the important business of eating, they had all adjourned to the veranda where Eb had laid out a number of tables for them and sufficient chairs. They talked amiably for some time and Matthew related some of his experiences which were funny, and Fred enlightened them with his experiences and his exploits among the natives when he worked for the Voluntary Services. Joshua and Nat were deep in conversation, as were Football, Tony and Dave. Marcel had unearthed an abundance of jokes and soon had them all laughing hysterically. Football's command of the English language was found to be greater than they thought, which surprised Matthew. Fred decided that he had met Football somewhere else before, and after some thought he remembered where it was. Some years ago he had taught in a village class, and he recalled that Football was there and was quick to pick up the speech, after he left the area he had heard that Football had been taken on as a teacher for only a short period of time before leaving to take up other work. The man in charge tried to find him to ask him to return but he could not find hide nor hair of him. However, he was glad to see that he was now in a position of authority and that he had the men well-organised. John had already reached that conclusion, and had said so to Klaus some time back. They all mixed well, and Eb and Nat filled in a lot of the background information for John, Joshua added a great deal as well. They had an impromptu football match, five to a side and they played it in front of the house, most of it in the dark. It was difficult enough to see the ball never mind the goal posts, but play they did and noted that old Eb was extremely fleet of foot. Dave, Tony, Eb, Joshua and Marcel won by seventeen goals to four over the wishy washy side of the remainder of them. Anyone who had innocently stumbled on this event in the darkness would have been surprised to say the least.

The night wore on and by the time that they had decided to call a halt to the proceedings it was three-thirty in the morning.

Next day on the morning inspection, Klaus noticed that some of the men were not at the place they had been the day before and he called Football on the radio, who ambled up to him and said,

"Yes massah! What you want?"

"Football! There are four men missing here, do you know about it?"

"No massah, but I find out," and he went off to seek out the supervisor. He returned after about five minutes or so with the man and asked him, in his language, where the men were. After a brief conversation he turned to Klaus and said, "He say dat de men not heah for de wagon this mornin', and dat dey are last seen in the evening."

"Ask him where they were."

Football spoke again, then replied, "He say dey ate by themselves at de separate table, not with de others."

"Why was that?"

"He say is because they not wish other mens to heah what dey say."

"Is that so! What villages do they come from, Football?"

"I go get de book!" and he went off to his hut not far away and returned with it, and opened the pages. He lifted his head up in an unspoken message to the supervisor who stepped over towards him, and together they went through the list of names, Football made a mark against the names as he came to them. "Dey is all from same place! Two villages, close togetha'."

"How far away?"

"Is 'bout fifteen kilometres, Massah Klaus, name of Duga and Bakare, other side of de Lake Kanji, neah de water's edge."

"Okay, Football! We go and look for them now! No good waiting to see if they turn up, we will take my Land Rover." He called John on the radio and said he'd wait until he came down, on his arrival he briefed him on the situation and the three of them set off along the dirt track towards the road.

The supervisor returned to his work but not before Klaus had given him a dressing down for not having reported the men missing. They took a rough road that cut across the bush. It was rutted and pitted with holes but they were able to reduce the distance by about five kilometres or so, and they turned on to a faint track that skirted the edge of the huge lake. Approaching it from above they slowed allowing some respite from the constant pounding on their buttocks as the wheels followed the contours of the ground. They stopped and got out and studied the village through their binoculars for a moment before proceeding. Football noted that the village appeared as normal, women were busy with their chores, the fires were evident, the smoke rose vertically in a plume, and all appeared to be tranquil below. Suddenly, he spotted a movement, and tapping Klaus on the shoulder, he passed the binoculars back to him and said, "Look now, massah!"

Klaus took the glasses from him and focused on the central clearing where two men stood talking to each other.

Football spoke as he watched. "Dey is two of dem, but I can't see de others!"

"Let's go on foot now, then," Klaus said quietly, and he went back to the Land Rover, lifted out his rifle from the grips behind the seats and slung it over his shoulder. The three of them moved through the bush and stopped at the edge of the clearing where the village began. They were just about to enter when the two men that they had been watching moved off into the bush on the far side. Football motioned to them and they detoured around the huts keeping under cover, Football bent low as he picked up their trail. He indicated off to the right. John and Klaus followed him as they wound their way in and out of the elephant grass for quite some distance. They stopped as they were drawing too close to them and waited a few moments then continued. Again they advanced and entered another belt of tall elephant grass. The trail meandered right and left and then descended a small hill, they stopped to view the area in front of them.

"There!" exclaimed Klaus, and they looked towards a mud-built hut that was just visible against the trees. Football borrowed the glasses and studied the hut in silence, then indicated that they should move forward. They descended the hill slowly and in silence until they were within about twenty yards of the hut itself.

"They inside!" he said, and motioning to John and Klaus to stay where they were, he advanced step by step towards the hut, taking great care as he went to keep down low and to where he placed his feet. The slightest sound of a twig cracking would alert the two men. He crept closer and was soon up against the wall of the hut, he stood perfectly still listening to what was being said inside. He remained there for about ten minutes or so, still listening to the low voices within. Klaus thought that it was an aeon and hoped that Football would return soon. He thought that he saw a movement and Football approached him like a shadow in the night, about a minute later he was back beside them.

"What are they saying, Football?"

"Dey say dat dey intend to break into de compound tonight, that is Massah Dave's, and steal de gold."

"Do they now? Anything else?" said Klaus.

"Dey say that dey meet tonight on de low road and climb up over de rock behind the compound."

"In that case, we'll be ready for them," said John.

"Let's go then, " Klaus added, and the three of them set off back through the elephant grass following in Football's footsteps and were soon back at the Land Rover, which looked ghostly white in the shaded area of the trees. Klaus drove straight back to John's house and there they called a meeting of the team and discussed what had happened.

"Rememba, I told you, John, that everything was going too smoothly!"

"Yes! Point taken, Klaus! Now let's see what we can do to thwart this little ploy. Dave, how many weapons do we have in the store?"

"Two dozen rifles, automatic, five handguns, Smith and Wesson, plenty of ammunition as well!"

"Good!" said Klaus, "I vote we set a trap for them, as soon as it is dark we'll surround the compound and lie in wait for them, that way we will get the culprits for sure!"

"There's only one area where they can approach from," said Dave "and that's from the rear of the fuel tanks, it's quite thick bush at that point for about twenty yards or so."

"Right then," said John. "We'll lie in wait for them, let them get in over the fence, once they are inside we'll make our move and catch them red-handed. Agreed?"

All were in agreement. Dave then said, "I'll leave the side door of the main shed unlatched, make it seem easy for them, and we could have some of our people inside as well just to be on the safe side, so we either get them there or when they come back out to the fence, where we can grab them.

"We need some illumination," commented Tony.

"I'll see to that," commented Matthew, "I'll get one of the generators up and rig up some temporary lighting. As soon as they appear, I'll start it up and we will have ample light to see by."

"An excellent idea!" commented John.

"What if dey is armed?" said Football.

"The only arms they have is machetes, spears or clubs," said Klaus.

"Dave," said John, "before you lock up tonight, move the gold to a safe place and fill the sacks with bricks but leave them exactly where you had them in the first place, as they obviously know where it is."

"Sure thing, John, I'll make sure that it is marked clearly as well!"

"Right! I'll go and get the lighting seen too," said Matthew, "a couple of those big spotlights should do the trick, we won't have any problems seeing them with those!" and he went off to arrange it.

Evening came around and the shift change took place, they withdrew the arms from the store and, once darkness had fallen, they assumed their positions around the perimeter fence but back from it, in the cover of the low tree line and the grasses that grew there.

They had agreed to keep a regular reporting system using the radios turned down low so that they could just be heard and no more as they didn't want to give the game away in the slightest. They waited for two hours.

"Maybe they're not coming," said Fred quietly, peering into the darkness. Outside the fence, the eyes of them all strained in the darkness as they peered into the bush. The moon now was well up.

"They're coming all right!" said Tony as a bird suddenly flew up in the air and beat a retreat into the trees far off. Now, they were all alert and looked in that direction. There was no further sign of movement until Football waved his arms and pointed off to the far right. They all strained to see whatever it was but nothing was immediately apparent and the silence was deafening. Then the elephant grass moved slowly and was pushed aside, unnaturally bending.

"They come," whispered Football. Those outside the building watched closely as the men drew nearer. There were three of them, one acting as a lookout, then a fourth man appeared. The glint of machete blades was seen in the moonlight as the men halted at the fence, looking around carefully as they stopped close to it. Then three of them quickly and agilely climbed over the fence and dropped silently into the compound. Klaus's finger crept silently on to the trigger guard of his rifle. The man signalled silently to the one remaining outside the fence, who remained there keeping watch.

"Damn!" said John, "I thought they would all be inside."

"Nevah mind, massah! I get him!" said Football, and without a word he slipped off his well-worn leather sandals, crept off into the darkness and taking a knife from the belt around his waist and placing it between his teeth, he disappeared from sight into the bush. All eyes now returned to the three men inside the fence. One by one, they darted from the fence line over to the wall of the building, crouching low as they ran. They crept up to the side door, all of them looking around as they went. Inside, Dave and two others lay silently behind a packing crate on the first shelf up from the floor and watched the doorway.

The men tried the door and found it open, one of them entered and they all slipped silently inside, pushing the door to as they went. Dave being directly in line with the door had a good view of them.

He recognised only one of them but remained watching. The three men went off to the left of the storage area. They knew exactly where to go, thought Dave, and he followed their progress. They quickly crossed to the metal cabinet in which the gold had been placed, but was now replaced with the heavy bricks. One of them searched around and finding a metal bar, they proceeded to lever open the doors, placing it under the lock on the door they snapped the lock open and forced the doors, now grossly distorted, aside. With a quiet cry of success they reached inside and quickly passed the bags to the man at the back, who fortunately did not look inside but set off towards the door dragging the sacks along the floor as he went. Dave reached for his radio and said quietly, with his finger on the transmit button, "On their way out."

John and Klaus looked at each other, made ready and continued watching. Matthew went silently over to the generator and placed his hand on the start button and watched the fence line. The door of the building opened and a face peered out, the head moving left and right as it viewed the line and then disappeared from sight. The three of them emerged and crossed over to the fence, dragging the bags as they went. Meanwhile, Football had crossed over and worked his way around to the rear of where the lookout was and had his knife ready in his right hand. Seeing the three men get closer to the fence, he moved forward quickly and came unseen up behind the man. He swooped down upon him, placing one hand over his mouth and placed the blade of the knife in the man's throat and pushed it inwards. A gurgling noise was only just audible and the man went quickly limp, Football pulled him back into the grass and allowed the body, spurting blood, to fall silently on to the grass. Football then dragged the body into the bush and hid it from view.

Now all eyes were on the other three as they followed their every movement. They were now only five yards from the fence.

Dave, who had followed them out of the building, called from the shadows on the radio, "Now!"

John waited until the first of the men had climbed up on to the top of the fence then pressed his button and said quietly to Matthew, "Now, Matthew!"

Matthew pressed the starting button home firmly and the generator sprang instantly into life, the floodlight bathed the area immediately, turning night into day in a few seconds. The three of them froze in their movement. One of them on the top of the fence, quickly threw the sack he was carrying over and down on to the other side. As he did so, Klaus took aim with his rifle and sighting the man squarely, he pressed the trigger. The shot rang out, disturbing the night birds which flew off in all directions. The man hesitated at the apex of the fence, then dropped over it into the bush and fell with a thud on the dark soil, shot clean through the head. The others ran towards where Klaus and John were in their blindness and the glare of the light, and as they approached them Klaus stood up and said, "So! Now we have you! Stand still!" The men froze again and they all moved forward and without any due ceremony, they quickly bound their arms to their sides and pushed them up against the fence.

Tony had kicked the machetes out of their hands and had gathered them up. The two men were now pushed roughly along, Klaus with his rifle placed at the side of the head of one of the men, and said, "What shall we do with them then, John?"

"We'll lock them up in here!" said Dave, now arriving alongside them and he indicated a metal container nearby. They were duly bundled inside, chained together now, and the door was slammed shut behind them.

"What happened to the other one?" asked John of Football.

"Oh, he try to get away, but he accidentally fell on de knife, massah," said Football innocently.

John and Klaus looked at each other but said nothing.

Dave killed the generator and they all left, telling the guard on the compound to keep an eye on the prisoners.

"We'll see to them in the morning," said John, "then we might be able to get to the bottom of it."

They all split up and went their respective ways to the sounds of the night insects. Football returned to his sleeping quarters but did not sleep. He lay awake thinking. What if someone else was to find out about the plot later on and try the same thing again? They could not release the men without risk, so he decided to remove any chance of that occurring. He arose, it was two-thirty in the morning, the moon was still high and most of the men were sound asleep. He slipped out unseen and, in the darkness, made his way up to the compound and around to the back of it. The guard was dozing at the front so he stole along to the container and silently released the locking mechanism, pulling the door open. The moonlight flooded in, falling upon the two men sound asleep on the floor. He stepped within and with two short movements he plunged his knife into each form, ending their lives instantly. He stepped out, looked around to ensure that all was quiet, closed the door and applied the hasp and lever, and left as silently as he had arrived, slipping away into the night.

Next morning, everyone in the team was up early. John and Klaus called on Dave at his house and they went directly up to the compound and over to the container so that they could get the men out for questioning. They opened the door and the early morning sunlight fell on the men only some hours after the moonlight had done the same. The two bodies by in a large puddle of blood, now congealed and to which an army of ants scurried in and out, invading the corpses and carrying off pieces of the flesh to their nest.

"Dead! They're both dead!" Klaus exclaimed, and they stepped backwards as the stench of the enclosed space hit them.

"Well! They certainly were not dead when we left them last night," said John.

They stood in silence for a minute or so deep in thought.

"Well! There's no doubt about who did it," said Tony.

"Who is that then?" asked John.

"It's got to be Football, stands to reason!"

"How do you make that out, Tony?"

"Well, it could have been anybody really, me or you, or Klaus, or Matthew, in fact, anybody that knew about the men who planned to steal the gold, but Football, I reckon that he didn't want the news of it to get out as he knew it would cause a lot of trouble so he must have done it, at least that's who I'd put my shirt on."

"Where is Football, anyway?" queried John.

"About this time, he would just be getting up, the night shift have not changed over yet."

"Give him a call on the radio," said John, and Klaus picked up his, and called him.

"Chief to Football!"

There was a short delay, then Football's tired voice answered, "Football heah, Chief, what you want?"

"Come up to the compound, Football, that is Dave's compound!"

"Okay, boss! I on my way, be about five minutes!" and the radio was muted. They waited patiently for him and soon the sound of the engine could he heard as he swung into the compound and getting out, he walked nonchalantly over to them.

"Mornin' massahs!" he called out as he walked towards them smiling, "what you want?"

"No need to smile, Football!" and the smile slid from his face.

"Come over here!" and he indicated the container. Klaus led the way and opened the door of the container again, Football leaned forwards and looked in but said nothing.

"Did you do that, Football?" he asked.

"Me? No, massah, I knows nothin' 'bout that but they is dead foh suah."

"We know that! But who did it, then?"

"Are you sure that you didn't do it?" John asked.

"No, not me, massah! I only sees to de man in de bush," and he pointed to where he had seen to the lookout the previous night. Silence fell on the group.

"All right then! Let's get these stinking bodies out before they stink any more and get them buried!"

"He's lying!" said Klaus, "he's handy with a knife, I know that."

"Well, it's too late now to get anything out of them, so let's get rid of the bodies."

Dave went off to get hold of an excavator and when it arrived, they dug a pit behind the storage compound and hastily placed the bodies in it. Klaus sent Football to get the man he had killed the night before, and he returned shortly afterwards with what was left of the body, most of it having been eaten away during the night by some animal. They covered them up and bulldozed the ground over them, removing any traces of them having been killed.

"Well, that's that then," said Tony, and they all went out of the gates of the compound and went off to their normal day duties as it was now eight-thirty in the morning.

"How are we going to report their disappearance, Klaus?" asked John.

"Put them down as having absconded, John, the money they are owed, I'll get Football to send someone to their villages with it."

"Yes. I suppose it's about all we can do for the meantime, then."

"Yes, John. I suppose you had better let Hendry J. know as well, just to keep it all legal."

"Yes, I'll see to that, Klaus."

Doc had not been involved directly in it so he decided to tell him that they absconded, he would then remove them from the register. The doctor, however, had an inkling of what had been going on but said nothing.

The work continued normally and there was no more mention of it at all, much to John's relief. The assayer had arrived, not before time John thought, and he had spent much of two days inspecting the gold and weighing it. In the end, he only passed it as eighteen carat and quoted John the price he could expect for it. John discussed this with Klaus and the rest of the team. They discussed the amount of the money and after a few comments, it was decided to share it out amongst the men. That having been agreed upon it was entered on their pay sheet and it would be paid out on the next pay-day which was in two weeks time.

"Maybe Football will not be too happy about it but then he can't complain at all as I reckon he knows that we think he murdered the two prisoners."

A week later Dave and Klaus loaded the sacks of the gold into a Land Rover, covered it with sacks of cement and took with them two loaded rifles. They set out for a bank which was about thirty-four miles away and, after a slow journey there, they collected the money for it and obtained a receipt. On their return they locked this extra money, in the form of huge bundles of notes, away safely ready for distribution when the time came. John recently had made up a fresh set of company reports and had also included a personal letter to Hendry J. mentioning the gold and the absconding of four of the work-force. He had also asked for a few truckloads of cement to be shipped up from the wharves at Lagos where it was normally stored after having been unloaded from the huge bulk carrying ships that regularly unloaded there. John recalled his short stay in Lagos, and in seeing the bulk carriers that had developed leaks and sunk in the shallows as the water penetrated the cement cargoes. Many of them rested there as monuments to the poor overall condition of the ships involved in this trade, and those that sank were only noticeable by the tops of their funnels as they protruded above the sea. Hendry J. had got on to it straight away, and said he would organise a 'crocodile' as he called it, and get it up to the site as quickly as possible. He was also pleased to read the company reports, particularly the ones referring to the finding of the gold. He forwarded them to the various offices by D.H.L. Service to the United Kingdom and the United States of America.

Up country from Hendry J., everything was running smoothly, and this time Klaus did not have any reservations about the fact. Pay-day had come around for the work-force and the men assembled after completing their respective shifts. They were very pleased, to say the least, with what they received. What with the new pay rate, and the added bonus from the gold find they returned to their quarters with beaming smiles and broad grins. Klaus had organised a type of banking system with Dave as they didn't want the men to hoard large sums of money in their accommodation and it worked very well. Doc had made progress with his medical cases, namely the ones with typhoid, and yellow fever. They had recovered slowly and would soon be able to return to work. Their pay had been retained for them, even though they were not working, and they of course, got their share of the find as well. As for those that had Aids, their symptoms varied from mild to serious and Marcel kept a close watch on them. Most were back at work but some were kept in the small ward in the clinic.

It was Harmattan time and the sun was often blocked out by the dust swept on thermal currents from the Sahara which caused everything to take on a dusty appearance, as if a fog existed. John couldn't see further than about a quarter of a mile and he was truly appreciative of the radios. The normal sweat patterns of the workers gave them a 'cracked' appearance and the dust laden atmosphere penetrated into almost everything. It got ingrained into the paperwork, in John's tea, stuck in his hair, and the inside of the vehicles resembled something like a miniature sand dune. To the workmen, of course, this posed no problems, they were used to it and carried on regardless.

Football reported to Marcel that some of the men were acting strangely. Klaus said that they were incapable of work; mistakes, only small ones, were being made but nevertheless some work had to be repeated. Marcel decided to investigate this strange effect. Marcel had some of the men into his first aid hut down town and had examined them, he emerged smiling. Klaus asked him what it was and Marcel replied, "They're drunk!"

"What? How?"

"I don't know, Klaus, but I can assure you, I know a drunk when I see one!"

Klaus called Football on the radio, and asked him to come over to the first aid hut straight away. He arrived, looking at Klaus's face, he said, "What wrong, massah?"

"Football! These men here are drunk!" and moved his hand at the group of them. "Where are they getting the alcohol from?"

Football looked unperturbed, and said, "Probably got de still, could be Guinea corn or palm wine, and if dey mixes it, it gives many sore heads!" and he smiled slyly as he said it and winked at Marcel, unseen by Klaus.

"So day must have this in the accommodation, Football?"

"I not know, massah! I not see any."

"Marcel! Come with me, and you too, Football!" They climbed into Klaus's Land Rover, drove to the accommodation area and pulled up at the row of huts and the sleeping quarters. They looked around but no evidence of a still could be found. Klaus decided to look further afield, and after another search, he called out, "Found it! Over here!" Marcel and Football followed his voice and went over to where he was standing. Through the trees and into the long grass they went and followed a well-worn path in the grass. At the end of this stood the still. Klaus looked in it and saw that it was full to the top, picking up a wooden ladle hanging on a string at the side, he dipped it in and tasted the liquid. A strained look came over his face and turning to Marcel, he said, "Mon Dieu! Pure alcohol!" He took another sip and spat it out. "They're drinking this, Marcel! Here, have a taste!" Marcel stepped over to the still and took a small sample and tasted it.

"Sacre Bleu!" and hastily hung up the ladle.

Football stepped over and did likewise, then smacking his lips, he said, "Is good!" then cast his expert opinion on it, "is very old method, tastes like the wine my father make, get you plenty drunk quick!"

"Well, we'll have to destroy it, if they all got drunk think of what might happen during their work! So I'm going to do away with it!" He went over to the Land Rover, lifted a pickaxe from the rear of it and with a few carefully aimed blows, he punctured the sides and the liquid gushed out on to the grass. "Any more?" he asked Football.

"Don't know, massah, but if I sees one, den I come and tell you."

A likely story, thought Marcel to himself.

"For the moment, that solves this problem, but I'm sure we'll find more of them." They left the accommodation and returned to the site. Subsequently, no other reports of drunkenness were made and it was forgotten about. Marcel informed John of the event and John had asked that he be kept informed of any recurrence.

The cement store had been replenished and the construction of the heavy reinforced sections had commenced. Most of those 'up top' now spent much of their time down town, getting stuck in and almost becoming part of the shifts at times.

A few days later the supervisor for shift number two was missing. Klaus had called him on the radio and there was no answer, so he called Football.

"Chief to Football! Where is Super number two?"

Back came the reply, "Football to Chief. He not heah, today, has gone to see his uncle in his village, is very sick! He mus' go and do de good magic to make him better!"

Klaus was just about to explode at this excuse but then he remembered about the importance of magic to these people, and replied, "Well, okay, Football! But if he is not back in two days you tell me! And take two days pay off him also! And find a replacement immediately! Understood?"

"Yes massah! I find!" and the radio fell silent.

Klaus looked to the heavens and hoped that he would not too many of these occurrences. Next day however, the supervisor had returned and Football had called Klaus on the radio to let him know. Klaus spoke to John about it and said that he wasn't happy again.

"Not another one of your feelings, Klaus! What is it this time then?"

"I don't know, but I'll tell you when I find out what it is."

A day later Tony was watching a group pouring concrete and it occurred to him that from a distance the amount of men there was very sparse. He went casually over to where the activity was and said, "Why are there not enough men here?"

One if the men looked up and said, "Dey gone, massah!"

"I can see that! Where have they gone to?"

"Into de bush," and he indicated with an outstretched arm.

Tony called Klaus on the radio, "Rock to Chief."

"Yah, Chief here, what gives Tony?"

"Better get down here, Klaus, more trouble!"

"Roger, be right with you."

Klaus jumped into his Land Rover and drove across to where Tony was, and Football appeared at the same time. Tony explained what the problem was and turning to Football, he asked him to question the man.

They conversed in the man's tongue and after much discussion, Football turned to Klaus and said, "Man say that twelve of them have gone to a village because de spirits tell them to."

"What spirits, Football?" asked Tony.

"It is de spirits of de ancestors, massah, dey say dey have to go and speak with the chief of the tribe."

"Where have they gone then?"

"Dey go to," and hesitated deep in thought, then recalling the name, he said, "is called Kapubara, is long way."

"How long?"

"Foah hours, massah, not many roads!"

Tony and Klaus moved to the side and discussed this. "Do we go then, Klaus?"

"Yah! We must, we need to know what they are up to, and if you ask me it's more of this magic mumbo jumbo that they believe in."

"Well, let's go and see John and see what he has to say on the subject."

They drove off uphill with Football in the back of the wagon, and pulled up outside John's office. John was writing as they came in.

"What's up?" he said before they could speak, "I heard you on the radio, don't tell me that it's more trouble?"

"Yes! Looks like it," said Tony, "it's these men again, they have gone off to some village because the spirits told them to."

There was silence for a few moments as John thought about it and no-one spoke. After another brief conversation they all agreed, including Football, that they would seek out the men and get them back, if that was possible.

John called Dave and Marcel and told them that they would be away for quite a few hours, that they would not be back until late in the evening.

"We'll take the long-wheel-based

Land Rover, and some arms too, just to be on the safe side." When they were all ready, Klaus got out the map and searched for the village and on finding it, he marked it with a cross. Football indicated the route that they should take, adding that after they had reached

Karengi, they would have to go across the bush. Klaus checked that both of the fuel tanks were full to the top and they also took on board two Jerry cans of fuel in case they had to make detours.

They set off westwards and headed for Doro and Luma and continued on the rough road towards Kubli. They carried on, heading for the border with Benin but still in Kwara State and came closer to Babanu, where they turned to the right and went on towards Karengi where they lost their way. Football got out and sought out a small village and asked the man where Kapubara was. The man pointed into the bush, and indicated that they would have to cross a hill and go down the other side, then they would see it in front of them. They had made good time, however, Klaus had started the driving and John had taken over at a later stage and they had almost arrived at the village, three and a quarter hours later. Now it was through the elephant grass, the Land Rover nudged its way through and the ground was hard and bumpy. As they went along the branches and the bushes scraped along the sides of the vehicle, and the ground under the wheels varied from soft and giving to hard and firm. Occasionally they had to stop and backtrack as the ground was too slippery. Klaus had taken over again, and being skilled at handling the vehicle he had forged ahead and attacked the terrain with a vengeance using the full potential of the drive system to their advantage. It was more like a cross country rally, John thought to himself as the wagon bucked and swayed on the uneven ground. They emerged on a bluff and looked down, the village lay below.

John took a quick sight through his binoculars, all looked peaceful so they proceeded and stopped in a clearing and decided to continue on foot from there. They got out and Football led the way, the two of them following behind him as he picked his way through the grasses and approached the huts with their tall conical roofs, there they halted.

"Too quiet to be normal," Klaus whispered. They remained where they were, watching and waiting. Some of the villagers were in evidence, met and parted, tots ran to and fro in their play. An old man with a staff, limped across the clearing in front of them and finding a vacant stool, he rested upon it in the shade. They then advanced and as they did so Football called out. From a hut at the side a man emerged, greeted Football and they spoke for a moment. Football explained that he wished to speak to the village chief about some of his people. The man went over to the far side and entered a larger hut.

While they waited Klaus's eyes were busy searching the undergrowth around the huts. They had been waiting for about five minutes now in silence and he noticed out of the comer of his eye, that there were movements all around them. Football too had seen it. Klaus whispered to them, "Stand still, do nothing!"

All around them, men had appeared from out of the bush.

"Do you see what I see?" asked Klaus.

"Yes," said Tony, "many men, no women, and they're all dressed up in their tribal war paint! See there!" and he nodded his head in the direction in which he was looking. The men around them, all stood in small groups armed with spears or machetes, and their bodies were daubed in green, white and yellow patterns, striped with black. Their faces, too, were marked to present a fearsome appearance to others and their eyes betrayed nothing but hostility. They waited. No-one moved and all was deathly silent.

After about twenty minutes, a man reappeared from the large hut and walked slowly towards them and stopped in front of Football. "De Chief will see you," he said, "you must wait, he will come." The man went over to one of the groups and joined them. All stood in silence.

After what seemed like an eternity, the wicker door of the hut was opened from within and a man stepped out and looked around as if to make sure that it was clear, then held the door ajar. A huge heavily built man emerged, evidently at some time in the past he had been very muscular but had now turned to fat. He moved clumsily, stepping out into the sunlight. He was dressed in a loin cloth, a brilliant red waistcoat, jewelled on the lapels and it sat astride his chest gaping, as it could not cover the vast expanse of it and the silver buttons were now long divorced from their button holes by the flesh between them. Around his neck hung a heavily carved ivory necklace with a bird's skull suspended from it on a braided string. Adding to this strange appearance was a very tall stovepipe hat, a relic from some pre-Victorian age but immaculate in its condition. It was worn askew giving him a sort of tilted appearance. His right arm held a spear tipped with ivory, and from which dangled a group of brightly coloured feathers tied together on a woven rope tassel. He spoke. "Me Stovepipe Charlie!" and he gazed around him as if he dared anyone to question that fact. "You wish to speak to me about my people!" and he drew himself up to his full height.

Football moved over towards him and greeted him, then said, "This men here!" and he indicated Klaus, John and Tony, "are from de big dam in de east!"

"Ah! Dutse!" he responded, "Ginna, Mamuna!" The men around him repeated this phrase while Stovepipe's face remained impassive.

"What's he saying?" asked Klaus quietly from behind.

"He is telling the men that we have come from the big ugly stone rock far away. They have heard of it."

Football re-engaged the conversation with Stovepipe and informed him that men who worked for them had disappeared, and he wanted to know if the Chief had seen them as they came from this area. Stovepipe waved his hand around in a half circle and said something to Football.

He turned to Klaus, and said, "The Chief asks, do you see the men here?"

Klaus, Tony and John looked around but in any case they would not have been able to identify any of them under all their war paint, it was impossible to tell. Football replied in the negative.

The Chief then conversed again with Football, who turned to Klaus and said, "He says that if we can identify any of the men here, as being your employees then you can take them with you."

"Could be any of them," Tony commented, "but they are here all right, I know."

"Ask the Chief, Football," said John, "why they are all dressed for war." Football asked the question and the Chief turned towards John with an angry look on his face and glared at him and raised up his spear. The men around closed in quickly round John and his men and only when he had lowered his spear, did the men retreat to the position they were in previously. The Chief spoke again to Football.

"He says it is only a simple tribal ceremony which the white man would not understand."

"Tell the Chief, Football," said Klaus, "that we mean no disrespect but if these men turn up here, will he send them back to the dam?"

Football translated the message. "He says that he will do that."

"Let's get out of here!" said Klaus. "We're not going to find out anything at all." Football thanked the Chief for the audience, the Chief turned around and waited for the door to be held open for him and, without looking back, he re-entered the hut and the wicker door was pushed to. The group of men melted away and John and his party retraced their steps into the bush.

As soon as they were out of earshot Klaus spoke, "There's something going on here! I can sense it! The Chief was lying through his teeth! He knows who our men are and they were there also, but for what purpose I don't know."

"Yes, I agree," said Tony, "that war paint was not for fun! Some simple ceremony indeed! More like some form of intimidation towards someone, namely us."

"What type of intimidation?" asked John.

"I don't know," said Tony, "ask Football!"

They turned to him and waited for his comment. "Is bad magic, massahs! This I know, we wait and see maybe?"

No-one added any comment so Klaus suggested they get started on the return journey and they set off across the scrub, Football leading the way. As they reached the clearing where they had left the Land Rover, Football stopped abruptly causing those behind him to cannon into him. He stood still, pointing to the Land Rover. In front of it a wooden stake had been stuck into the earth, it was about five foot in length with the top pointed. It had been inserted through the base of a human skull, protruded through it and poked out of one of the empty eye sockets, the skull leaning sideways with the jaw hanging open. Tied to the pole, hanging upside down, was a large black bat, dead and crawling with lice.

"Christ!" said Tony, "what manner of thing is this?"

Klaus walked up to it and prodded the bat with his rifle, whereupon part of it fell off on to the ground. Football looked terrified.

"What does it mean Football?" asked John.

"Is a warnin' massah! Best not to ask too many question," and moving quickly past it he added, "we go now, massah!"

Klaus muttered something under his breath and went over to the Land Rover and climbed into the seat. The others followed and they set off through the grasses and scrub. They drove for some distance in silence, each of them busy with their own thoughts on what they had experienced, and it was only when they reached the point where they joined the road again that the silence was broken by Tony.

"There's trouble brewing for sure, John, I think that we'd better be on our guard from now on."

"Yes, Tony, but they're hours away from us, I can't see how they can affect us really," added John.

"It's not that I'm worried about," said Klaus, "it's this bad magic that Football is speaking of that may infiltrate the workers."

"You mean poison the men against us, Klaus?" asked Tony.

"Yah! But how I don't know. Anyway, I will re-organise the shifts. There are still some men who come from that village, or if not that one from ones nearby, if we split them up between the shifts then there will be less chance of them getting together and organising any disruption, what do you think?" They all looked at each other and there was silence for a moment.

"I agree!" said John, "Football, you know the men?"

"Yes massah!"

"When we get back you point out to me the names in the book, and then we will take the necessary action."

"Yes, massah!"

"What about this war paint, Football?"

"Is somethin' to do with de old cult, massah, long time back!" and he hesitated for a moment as he tried to recall what it was. "Is de men with de leopard claw, massah, is de work of de Juju men, is bad magic!" and he shook his head as he said this. They all fell silent again and they drove on into the fading sunlight.

Klaus pressed harder down on the accelerator and increased their speed in the almost empty road. They carried on, Klaus electing to continue driving instead of changing over drivers and they were soon approaching the turn off to their site. Klaus drove straight to the accommodation area and dropped Football off saying, "We'll separate the men tomorrow, Football, but say nothing at all to them tonight!"

"Yes, massah! See you in de mornin'," and he went off to his quarters. The remainder of them drove off uphill to John's office and went inside.

"Well," John exclaimed, "a nice sort of situation this is!"

"It's all we need!" added Tony, "I can't see why this is directed at us as we haven't offended any of the local tribes at all, have we?"

"Not that I know of," commented John.

"This blotty Juju magic is all behind it," said Klaus, his voice sounding more guttural than ever. "We'd better keep our eyes skinned for any sign of trouble."

"Let's talk about it in the morning, then," said John. "I'm bushed, so to speak," and he stood up. Tony got the pun straight away and smiled as they all exited and went their separate ways. John drove down to his house and, on entering, he poured himself a large whisky as he felt he needed it. After the episode with the skull his nerves were slightly shocked and he wished he could understand it all as it seemed to be disjointed, too complicated to make any coherent sense out of. He ate his evening meal mechanically. After the coffee and biscuits, he called Eb over.

"How long have you been living in this area, Eb?"

"All my life, massah!" he said in a drawn out phrase, "my village is only 'bout four miles away, up above the big rocks."

"What do you know about these Leopard Men, then?"

Eb sat thinking for a while, then said, "Is a long time ago, when I is young man," and he smiled as he said it. "It was not in this area but ovah in Calabar in de Cross River State. De tribes have argument and some of de men, they dress as de leopards, that is with de leopard skins on de backs and on de head," and he put up his hands to indicate how it sat. "Dey catch and kill men of de other tribe, dey tie dem to de stakes and den rip out de throats," and he indicated with a grasping and tearing movement of his hand how it was done. "Is not nice! Is de work of de men who knows about de black magic, is very old, as you say, superstition? Yes! But it not happen here, is very far away."

John then related to him what they had seen at Kapubara, and Eb sat silent for a while and thought about it.

"This man you call Stovepipe? I have heard of him. He became Chief of de people by killing his two brothers for the money dey have and also he kill his father too, so that he can be Chief. He is not a good man! Is into evil ways."

"How about Juju men?"

Eb sat silent again, looking at John once or twice before answering. "Some of dem, dey still remain but only a few in some of the villages. Most of dem is young mens, eager for power, dey are the ones who are as you say, easily made into these Juju peoples. They are promised power and riches for evah."

"Do you think then, Eb, that these two different things are linked together?"

"Is possible, massah! But these Leopard Mens you speak of I not think they are heah, but I will ask in my village. There is a man who travel far," and he waved his hand around again as he had done in an earlier conversation, "and he heah much talk, he will know."

"You do that for me, Eb. I would like to hear what he has to say as we must find out all we can about these people or else it will have a bad influence on our workers."

"Yes, massah," said Eb, "I will let you know, I will go find out," and he went off into the kitchen, then out to the laundry to carry out his last task for the night. John went out on to the veranda and wrote up his report for the day which now was somewhat lengthened, mentioning the search for the missing men and the skull on the stake. He had a few more whiskies then went to bed and slept an uneasy sleep.

He was up early and sat waiting while Nat hurriedly cooked his breakfast for him. The massah sure was early today, he thought as he turned the eggs over in the pan and John left shortly afterwards and drove up to the office site.

Klaus was also in early and they waited for the time for the shift changeover when Klaus called Football on the radio, asking him to bring up the book of names and they sat in Klaus's office going through them. John called in everyone else and they crowded into Klaus's small office, Football ringed the names of the men in the book and made a note of their numbers and the villages. They all discussed the plan and Klaus extricated the three names which were most relevant to the place they had visited.

"You'd better separate any living close by as well, Klaus," commented John. Football looked again through the list and found those that this applied to and noted their names. That made a total of eight. Klaus worked this out and passed a sheet of paper over to Football who silently took it, and after a brief conversation at the door he set off for down town and implemented the changes.

It was decided however, that they could not do much at present, and so they waited to see if there were any other developments. As expected the men had not returned, not even to collect their pay, an unusual occurrence to say the least.

Some weeks had passed by since their visit to Kapubara, but Klaus still had his misgivings and on every shift change he had Football check to see if any of them were missing, but so far none were. He was, however, watchful for any sign of trouble as he was guarded against being lulled into any false sense of security, and remained vigilant on each and every day.

Quite by accident, Doc on his normal walkabout in the morning by the first aid hut had come across a man with a cut on his neck and took him over to the hut for treatment. As he was administering it, Football passed by and seeing that Doc was there, stuck his head through the door to speak to him. His eyes fell upon the man and, waiting until Doc had finished, he waved him over and said, in a low voice, "Dis man you have heah, he is one of dem from Kapubara!"

"Are you sure?" Doc asked.

"Yes, massah! His name is Obidawe! Ask him how he get de cut in de neck!"

Football and Doc went into the hut and Doc looked at the cut again, noting that it was a fine line as if a sharp knife had been used. They questioned him and after a few minutes they had got an explanation out of him. He had apparently been asleep and he was awakened by a man who held a knife to his throat who told him that he was to cause trouble. He had refused and then the man had cut his neck as a warning to him and to others. Marcel decided to treat him and, applying a few quick stitches to the skin, they sent him back to his accommodation. He and Football then went up to see John and informed him of what had happened. John listened to this then called on the rest of them to discuss it. They decided that they would set a trap at the rear of the accommodation huts. They went down to them and Football pointed out the cots where the men from the Kapubara area slept. That night they lay in wait in the darkness but no-one came. After a few more nights of this they abandoned it as there were no further visits.

Eight days later, however, the same man was missing at the start of his shift and the supervisor had called on the radio to report the fact. Shortly afterwards he was found behind the accommodation area, deep in the tall grasses and tied to a tree. Klaus and Football went to see where he was found and there they discovered that he was indeed dead, his head hung down on his chest. When it was lifted up they saw that his throat had been cut away, or rather, as Klaus said afterwards, ripped out, the vocal cords exposed and the neck now a mass of flies. He was quickly cut down and taken away to Marcel's clinic where he had inspected the body and would give his opinion shortly afterwards.

"Whatever it was," said Marcel, "it was something very sharp, see how the throat has been punctured, not cut, and torn in a downwards motion?"

Klaus and John viewed the grisly sight and felt squeamish after having done so.

"And another thing," added Marcel, "the tears are all in one direction, downwards, it looks as though it's one of your Leopard Men you were talking about."

The man was buried the same day, and from then on they paid particular attention to the remaining men from that area.

A week later, two figures were seen late at night, making their way through the bush as the moon shone down upon them approaching the accommodation. Football and some of the men who were off duty, slipped into the grass and followed their movements. They crept up behind them unseen, and allowed them to go to the low-lying area adjacent to the huts then pounced on them. They were quickly tied up and dragged into the light. Football looked at them, and said that they were not any of the workers so they were taken away and locked up. John and Klaus went to see the men and Klaus interrogated them. They spoke broken English and it was not long before Klaus extracted from them why they had come. They were from the village where they had seen Stovepipe, and after Klaus had threatened them they admitted that they had been sent to entice the workmen away. They had a quick discussion about what they were to do with them. They locked them up, Klaus saying to Football sort of half-heartedly, that he expected to see them alive in the morning.

Next morning, Klaus proposed that they return the men to the village where they had come from, and after much arguing it was decided that they be taken back to the village. Klaus and Football both volunteered to do this and they set out with them in the back of the wagon, securely tied to the upright pillars of the canopy. The intention was to take them back and warn Stovepipe at the same time. Klaus and Football, however, had another plan, and they drove there taking a detour, coming out at the village on the opposite side to where they were before. They pulled up just out of sight of the huts and, having a quick look around to make sure that they were not seen, they tied the men up to two trees. Football went into the hut and told Stovepipe, not now dressed in his finery but in dirty trousers, that the men had been returned and warned him not to send anyone else to the dam.

"Do you think that he will take any notice of this, Football," Klaus asked.

"No, I not think so," he replied.

"Well, we'll make sure that he does, then!" Klaus commented, and without further ado he crossed to where the men were tied and Football drew his knife and cut their throats, the blood cascading down their torsos and splashing on the ground. In all it only took a few seconds. Football wiped the knife in the grass and they leapt into the Land Rover and quickly but quietly drove away from the village. On their way back they congratulated themselves on a job well done, and when they arrived at the compound they reported to Tony and John that they had handed the men back and that they didn't expect any further trouble. From that day onwards, there was no repetition of the nightly visits. Obviously, thought John, the warning to Stovepipe had worked.

From then onwards for some time, it seemed to be a period of tranquillity, and with no worries they had more time in the evenings for the social occasions. They kept in close touch after working hours and John had sent word down to Hendry J. that he was welcome to come up and see how things were for himself. John had expected a refusal but by some miracle Hendry J. had managed to escape from behind his desk, which must have been a shock to everyone, and had organised to take a four day break away from it all.

On a Tuesday he arrived, having driven up from Lagos the day previous via Ibadan and Ilorin. He stopped at John's house on arrival but was directed up to the site by Eb. He pulled up, got out and went into John's office unannounced. Klaus and John had been studying sets of figures and did not see him enter. They broke off to give Hendry J. a hearty welcome.

"It's good to see you, Hendry! Now sit down and tell me the secret."

"What secret?"

"The secret! About how you managed to get away from your office, let's face it you are married to it, aren't you?"

"I just stood up," he said, "like this," and did a quick repeat of the exercise, "and walked out of the door!"

"Well I never!" said John.

"Ah!" said Klaus, "did anyone see you leave?"

"Yes! I just told them I was taking a few days off!"

"No-one fainted, then?" asked John, taken aback.

"No!"

"Amazing!" and turning to Klaus, he said, "We must get on to the *Lagos Courier* and have them do an article on it, eh? Should double their circulation I would think!"

"Yah! If not treble it!" added Klaus.

"All right you two! Stop taking the mickey! I'm here for a rest, not an interrogation."

They all laughed at this and John passed a cup of coffee to him and they all sat down again.

"Tonight we are having one of our usual social evenings, Hendry, so we will all meet up there but in the meantime we can go down town and you can have a look around there for yourself."

"That would be fine, John," he said, and sipped his drink. After ten minutes or so had passed they went down and he spent some time looking at almost everything and talked also with some of the men there. He went back up top and met Dave and Tony, and they were soon deep in conversation with them. Marcel happened by and he disappeared into the clinic with him and was gone for quite some time.

"Well, I'm impressed, John, quite a well run outfit you have here now, that will go down well with the owners. I see that your men are on top of the job."

"Everything is ahead of schedule, Hendry, mind you, we've had a few upsets, but all in all, it's going well."

"Yes, at this rate, you should be well ahead by this time next year, so we will be able at this rate to have an earlier completion date perhaps. The company will be impressed with that if you can achieve it." The evening approached and they closed up for the day and set off for the residences.

They all assembled at John's house at eight in the evening. Eb had 'the big meeting table' as he called it, out and had arranged tables, glasses, food and just about everything else he could think of for them all. The conversation flowed and Hendry J. spoke with Eb and Nat at length, Eb every now and then breaking off to serve the drinks in a truly diplomatic fashion. The talk ranged from work to tropical diseases, Marcel being of course, foremost in this discussion. The dish of tasty black pepper chicken pieces was passed around, followed by other meats, home-made potato crisps and various titbits. At four in the morning they halted, it hardly seemed worthwhile going to bed but they dispersed for a few hours respite and got some shut-eye as the sun arose.

Hendry J. spent the next few days relaxing and then returned to Lagos well-satisfied with his visit on both fronts, and pleased that the project was in safe hands.

Chapter Six

Owing to the progress that had been made to date, it was time for the access roads to be constructed. Hendry J. had informed the company and the contract, having already been awarded to Julius Berger, was initiated. A fleet of huge earth moving vehicles had assembled, moving from their depot just outside Abuja, and a train of trucks with trailers brought in the equipment necessary for the heavy engineering that would take place. A team of surveyors had arrived and their tripods were dotted about here and there. The markers had staked out the line of the roads and now a wide swathe had been carved out of the jungle and the surrounding bush to join up with the local road at the bottom of the hill. Up top also, the surveyors were in evidence and the road that would eventually cross the top of the dam itself was pegged out. Further away the same was happening where the main road met with the local one and the ten miles or so to the dam site had been planned. Already the red earth that had been gouged out of the land was piled up at the sides, and gradually this feature was extended through the bush. Some of it was removed for reconstitution at a later date, and for landscaping material. Crushed rock was ferried in by the truckload and soon a temporary wide track had been laid adjacent to where the new roads would run. The construction teams took great care to avoid the local villages and cultivated areas where necessary, and the sound of the earth moving vehicles was now common to their ears as they went about the task of forming the road to Kaminoriga.

After a few months work, from up top the new road line could easily be seen snaking its way towards the east side of the valley. The men who worked for Julius Berger were of a multinational mix. There were Nigerians, Cameroons, Italians, Mexicans and a host of other nationalities, all supervised by the few German staff who oversaw them. New friendships had been cultivated, and John's team and Julius Berger's had met frequently. Socially they became involved with each other, too.

There had not been any cause for worry for a long time now, but Klaus was ever watchful for the slightest indication of trouble in any form.

Football had got control of the shifts firmly in his grasp. Over a period of time, some nineteen men had left, all voluntary, for various reasons ranging from sick families, family deaths, and general unsuitability for the work which was physically demanding. John decided not to replace them as it made little difference to the shifts, and the back-up shift was always available in event of difficulties or emergencies. Monthly, the shifts themselves vied for pole position in their efficiency. They were judged on the quality of the work and their attitude to the safety aspect, and the competition was fierce at times. The supervisors that had been chosen by Football had proved to be natural leaders, and as time went on John upped their pay to reflect their position.

Matthew was constantly at work, moving temporary lighting, repairing the numerous electrically powered tools and also getting involved in anything that was going on. He had rigged the alarm system up and, in the event of any danger, the klaxons would sound their ear-splitting shriek which could easily be heard above the loudest sounds produced by the equipment being used. The valley itself also served to convey its sound afar.

The rainy season was now almost upon them and this occasionally halted work when the ground got so wet that it turned to a quagmire. The numerous herds of bush cows came and went. The fact that the new roads were being constructed did not deter them, and the men who were working on the new roads turned a blind eye to them as they passed through the middle of their operations. They were accustomed to them, a form of necessary evil, as they put it.

During one of the night shifts it was reported to Klaus that some of the men 'had gone off' and he went to investigate this occurrence at ten in the evening. The supervisor spoke good English and told him that they had gone away after they had been working for two hours. He dug out Football and they checked the register. The men were all from the north but from different areas. One of them was from Swate, which was about fifty miles from Kapubara, the second one from Gwarnba and the remainder of them had come from the Culbin Ka River which was far to the east. There didn't seem to be any from Kapubara but Klaus was nevertheless suspicious. He went up to see John and they held a short discussion about it.

"They're all from the north, but I suspect that it's definitely got something to do with Stovepipe Charlie!"

"I wouldn't be surprised, Klaus. I thought that as well. I think that we will keep that in mind and if the men reappear we will take action then, eh?"

"Yah, I agree," said Klaus, and left to return to the site down town.

The next day a similar occurrence took place, but this time a different shift was involved. The absence of the men, two of them, was not noticed until they were boarding the trucks that were leaving the site on the shift change. Klaus and Football again checked the register and annotated the names. One of them was from Sagbana which was across the border in what was previously Dahomey and of the old Hausa Banza region and he belonged to the Borgawa tribe. The other was from Senefeluna and was a Nupe.

John, again, was alerted to this by Klaus and they summoned Football for a discussion. Klaus got out the detailed map of the area and Football marked upon it the areas where each of the missing men to date had come from. John asked Football to mark also the area where the recent murders had taken place, and he did so. They stood looking at it for a moment in silence, then Klaus picked up a pencil from the desk top and drew a line from each of the points to its nearest neighbour. He stood back and worked out in his mind the area of land indicated. It was roughly three hundred and ten kilometres.

"Too wide to show any pattern, John, but I still feel it is all linked anyway." They looked at Football and waited for his comment.

"Not suah, massah, maybe dey are!"

"Well, I think so anyway," said Klaus not waiting for any further comment.

John thought for a moment then said, "Let's wait and see, Klaus. I know you're eager to get on to it straight away but I want to make sure first, we don't want to go off half cock on it. I'd rather be a hundred percent certain." That comment being made, they decided to wait for one more further development and if that occurred, they would go into action.

They did not have to wait long. Ten days had gone by and the evening shift had told the supervisor that they had seen something moving in the shadows near to the site in the low scrub below the base section. The hand portable floodlights were got out of the temporary store and a search of the area was carried out. Nothing was seen but later on in the shift, at four in the morning, a similar report was made. This time Klaus and Football and Matthew were called and they picked out about twenty of the workers to form search parties. They formed into two groups and covered the same area again but discarding the light and using their eyes. This time no-one was seen but Football said that he had heard voices carried faintly on the wind from the bush. He also commented that he had heard one of the voices before but he could not identify who it belonged to.

Next day they held another meeting in Klaus's office and reviewed all the information that they had to date on these occurrences.

"How many men do you think you heard altogether, Football?"

"Two, massah, maybe three voices, very low, difficult to heah."

"You mean they were whispering, then?"

"Yes, massah! But very quiet and I think I knows wheah I's heah dis voice befoah!"

"Where was that then, Football?"

Football looked around them, before replying, "I heah dis voice when we is at de evil place!"

"You mean Kapubara?"

"Yes, massah!"

"Whose voice, then?"

"It is de voice of de big man, Stovepipe!"

A silence fell on them all for a moment then Klaus broke it by saying, "I knew it had to have something to do with him, I've suspected that all along!"

"Are you sure, Football? You couldn't be wrong, could you?"

All eyes turned to him again.

"No, massah. It is de man! Dat I is suah of!"

"Well," said John, "we could go back up there again but it's too far to be trawling back and forth, don't you agree?"

"The question now then is what is Stovepipe doing down here? It is a long way from Kapubara and he didn't come all the way here for nothing."

They thought about this for a few moments before Matthew spoke. "I could extend the range of the lights, say place them further afield and camouflage them so that if he appeared again in the area around the workings, we may be able to see him and perhaps capture him, don't you think so?"

"Perhaps we should do this, John," said Klaus. "It will give us more security anyway and we can always be ready for him if he comes again."

The next night, with the lights now extended, they assembled at the edge of the workings and kept watch. Nothing occurred, so they repeated the exercise over the next two nights but all was in vain. They discussed it again and most were in favour of giving it up, but Matthew insisted that they try it for one more night and this was agreed upon. They deployed the men once again and lay in wait. About two in the morning, Klaus received a short message on the radio, "Someone was in de bush!"

The watchers moved over to the part of the site where the intrusion had been spotted and they gradually inched forward into the cover of the grasses.

"Off to de right!" a voice whispered, and all eyes panned to that side. Now they lay silently in wait. Ten minutes had passed in total silence, then suddenly one of the men pointed to the left and with his arm indicated that whoever it was, was crossing in front of them and was now centrally located. They all strained their eyes but could not identify anything. Football and Klaus had each brought with them a hand searchlight and they held them in readiness. In the silence only the crickets could be heard. Now, some of the men had their ears to the ground and one indicated that someone was moving directly in front of them. He listened again and this time held up his hand with three fingers outstretched.

Football leaned over to Klaus and whispered, "He say dat de three men is now moving very slowly."

Klaus acknowledged the information without speaking but kept his eyes on the point ahead of him. A further ten minutes passed and there was still no movement. Klaus decided that they would have to rush them to flush them out. He signalled to his men who were all crouched low, having risen from their prostrated positions behind the bushes. He stood up, and called out loudly, "Go!"

They all rushed forwards as fast as their feet could propel them. Klaus's searchlight stabbed the darkness ahead as they ran and then the three figures emerged from their cover and made off through the bush.

"Stop!" shouted Klaus, but the men took off now at a greater speed but not before the high intensity beam caught them in mid-flight. The larger of the men looked back as he ran. The light fell on his features and Klaus could clearly see that it was Stovepipe Charlie. Football instantly shouted the same name as they pursued them. They pounded through the bush, Klaus firing a few shots in their direction hoping to bring at least one of them down but he was unsuccessful. The three men managed to give them the slip in the darkness and despite a thorough search, they could not locate them again.

"That was him all right, Football! I'd recognise his features anywhere!"

"Yes, massah, it was him."

"Okay then, let's get back to the site," and they recalled the men who were still searching in the bush for the three. Klaus and Football went directly to John's house, who had been alerted by the sound of gunfire. They deferred any further action until the morning when they would, in daylight, scour the area for any clues. Football said that he would get two good tracking men from one of the other shifts to assist and they agreed to meet at six in the morning, as soon as the sun had risen.

They assembled down town at that time, and the two trackers moved slowly into the bush, bent low, and followed the foot marks in the soil. They conversed for a moment pointing in one direction, then set off again. John and Klaus followed behind while Football went on ahead keeping about four yards back from the two trackers. The three of them stopped and talked in one of the lesser-known dialects.

"What are they saying, Football?" Klaus asked.

"Dey say massah, dat de three men, dey run off in different directions then dey meet and go into de bush in single file, one small man, two big men, one of them verrah heavy, massah. Dat be Stovepipe Charlie!"

The trackers continued then stopped as the trail petered out, and they returned to the point where they had spoken. There the men looked around then suddenly one of them called to Football, pointing to the ground, and he went over towards them.

"What is it?" asked Klaus as he and John approached them.

"You come, massahs! See this!" called Football over his shoulder. They arrived at the point and the trackers indicated the marks in the soil.

"Well, Football! I can't see anything, what is it then?"

Football, turned to John and said, "It is de marks of de Leopard Men, massah!"

"Come on now, Football! You know that there are no leopards here now, they were all killed by the hunters years ago!"

"Yes, massah, but it is not I who says it, it is de men heah, dey can tell de tracks, it is foh suah de tracks of a leopard but is also a verrah big one!"

"So! You think then that what we have here is the name the people give to the leopard murders, then?"

"Yes, massah, dat is what de men say," and he turned and asked them again and the two trackers nodded in confirmation.

John then spoke, "It all fits together then, eh, Klaus?"

"Yes, they seem certain anyway," Klaus replied, then turning to Football, he said, "Take the two men downstream and see if you can find any other tracks."

"Yes massah!" and the three of them went off towards the river.

As they went John called to them, "Football! Go to the village where the women do the washing and ask the head man there if they have seen anyone unusual around lately"

"Yes, massah," he replied and they disappeared from sight in the tall grasses.

Klaus went after them, caught up with them and gave his rifle to Football, "Take this, just in case and if you have to use it, do so!"

Football looked at it for a moment, then taking it slowly from Klaus, he replied, "Yes, massah!"

"You know how to use it?"

"Yes, massah, I can shoot."

"See you when you get back then, see what you can find out Football, someone must have seen them!"

Football raised his hand in understanding as the three of them loped off along the path by the river bank.

John and Klaus went off back to John's house and Nat cooked them breakfast, then they left to go up top to their offices.

"We'll wait until Football returns and see if there is any other information at all before we decide what to do next," said John.

"Yah! Give me a call on the radio when they get back, John," Klaus replied and went up the steps into his office.

It was two and a half hours later when the three of them returned and leaving the men at the accommodation, Football carried on up the winding path to the top and arrived at John's office. John shouted across the compound to Klaus, who came over right away and the three of them sat down on John's table.

"Well? What do they say?" asked John.

"Well, massah, we's find more of de tracks de same, down by de river and we follows dem foh 'bout foah kilometres down de stream, den dey stops."

"And?" added Klaus.

"In de village, I axes de headman, an' he say he not see anyone but de wimmen, dey see de men passing far away on de way towards us, at de dam dey see them later. Den dey also see dem coming back and den dey see in de evening de smoke of their fire high up on de bluff befoah de river bends."

"I knew it," said Klaus.

"Seems as if they have been watching us for some time then," added John.

"Okay Football, thank the trackers for me, and tell them that we may need their services again soon."

"Yes, massah," he replied and went off down town.

Klaus looked at John, questioningly, and John looked at his watch.

"Get all the team up here, Klaus, at, say, an hour after midday and the four supervisors as well, we'd better have a serious discussion about this."

"Oh! That is a good idea, John. I'll go and get that seen to and detail the substitutes," and he left and drove out of the compound.

At the appointed hour they all assembled in John's office, crowding in. John had managed to find enough seats for all of them.

"Do we need any translation, Football?" he asked indicating the supervisors.

"No massah, they all understand but I will speak with them if necessary."

"Good," he replied, and taking his notepad over towards him, he glanced at it and said, "As I see it, we can do a number of things. We can lay in wait as before, and hope to capture Stovepipe and his friends. We can go to the village and capture him, but that is very risky, or we can wait until something else happens."

Tony spoke up. "I'm all for the second one," he said.

John looked around them, then said, "How about the rest of you?"

They all looked at each other and without being prompted, they all made their thoughts known in turn. Klaus elected to go for the second one, so did Dave, the four supervisors indicated that they go and get Stovepipe, Joshua said the same. All, in the end were in agreement and Marcel, now being involved directly, went along with this decision.

John then said, "All raise their hands then, if we are to go and seek out Stovepipe at the village."

They did so.

"Well! That's pretty convincing then."

"It is the only way, John," added Klaus, "he is the root of the trouble, and by getting him we hopefully can stop it once and for all."

"A bit on the risky side, though," John commented, "some of us could get injured."

"We'll just have to make sure that we don't then," Dave stated.

"There is a way of removing Stovepipe," said Football.

"And what is that, Football?"

"It is the African way, massah."

"You mean a slit of the throat?" said Dave.

"No, massah, jus' old African ways."

At this time, Marcel, who had been standing at the rear, spoke up and said, "You mean poison, don't you Football?"

Football did not answer, but his silence was enough to confirm that this was the method.

Marcel spoke again, "A quick acting poison, Football?"

He nodded but did not speak, then turned to the supervisors and latched into their common dialect. They conversed between themselves. One of them explaining how they would do it, while the remainder of them watched in silence, following the movements of the men's arms as they described the actions. Marcel had cupped his hand behind his ear and was listening intently, and had caught the name of the poison during their conversation.

Before Football could speak Marcel interrupted, "They are speaking of using a poison which is made from the leaves of a tree. I think it is one of those that I have heard about and it's quick acting and very concentrated."

"Is this true, Football?" asked John.

Football looked at Marcel, then said, "Yes, massah, is true, dis poison, he go verrah quick, kill in seconds!"

John looked at Marcel for a further explanation and he spoke without prompt, "It flows round in the blood, gets into the lungs and causes the tissues to collapse, death is certain, I would say in about one or two minutes."

Football agreed with this, then turning to Marcel, he said, "How you know, massah?"

"I have seen this used before, Football, a few years ago." He looked around, his eyebrows raised.

Here was a fine kettle of fish, John thought to himself. Here we are all mixed-up in death, murders, plots and the like and goodness knows what else may come! Previous to his coming out to Africa, he had never envisaged anything of this nature at all, if he had they would have been considered totally unacceptable. Now, it was all too relevant but seemed to be the only solution to their current problems. Looking around the table he asked for any further comments.

Marcel said, "I can't condone murder but if we can do it without arousing any suspicion, then I'd say, go ahead."

"There is the other way, massah, also," said Football.

The eyes turned to him again and waited for the explanation.

"Long befoah de white man come," he said, "de men use de bow and de arrows and on dem dey put dis poison."

"Sounds like an ideal solution," said Dave.

Tony raised his eyebrows.

Marcel nodded his head as he obviously understood.

John thought about all of this, then spoke. "Let's not get too carried away by it all. I suggest that we sleep on it for a night and then if we're still in the same frame of mind, we will go ahead with it, agreed?" They all looked at each other, no-one spoke, so John interrupted their train of thought, and said, "Tomorrow then."

At this point they abandoned the discussion and all trooped out to their duties. After they had gone, John spoke with Klaus on the steps of his office, "That is, if nothing else happens in the meantime!"

The following morning Klaus met John outside his office and said to him, "Well then, John, what is it to be?"

"I agree with what we discussed, yesterday."

"Gut! That is what I expected to hear, if we delay there could be more trouble, that I know for sure!"

"Yes, I agree, let's get it organised then, Klaus, you go and see Football and make the arrangements."

Volunteers from each of the shifts were recruited and they set off into the bush to locate the plant that produced the poison, and after a few hours they returned with a huge bunch of leaves. Marcel surveyed it, and thought to himself that there was enough here to kill an army. The men started a fire, erected a tripod over it and placed the leaves in a large metal pot suspended over the flames, adding water to the leaves as it heated. They gradually added more leaves as it steamed and gave it an occasional stir with a stick. An unpleasant odour crept out of it and filled their nostrils.

Once this pungent smell had occurred, they compressed the leaves and allowed the brew to ferment for some time, before straining the liquid which by now was white and sticky. They poured it out of the bowl into a narrow necked jar and plugged it with a stopper made from the bark of a tree.

Klaus had been watching this process. "Is that it, then?" he asked Football.

"Yes, massah! Is enough! Very potent, needs only a little to work!"

"Why did we make so much, then?"

Football grinned, and said, "We keep for another time, eh?" and grinned widely.

Knowing how devious Football could be, Klaus just nodded without adding any further comment. He thought about this for a moment then turning to him, he asked, "How does it work, then, Football?"

"We take de short arrow," and he picked one up from a pile of them on the ground, "we dip de point into it, den fire it, it is easy! When it hits de man he will feel nothing but after a short time," and he hesitated to find an explanation for Klaus, he continued, "is about the time of a bird's call, de man, he became weak, and fall to de groun', death follow plenty quick! You understand, massah?"

"Yes, I understand. I hope it works well, Football!"

"It will, massah, this I knows!" and he spoke in a tone of conviction.

"Maybe it will be tonight, Football, maybe tomorrow."

"Okay, massah, we wait, we will be ready," and he went off with the men, the poison and the arrows to the accommodation area. Klaus returned to John's office to tell him that the preparations had been made, the men, vehicles, arms, radios, poison and anything else that was necessary.

"Thanks, Klaus."

"Better be ready for tonight, I think," said Klaus.

"Right, I will be," said John, and continued his writing.

That night Football had his men ready and the shift change had taken place as the sun set. They waited patiently with the trackers accompanying them. It was nine-thirty when Klaus received an urgent call on the radio. John, Tony and Dave had heard it also.

"Trouble down at the accommodation!" shouted Klaus as he raced across to his Land Rover. They all scrambled aboard and set off rapidly down the hill, Klaus driving as if he was taking part in the Grand Prix, the remainder of them hanging on for dear life as they swayed and rocked as the vehicle flew over the indentations in the road and swung off on to the track leading to the accommodation. They arrived to find that someone had broken into the sleeping huts in the darkness and had kidnapped some of the workers in their sleep, and they had been carried off into the night. On the doors of the two huts concerned, a spear was stuck, penetrating the wood. Football crossed over and pulled them out, and looked at them in the light of a torch. He studied the engraving on the shaft carefully and the long bird's feathers that were attached to them.

"Is from Nupe! But not from here, is from tribe further away up in de hills."

"Well, it doesn't matter, Football, let's get after them!" cried Tony, and set off toward the bush. They cocked their rifles and not waiting for anyone, they quickly entered the bush and fanned out. The trackers went on, and even in the dark they could discern the tracks as they loped along bent low with the rest of them following on behind.

"How can they see the tracks in this light?" asked John, "I can hardly see my feet, never mind anything else!"

"These men know their stuff," called Tony from close by.

They advanced, Football called to them that the men had gone in a certain direction and they wheeled towards it. As they approached the side of a rock escarpment Football spoke, "De men go this way!" and then they halted as the trackers backtracked slightly and studied the ground again.

"De trackers say dat der is ten men, maybe twelve, all gone ahead, and dey are running."

"Right, let's get going then," said Klaus. "We must catch them at all costs!"

Now they were out of sight of the dam and deep within the trees and long grasses. They sped along brushing through the undergrowth on the run then the trackers stopped suddenly.

"What is it?" asked Klaus, drawing up short behind Football.

"Men up ahead, not far," he whispered. "De trackers heah de voices!"

They continued on now, slowly and crouched low, taking great care as to where they placed their feet. The slightest sound made by stepping on a dry branch would betray their presence. Football indicated a halt and they stood still, listening for the slightest sound. On the breeze faint voices could be heard just ahead of them. They advanced crouched low and keeping back from the trackers who were on their bellies on the ground. Suddenly a cry of pain was heard cutting through the silence. Football pointed directly ahead and they detoured around a large black rock which brought them into sight of a clearing in the trees.

In the faint moonlight figures could be seen, most were dressed in leopard skins, the heads of which were on the tops of their heads. The eyes glowed bright in the darkness, yellow in colour. Their bodies were daubed with strange symbols giving them an awesome appearance, and on their feet each wore a dark skin and from them protruded long white curved claws.

"It is the Leopard Men!" whispered Klaus.

Footballs eyes opened wide as he stared at them, then said, "Yes, massah! Dat is dem!"

Against the trees four men had been tied individually to them. Klaus noted that the trackers description of the number of them had been correct. The men were bound and had been stripped of their clothing, their black skins shining in the moonlight. At the front of the group a large man was prominent.

Football pointed and whispered, "That is Stovepipe!"

Klaus nodded. They remained crouched down and watched the proceedings. Those dressed in the skins then started a ritual dance during which a ghostly white skull on a pole was waved around the head of each man in turn. The men danced in a circle, stopping every now and then to recite a chant. Then a spear was thrown at each of the men, none striking them but coming perilously close to their heads. Those tied up were speechless but their faces displayed a look of abject horror as the weird dance progressed. The chanting stopped and silence fell upon them all. Stovepipe's deep loud voice was then heard.

"What's he saying?" asked Tony.

Football listened for a while, then whispered, "He is offering de souls of de victims to de Leopard Men, they is going to execute dem!"

"Are your men ready?" he asked Football.

"Yes massah! We ready!" and Football signalled with his arm.

The men with the bows and arrows took out the jar and, unstopping it, they each dipped the heads of the arrows into the neck of the bottle and placed the arrows on the bowstrings in readiness.

From amid the dancers one of the men walked towards the intended victims and picked up a long machete. He looked up to the moon and spoke some strange words. Then he walked forwards and stood in front of the four trees. He raised his arm ready to strike at the first man. Klaus had his rifle sights trained on the man and was ready to shoot if necessary. Football gave the signal to wait.

The man advanced towards the first man and slowly but deliberately he drew the blade of it across his chest, causing the incision to spill blood on to the earth. He repeated this on the other three men, the incisions diagonal from shoulder to waist. The blood spilled out angrily and two of the men shrieked in pain or fear. Then each member of the group stepped forward and in turn they cupped their hands at their waists to catch the blood and drank of it. They then held their hands up to the moon and repeated the chant. Each having done this, they stepped over to the men and picked up their spears. They glinted in the moonlight, and on a command from Stovepipe, they drew their arms back and prepared to hurl them at the victims. Stovepipe stepped forwards and glaring at the four men, he uttered something unintelligible at them. The men slowly pulled their arms fully back.

At this point Football waved to his men. Their bows strung and their arrows laid out on a flat rock beside them, the heads of the arrows overhanging the rock to avoid accidental contact with them. They each took aim. Stovepipe's voice had given the order, and as the spears moved forward, the quarrels of the bowmen sped silently through the air towards the spear throwers. No sound was heard as they found their targets, each man toppling over onto his face as the arrows penetrated their bodies, some carrying on through and emerging at the other side.

Each of the men had halted in mid-delivery of their spear thrusts and toppled over, seemingly in slow motion, as the sharp arrows penetrated their chests. The remainding Leopard Men spun around to see where the attack had come from, then began furtively looking around for the source. The other missiles were unleashed and they sped across the short distance and thudded home. The men fell where they stood. The one aimed at Stovepipe bounced off his collarbone and penetrated his neck, going in at one side and out at the other. He pitched forwards, keeled over and fell to his knees, frantically clutching at his neck and the protruding arrow. The blood oozed over his hands, his eyes rolled as the whites of his eyes shone in the moonlight.

Klaus burst out of his cover and before anyone realised it he was half way across the clearing. His hand dropped to the safety catch as he ran, he flicked it to the off position. Stovepipe was still on his knees, his face towards the tied up victims, who looked on in shock at what was happening before them. Their would be executors fell as if cut by the swathe of a scythe. Klaus reached Stovepipe and standing to face him, he levelled the muzzle of the automatic rifle at his head. He looked directly into the face of the man and it was only then that Stovepipe recognised who he was. Without waiting for a cue he pressed the trigger home and held it down. The volley of shots shattered the extreme silence of the night and the flashes of the blinding light from the muzzle lit up the ground. Stovepipe's face instantly disappeared in a scattering of flesh and bone as the bullets tore into him, bits flying off all around. Klaus kept his finger on the trigger until the total magazine was empty when the firing ceased. The corpse lay on the ground the head blown apart, the jaw bone lay at an acute angle. Klaus stepped forward and kicked the leopard skin from his body and with the butt of the rifle he ferociously mixed what remained of Stovepipe's head into pulp. Everyone sprang forward. Less than half a minute had passed since the first arrow had flown. The men at the trees were quickly freed and Marcel was in immediate attendance, gave the men pain killing injections and had carried out some neat sewing up of the incisions.

John crossed over to where Klaus stood by the now dead body of Stovepipe, and looking down at what was left of his head, he said, "Christ, Klaus! That's a bit on the heavy side, isn't it?"

Klaus looked at his still smoking weapon and turning towards John, he replied, "No! he deserved it," and after a fleeting thought, he added, "every bit of it!"

John did not reply but had to turn away as the scene made him feel violently sick.

Tony came over and briefly glancing at the remains, commented, "Nice one, Klaus!"

Football and his men were busy making temporary stretchers out of branches for the wounded men, and surveying the bodies lying on the ground, he commented, "Good poison, massahs!" and grinned widely.

Marcel came up to look at the remains of Stovepipe but only cast a passing glimpse at him as John said, "What do we do with this lot now?"

"I will take them all up top," said Marcel.

At this point, Football, who was standing at the side of the group spoke. "No need, massah, we have a way of getting rid of the bodies." No-one knew just what exactly Football meant by that comment, but after a brief pause, they decided to let them attend to it.

Shortly afterwards, they all left the clearing with the men on the stretchers and retraced their steps through the bush to the accommodation area. Marcel went on ahead to prepare his ward in the clinic for the men. The trackers and the bowmen however, had raced ahead and had spread the news. This was disseminated and like wildfire it spread to the workers, even to those on the work face. All were in a jubilant mood and the only subject of conversation for the following days was the killing of the Leopard Men. Some of it was embroidered upon and gradually, over a period of time, it grew into a sort of legend. It had spread to the surrounding villages and any of the workers who visited them were warmly welcomed by the villagers.

Next day when John and Klaus had gone about their normal day's walkabout all the men who were working stopped as they approached and applauded them. Afterwards John was sitting at his desk, writing up the report of the incident when he stopped in mid-sentence. He could clearly hear the sound of singing again, and putting down his pen, he went out and crossed over to the roadside. He gave Klaus a shout, and he came over to see what it was that John wanted.

"Hear that?"

"A good sign, and a good omen, too," said Klaus.

Football had taken a truck down to the spot where the grisly event had occurred and removed the bodies. The ants had by now invaded them and they had already started to decompose in the sun, but they gathered up the putrid remains and took them up to the construction site. Later that morning they were to be pouring concrete and as the mix was being prepared, the bodies were hacked up into pieces and poured into the large moulds with the mix. Once the mix had set there was no sign of them. The men that were involved were sworn to secrecy but they themselves thought that it was a fitting end to the Leopard Men.

Later Klaus asked Football if he had buried the bodies.

"Yes massah! We bury them good! They is deep down in de ground, no more problems with these men!"

"Good!" said Klaus, but never did he ever find out about the method of disposal.

The main road, one of the various access roads, had been formed and even at this early stage, a surface had been laid and a length of it was already in use. News of the delivery of the turbines was received and Klaus had made preparations for their receipt and storage down town, adjacent to the first aid hut. An installation team was also due out and Klaus had his work cut out for him with the numerous preparations.

Tony and Fred were still busy with the hammerhead excavations and preliminary work had commenced up high on the framework for the hammerheads themselves, at the curvature points.

Marcel had sent the four men back to work after some three weeks in the clinic and, surprisingly enough, their wounds had healed quickly. Now they sported the long diagonal scars on their chests but this took on a new meaning to them. They grew in importance as the men who defied the Leopard Men and they were treated as heroes amongst the workers. At Marcel's request Football had given him a sample of the poison used on the night and he analysed it that night, he was amazed at the lethal content of it which had given him food for thought from a medical point of view. This was something entirely new for him and he sat down to work out the effects of this toxin on the human body.

The end of the year was almost upon them and John realised that the time had flown since first he arrived here, the annual report was due. So he set to collecting up the various information and facts that would support it, referring to his copious notes made as he had observed items on his inspections.

The height of the sheer face of the dam was now apparent by the lattice work of scaffolding that followed the curve across the valley and protruded upwards, it seemed, into the sky. Owing to all the recent events there had not been a social night for some time so it was mooted one take place. They drew straws to see whose house would be the venue, and again it came out as John's. Eb got out the big table again and after he had heard that he was to host it, John commented that it must be a fix to which he received the reply, "The only house big enough to hold us all, what better!"

For Christmas it was decided that the work would be scaled down and eventually stopped, thus allowing all of the workers to travel to their villages for the Christmas festivities. As the work was well ahead of schedule they could afford to have a stoppage and so it was arranged. The social evening was held six days before Christmas Day and was a roaring success. John had all the supervisors attend as well, and Nat and Eb had conjured up a veritable feast of food for them. The native supervisors were amazed at this sea of food and the look on their faces was not to be forgotten. Naturally the conversation turned to the Leopard Men and according to Eb, the news had carried, 'like the bush telegraph' he said, and relations of relations had spread it much further than John at first had thought. Even the truck drivers from the south of the country had heard of it and so the story had spread far and wide. During the course of the evening John had asked Klaus how he came to be so handy as he put it, with his automatic rifle.

"Ah!" he replied, "it is the military training, John. It comes in handy every now and then."

"Yes Klaus, but you must admit that you fired a few more rounds than was necessary at the time!"

"Perhaps, but I just wanted to make sure that we would not be bothered by him again."

The food and drink was consumed only to be quickly replenished again by Nat who must have been cooking for about a week, thought John, as the empty plates were quickly replaced with full ones. The beer and the wine that they had got in added to the overall merriment, and the celebration, as it turned out to be, for the dispatch of the Leopard Men, went on and on. Eventually they decided to call a halt as by now it was almost four in the morning. Needless to say the following day was a write off as far as the management team was concerned.

But Football and Klaus had gone down town and had assured themselves that the work was still progressing. This event had brought on a sort of holiday atmosphere and those villagers who did not want to travel the long journeys to their homes, organised celebrations of their own down in their camp. Everybody was happy and John was able to sit back, having written his yearly report, and heave a sigh of satisfaction.

Christmas week came around, although it hardly seemed like it with the sun still streaming down each day, a warm breeze accompanying it. All over the country relatives travelled to the far corners to see their families at this time of year, some would trek for hundreds of miles even if it meant that they would only be at their homes for a day. Marathon taxi journeys were made, some of the men only arriving on Christmas Day itself.

Chapter Seven

After a week of respite, the time came around for the resumption of work. Only a few days remained of the current year but by the first day of January all the men would be back at work, the odd one or two taking slightly longer from those villages that were far afield.

The access roads were now progressing at a fast rate and the supply vehicles no longer had to make a detour around the jungle, but instead took the shorter route on the temporary road which was less than half a mile downstream. This had not been welcomed by those living in the nearby village but once they realised that they could now secure passing trade, numerous enterprising members of the people there had set up stalls and were doing a steady trade in the selling of fruit and chilled drinks, and the fresh fish from the river was now smoked in quantities and sold by the wayside. Many of the truck drivers stopped to buy and day by day the income of those that lived there went up.

To Klaus's and John's surprise all the men had returned from their homes on time. They had expected Football to notify some absences but he had said that all were here. Football commented that this was a good omen and that it showed they had confidence in their leadership. This man is more educated than I first thought, said John to himself.

The 'big ugly rock' that Stovepipe had referred to was now visible for some distance from downstream and the villagers there could see it rising high above the trees. The scaffolding was now densely populated with a mass of busy men. Numerous lifts, ramps and walkways had been temporarily erected, and a conveyor system for the large quantities of concrete had been put in place, the mix was now conveyed to the point where it was required by a moving bucket system. The pinning of the large steel reinforcing plates had started to give strength to the concrete sections, Tony and Klaus had been busy with their calculations and the measures they would have to take to allow for the effects of any earth tremor that may, or may not occur, this enabled them to arrive at a final figure for the stress factor.

Marcel had an easier life now that the number of injuries had fallen following the issue of the safety equipment and he had frequent helpings of laughter when he discovered that some of the workers, the less intelligent ones, wore their equipment while sleeping. Somehow the vividly coloured vests had taken on a new meaning, men slept with their boots and hats on and even wore them when eating their meals. It was not uncommon, therefore, to see rows of safety helmets at the tables as the men supped.

Bombay had taken on more cooks and the smell of roasting meat hung on the wind. John could smell it from his house and sometimes it was more appetising than what he was served with. He could not fault the cooking of his two servants, however, and he was surprised to see so many what he called traditional dishes, appear on the table in front of him. The fact that the leftovers disappeared the same night as Eb and Nat left did not worry him in the slightest.

Down at the nearby village, John had heard through Eb that there was quite a few of the people there who were sick so he had asked Marcel to go down and see what he could do for them. Marcel now spent more of his time there, and had become a welcome figure in the surrounding area. His knowledge of the tropical diseases had come to the fore and his services were now in even greater demand. A number of cases of leprosy were in evidence but all were treatable. He was also kept busy with numerous pregnancies which took up more of his time, and immunisations for the workers led to the same service for the villagers. This was in addition to the voluntary services who had included health issues in their farming projects. The spread of Christianity was a lesser goal but that was left to the missionaries. Marcel had found that the local remedies for some illnesses were very effective, and he had made careful note of them and the preparations used, the plants they were derived from and other salient details.

The Bororoje came and went as regular as clockwork, they could almost set the calendar by them, perhaps a day or two either way, but they always appeared when expected. Julius Berger's men had taken their movements into consideration so that when they came along work ceased temporarily and resumed as soon as they had passed by.

A number of breakdowns had occurred on some of the trucks and the mechanics had a busy time repairing them. It appeared to stem from contaminated fuel, and the problems continued. Klaus had started to take an interest in the number of occurrences and had traced it back to certain deliveries, after a further period he had arrived at dates which were significant. The fuel was one of a batch of regular deliveries which were sub-contracted out and it was not in the least surprising to find difficulty in tracing the supplier. He and Football decided to go and seek out the suppliers and they set off in a Land Rover. Their investigations led them to one man and obtaining directions as to where he was located, they set out to find him. They arrived at the address they had been given and pulled up outside of the mud brick hut. He, however, was not there and enquiring of two youths who loafed nearby, they indicated that he could be found in the local bar. They sought it out and entered, looking around as they did so and it took a few moments to locate him as the light within was dim to say the least. He was squatting on the ground in the company of others and they were engaged in the traditional African game of moving a number of beads from one hole to another and then, in a complicated sequence, into others. As they approached, the game stopped. The man got up and the three of them moved over to a rickety table and sat down on the equally rickety chairs that were scattered about. Football questioned the man in his own dialect as to the source of the contaminated fuel, the answer to which was a shrug of the shoulders. He was only the middleman, he explained, the fuel was collected some twenty miles away and taken by tanker from a large underground tank.

After a brief conversation they elicited the location of the place and drove off to find it. After a short search they came across it, being evident by a stream of tankers going in and out of the gates. They went in and over to the boy who was in charge of the loading and asked for the boss. He pointed a finger at the hut at the side of the compound. There, Klaus and Football found an old man, grey-haired and wizened, who looked as though he might die at any moment, so frail was his appearance. Football spoke to him and told him that they were not going to buy any more fuel from him as it was contaminated. To this there was no reply, only a far away look from the man's empty eyes, resigned to the fact that he had lost a customer.

"Come on Football! Let's go!" said Klaus, and led the way out.

"Where we get de fuel from now, massah?" Football asked.

"We'll go and see Julius Berger and buy our fuel from them, that way we will be guaranteed that it will be clean and on time."

"Okay, massah," Football replied, grinning.

They drove back towards the dam and as they came to the new access road, they branched off and went into the Berger camp. On the way they passed a long line of schoolchildren, walking along the roadside in single file, each chewing a length of sugar beet about a foot long, this being vital to their diet and a daily habit for most of them. Moving along the road were a long line of trucks on the back of which were painted the more common variety of sayings. 'No Singing, No Dancing', another, 'No man is an Island', and the most thought-provoking one declared, 'Man who is always right is in danger'. The trucks themselves leant over at crazy angles owing to their unbalanced loads and they had noted a number of them capsized along the roadside at the numerous sharp bends. They sought out the Construction Manager and after a brief conversation, they obtained the undertaking to supply the fuel by tanker. This achieved, they returned to the site and informed John of the arrangement. Dave was pleased as he had been fed up with the drivers continually complaining about the shortages and the contaminated fuel.

That evening after the shift change, all was quiet save for the noise of the machinery operating down below as the night shift commenced their routine. The noise drifted up on the thermal currents, the warm breeze wafting up from the valley floor. John sat eating, the window wide open to catch the breeze when Ebenezer came rushing in shouting, "Come quick, massah! Big fire in de bush!"

John leapt out of his chair, grabbed the radio and ran towards his Land Rover. As he crossed to it, he could smell the acrid smoke on the wind. He called Klaus but he was also alerted to it and had already passed a message to sound the klaxon, whose strident notes could now be heard shattering the silence. The off-duty workers had come running and were climbing into the trucks as they gunned the engines and made for the road that led up to the storage area. In order that he could ascertain where the fire was, John proceeded uphill to a point where he could see out over the valley. A rapidly advancing wall of flame was evident on both sides and had spilled down to the valley floor itself. Numerous beams of light stabbed the darkness as the vehicles headed for the fires, the smoke now dense in places. John reached for his radio and called Klaus. "Chief! You there?"

"Yah, Kingpin! I'm up here on the east side. Big fire! Advancing rapidly. Difficult to see where it is going, but it's got quite a hold."

"Have you got any beaters, there?"

"Yah! I have thirty or so, there are more on the way."

"Okay, Klaus, stay with it, I'll see what I can do from this side."

"Rock is on the west side, Football is down below, and Doc is in the clinic."

"Good! Call me on the radio if there is any change."

"Roger."

"Boxer, Boxer! Where are you?"

There was a short delay, then Dave replied, "Up on the east side! Higher than Klaus, it has now split into three parts. I need some more beaters up here." A few seconds later he called again, "The main front is approaching fast. It is near to the fence of the storage compound! I'm worried about the fuel, John!"

"Roger, Dave. Sparks from Kingpin."

"Sparks, here! Okay, John! I got all of that, I'm on my way over to Dave with a truckload of men. I'll be there in a couple of minutes."

"Roger, Sparks, make it as quick as you can."

John did not wait for a reply but headed off to the point where the road ran close to the storage compound. He drove as fast as he could, breaking through the ranks of smoke which by now were advancing upwards at a fast rate and as he got closer he could feel the heat on his skin. He drove in through the now open gates of the compound and screeched to a halt, leaping out of his wagon and sprinted over to the fence passing the hose reels, now run out, that were being applied to the nearest flames. The huge water tank which towered above him was lit up, its huge size casting a dancing shadow on the ground behind him. He passed through the access gate and into the bush behind the compound where he could see men silhouetted against the ground as they struggled to contain the fire. The men were beating towards it, knocking out fresh pockets of flame and advancing towards it as best as they could. There seemed to be little wind which was a blessing, however, that did not seem to deter the flames as they leapt as if by magic, over to the dry pockets of grass and spread the flames in new areas as fast as they could extinguish them. With a loud swooshing noise, an area erupted into flame drawing with it clouds of dust which coloured the smoke as it reached to the sky. The loud noise of the crackling drowned out their voices and it was difficult to make others understand what was happening. He worked his way around the groups of beaters and made his way towards Dave who was busy beating a bush into submission. A moment later a shout went up as Matthew and his men arrived upon the scene. They sprang into action and with a renewed effort, they managed to hold the line and gradually drive it back towards the jungle. They had now broken the line of fire and they had set to digging a trench to provide a gap where it could not cross.

A burning palm frond spiralled upwards and fell into an unaffected area but the beaters had spotted it and quickly extinguished the flame. Within moments fresh outbreaks occurred and they had to redouble their efforts.

"Fiah at de fence!" a voice called out, and all looked immediately at that area. They wheeled about and moved backwards to tackle this but it was now out of control and, fanned by its own wind, it flared again close to the fence.

The sound of a horn blowing attracted their attention as Klaus appeared and grabbing a beater he applied himself to the task, "All under control on the east side, John!" he shouted.

"Get some more men over here, Klaus!" John called.

"Yah! Okay!" and grabbing his radio he called and shouted into it. The trench that they had dug was of little use as the fire had now jumped behind it, and the two pockets of flame had now become three. Men broke off to tackle this as it licked around the fence and had threatened to jump the fence itself and enter the storage compound.

With a superhuman effort they drove it backwards about eight yards or so and forced the flames back towards the bushes. Another clump of elephant grass went up with a swoosh and blackened pieces of it fell to the ground and rained down upon them. Lizards in their dozens scuttled for cover over the feet of the firefighters but the men heeded them not. Ghostly shadows could be seen in the dense smoke and by now all men looked the same, blackened by the smoke.

John grabbed for his radio and called, "Rock! Come in!"

"Rock, here! Fire under control on my side. I'll work my way over to you and attack it from the other flank."

"Roger."

They were winning now and able to move forwards. Still the flames made jumps here and there but they contained it. It had now spread sideways and thinned out but had extended the line again. A full hour had now passed and the men fought doggedly on as Rock's contingent of men arrived. They stopped, formed a circle and advanced and now they were gaining the upper hand, advancing inwards, bringing it under control. Eventually they mastered it, and after a further half hour they had extinguished it, although smoke still billowed up into the sky. John looked around, on either side the jungle had now disappeared and all that remained were blackened stumps of trees and numerous patches of scorched grass. They continued their efforts for a further half hour lest the fire rekindle itself and when they felt it was safe, they stopped and sank to the ground exhausted, catching their breath and clearing their lungs of the smoke that had invaded them.

"Any injuries?" John called out.

A few had minor burns and scrapes but that was all, luck having played an important part in their efforts. A party was formed and they went off to check on any sporadic pockets, but returned soon after to report that all was well.

"Phew! That was close, John." commented Dave as he crossed over to where John stood.

"Yes! Not the sort of thing I'd recommend for after dinner!"

"A gut effort all round!" commented Klaus, "I think we should suspend work tomorrow and let the men have a rest."

John thought for a moment, then agreed and called to Football who was about two hundred yards away and informed him of the decision. He in turn passed it on to the men. Shortly afterwards the men wearily climbed into the trucks and when they were fully loaded, they snaked their way back down town to the accommodation and a well-earned rest.

Klaus told one of the men to go up to the top and look out over the valley to ensure that no other fires remained. He was not gone long when he returned to report that all was normal. This being so, they called it a night and went their respective ways.

John made his way to his house where he was met by Eb and Nat at the doorway.

"Is de fires out now, massah?" they chorused, a note of concern in their voices.

"Yes. All out now," said John.

Suddenly Eb burst out laughing.

"What are you laughing at, Eb?"

"Is you, massah. You is jus' like de rest of us now!"

John looked down at himself and quickly caught on as to what Eb meant. He was indeed black all over and as he grinned at this, his teeth shone in the light.

Nat grinned and said, "So! Who is de massah now, eh?"

They all laughed as John went upstairs to have a shower, and as he did so he heard Nat say, "I go and put de coffee on foh de new black man!" and he could clearly hear Eb laughing at the statement. He returned downstairs and took the proffered coffee and sat down.

"Was it big fire, massah?"

"Yes, Eb, it took a long time to get it under control."

Nat thought for a moment, then said. "We has de big fiah like this many years ago, but it was deep in de bush and many people die in de villages!"

"Yes!" added Eb, "I remembers it, was maybe fifteen yeahs ago."

John got up and went over to his desk, and while everything was still fresh in his mind, he wrote his report, then went upstairs to bed.

As he went up the stairs, Eb commented upon how beautiful he looked and he smiled and said, "Maybe I change de name to Sambo, eh?"

"Good night then, Sambo!" the two of them chorused.

He awoke in the morning to the sound of Klaus's wagon pulling up outside, and he heard Eb call out, "De massah Klaus is heah!"

He had slept soundly even through the cocks crow from nearby. Klaus entered and they discussed the nights events. The fire breaks would have to be extended and widened, they would move the high value items away from the fence and also relocate the bulk storage tanks for the fuel. As the men had been given the day off he decided that he needed a break and earlier they had decided that at some time they would pay a visit to the falls at Minnah. He said to Klaus that he would be up to the site shortly and Klaus departed to see to some of his paperwork. When Klaus had gone he turned to Eb and said, "You two are to take the day off."

"But what about de breakfast, massah?"

"That's okay, I will see to the breakfast myself."

"You shoah, massah?"

"Yes, everyone else has the day off, so you two must as well, okay?"

"Yes, massah," they replied and without further ado they left closing the door quietly as they went.

John went into the kitchen to cook the breakfast. He put the frying pan on the stove and with the practised art of breaking three eggs into the pan, he cooked them then added the bacon. Some years ago, a friend of his who was a chef, had shown him some tricks of the trade which he had not forgotten. He brewed up some strong black coffee and picking up a knife and a fork from the dish rack, he carried the plate and the mug through to the table and sat down to eat. Seeing that it was quite a bright day outside, he transferred himself to the table on the veranda. A snake which had been basking in the morning sun moved as he sat down and raised its head as he came into view. It stared at John and he stared back at it. He moved his arm quickly and the reptile on seeing this, silently but quickly slithered off under the veranda to search for some tasty morsels. John ate, taking a swig of the coffee, then went back indoors and locked up.

He crossed to the Land Rover, dusted off the seat and set off along the road, the gear stick rasping in his hand as he changed upwards through the box and headed for Dave's residence. Eight minutes later he turned off the road and made for the house, the grasses scraping against the side of the vehicle as he approached it. He sounded the horn. A young black boy was busily engaged in beating a well-worn rug to death and he looked up from the flailing and in mid-swipe he called out, "Visitor come, Massah Dave!"

Dave stuck his head out of the window to see who it was and raised an arm in recognition, then moved over to the door and emerged into the sunlight.

"Hi, John! What brings you up here at this time of morning?"

"Remember that trip we spoke of some time ago? To the falls at Minnah?"

"Yes?"

"Fancy it for today, then?"

"Well, yes, now that you come to mention it, come in while I get dressed, it will only take a few minutes."

He reappeared and said that he would give Fred a call as well, and reaching for his radio, he spoke into it. Fred replied almost at once, and on hearing the venue, agreed to come along.

"When?" he asked.

"Well, now."

"Roger! Be down in five minutes!" he said, and the radio fell silent.

Dave looked out of the window and called to the servant, "William!"

William stopped beating the rug and in the cloud of dust he replied, "Yes, massah," and crossed over to the house.

"I'll give Doc a call as well," said Dave. Doc replied in the affirmative and said he would be there shortly. They waited for the two to arrive while William had gone into the kitchen to make some sandwiches and he was busy sawing away at the bread as he constructed them carefully.

"Do enough for us all, William!" Dave called out.

"Yes massah! I do de big ones! Plenty of bush meats in them!" and he stuck his head around the corner of the door and grinned widely.

"Never mind the bush meat, just make them edible!"

"Yes massah! I makes!"

"We'd better check them before we leave," said Dave, "he'll put anything in them!"

John laughed at that.

"He's good though," said Dave, "but it is very difficult to have a serious conversation with him though, he makes a fool out of everything."

Dave applied a pair of battered sandals to his feet and adjusted the well worn leather straps, unslung his camera from the hook on the wall and checked the film remaining. The sound of a vehicle pulling up outside attracted their attention and they looked out.

"That'll be Fred," said Dave, just as he appeared in the door frame and entered saying,

"Okay, peoples! Let's go!"

"So! You're a bright spark as well, eh?" asked Dave, "you weren't so bright when I called you up a short time ago."

"Yes! But you see I am alive and well now and I'm ready for the off!"

As he got no instant reply from this statement, he looked at the two of them.

"We'll be ready in a minuet, or a waltz, whichever is the quicker," said Dave, "Doc is coming as well, he should be along soon."

"Ah! A foursome then? Whose wagon are we going in then?"

"Mine," replied Dave, "we'll leave the others here."

William drifted in from the kitchen and produced the large parcel of sandwiches all wrapped up, and commenting, "Heah is de bush meat, boss, which you odah!"

"Thanks, William, we'll be away for most of the day, be back about sundown."

"Yes, massah. Okay, massah, I has de big party! I invites all of de village down, we drinks de booze, smashes all de furnitures and de crocks!"

"Okay, William, you do just that, but tidy up before we return, okay?"

"Yes massah! I does that," and he grinned as he said it. They all laughed and made for the doorway.

"Nut case, he is," commented Fred as they went out.

A horn sounded and Doc's Land Rover appeared around the bend and came to a halt.

"Well, messieurs! Are we all ready?"

"Let's go then," said Dave, and led the way round the comer of his house to his wagon. They all climbed aboard as Dave called back to William, "We are off now! You can go back to sleep!"

William smiled and gave them a wave from the window and as they pulled away, he ran out of the door and holding a handkerchief to his eyes he pretended to wipe the tears from his eyes. They all laughed at this and Dave shook his head as they turned on to the road.

"I reckon that it will take us about two hours to get there," said Dave. "I'll go by Mogwa, Akerre and Zungeru, it'll be quicker."

They went off downhill and followed the lopsided sign for Mogwa which skirted the Naja hill. There was little traffic on the road at this time of day, and they made good progress.

They were entertained by the 'no sayings' again and they pointed them out as they went along, most of them painted in flowery writing. 'Be careful! Many have gone before!', read one, and another 'No man is an island'. They came upon a truck packed to the gunwales with bush cows, their long pointed horns protruding over the edges and giving the truck the appearance of a forest of horns on wheels. On this one the saying was 'He who endures will win!'

They continued on, the hot wind flowing through the window and out of the rear of the wagon. They passed by a file of women with basins of cooled goats milk on their way to the market. The younger girls clad only in a cloth around their waists, beamed widely as they passed by. Dave gave them a wave and they waved back in return. They had now reached the centre of Mogwa itself where life was in its daily routine. Groups of people stood around talking, women pounded yams and a boy with two chickens tied together at the feet, held them up for passers by to see, calling out that they were for sale. An old man stepped wearily along resting every few yards on his staff, his eyes following the white man's wagon as it passed by. They branched off at a side road to Bokani and then followed the old road which was uneven and bumpy, and wound left and right as they crossed a low lying area and continued on to Akeffe. Here, sections of cheaply laid tarmac were interspersed with long patches of hard packed sand, uneven and dotted indiscriminately with well worn potholes. The suspension took a hammering as the vehicle twisted and bucked as they negotiated the hazards. Here and there the road had completely disappeared and a roughly hewn track through the bush had to be negotiated with care before they came upon the remains of the road again. A number of crossings of small streams was necessary, most of them being six or eight feet below the level of the road, and when this occurred water lapped in at the bottom of the doors, leaving the floor of the Land Rover swimming. A few crudely designed concrete bridges which were barely wide enough for any vehicle to pass over, provided flimsy support and as they crossed these nothing could be seen on either side, the margin of error being minimal. Below them they could see many wrecked cars that had fallen prey to these narrow crossings in the hours of darkness. Around the next corner a truck which had been fully laden with mangoes had toppled over in the middle of the road, and a crowd of local people were busily engaged in filling their baskets with the fruit, this being the custom, otherwise the fruit would have lain and rotted there. Streams of bodies were in evidence and soon the load would be completely removed. John smiled to himself as he viewed the event. You had to give these people ten out of ten for initiative, he thought. Now they had arrived at Kutewenji where they stopped at the roadside for some cool drinks. As they sat drinking them they were surrounded by a group of people, most of them children, all hawking their wares and shouting in order to attract their attention, and to outdo their opponents.

"Chocolate, massahs!" "Fresh orange! Very juicy!" "Big grapefruit, verrah cheap!" They declined all of these offers, which of course did not deter the sellers. They continued with the cries of, "Boiled eggs! Still hot, massahs!"

Dave and Fred called them over and a boy forced his way with difficulty to the front, and lowered the tray so that they could inspect them.

"Are these fresh?" Dave asked, picking a few of them up in his hand.

"Yes, massah! All fresh, I just squeeze dem out of de hen a few minutes!" he replied. They all laughed at this and the boy grinned.

"How much then?" asked Fred.

"Foah for eighty kobo, massah!" the boy replied.

"Sounds like a decent price," commented Dave. "We'll have some of them then."

"How many you want?" asked the boy.

"Sixteen," replied Fred.

The boy's eyes opened wide in amazement and with a "Yes massah!", he quickly counted out the amount and handed them over the heads of the others and through the window. Dave passed over the money and they waited for their change. The boy pushed forward and handed it to them, but Fred replied, "That's okay, you keep it!"

"Thank you, massah!" he replied, "God bless you, massah!"

Needless to say, the remainder of the crowd pressed forward, eager for a sale but when they realised that nothing else was forthcoming, they melted away to await the next arrival and an attempt to sell their wares. A truck pulled up at the petrol pump nearby and the sellers all rushed over towards it. As they drove off, John suggested that they get some fresh oranges as well and he called out to one of the girls there. She was, he reckoned, about four years of age, and although still young she knew her onions and was a shrewd bargainer. She lowered the tray of oranges that she balanced on her head. They picked twelve of them.

"How manys?" she asked.

"You know what twelve is?" John asked.

"Yes, massah! I knows!" she replied, "I'se go to school you know!" and she counted them out quickly, then repeated this for their satisfaction. John smiled at the comment.

"Okay, massahs, dat be ten niara!" she stated.

"What?" said Fred, "that's too dear!"

"You not gets them any fresher anywheres else!" she replied.

John having a soft spot for children, said, "Well, that sounds like a hard bargain to me, but okay, are you sure that they are fresh?"

"Yes, massah! You not hear me de first time? I tell you dey are plenty fresh!"

"Okay," said Dave, "but if dey not fresh, we come back!"

"You be okay, massah, dey is de freshest you gets heah!"

Fred handed over the money and she took it with a smile and handed the fruit over to them. She ran off over to the others holding up the ten niara note and boasting of the big sale she had made to de white mens. All heads of the sellers turned towards them and they craned their necks to see which of the white men had been fool enough to pay that money for the oranges. They pulled out on to the road again, as they did so Fred commented, "Mug of the week!"

They all grinned at this as they joined the traffic flow.

"It's peanuts to us," said Dave, "but a fortune to them."

"I just couldn't resist the smile on her face," said John "that alone was worth the ten niara."

They drove onwards, Doc commenting that now John had a friend for life. They negotiated the bends in the road as it swung alternatively left and right, then went downhill, and soon they had reached Akerre, crossing over the River Mariga as it flowed southwards to join the larger Kaduna which in turn would flow into the Niger itself further on at Muragi. Now, the quality of the road had improved having been recently repaired in places and tarmacked as well and they were able to increase their speed and soon afterwards they passed through Katanku and went onwards to Zungeru. They took the lower road to Baji as it had less traffic on it and continued onwards to Minnah itself. This was the largest town for some distance and was famous for its street lighting and had been a cosmopolitan centre of trade for many generations. They continued and proceeded along a newly constructed stretch of highway which went alongside the airstrip, which itself would soon disappear to be replaced by the new airport planned some years before.

They passed through the large city gate which towered above them, its pink marble slabs shining in the sunlight. There they joined the throng of vehicles that weaved in and out along the road, avoiding occasionally the huge pot holes. It was now akin to cross-country driving and they had to edge their may through the various types of transport that were on the road. There were buses, bush taxis, carts pulled by donkeys, motorbikes, men on foot and the odd dilapidated bicycle here and there, this mass competing with each other for every inch of space available. These weaving streams mixed and parted repeatedly. They headed south, now watching for the sign that indicated where the marble quarries were and noted that the next sign on the road indicated 'To Paiko'. Here the road had straightened out, then rose and fell regularly before levelling out and leading on to long stretches of tarmacked surface. They slowed now, watching for the sign and soon they came upon it. 'Minnah Marble Quarries' it declared.

"Close now!" said Dave, as they went onwards. They turned off the road at the sign, only just visible, and headed along a dusty track that weaved along a further fifty yards or so. They came to a halt.

They got out and followed the well-worn trail that led downwards and wound in and out of the undergrowth, and there they came upon a sign that declared that the falls themselves were just a mile ahead. Further on they rounded a bend and were able to see a hut with a thatched roof set upon a rise in the ground, and they headed for this. A slight breeze had sprung up and some tall trees offered some welcome shade. They approached the hut and entered. Inside, upon a table a well worn book lay, accompanied by an equally well-worn pencil. Fred crossed to it and bent to inspect it. He thumbed through the pages, read the contents with interest and noted that there were about ninety years of signatures in it, all visitors to the Falls and that they had each appended their names in it and their country of origin.

A shuffling noise behind them heralded the arrival of the attendant, who was an old man with glaucoma in both eyes and looked extremely feeble. He spoke, however, with a strong, clear voice in perfect English, and said, "Welcome, masters!" and hesitating, he said, "please sign the visitor book."

They each did so and then the old man beckoned to them and turned the pages of the book and bade them read some of the entries. With a toothless smile he pointed to the writing there, "You look, massahs! Many famous people come here," and he pointed the names out to them. They thanked him for the information and the man hesitated for a moment, then John realised that he was waiting for a tip, and reaching into his pocket he withdrew a five niara note and handed it to him. The man smiled and said, "Thank you, mister," and as silently he disappeared from sight, it seemed as though he had vanished into thin air, thought John to himself. They went down a sharply descending path and after only a few yards they could hear the roar of the Falls. They came immediately into sight as they turned the next corner. The sheer rock rose sharply above them and Dave reckoned that it was about two hundred feet higher than where they stood. The water cascaded down not in torrents, but in a steady flow and splashed noisily into a pool at the foot. Numerous fingers of water fell at other points and a curtain of spray hung in the air which had caught the rays of the sun and had produced the spectrum of the rainbow and which remained permanently all around. It was extremely cool here and very relaxing. Further on they descended a steep path, managed with some difficulty to reach the bottom of it and were able to walk along under the falls themselves for a distance which provided a spectacular view as they looked back up at them from below.

Marcel was busy with his camera as they climbed around. There was no-one else about and they had the run of the area to themselves. Fred was away off to the right hand side, bending low over the rock formations and the sound of the geologist's hammer, striking the rocks, echoed off the others. Fred examined the pieces he had chipped off carefully with his eyes. He had brought along a stout canvas bag and every now and then he would place a sample of the rock within it. The sun beat down but the air was cool. John was up to his thighs in a pool making his way over to the far side where he had spotted some unusually brightly coloured flowers. Doc was painstakingly pursuing a brightly coloured butterfly across the rocks and which somehow eluded him for most of the time in his efforts to capture it. Fred had ascended the far bank in his search for specimens and had by now almost reached the top of the falls. He shouted down from there to say that the view from where he was, was really spectacular. He disappeared above the rim and his voice faded away. About an hour later, they met up and sat down to eat their sandwiches that William had prepared.

"Isn't it nice here?" asked Dave, "so tranquil, I could come here every day!"

"Indeed!" commented John, "pity it wasn't closer to us, eh?"

"You were away a long time," said Dave to Fred.

"Yes. There's some really interesting species of rock here. Thousands of years old at least. But I'll find out about that later once I've studied these samples," and he tapped his bag by his side.

After they had eaten, they again went their separate ways. Dave stretched himself out on the grassy bank and fell asleep while John dangled his feet in a nearby pool. The hours slipped by, and all too soon it was time for them to leave on their return journey.

They collected up their bits and pieces and climbed back up to the point where they had left the Land Rover, boarded it and set off up towards the road. They entered Minnah again, then struck off on a side road and headed for the route they had come upon. They headed for Kateragi and Ebba to bring them out on the main road near to Egbati. From here they sped onwards through Bida and Batati and arrived at Mogwa a few hours later. They were in a happy frame of mind and they sang as they drove along, going through numerous versions of songs. Marcel had come up with a number from his native country as well and the singing seemed to have shortened the journey. Now they were at Eban Bannaki and there they took a side road and bumped along it, which brought them out close to one of the new temporary roads that Julius Berger's men had constructed.

Marcel had them all up to his house and they started telling stories which had rounded off the evening. It was now eleven and they each retired to their respective houses. Dave was relieved that William had not smashed up all the furniture in his absence, and that all of the crockery was intact. When Dave appeared William had feigned more tears at his reappearance. To this Dave smiled, went upstairs to his bed and slept like a log.

Chapter Eight

The sweet sound of bird song heralded the new day with a cloudless sky and not a hint of a breeze. John awoke, and downstairs he could hear voices. Nathaniel and Ebenezer were going about their daily routine, preparing the breakfast and setting the table. He lay for a while listening to the stillness of the day outside and looked at the clear blue sky. The sun's rays strayed into his room and bathed the far wall in light while outside the trees changed their hues. He got up, stretched himself and went into the shower. Shortly afterwards he went downstairs where Eb and Nat both greeted him.

"Good mornin', massah," they chorused, as if it had been rehearsed, "You have a nice holiday?"

"Morning boys!" he answered. "Yes thanks, what did you two do then with your day off?"

Eb spoke up, "I go to see my sister, not far away, I spend de day with de family and we talks of old times and things."

"Good! And how about you, Nat?"

"Me? I jus' stay at home with de family, go nowhere, dat's all."

"Well, we all need a break now and then so I think we have all enjoyed ourselves." He went and sat at the table and Eb appeared with the coffee pot and poured him a cup, while Nat cooked the bacon and eggs for the massah. John ate heartily and he went out and sat on the veranda for a while. There it was still and quiet and it reminded him of the previous day's outing to the falls.

A lonely figure appeared from out of the bush far away and approached slowly. As he got closer he could see that it was an older man, walking at a steady pace. He was from the local village and carried the traditional hunter's spear and a well-worn leather quiver and a bow over his shoulder. As he came level he called out, "Hello, Baturi!"

John raised his hand in greeting and called, "Good morning!"

The hunter smiled. His hair was long and grey, but despite being old the man was in extremely good physical condition and carried on walking past the house and as he reached the bend in the road he turned and waved again to John before disappearing around it. He was soon lost from view behind the bushes and all was undisturbed and silent again.

John got ready for work, it was still early but he had decided to get an early start. He went out to his Land Rover and dusted off the seat and climbed aboard. He waved to Nat and Eb as he set off and went up the hill at a leisurely speed. Arriving there he went into the offices, extracted the latest Sitrep and studied it. He then went outdoors and viewed the site through his glasses. The oncoming shift was just arriving and were in the act of climbing down from the trucks and making their way over to the site itself, the men splitting into groups according to their tasks. On the faint breeze that had now sprung up he heard the note of the shift change siren as the bodies disappeared from sight into the workings themselves. He could see Football there moving around, pausing to talk now and then to the men and indicating with his arm where the effort for that day was to be made. John picked up his radio and pressed the transmit button, "Chief from Kingpin, I'm going down town," and did not wait for a reply, but headed on down the hill, passing Dave and Doc on the way who gave him a wave and called out as he passed,

"No sloping off to the Falls, now!"

He smiled at this and drove on. He arrived in the assembly area of the site down town and parked alongside the first aid hut. Every one of the men greeted him as he approached them and he acknowledged their greetings. Over a period of time, he had got to know quite a number of them on first name terms and this went down well with them all. He inspected the numerous activities at random, stopping now and then to speak to them or to lend a hand if it was needed. He called Football on the radio and asked him to meet at level two, a system he had devised to avoid confusion of location. Across the face of the dam there was strung a number of walkways and vertical staircases, and looking down Football spotted John and made his way towards him.

"Hi, Football! How are things in general?"

"Okay, massah! De work goes well, we is ahead of de schedule so no problem on dat front!"

"Good! Any other problems then?"

"Only one, massah!"

"And what's that then, Football?" he asked as he trained his eyes on the face through his glasses.

"One or two of de men have said, massah, that they have paid de moneys again!"

"Money? What money?"

"They say it is foah de extra things, massah."

"What extra things? We don't charge anybody for anything extra!"

"I go get one of de men, massah. He can explain."

"You do that, Football," he said still looking through the binoculars.

Football went off to the other side of the workings and calling out in one of the lesser-known dialects, he had his request relayed across the face of the dam. The calls got fainter and fainter as the message was passed on, and eventually a man broke off from his work and started to make his way along the walkways over to where Football was waiting. This took about ten minutes or so and another few before he appeared at the side of John.

"This is de man, massah," said Football.

John turned to him and in English said to him, "Well, what is this money you speak of?"

Football translated and then said, "He say it is de money foah de protection."

"Protection? What protection?"

Football conversed with the man again and he pointed down the valley.

"What does he say, Football?"

"He say, massah, dat he and some of de men, about nine or ten of them in all, has been asked by some of de other workers to pay de protection money."

"For what?"

"Is for de protection against de evil spirits, massah."

"What evil spirits?"

"He say his friend Obi knows."

"Go and get this Obi then!"

"Yes, massah!" Football issued a command, and again the word was passed along the lines until it reached the man called Obi. He eventually arrived and stood in front of John, looking down at his feet.

"Well," said John impatiently.

Football spoke with Obi, and the man looked up and then at John before replying.

"Well? What does he say, Football?"

"He say, massah, that a man he has not seen before come to him in de night and dat de man he say that to be protected from the evil he must pay de money."

"Who is this man?" asked John.

The two of them conversed again, longer this time and then Football turned back towards John and said, "The man is from another shift."

"I see," said John, "and who else has been approached by this other person?"

Football put this question to Obi and Ade. "They both say that the man is here on this shift."

"Go and get him, then!" said John, and indicated that they do this immediately. While the men went off, John spoke on the radio to Klaus, "Chief from Kingpin! Where are you?"

"Here, in Dave's compound."

"Okay then, Klaus come down town straight away will you, we have a small problem to contend with."

"Roger!" was the reply.

While he waited the arrival of Klaus, he thought about what had been said so far, and he was trying to guess what the next move was of these people who demanded the protection money. This had sinister overtones for sure!

Klaus arrived in a cloud of dust, and swinging his arms about to dispel it, he stopped alongside John, "Guten morgen, John. What is it then? More trouble?"

"Looks like it, just hang on a minute while Football gets the man I want to question." As he said this, he espied Football and the man approaching and waited patiently as they drew up level with them. "Okay, Football, ask the man what is going on, and is this the man that spoke to our men?"

"Yes, massah!" and he latched into the dialect of the three men. They conversed for a while and John and Klaus waited patiently as the conversation took place. Eventually Football ceased talking to them and turned towards John and said, "Some of the men asks the other men for moneys, but de other men, dey say it is not the same man, one of this men say he is different."

"That sounds as clear as mud, Football! Can't you get something sensible out of them?"

"Yes, massah," he replied sheepishly, and latched once again into the dialect. After an inordinately long discussion, during which much pointing and gesticulating took place, Football eventually returned to English and spoke to John while the men argued amongst themselves. John, with arms folded, awaited the verdict. "They say that the men who ask for money are outsiders, massah, not of our workers!"

"At last we're getting somewhere!" decreed John, "right then, what are the names of these other men?"

The men conversed again and John waited for the translation.

"Dey say massah, that de name of de mens is Akitoye and Shango."

"Are these men here, the only ones that have been asked for money?"

Football put the question and back came the answer, "Yes, massah."

"How long ago then was this?" asked John.

"Two nights back, massah."

"Okay then, Football, send the men back to work."

"Yes, massah!" and he spoke a word and the men went off along the walkways.

The three of them stood for a moment in silence, then Klaus spoke, "I have not heard of this before," and turning to Football, he said, "You should have told me, Football!"

"Yes, massah!"

"Well, never mind that for now, let's see what we are to do about it."

"I say we go down to the accommodation and see how many others have been spoken to," said Klaus.

John thought about this for a moment, then agreed, and they all climbed into one of the Land Rovers and set off down to the camp site. Ten minutes later they pulled up at the huts and alighted.

The chief cook hailed them from a distance, "Welcome, massah! You wants de coffee?"

"Yes!" replied Klaus, and they stopped where they were.

"Jus' comin', bosses," was the reply, and he reached out for three mugs and filled them with the steaming brew.

"Where are the men who are not sleeping, Football?"

He pointed to a long low hut with only three sides, and they made their way over to it. The cook caught up with them and handed out the coffee while Football stepped into the shade and spoke with some of the men inside.

Football returned with a group of men and they all stepped out into the sunlight and crowded around while the discussion progressed. Football spoke for much of the time, and then the men spoke. Just as John was about to ask what the information was, a voice from the rear of the small crowd spoke clearly and all eyes turned towards the direction from where the voice had spoken. The small man who spoke said, "The men have been visited by de Juju man!"

"What Juju man?" asked Klaus.

Carrying on without regard, the man continued, "He speak with one of our men here!"

"Where is this man?" asked John. The small man pointed to the river.

"Go and get him, Football!" said Klaus, and he went off at the trot down to the river bank. The small man put on a pair of well-worn sandals and followed Football down the track.

"I don't like the sound of this," commented John.

"Me neither!" said Klaus.

"We'll find out soon enough," said John, and they stood in silence awaiting the arrival of the man. Those who had gathered around also waited in silence. They did not have to wait long as Football came into view accompanied by the small man and another, who held a large fish between his thumb and his index finger of his right hand. The fisherman laid the fish down at his feet and greeted John who reciprocated.

"What is your name?" asked Klaus.

"Is Sambo, massah."

"Okay, Sambo, what is this about Juju men?"

"He come last night boss! When I is down at de rivah fishing."

"What did he say then?"

"He say he is a Juju man, an' his name is Possou."

"What else?"

"He say dat de magic is verrah strong and I must pay de protection from it!"

"What sort of magic is this, then, Sambo?"

"Dis magic, massah, it make men sick! Can turn you into snake!"

Klaus and John looked at each other, but said nothing.

"Did you give him money?" asked Football.

"No! He say he come back tomorrow for de money!"

"What time?" asked Football.

"At time de sun go down," the man replied and pointed to the sky.

"Well at least that gives us time anyway," commented John, "we'd better have a plan as to what we are going to do then."

"Okay, Sambo!" said Klaus, "we will come and see you tomorrow before de man comes."

"Yes, massah!" he replied, bent to pick up the fish, and entered the hut calling out as he went, "Fish for de meal tonight!"

The three of them left the hut, handing back the now empty mugs of coffee, walked back over to the Land Rover and stood for a while beside it.

"What do you make of it, Klaus?"

"I've heard about this but it was way back at the start of the work."

"What was that, then?" asked John.

"It was old stories of men putting spells on other men," and he turned towards Football for confirmation.

"That right, boss!" Football commented.

"What do you know of this then?"

"I knows of de people who pay de money to de Juju men. Long time ago."

"And what happened to them?" asked John.

Football thought for a while, then added, "Dey suffer with de magic, massah, get ill, de crops go bad, and de cattle die!"

"I don't believe that for a moment," commented Klaus.

"Well! We'll put a watch on the huts then and see if we can catch this Juju man, then we may be able to get to the bottom of it!" said John. "Let's get back to work, then!" and they returned to the site.

When John reached his office, he called in the rest of the team and they sat in his office around the table. John gave them the details of the event and asked for comment.

Dave said that he was not surprised at this at all.

"Why is that, Dave?"

"Well, up north a few years ago there was a lot of trouble with these Juju men and some of the villagers at the time said that they pretend to be priests and were asking for the money to save them from the evil spirits."

"Really!" said John.

"Yes. And they made quite a killing at it as well, got money from just about everybody before they were caught and hanged, then it finished and was not heard of again."

"Sounds like the same sort of thing, then," said Tony, who stood by the door.

"I've heard of this also," said Doc, "but not in this area, it was away in the southeast, down by Cameroon."

"What do we do, then?" asked John.

"Same as before," said Dave. "Lay a trap and then we can extort the information we require."

"Anyone disagree?" asked John. There were no objections, so they called Football on the radio and asked him to come on up to the office.

He arrived and entered, "Yes, massah! What you want?"

"We want to catch this Juju man, Football, can we get that organised?"

"Yes, massah, is no problem!"

"What effect do they have on these villagers, Football?"

"Dey tell de wimmen dat dey will have de bent babies."

"You mean deformed?" asked Doc.

"Yes, massah!"

"And what else?"

"Dey tell de wimmen dat dey mus' fry an egg in palm oil and kerosene and den mix it, then dey mus' read psalm ten two times, and pray for forgiveness, while dey rub de mixture all over de body."

"And do they believe this?"

"Yes, massah! Dey believe!"

Tony commented, "Sounds bloody stupid to me!"

"Anything else, Football?"

"Yes, massah! I heah of other villagers where de Juju man has been and dey tell them to give money and get a green candle, light it at de both ends and let it burn, and when it is finish, they mus' bury the wax in de cloth an write JIHEJE on it."

"And what does that do, Football," asked John.

"Keep de spirits away," he replied.

"God! What rubbish! The sooner we get rid of this sort of thing the better," said Dave

"All right, then, Football. You and Klaus set your trap, you seem to be good at that sort of thing but let me know what you've decided first, okay?"

"Yes, massah!" he replied.

The meeting broke up and as they went out of the door Tony commented that it was all beyond belief. Dave added a further comment, saying that it never rained but it poured and that these things usually came in threes.

"Shudder the thought!" added John.

The remainder of the day proceeded as normal, and it was late in the afternoon before Football had laid his trap and had organised his men. He had selected a total of ten of them who were fluent in most of the dialects just in case they were needed, two of the men were ex-hunters and adept at following trails even in the darkness. Some of the group were men who had been asked for money so that they would be sure of his identity, and the rest of them were heavily built young workers who were eager to get their hands on the Juju man. They had issued the radios and had lain in darkness for some time near to the huts. Matthew had rigged up a tripwire system that would switch on the lights so there was little chance of the man escaping. John elected not to be present but said that he would listen out on the radio. The evening shift came on and the men coming off shift went back to the mess hut for their evening meal and laid down to rest. John went up to his house, and said that he wanted his meal earlier that evening.

Eb replied, "That all right, massah, no problem! I fix for you right away!" He ambled off into the kitchen where he saw that Nat was sitting, sleeping, in the chair behind the kitchen door. Lifting one of the heavy pans from the rack, he brought it down heavily on the edge of the sink with a loud bang.

Nat started at the sound and jumped up in panic. "What up?" he shouted, taken by surprise, and as he came upright he knocked the teapot flying across the kitchen floor.

"Wake up, Nat!" shouted Eb, "de boss want his dinner, chop chop!"

"Yes! Okay! No need to shout, I hear you, it is prepared!" and he went over to the table in the middle of the floor. "Why for this early?" he asked.

"I no know! Jus' say as quick as possible! Something up at de site I think!"

Nathaniel grunted in response, still not fully awake, and set to the task.

Ebenezer grinned to himself and calling out through the kitchen door, he said, "Dinner ready massah! It come now."

Nat gave him a cutting look as he had not got it ready at all and he was caught on the hop.

"Okay, Eb!" John replied, "I'm waiting for it!"

Eb had to suppress the will to burst out laughing, while Nat muttered under his breath as he hurriedly placed the food on the plate. Ebenezer took the food through and placed it down in front of John, who thanked him for getting it so quickly.

"No problem, massah! I jus' kicks de cook a bit."

John realised that some thing was going on and replied, "Good for you, Eb!"

Eb went back into the kitchen and said to Nat in a rough voice, "De boss he say you has to wake up, too busy sleeping all de damn time."

After John had eaten, he called through to the kitchen and asked them both to come through.

"What he want now?" asked Nat ruefully.

"Probably going to give you de sack for de sleeping!"

"Ha ha! But not funny!" replied Nat as they went into the dining room.

"Come and sit down here, both of you," John called to them.

They did so and Eb said, "Yes, boss! What you wants?"

"Ever heard of the Juju men around here?" asked John.

They both looked at each other, then Nat said, "Well, long time ago, was ten, maybe twelve years."

"Where abouts then?"

Ebenezer then spoke, "Was over in Dahomey! Juju men there very strong," and he hesitated as he thought. "Was in de place called Boni."

"Go on," said John, "I'm listening."

"Well, was in Boni, as I say, and der a number of de men dey get rich plenty quick and dey claim to have de magic powers, and dey spread dis word roun' all de villages."

"Is de magic, boss! Dey put de spells on de people and den dey lives in fear. The villagers give dem money and food and many other things, and some of dem give up de women to dem also."

"And what happened after that?"

"Well, de crops dey were burned and the cows stolen."

"I see!"

"Why you ask, boss?" said Nat enquiringly.

"We have some trouble here, you see, and the men have been asked for money to protect them from the evil."

Eb and Nat looked at each other.

"What is the names of the Juju men, then, Nat?"

Nat thought for a while, but could not remember.

Then John said to them, "I hear that they are well-known though."

"I remember!" said Eb, "is old names!" and he thought for a moment. "Dey is called Akitoye and Shango, and de other name is Dosimu."

Nathaniel spoke up again, "Yes, dat is all old names, dey are also old names of kings of dis country, or chiefs, dey is de names from de old tribes many years back."

"Sounds like the same," said Eb, "is few years ago but sounds like it is de same mens again."

"Is not few years!" said Nat, "Is twenty, I say!"

"Okay, don't argue about it! At least now I know what we are up against."

"Last time boss, de villagers, dey form war party and dey hunt de men down and when they catches them, they cut them opens and lets them bleed to death. Yes! Dey deserve it! Den de Juju men is not heard of again!"

"Well then, tonight we are going to set a trap and we hope to catch one of these Juju men then we will find out what is going on, it could be those you spoke of."

John arose from the table, and Nat and Eb got up also and went off into the kitchen, speaking to each other as they went. Nat called back through, "I hopes you gets them, massah!"

John went out on to the veranda and sat on the chair. He picked up the radio, switched it on and turned up the volume control. It burst into life. It was Klaus calling to Football and they were in the process of positioning the men in the bush down by the track that led to the river. They had spread the men out and most of them had good vantage points in their immediate surroundings. John sat for hours listening for some call on the radio, but none came. He fell asleep and later woke to the radio which was now calling him. He grabbed for it and answered.

"Klaus here! Nothing to report we've been here for almost five hours and no sign of anyone."

"Roger! Do you want to continue?"

"No! We call it a day, John, try again tomorrow, eh?"

"Roger, Klaus, thanks!" and the radio fell silent. John went to bed and fell asleep quickly.

He awoke at his usual time and Eb appeared with the tray and a cup of tea as John struggled upright.

"Did you get them?" he enquired.

"No, nothing Eb, dey did not come. We try again tomorrow, I mean tonight."

Eb nodded and went silently off down the stairs, and John heard him pass on the information to Nat.

At six-thirty John made his way up to the site, calling on Football as he went.

"Kingpin to Football!"

"Yes massah."

"Meeting at seven-thirty up top, Football, you be there."

"Okay, massah, I is!"

Doc's vehicle was already outside the clinic. Today was the weekly sick parade as he called it, when he attended to any minor injury that had not been seen to at the first aid hut. John went over to the clinic and climbed the steps. There were a number of men there who all greeted him as he passed by. The clinic had not yet started but even before he got near the door he could hear Doc laughing uproariously at something. He pushed the door open, and entered. Doc was sitting at the table and on it was an open newspaper. He was sat holding his head in his hands, the tears streaming down his face.

"What's this, then?" asked John as he pushed the door to behind him.

Seeing John, Doc waved him over to the table and indicated that he sit down and he did so.

"Well! " said John, "what's so damn funny?"

Doc pointed silently at the paper and again burst into more uncontrollable fits of laughter, the tears running down his face and dripping on the floor.

"Well then! Come on! What is it?" and walking round the desk he came alongside him and looked over his shoulder to see what the source of amusement was. Doc lifted up the copy of the *Lagos Weekly* that he had in front of him. John looked at it but could not see anything that was funny from where he stood. There was only a page of adverts that lay open.

Doc managed to contain himself and with a superhuman effort he got a grip of himself, and still half laughing, he said, "Have you seen this?"

John looked at it but could not see whatever it was that Doc was referring to. He started to explain, and even as he did so, he burst out laughing again.

"It's these adverts! I've never read anything so funny before in my whole life!" John looked at the medical section that was next to where Doc's hand was and cast a glimpse at it.

"What's so funny then?"

"Just listen to this," said Doc, and started to read it out loud. "Venereal diseases, medicines available for Gonorrhoea, Syphilis, Herpes and weak organ. Also for Gono, Scrotum Gono, Big Testes, Bloodish Gono, Itching Gono, Milky Gonocacal, Cut Cut Gonococcus, Quick Quick ejaculation," and at this point he burst out laughing again, then containing himself again, he continued amid more tears, "Boil Syphilis, Scratch Syphilis, Burning Herpes, Weak organ," and the tears flowed again, "Small organ, Weak and black Menstruation and Unsteady pregnancy!" and at this last description he held his sides as he laughed out loud. Then he continued again, "Hot womb!" and he was now in uncontrollable fits of laughter, "Piles of all types, Diarrhoea and Diabetes!" and he hung on to the table to prevent himself falling off his seat. "Have you ever heard so much rubbish! If you get these all at once I reckon you'd be past treating!" and he burst out laughing again. "This is the sort of thing we have to put up with in this country!"

"Well, I suppose that is funny, Doc, but I don't exactly share your enthusiasm for the joke."

"Well! You wouldn't, John, not being a medical man but I think that I will never be the same again after reading that!"

John smiled politely.

"Now, my friend, what can I do for you today?"

"Oh, nothing, it was just a social call but I think that by now those waiting outside will have thought that you have, as we say, flipped your lid!"

Doc nodded, grinning, and reached in the desk drawer for his scissors, cut out the advert and pasted it up on the wall of the treatment room. Turning back to John he said, "I heard of the trouble we are having, sounds like these Juju men are definitely up to something."

"Yes, I'm afraid so. But we'll get them yet and put a stop to it."

"Yes! And the other people."

"What other people?"

"You don't know?"

"No, tell me then, Doc!"

"Well, I've been going through the files, and came across a report from some time ago, which is about Klaus."

"What sort of report?"

"It says that he has a high alcohol content in his blood."

"Oh yes? When did you discover this then?"

"Last week, John, so I had him in for a routine check as I called it and the sample confirms it."

"Well, I've never seen any sign of this," said John.

"Perhaps not, but as a doctor I have to take this seriously, John, so now I am telling you."

"Yes, thanks, eh, does he know about this?"

"No, not at all."

"How long do you reckon then that he has been in this state?"

"Difficult to tell, maybe a few years, the content is higher than normal you see, he must be drinking a lot of it to show up."

"That's all I need!" commented John.

"It is possible that he is normal at work, as I have not, as you say, noticed anything unusual about him at all."

"Well, thanks for telling me, Doc, I'll keep it in mind and also will keep an eye on him for a while, just in case."

"Okay John, see you!" as John left, and Doc called the first man inside for treatment.

Later on, John met with Klaus and Football but made no mention of Doc's conversation.

"Right then, Klaus what do we do tonight then?"

"Same again, John. We'll lie in wait for them again, and if they do not appear tonight then we will do the same each night until we catch them."

"Okay then, Klaus, I'll leave you to it. Football here has it all arranged, I know. Just call me at any time when you catch someone and we will see what we can find out about these Juju men!"

"Yes, boss!" replied Football, "We gets them, you no worry!"

The two of them left, and John continued with his progress report in the office.

Marcel had both Dave and Matthew in for treatment - Dave had tripped on a pallet and had stubbed his toe and now was only able to hobble about like an invalid. Matthew sported a twisted arm while in the act of fishing out some old electrical wiring in a working at the side of the dam. Apart from that the day passed quietly.

John ate early, anticipating a call that night if anything happened, so he kept his radio at hand. The hours dragged by after darkness had fallen and by eleven in the evening he was getting restless in anticipation. He occasionally paced up and down the veranda only to return to the seat at the far end of it where he would sit peering out into the darkness. The cacophony of the frogs croaking broke the silence as he strained to hear an expected sound but none was heard. The hours drifted on and it was now almost two in the morning. The moon was high and all around was bathed in bright moonlight, reaching out to cover every nook and cranny of the valley.

Down below, Klaus had deployed the men and they all lay in wait patiently, lying perfectly still, their eyes straining into the shadows for some sign of a movement. Klaus scanned the area through his binoculars, shifting his view now and then to different areas and panned right and left at regular intervals. Football's eyes followed the tree line and the bush around it. A deathly hush was apparent and only occasionally they could here the voices drifting up from the village downstream, borne on some faint zephyr. Now it was ten minutes after three in the morning and Klaus had noted that as he peered down at his watch, half hidden in the grass. Suddenly a shrill cry emanated from some disturbed bird as it flew up startled, and flapped noisily away to their right. All eyes followed the reverse of its track and focused on the spot where it had emerged from. It continued on, squawking its warning call. Now all the eyes were scanning the area by the river but there was no sign of movement at all. They were all on tenterhooks, ready for action and Football shifted his weight as he changed to a crouching position. Ten more minutes had passed, and Klaus scanned the area for the umpteenth time. This time, however, he spotted a movement, ever so slight but still it was a movement. He focused on the spot and watched hawk like. Slowly he noticed the grass part and a head appeared, peering out and carefully looking around as it viewed the area. Then a second head appeared and imitated the first. Slowly the two men emerged into the moonlight, crouching low and broke cover and crossed to the taller grass nearby which they moved through slowly, pausing every now and then to assure themselves that all was still clear. Klaus picked up his radio and pressed the transmit button and called to all and John that the intruders were in sight. He whispered into it, "Klaus to all! Two men approaching the rear of the accommodation block from the riverbed!" and released the button again. The two men stopped and pointed in the direction of the row of huts and keeping low they crept closer. John meanwhile, had leapt into action and had driven off downhill as fast as he dared letting the Land Rover pick speed but keeping the noise of the engine to a minimum as it approached the bottom of the hill and the turn off for the accommodation area. He stopped on the track to the huts and got out, quickly but quietly he made his way along the track in the shade of the trees. The men who were watching down below had now swung around behind the intruders and now were closing the net as they advanced in the form of a purse string around the two men who by now were almost at the huts themselves.

Klaus allowed the two men to reach the hut nearest to them, the intruders now darting forwards in short quick movements. One of them was stockily built and short and wore a faded blue tee shirt and brown torn trousers, the other a tee shirt and black shorts. Each wore a piece of cloth tied around their foreheads and carried a machete whose blades glinted in the moonlight. They advanced to the door of one of the longer huts, looking around as they did so, and hesitated as they carefully pushed the door open and stepped inside. They saw the rows of sleeping forms and looked carefully along them as they stealthily made their way along the centre of the hut. A few snores emanated from the men. Outside, the net had closed and Klaus's men were now grouped around the door of the hut itself. Some of them went around to the rear of it and covered it in the event of an escape attempt. Klaus crept to the open window and, keeping his head below it, he pressed his ear to the wall and listened.

Inside, the two men came to a halt alongside one of the younger men and, reaching down, one of them awakened him with a shake of the shoulder. The man started but froze as the keen edge of the machete was brought fully up under his windpipe. He stared up at them. The two men indicated the door in silent movements and slowly the man got up and accompanied them over to the doorway in the shade. Reaching there, they stopped. The door opened and slowly the three of them stepped out onto the hard packed earth and started to converse in a low voice and in one of the more obscure dialects.

The young man had the machete kept against his neck as they spoke. Klaus moved around to the opposite side of the hut and crouched behind a bush. He could not hear what was being said but the three of them moved, the intruders having obviously received the required answer. They all stepped out into the moonlight. Football had been listening intently to all that had been said and as the men moved away from the hut, he signalled with a wave of his arm and the net grew tighter, unseen by the three who now were approaching a pathway that led off into the bush.

"Do we get them now, massah?" whispered Football to Klaus.

"No, we follow them, but close behind."

They all moved forward silently and keeping about twenty yards behind the trio, they proceeded along the path which wound in and out of the grasses. The three, however, did not go back towards the river but instead took a path that led to the messing huts, the trio stopped by a tree trunk and stepped into the moonlight. There they moved on a few paces and entered one of the huts which stood by itself, cursing on entering, as they stumbled over some of the low eating stools that were scattered around. One of the men called out the name of one of the cooks and after a short silence, a voice was heard and a few moments later, the cook appeared, conversed briefly with them, then disappeared and returned shortly afterwards holding a cloth bag in his hand and a few more words were exchanged. Then the men made off through the grass towards the river, closely followed by Klaus, Football and the others. Football waved the men ahead and they outflanked the intruders. Now they had increased their speed but those around matched it. Klaus whispered again into the radio and the purse tightened more. As they emerged from the grasses on to the river bank, Football hailed them in a loud but clear voice. The men froze instantly and looked around. One of them shouted something and the two of them set off for the river bank as fast as they could go, but hot on their heels, the pursuers gained upon them. They fell upon the two men and after a short struggle they were overpowered in a flurry of arms and legs and unceremoniously tied up tightly by Football's men.

Klaus was hard on their heels and they dragged the two of them to their feet.

"All right then, Football! Let's see what they know!" and he nodded towards them.

Football licked up the bag and shook the contents out on to the ground in a pool of moonlight and they all gathered around as they gazed upon the items. Klaus bent down and picked up the first of them, it was a child's skull, showing ghostly white in the darkness, he turned it over in his hands and noted that it was pierced at the top where an arrow head or something similar had broken it. Football and his men looked on in awe. Klaus put it down and unfolded the skin of an animal, it was shiny, and he spread it out to reveal the familiar spots of a leopard still attached to the head.

"What's this for?" asked Klaus.

"Is for de ritual, massah. Dey wear dis on de head and de skin it hang it down de back."

"Like this?" and Klaus put it on. Some of Football's men stared at it wide eyed and shrank back.

"This scares you then?" he asked of them.

They nodded in silence, then one of them answered, "Is de sign of de Juju men, massah!"

Klaus tore the skin off of his head and flung it on the ground and then went through the remaining items. The machete, he noted, had its blade honed to a fine edge, then there was a necklace of monkey skulls joined together by strips of leather, a knife, a bag of yellow-coloured powder, then a smaller bag tightly drawn together at the neck. He took hold of the strings and with both hands separated the strips. He looked inside, then dropped it quickly and uttered the phrase, "Mein Gott!" For a moment he stood looking down at it while the others crowded around, then with the toe of his boot he tipped the bag over so that the contents spilled out on to the ground.

A nauseating smell greeted the nostrils of those around as a human heart, glistening in the light, toppled on to the ground. They could see the congealed blood and the scraps of tissue that still clung to it. All stood in silence looking at it, it was revolting!

Football, was the first to respond, "They are de Juju men, massah!"

On hearing this the two men although tied up tried to wrench themselves free but the men holding them cuffed them roughly and held them fast.

Football looked at the men and then turned to Klaus and said, "We kill them now! Best get rid of them, plenty quick!"

Most of the men reached for their weapons instinctively, and Football stepped towards them and raised his machete up as if to strike at them.

"Wait!" called Klaus, "we need to find what others there are also. If we kill them now, we will never find out."

Slowly Football lowered his arm and the other men stepped back a pace. A few murmurs of dissent were heard but they all lowered their weapons. Football spoke. "The massah is right! We find out first, den we kill them!"

"Okay Football, but not here! We take them up to the camp, lock them up for the night and then we will question them."

"Okay boss!" replied Football, and with a flick of his head the captors bundled the men roughly along the path and towards the camp. John met up with them as they approached and, coming abreast of Klaus, he asked him to describe what had happened. Klaus did so as they approached the accommodation huts.

"Well, at least your trap was a success, Klaus!"

"Yah! We caught them, I knew somehow that they would be tonight, we will get the information out of them later today."

"Good Klaus, but remember that I want to be there when you question them."

"Yah! Stimmt!" and turning to Football, he said, "Get that man from the cook's hut also."

"Yes boss! I get!" and he went off in that direction.

Klaus then described what had taken place at the hut and mentioned the bag of horrors that they had witnessed.

After hearing the descriptions, John added, "Definitely the mark of the back magic, then."

"Yah! For sure!"

"You'd better let Doc see this heart, Klaus."

"Yah! Will do." and he called out, "see you later!"

John drove back up to the house and Klaus went of to see Doc. John was pleased and he felt that, at last, they would get to the bottom of the Juju business once and for all. When he arrived at the door, Nat and Eb were still up and obviously awaiting his arrival.

Nat produced a pot of tea despite the fact that it was early in the morning and they all sat down together at the table.

"You get them? Yes?" asked Eb.

"Yes Eb, we got them, and later this morning we will question them."

"Good!" replied Nat, in a satisfied tone of voice.

"Klaus said that they had a bag of black magic things and in it was a heart."

Nat looked up in surprise, "A heart?" he queried.

"Yes, Nat. That's what I said."

"Den dat is de Juju men for suah!" he replied.

Ebenezer thought for a moment then said, "This heart. They uses this to frighten de peoples, dey say it is de heart of de devil and can cast bad spells on all who look upon it for long, long time." A faraway look came over his face, and then he lapsed into silence.

"Well! Whatever it is, Eb, you can be assured we will get to the bottom of it all. Now I am going to bed! I see you in the morning," and he got up from the chair.

"Yes, massah, " they chorused, and rose up also.

What remained of the night passed quickly by, and soon John awoke to the calls of the early morning birds in the trees opposite the veranda. He arose and showered, dressed and went downstairs to the kitchen. There, Nat and Eb were already preparing breakfast and Eb passed a cup of coffee over to him as John went to the writing desk and wrote up what had happened that night.

Shortly afterwards, Nat called out, "Come an' get it while is hot, massah!"

John put his pen down, crossed to the dining table, sat down and addressed the bacon and eggs. He washed the breakfast down with some more coffee and took a cup with him out on to the veranda. Further up the hill, two bush men herded a small group of cattle across the road and off into the trees, disturbing some bats as they flitted around in the tree tops. John reflected upon the night's events and surmised that it would be interesting to see what the men had to say for themselves.

Soon it was time to leave, and he called out a good-bye as he crossed to his vehicle and climbed aboard. He headed uphill, waving to the village women as he went on their way down for water. They smiled in return, showing their fine white teeth, and waved back to him.

He arrived at the office and pulled up in a small cloud of dust, made his way up the steps of Doc's office, and entered. He was busy at this early hour, four or five of the workers being in attendance all of which had cuts or bruises of some description. Doc waved to John, indicating that he would be about fifteen minutes before he could stop to talk to him. John went out and over to Klaus's office and entered it. Klaus however was not yet there so John returned to his own and dropped off his report book, then gathered up his binoculars and crossed to the roadside and viewed the area down below. After studying it for a few moments, he was satisfied with what he saw and crossed back over to Doc's clinic. John pushed the door open, noting as he entered that all the men had now left.

"Et bon jour, Marcel!" he called.

"Et vous," replied Doc.

"Did you hear of last night's events, then?"

"Yes! Very suspicious, eh?"

"What about this heart, Doc, have you seen it yet?"

Marcel waved him over to the surgery and entered, John following on. On a stainless steel tray sat the heart, like a piece of meat displayed in a butcher's shop. John felt slightly sickened by the sight of it and said so.

"It's very recent," said Marcel, gazing down upon it, "from a man about twenty-five or so years, I'd say, a large man, but healthy too."

"Can you tell all that? Just by looking at it?"

"Mais oui! But this man, I would say, was not yet dead when this heart was removed."

John looked at him in disbelief.

"Are you sure?"

"Yes! Certainement!" and added, "but if he was not yet dead, then it is certain that it was removed, or should I say, butchered as he was dying."

"Why do you say that?"

"Well," and he hesitated as he picked it up in his hands, "see how much blood there is in it," and he squeezed one of the openings in it and some of the blood flowed out freely.

"Also in one of the valves there is a lot of congealed blood, so you see, the organ was still in the process of pumping when it was removed."

John was now looking exceedingly pale in the face as he nodded silently, making a mental note of what Marcel had said.

"I will keep it here in the fridge, John, and I will examine it again later in detail, and then I will give you a report on it."

"Yes! That'll be fine, Marcel, thanks," and he got up and left the clinic and crossed back over to his office.

There, even as he started to write up some notes on this, he still felt heartily sickened by the event. The sooner we can eliminate this Juju stuff the better, he thought to himself, then we can all return to normality again.

At this point Klaus had arrived in the compound, and he pulled up in his usual cloud of dust as he spun the vehicle around in a tight circle in front of his office. He emerged from the cloud and went over to John's office and entered.

"Ah! Good morning, Klaus. I have just spoken with Doc. He tells me that the heart which was in that sack was cut out of a man's body while he was still alive! Can you believe that?"

"Yah! This Juju people have no scruples at all."

"Well! Let's get these men out of the calaboose and see what they have to say for themselves."

After a brief conversation, Klaus said that Football and the men and their escort would be up in about fifteen minutes time. While they awaited their arrival Klaus went over to the clinic and asked Doc to come over to John's office when the men arrived. Not long afterwards a fresh cloud of dust heralded the arrival of the prisoners. Football climbed down from the front of the Land Rover and pushed before him the two captives and the cook who was seen to have spoken with them the previous night. Two other guards roughly pushed the men towards the office and up the steps. They all entered through the doorway and crowded into the shaded interior. John surveyed those arranged before him. The two captives looked frightened as they were pushed roughly forward to stand immediately in front of him.

Silence returned for a few moments before anyone spoke. The cook was bound tightly with rope and Football gave him a kick in the leg as he dragged him to the front.

"All right Football! I don't think he will attempt to go anywhere."

He was brought up level with the two prisoners.

At this point Marcel entered and came around the back of the desk to face them. He stood looking at the men, then as his eyes ranged along the faces, his gaze came to a halt at the face of the cook.

"What happened to his face?" he asked Football.

"I don' know, massah! Mus' have fallen last night, I think."

John looked at the man's face and noted the swelling above the eye, as if he had been struck a heavy blow with some type of weapon. John looked at Football. A likely tale, he thought to himself. Klaus shrugged his shoulders as John looked at him and raised his eyebrows in a form of comment.

"Right then! Let's get on with it," said John.

"This man no speak English, massah!" Football commented.

"Okay, Football, you translate for him but no nonsense! I want honest answers, not concocted ones. Understood?"

"Yes, massah! I get de drift."

"Okay! Proceed."

"Before you ask him anything else, I want to know where they got this heart from."

"Yes, massah!"

Football latched into the dialect and a short conversation ensued, and after a few moments Football turned to John, and said, "Dis man, he say dat je is told to keep the heart to use later."

"Yes. But what for?"

Football again conversed with the man and turned to John again. "The man he get de heart from de cook."

"Where did the cook get it from?"

Football asked him in a gruff tone and the man answered. "He say he get it from a man who is passing by."

"Passing by? We have no men who pass by, Football!"

Football spoke with the cook again, then turned back towards John and said, "He say dat de man is passing by an' he ask for food, and when de cook gives it, de man he hand over de bag and say that he is to keep it and another man will come later to collect it. He also say dat if he do not do this den de bad magic will fall on him, and he will die."

John and Klaus looked at the man for a moment, who shifted uncomfortably.

"Okay," said Klaus, "ask him if he knew what was in the bag."

Football spoke again and the man shrugged his head in response. "He not know, massah!"

"Does he know that the bag was bad magic?"

The man nodded in reply and bent his head low, as though ashamed. "He know, but if he tell anyone den he die de bad death."

"What kind of bad death?" asked John.

Football spoke again at length with the man and all around waited patiently for the reply. "He say that if he tell den de men will pull out his eyes with de hook an' den cut open his belly and he bleed to death, then he will be in the power of de magic men and dey will possess his soul."

A silence fell upon all of them for a moment while they contemplated the answer.

"He believes in all of this?" asked John.

"Yus sah! He believe! Now he thinks he will die because he has told of it."

"Well!" said John, "They've definitely poisoned his mind that's for sure, probably his soul as well as far as he is concerned." They all remained silent for a few moments, then John said, "All right, Football, take him away and lock him up again for the moment."

"Yes massah!" and he gave the man a push towards the door, one of the guards placed him in the back of the Land Rover and stayed with him. They all remained silent and no-one spoke for a while, their eyes carrying on a conversation amongst themselves.

"C'est pas bon!" exclaimed Marcel, speaking to no-one in particular.

"Yes Marcel," replied John, "but we'd better have these two intruders speak and see what they have to say for themselves."

Football called for one man from the back of the room and he was brought to stand in front of John.

"Do you speak the dialect of these two, Football?"

"Some, massah!"

"Right, then, let's see what we can elicit from them."

"One of de men, he speak some English, massah!"

"Good," replied John.

"What is yoh name?" he asked the man.

"Shango!" he replied.

Football spoke in the other dialect, and after a pause the man replied. Football said that he was from Dahomey, then asked him what he was doing here as Dahomey was far away.

"He say that he is part of the brotherhood, massah, and dat he comes on de command of de priest of de magic men."

"How many of these men are there in this brotherhood?" asked John.

Football put the question, and waited for the answer, "He say many men! All races! In de big wide brotherhood."

"Ask him who is the leader," said Klaus.

The dialect continued and Football had to repeat the question three or four times before he got a satisfactory reply.

"He say he not know, he only get de message and he do what he is told."

John thought on this for a moment, the man obviously knew more than he was prepared to say, but without actually resorting to some form of torture they would not be able to extract the information they required.

"Okay, Football, take him out. Let's have the other one and see what he has to say."

Football executed the transfer and the remaining one was hauled forward and stood in front of the desk

He was a heavily built man and had a flat nose. John formed the opinion that he was of mixed race and that he did not look like the normal African man, perhaps a cross between African and Arab maybe.

Before John could speak, Klaus started and said, "What were you doing down by the river, last night?"

The man looked sullenly at him then after a pause, he said, "I come to collect de bag."

"What for?"

"To take to the village."

"What village?"

"It's called Rikka."

"There is no village of that name, that I know," commented Klaus.

Football thought for a moment, then said, "Der is, is not far away, is small one not many people live there, go three bends of the river."

"Are you sure, Football?" asked John.

"Yes massah! Is called Kamino Rikka! I have been there, but dat is many yeahs ago!" Football continued the dialogue, then turned back to Klaus and said, "he say dat the place is the meeting for de brotherhood when de moon is full."

"So it is some sort of ritual, then?" asked John.

"Yes massah!" and he spoke again with the man. "He say his name is Nanda and he is of the Itsekiri people from Benin."

"I've heard of them," said John, "something to do with slave trading, yes?"

"Dat right, massah," said Football, "was long time ago. De chief he was called Nana, he fight de British an' he sell many slaves to many peoples for de money."

"Putting two and two together," John said to Klaus, "I bet that this has to do with trading for slaves, then, all this magic mumbo jumbo."

Football asked this question of the man and obtained a nod of the head in response.

"Now we're getting somewhere!" John commented.

Football continued to question the man who now was freely giving information out.

Probably to save his own skin, thought Klaus.

Football spoke again. "He say that when de moon is full, den dey have de ritual!"

"What ritual?" asked John.

The man spoke again at length, and Football took it all in. "He say dat at the turn of the moon, they sacrifice a male person to show a sign of loyalty to the brotherhood. Then de brothers," and he hesitated as the man continued the description, "dey drink de blood of de man and swear to follow the brotherhood until they die."

"And what happens if they do not do this, Football?" asked John.

"Then they is marked men for the rest of their lives, and when de next moon come den dey are de ones to be sacrificed."

"Well! We must get rid of this evil, Football. We will do something about it." said Klaus.

The tone of Klaus's voice reminded John of a quote by Kipling,

'Clear the land of evil, drive the road, and bridge the ford.'

How appropriate that statement was! A similarity to the project of building the road to the dam and bridging it at the ford in the river!

Klaus continued, "When does this ritual happen next, Football?"

He spoke again with the man and turning to Klaus, he said, "At the next turn of de moon."

"When is that?" asked John.

Football looked at the ceiling as though drawing inspiration from it, then said, "Is nine days, massah."

"Then we must be ready for it," exclaimed John.

The prisoner then spoke unprompted, in clear and precise English. "Many men present at the moon's turn. Powerful magic then. You will not succeed!"

"We shall see," commented Klaus in a menacing tone of voice. "Okay, Football take him away and lock the two of them up! When the day comes we will be ready for this sacrifice, and then we will put an end to it all."

After the men had left, Doc, Klaus and John remained in the office and went over what they had heard.

"We will have to have a look at this place, Kamino Rikka, better go tomorrow, I think, so that we can lay our plans carefully, we may need a lot of men."

"There are plenty!" Klaus commented. "There will be no shortage of volunteers. That I can assure you of!"

"I suggest that tomorrow we go down there on the pretence of carrying out a geological survey," said John, "that way we will not arouse any suspicion."

"No problem!" commented Klaus, "I'll see to it and get Rock to organise it."

"Thanks, Klaus, " John replied and Klaus left. John went with Doc over to the clinic to see what else he had discovered from the grisly remains.

"There's not much else, John," he said, "but there must be some remains about somewhere that match the rest of the body."

"I bet you we find them at this village Kamino Rikka, Doc."

"Perhaps," he said noncommittally.

They went about their normal tasks and the days passed slowly until it was almost near the time for the turn of the moon.

Meanwhile, they had set out on the survey, leaving Matthew in charge of everything. They drove off downriver, following the bank as closely as they could and abreast of the river's course. They had been driving slowly now for almost three-quarters of an hour, passing numerous villages on the way, skirting most of them, but so far they had not come across the village they sought. Espying a herd of bush cows, they drew level with it and stopped. As the lead herdsman approached, they hailed him and asked of the village. He hesitated for a moment, then pointed down the valley and indicated that they must go up the bank to find it. John thanked him and Klaus handed over a few packets of cigarettes to him and a box of matches. His eyes lit up and he beamed a smile at them and, with a friendly wave, he returned to his cows. They climbed back aboard the Land Rover and went on downstream. There the track took a sharp twist and then followed a series of steep uphill hairpin bends which necessitated the full use of the gearbox and the lock of the wheels. Far below, the bush cows were now just moving dots on the landscape. They were now about a hundred feet up the wall of the valley and here the elevation decreased as they reached an area where the ground flattened out. Being unable to drive on any further, they all got out to continue on foot. They pushed the vehicle into the shade of some leafy trees and walked on. To their surprise, rounding a bend they came upon a clearing where they stopped in their tracks. Evidence of recent footprints was there and the path was a well trodden one. The path twisted as it went on and soon they came to a deserted clearing and a collection of mud huts in the trees.

Football moved forward cautiously and called out. The only response was silence.

John noted that although the wind was blowing gently, not a leaf moved on any of the trees.

"This place gives me the creeps!" said Fred quietly. "See how the sun is shining? Yet there is no heat here, it is cold."

They all felt the feeling, and they stood still for a moment while they pondered on their next move.

"Not even a bird singing!" added Klaus.

"Well! Let's look around," said John, and moved on towards the hut.

"Over here!" called out Dave and he beckoned to them to come over. They moved towards where he stood pointing at the ground. A trail of dusty footprints and marks of something heavy having been dragged along were evident. They followed the trail, then came to a halt as the prints petered out. Football then pointed to the grasses at the side of the path and they looked into them. There bloodstains were prominent and covered a wide area, the stains stood out against the different colour of the red soil. They all looked at each other, but no-one spoke.

"Over here! More of them," called Doc. The eyes panned left to where he was stood as he bent low to touch them, and rising slowly he followed the trail of them slowly. They led towards the hut at the end of the path and as they approached it the stains became heavier, and close to the point where the path widened out, he noted that the grasses were soaked recently in rivulets of blood. He bent low again, and fingered the trades of the grass next to him.

"Human blood!" he declared, "recent too, only a few hours old, if that."

"In this heat?" asked Dave.

Doc looked up at the sun and thought for a moment, "Yes! Even in the heat it will stay semi-congealed."

"Looks like something was propped up against this door, John!" Dave added.

They all looked at the door and the long stains running down to its base. A faint breeze whispered, unannounced, and with it the odour of something foul wafted past their noses. They all looked at each other as if someone had broken wind, but the obnoxious stench only came from one direction. Marcel stepped forwards and stood directly in front of the door.

He bent low and sniffed at the door, then straightening up, he said sombrely, "Ce est ici!"

"Are you sure?" asked John.

"Mais oui! It is in this hut, smells like flesh rotting in the heat."

"Let's have a look then," exclaimed Dave, but no one would move, least of all Football whose eyes were large with fright.

Klaus stepped forwards, brushing past them all and put the weight of his body to the door and gave it a heave. The door scraped open on the bare soil as it came ajar, the stench billowed out and over them all. Klaus hesitated for a moment, then pushed the door fully open and stuck his head inside. In the shadows he could just make out what seemed to be a heap on the earthen floor. The stench was appalling and he gagged at it as he struggled to move back into the fresh air. The light from without fell on the inside of the hut, forming a triangle on the floor. A sudden flurry of wings was heard and he instinctively ducked low as a buzzing cloud of flies emitted from the thing on the floor and swarmed out of the doorway past him. The others ducked low as the insects dispersed.

Doc moved forwards cautiously and looked inside. On the floor the remains of a corpse lay, the entrails torn out and stretched over the whole area of the floor. A group of rats, totally unperturbed by this intrusion, continued their feasting on the rotting mass. Here was the owner of the heart, thought Doc to himself as he backed out of the doorway. They all stood silent, looking in, the rats still gorging themselves. Klaus threw a large stone at them, and a loud squeal was heard and the rodents gave up their task and scuttled out of the door and off into the undergrowth.

"Jesus!" exclaimed Dave, "how long has that been there?"

"I can't say," said Doc.

"This is the place of the sacrifice, then." said John.

"Let's get out of here!" said Fred, "before I spew up all over us!"

"Oui!" said Marcel, and reached his hand behind the door and slowly pulled it closed. They all backed away some distance and stood in silence for a few moments. Football was standing as far back as he could get, some fifteen yards or so away from the rest of them.

Klaus shuddered at the thought of what he had seen, Dave's face was an ashen white in colour, and everyone was visibly shaken. Only Marcel, practised in dealing with the human body, was unperturbed by it all, and said, "Not a pretty sight, my friends! It is obvious that this is the custom of this brotherhood they speak of, so we must make sure that it does not happen again. N'est pas?"

"Yes!" replied John. "I think we will leave now, eh? We've seen enough for today."

They started off back along the path they had come on and into the scrub and the bush. They arrived back at the Land Rover and all climbed silently in, and they started to meander their way back down the narrow track, driving with extreme care as the vehicle slanted downwards at a perilous angle as they negotiated the sharp corners.

On the way, Dave broke the silence, and said, "Did you notice that we never saw a single soul apart from the herdsman at the bottom of the valley?"

"Yes! I noted that!" said John, "certainly a place that few go to, I'd say!"

"It's as if everyone except us knew that it is not a place to be frequented!" added Tony. The blanket of silence fell upon them again and they continued their journey back along the valley floor to their site. They stopped off at the camp to let Football and his men off, then continued on to John's house where they all dispersed in silence.

Klaus and John stood by the entrance to John's house doorway and John said, "Well, now! We have to get these people once and for all, eh, Klaus?"

"Jah! The sooner the better, eh?"

John nodded, then said, "We haven't got very long, though. We'd better be ready for this full moon, Klaus."

"Ve vill be!" he replied, and he crossed to his Land Rover and climbed aboard, banging the door to as he drove off uphill.

John turned to Nat, who was standing at the door, and said, "Nat, I will eat early tonight."

"Yes, boss!" he replied "I go get de dinner prepared quick quick." The meal was served soon afterwards, but John had lost his appetite and ate mechanically, staring into space as he did so. Eb cast a wary look out of the kitchen door, and he and Nat exchanged glances in silence. Then, the two heads appeared round the door jamb, and looked at John. "Is de food all right, boss?" asked Nat quietly.

John looked around at them and seeing the two inquisitive faces, he replied, "Yes, the food is fine, it's just that I'm not all hungry, that's all."

Nat and Eb looked at each other again, puzzled by the reply. "Can I gets you somethin' else, massah?" asked Eb.

"No, Eb, that will be all I think."

"Yes, massah!" they chorused and retired to the kitchen table in silence.

"Can you two come through here?" John called out.

The two of them emerged cautiously through the doorway and stood side by side, like a pair of dummies in a museum.

"Come over here and sit down," called John and pulled out two chairs at the table. They sat and then John spoke to them, "Now then, today I have been to the village where the brotherhood carry out their rituals." The two of them looked at each other in silence, then looked back at John, and awaited the next revelation. "Tell me! What do you know about these ritual killings that take place on the full moon?"

The two of them stared at each other again, and silence reigned for a few moments before Eb responded, shaking his head slowly from side to side, "Is bad, massah, verrah bad! Was long time ago. I have heard of this befoah, but not for long, long time."

"When was that, then, Eb?"

"Many moons! When I was young."

"And?"

"Der is a village, neah where I live, some young men were taken in de night and de bodies of dem, dey are cut up, like butcher meats, was taken by de evil people, and we never see de men again."

"Who took the men then, Eb?"

"Is de men with de yellow eyes.

"Yellow eyes?"

"Yes, massah! Is de men who is called de Leopard Men."

"You know of this as well then, Nat?"

"Yes, massah!"

"Tell me then. I need to know all there is to know about them."

"Well! Once, in my village, we had a visit from these men, but our headman and de rulers, dey beat them off, they not come back but they was there, foh suah."

"Was this the same time as Eb told of?"

"No, massah! Dis is different time. Ten yeahs, maybe."

Ebenezer looked at Nat and said, "Yes, that is 'bout right. Ten years or so."

"I see," said John, "so this is nothing new, then?"

"No, massah, is verrah old!"

"Well! We are going to try and catch them at their ritual."

"You mus' be verrah careful, massah," said Eb quietly, "it is dangerous!"

"Yes, I know, Eb! But we have a duty to stamp it out once and for all."

"I hopes so, massah," Nat replied, and without a further word, they arose and went back in to the kitchen. John could hear them talking in low voices later on, so he left them to their own discussions on the matter.

John went out onto the veranda and sat on the chair. It was cool as usual and he sat thinking for a while before rising, and went to bed early for a change.

The morning came creeping into the day bit by bit, bringing with it the sounds of life. For some strange reason, John realised that it was to be a day of foreboding, a portent perhaps. It was also dull and overcast and none of the birds sang as usual in the tree opposite the house. He looked out, sure enough they were there, but muted. He arose and dismissed all of this from his mind, showered and went downstairs, had his breakfast and, calling out to the two servants, he set off for his office up top. Klaus was already in and had left a note on John's desk to say that he would be down town if needed. John crossed to the escarpment and looked down at the site. All appeared normal so he recrossed the road and went towards his office just as Marcel arrived outside his clinic. John went over towards him.

"A grisly business that yesterday, eh, Marcel?"

"Oui! It is not something I would wish to see every day, mon ami."

"Nor me either. Apparently, according to my servants, they have come across this before, but a long time ago."

"That does not surprise me, John. I have also heard tales such as these from people I have met in the embassies."

At about nine-thirty, Klaus arrived at his office and John called on him to come over.

"Did you notice the weather today, Klaus?"

"Yah! Not good! I notice it, and also the men down at the site. They have reported that the men are not happy but I told them to get on with their work, and that soon we would be able to dispel their fears."

"Good for you, Klaus!"

They had a brief discussion on a few points of the construction base and then they each turned to their respective duties. John spent the remainder of the day with Dave, ensuring that they had sufficient stock for the next phase of work that was almost upon them. Dave had it all collected up and placed strategically in the compound ready for quick access. Matthew called in with a box of faulty light fittings and reported that some of the boxes of the correct ones were deficient of some of the contents.

"Probably fell off the back of the lorry," he commented.

"You mean stolen!" said John.

"Exactly that! It happens all the time."

Here in Nigeria, there was always a market for 'things that fell off lorries'. The black market was rife, money talked and corruption had reigned for a number of years from the time that the British pulled out of the country. Items were, as often as not, stolen to order. Dave being aware of this, had stored his items safely and it was like Fort Knox in some of the valued item areas.

Evening approached and the shifts prepared to change over. Klaus elected to stay behind to oversee the continuity of the shift change as it was critical as per the planned work programme which they were following.

John drove to his house and entered, the door swinging gently to and fro as it rebounded off the frame. Eb poked his head around the kitchen door and, on seeing John, he retired to the kitchen and put the tea on the stove. He made the pot of tea, carried it through to the lounge where John was sitting and poured out a cup without speaking and passed it over to John.

Looking up, he said, "Thank you, Eb! I could do with that, it has been a strange day."

"Yes, massah! I have noticed!"

"Why do you say that, Eb?"

"Don' know, massah, but suah is strange today, I notice when I is comin' to work on de path in de bush."

"Are you there, Nat?" he called.

"Yes, massah! I here!" and he appeared from the bowels of the kitchen, a cloth in one hand and a dish in the other. He stopped alongside John, and said, "Okay! I's here massah! Wha' you wants?"

"Eb, here, says this morning is strange. What did you think?"

"Well massah, is verrah quiet, birds dey am not singin' there, I sees them!" and he pointed up to the sky.

"Yes! I noticed that as well. Is that all then?"

"Yes, massah, dat is all."

"Thank you, Nat," John said and Nat shuffled off back to his chores. John went over to his desk, and commenced to write up his daily report, adding in the strange feelings that the men had reported. Eb called that dinner was ready and John broke off from the report and wandered over to the dining table. Eb brought in the dish of fish kedgeree and dished it up onto the plate. It smelt delicious and John got stuck into it with relish, followed it with fresh cut pineapple and custard and coffee, and then retired to the veranda.

In the still of the evening the cacophony of frogs was in full swing and the air still and hot. He relaxed and picking up a book he sat reading for about fifteen minutes or so. Out of the corner of his eye he was conscious of movement in the bushes further downhill from the house. He put the book down on the table and watched.

The sound of branches being pulled aside and then springing back into place again caught his attention and he focused on the point where the sound had emanated from. No movement was visible so he returned to his book. Shortly afterwards he heard the same again, put down the book and awaited developments. Now the sounds were closer at hand and he sat expectantly. Far away to the left he detected a movement, it was a single person moving upwards through the bush on the pathway from the valley floor. Probably a hunter he thought to himself. He waited for the figure to appear and slowly a silhouette came into view and approached, it being unrecognisable in the darkness. It came closer to the roadside, then the grasses parted and the figure appeared. It was Football! John wondered what he was doing up here at this time of night so he waited for him to draw closer. Naturally, it was shorter to climb the path than coming up by the road but you had to be fit to undertake the climb as it was very steep in parts. He emerged into the light of the lamp outside the house and approached the point where John was sitting. He stopped when he spotted him, then continued again until he was level with him.

"Hello, Football! What brings you up here at this time of evening?"

Football raised his arm in recognition and as he drew closer, he replied, "Evening, massah! I come to speak to you."

"Come on in then, Football!" Signalling to Eb, he said, "Bring me two cold beers, Eb."

"I's comin'!" was the reply.

Football stepped up on top of the veranda and John pulled out a chair for him and bade him sit down. Eb appeared with the refreshment and poured the beer into the glasses. Football sat down catching his breath first of all, then taking the beer from the table, he took a long swig of it to refresh himself.

"Well then, Football, to what do I owe the honour of this visit then?"

"Well, massah, is about today."

"What about it?"

"On all of de shifts de man are afraid."

"Of what?"

Football hesitated for a moment, then replied saying, "I don' know, but all de time dey is workin' dey is quiet de whole time."

John did not reply but thought it strange. It certainly tied in with what others had noticed and bore some relevance.

"I see!" said John. "What do you think about it then?"

"Is bad magic aroun', massah!"

"You think so?"

"Yes, massah, I knows."

"What kind of magic, then?"

"I don' know, de men, dey not speak all de time, even when dey is workin'."

"I see!" said John. But, of course, he didn't see at all. "Well, I'm sure it's nothing to worry about, Football. Tell you what, if you see something really odd you call me on the radio, okay? And then we will attend to it right away, will that satisfy you?"

Football thought about this for a moment, then replied, "Okay, massah! I calls you if that happens."

"Good, Football! Now carry on enjoying your beer, eh?"

Football smiled at last and raised his glass again to his lips. John and he remained talking of other things for about an hour, then Football took his leave and retraced his steps to the steep path and was soon lost from sight. The remainder of the evening passed by without incident, and John slept soundly.

In the morning John went to work early again and met Klaus on his way up. They both stopped and got out of their vehicles and met at the roadside in the still air.

"Morning, Klaus," he called out.

"Morning, John! All seems to be back to normal again, but the men are not their talkative selves today, that is strange. Yesterday, it was the same."

"Yes. Football came up to the house last night to tell me of it."

Klaus raised his eyebrows but added no comment, but after a few seconds he added, "There's something bloody funny going on, though."

"What kind of funny?" asked John, intrigued by the statement.

"I don't know." he replied.

"Well, something's put the wind up them, that's for sure!"

"Yah! Dat is the problem, mein herr," and he shrugged his shoulders as an added gesture.

"Well, no doubt we will find out soon enough, Klaus."

"Perhaps!" said Klaus, "anyway I am off down town and I will speak with Football," and he got into his Land Rover and gunned the engine back into life.

John watched Klaus later on as he and Football met up, but through his binoculars he could not discern any signs of trouble. He ranged them back and forth across the site but all appeared normal. Later on he met with Klaus again up top, and asked him if he could see anything apparent.

"No! Nothing, John, but I still have this feeling that there's something happening."

"Yes. Me, too," added John.

"You know, John, that tomorrow is the night of the full moon?"

"Yes! We'll have Football up this afternoon and we can go through what we are going to do then."

"Yah! I will call you when he comes up, John."

The afternoon arrived with amazing speed and John called on the radio for all the team to assemble at his office. He waited for the replies to come back to him from the men who were all scattered about over a wide area. They arrived in dribs and drabs and when all were present, he called for silence.

"Tomorrow is de night of de full moon," he stated loudly, "and we know that this is the night when these brotherhood people are to carry out their rituals."

He looked at Football who nodded in silence, then spoke. "No, is wrong, massah! De full moon is tonight."

John looked sharply at Football, then all eyes turned automatically to the calendar on the wall, next to the description of a Nigerian road. Their eyes fell upon it and stopped at the date. Next to the date, was a symbol which indicated that it was the full moon.

"Christ!" exclaimed John, "then it's tonight!"

"Yes, massah! Is tonight!" said Football.

"Shit!" exclaimed Dave, "that doesn't give us much time, then."

They then laid the plans and agreed to meet up at ten in the evening down at the accommodation huts.

"Do you have your men available, Football?"

"Yes, massah! I keep them off de shift. We has de big men, plenty of them and we will take de special weapons with us."

"What special weapons, Football?" asked Dave.

"Oh, de usual, massah, de bows and arrows, de poison, and others."

John smiled as he said this, then added, "Well, I don't know if we will be needing these, Football, but take them anyway. Are we all prepared for what we may come across tonight?" He looked around at the faces of those assembled but no-one indicated anything negative.

Doc spoke up then, "Be prepared for some more blood and things, my friends. I think that we will all see some of it tonight, perhaps."

"As long as it's not ours!" commented Tony.

The evening flew by and soon it was half past nine. They all met up down town at the huts and Klaus noted that the men that Football had assembled were a fearsome looking bunch. Football obviously meant business.

Machetes were prominent, glinting in the dark, a few bolas hung on belts and a variety of clubs and shotguns were slung over their shoulders. Klaus carried out a head count and, including the management team, there was a total of forty-nine.

"Don't you think we have too many, John?" he asked.

John looked around, then glanced at the number of vehicles that they had at their disposal and did a quick calculation. "No! We have enough transport I'd rather we had too much than too little, the more the merrier. At least with this number of men we will be sure of thwarting them at their practices. Let's go then!" John called out and the shadowy crowd melted into the vehicles, only the sound of weapons striking the sides of the vehicles was heard. John surmised that it must look as if they were going to war, judging by the number of weapons and the looks on the faces of Football's men.

The vehicles were actually overcrowded but no-one complained and the convoy set off along the path, bucking and swaying before it reached the metalled road, then headed downstream. The moon had now risen above the level of the trees and had bathed all around in a pale light. The convoy nosed onto the track that followed the bends of the river and they drove with their lights off so as not to attract attention. The light of the moon was adequate to see by. The track was difficult to follow but their keen eyesight kept them on it as they advanced slowly, keeping the noise of the engines low as they passed by one of the smaller villages on the river's bank. Klaus was in the lead Land Rover and was leaning out of the window, keeping his eye on the track as they went along. The river bank rose and fell and their movement resembled a roller coaster. Soon they were at the third bend and they started to climb steeply upwards, and steadily increasing their height as they passed the other bends in the river. They stopped at the same point as before and carefully hid the vehicles by camouflaging them with branches of trees. They remained there listening for a moment in case they had been detected, but all was deathly quiet. Now they advanced on foot and crept along the pathway, treading lightly in case the noise of a snapping twig would betray their presence. Football and two of the men covered their tracks as they went and soon they arrived at the huts where they had come across the decomposed body. They fanned out in a wide arc and settled down in the grasses to wait. Football deployed the men again in the form of a purse string, and each group was made aware of the signals to be used. John looked around. They were certainly well camouflaged and he could not see any of Football's men at all, only his own team. They all copied the technique of cover and to anyone looking on, all appeared as if normal. The bright moonlight cast few shadows as they waited patiently. Klaus looked around, but all was quiet and it remained so for some time.

Dave looked up at the moon, it had climbed higher now and was almost directly above them, creating few shadows. He looked at his watch and noted that it was only eleven in the evening. He held the face closer to his eyes to determine if the second hand was actually moving as it seemed to be stopped, but he was just able to discern the movement. Suddenly, a whispered voice was heard, away to his left, "Someone coming!"

Instantly all were alert, staring into the darkness at the point where the voice had spoken. They could not see anything, but then, far off to the left, a file of men had appeared. Slowly, they advanced into the moonlight and a reflection from something metallic being carried was seen. The file of men crossed an open tract of ground and continued on towards them. They pressed their bodies closer to the ground, it seemed as if they were pressed into the earth itself. Football put his ear to the ground and concentrated. Many men he decided after a moment, twenty or so at least, and some of them heavy footed. He raised his head and looked at the file now, which was much closer as they ascended the hill in front of the huts. They advanced passing close by where Klaus was laid and now the features of the men could be clearly seen in the light. A tall muscular man led the file carrying a long staff upright in his right hand. He led the way to the clearing at the centre of the huts and the remainder of them followed on. Klaus counted them as they passed by. There were eighteen of them, as they came to a halt they formed a circle and on the word of the leader, they each donned a head-dress. This was the head of a leopard, and the skin draped down across their shoulders and down their backs. The eyes in the heads shone yellow in the moonlight, and the dark shadows of the men on the ground presented an eerie picture. The ceremony commenced and words were spoken. Football strained to hear what was being said but he could not understand the words as they were in a strange dialect unknown to him. The men all spoke then in unison, and answered some question put by the leader. A chant followed, then silence fell upon them. The tallest of the men turned towards the direction from which the moonlight came and, raising his hands, he uttered some strange sounding words, directing them at the moon itself it seemed.

Football remained listening, trying to make some sense out of the words being spoken but it was all meaningless. The man who addressed the Moon, then held his staff up towards it and uttered more phrases, then lowered his arm and his head and turned back towards the men in the circle. A signal from one of them caused a stirring back in the low bushes by the trees and three men appeared. One led the second who was bound tightly with rope and was prodded on by the third man, the three of them advancing towards the circle of men by the huts. The circle opened as the men approached, allowing the three of them to enter, then the circle closed again. They turned the bound figure around to face the leader and Football strained his eyes to see if he could identify the man. He did not recognise him, but reckoned that he was about eighteen years of age.

The monologue recommenced and the circle closed inwards towards the man in the centre. A sack was then produced, and from it a bowl and a long machete were removed. The blade glinted in the moonlight. Football signalled to the men to be ready and they stirred, ready to pounce. All of the circle spoke as one for a few minutes, then fell silent. The tall muscular man lifted up the machete and approached the bound captive. He raised the machete to the moon and uttered another strange sound, then, turning slightly, he started to bring the bladed weapon down in a long slow arc. It was as though it all happened in slow motion.

Football stood up quickly and called out to his men. As one they all sprang to action and emerging from their cover, they closed the distance between them in what seemed like a few milliseconds. The men in the circle whirled around to see where the cry had emanated from and too late they realised that they were surrounded. A hail of spears flashed in the moonlight as they winged their way towards the circle of men. John had seen them fly across the clearing as he arose from his hiding place but he was unable to call out, such was the rapidity of their course. Some of the spears found their mark with deadly accuracy and the remainder of the men fell upon those in the circle with clubs and machetes. Within seconds they all lay dead, their blood spilled on the dry earth. The ferocity of the attack caused the blood to splash across a wide area. The leader stood mesmerised by it all while the attackers fell upon him, pulling him down to the ground. He fell to the ground, at least his torso did, headless. This followed soon afterwards and it came to a stop the head pointing up at the moon, the eyes staring widely. Spears protruded from his body at numerous angles, some having passed through his rib cage and out at the other side. Klaus and John drew level with the blood bath and extricated the would be victim from the heap of bodies. Their feet splashed in the blood as it gurgled out of the corpses and welled up against one of them.

Dave arrived at the scene and, looking around him in horror, he said in a loud voice, "Christ!" then felt violently sick as the stench of the warm blood greeted his nostrils. They managed to pull the bound man free from the milling throng, and as they did so, Football called out in a loud voice, "No more Leopard Men!" His men remained in the puddle, they were obviously enjoying every moment of it and stayed there hacking what was left of the bodies into small pieces. Finally, John looked at the heap which now only resembled a heap of butcher's meat, such was the result. All of a sudden the carnage stopped, and Football's men leapt around whooping with glee at their achievements.

Klaus looked at the man they had rescued and called Doc over. He approached the man and looked into his eyes. Drugged he was certainly, and his face had a zombie-like appearance. They laid him down while they watched Football's men finish their carnage, then, when all was quiet, Klaus asked Football what he was going to do with the bodies, or rather what was left of them.

Football replied by raising his arm, and two of the men broke off and went over behind a tree. They returned carrying two Jerry cans of fuel and commenced to pour it all over the remains. One of them struck a match which flared briefly as it arced down on to the heap. All of a sudden the mass went up in flames with a swooshing noise and the flames leapt high, lighting up the area for some distance. The fire raged and gurgled and spat as the blood boiled and they all had to retreat some distance away from it. The smoke billowed upwards and all of Football's men, to a man, stood watching as the flames consumed the Leopard Men.

"Well, I think we've seen enough!" said John, and they retired with the drugged man to the edge of the clearing. They climbed back aboard the Land Rovers, the men now all singing loudly in celebration. They left the scene, the bodies still in flames, sizzling and sparking in the intense heat. As they left, they looked back and atop the pile of flames a skull was prominent, smoke emanating from the eye socket, a chilling reminder of the Leopard Men.

The singing continued all the way back to the accommodation site. While they drove, John surmised that none of the team was really necessary there. Football and his men had done the deed and the rest of them had been voyeurs in effect.

They all disbanded for the night and when John reached his residence, he found that Nat and Eb were standing at the door awaiting his arrival. John allowed himself a half smile as he entered the house, and Eb walked towards him and said, "No more Leopard Men now, massah!"

"How do you know that, Eb?" he asked.

"I know! I know! De bush telegraph, he tell me," and waving John over to the table, he said, "Come, massah! Nat, he have de drinks ready for us."

Nat stood there, a huge grin on his face, beaming from ear to ear.

"Who told you the news, Nat?"

"No-one tells, massah, but we knows!" and he handed a whisky over to John who took it from him, still amazed at their perception of the outcome of the visit.

"It is two-thirty in the morning Nat! It's a bit late for drinks."

"Not tonight, massah! We can drink all night if you wants!" and he grinned again Nat and Eb then plied John for the details of the event, and sat enthralled as John related the train of events, trying to relate everything that had happened, including the grisly end.

Eb declared that was the end of it all forever, and that the news would spread far and wide.

"I hope it doesn't!" commented John. "I'd like to keep it quiet really."

"Not much chance, massah! De bush telegraph, it verrah efficient. You will see!" and he took another swig of his drink, and went off to the kitchen, doing a little dance as he went along the floor.

John awoke later that morning after dozing off in his bed for what seemed like five minutes or so, and looked out of the bedroom window. The sun was up, all the birds were singing sweetly and all in all, it seemed a brighter day for many reasons. The usual crowd of bats flitted around the tree tops just down the hill and the air was fresh and clean. He dressed and went downstairs where he was greeted by Eb, still grinning and singing as he went about his normal daily chores now with a spring in his step.

Eb served breakfast and was able to relax, completely safe in the knowledge that they had got rid of the brotherhood once and for all. After breakfast, Nat took the tray of tea out on to the veranda and set it out on the table for John. He went out and sat gazing out over the valley. Far below he could hear the singing of the village women as they set off for water. John called for the two of them and they both emerged from the shade of the house.

"Come and sit and have a cup of tea as well, you two!" he called.

They did so, and John asked them how they knew of the news so early.

"Is as I say, massah! And is as you say, de jungle drums!"

"But we have no jungle drums, Eb!"

"Maybe! But de people in de village downstream they all knows already, massah!"

"Do they now."

"Yes, massah, they knows and many others too!"

John set off for the site and on the way passed the usual girls on the road in single file. As he came abreast of them, they all stopped and raised their arms in a form of salute to him as he passed by. He slowed slightly as he realised the meaning and then continued up the hill. As he drew up at the turn off for the office, he passed a solitary hunter out early who called out to him, "No more Leopard Men, massah! " and grinned. John acknowledged his message with a wave and drove over to the office and got out of the Land Rover.

Marcel and Klaus were already in and they beckoned him over to where they stood outside the clinic. "Seems as if everyone knows all about it, John!"

"Yes! So I see."

"News travels fast here," added Klaus, "my servant knew before I could get the chance to tell him."

"Mine too!" replied John.

"Well, I'm off down town, John," Klaus said and climbed into his vehicle, banged the door to and drove off round the bend.

A few moments later the radio broke the conversation, "Klaus to John!"

"Yes, Klaus!"

"You'd better get down here fast, John."

"What's up?"

"Just get here, pronto!"

John crossed to his vehicle and climbed aboard followed by Marcel. As he drove off downhill, he called again on the radio to Klaus.

"Klaus! Where are you?"

"Down town, at the assembly area!"

"Roger."

John looked across at Marcel as they rounded the series of bends before the road reached the bottom of the hill, and said, "I hope this is not more trouble, Marcel, I thought that was the end to it all last night."

"We shall see soon enough, John," he commented as they rounded the last bend and set off along the rutted and dusty track to the assembly area.

They swung into the wide area, and were confronted with a huge mass of people. All of the workers must be here, thought Marcel as they drew to an abrupt halt.

John got out and did a quick scan with his eyes and spotting Klaus, he made his way quickly over to him. "What's up, Klaus?" he said as his view took in the face of the dam, and it was only then that he got an inkling of what was happening.

There was no-one at the face. Not a soul was in evidence, no manual workers, no-one on the walkways and no-one at the base of the dam either. The men all stood in a huge semi-circle, and as soon as John approached they broke into a loud cheering. John was taken aback but seeing Klaus approach, he relaxed slightly. "What's all this then?" he asked, suspiciously.

As he spoke the assembled throng fell silent. Then a loud cry went up from the front of the mass of bodies assembled.

"Gaisuwa Sarki!" followed by, "Ya tsayer! Muquenta!"

Silence reigned for a few seconds only, then another cry went up "Rankai Dade!" then to a man they all raised their right arm high above their heads. This was repeated again and the men raised their arms again. John looked around at them, realising that he was being honoured in some fashion but before he could respond, more cries were made. "Gaisuwa Sarki! Gaisuwa Sarki!"

Football approached and stood in front of John. "The men, Massah John, they salute you! They say that you are the great chief! You have delivered them from the Leopard Men!"

John still taken aback, responded. "Tell them it was not me who rid them of the Leopard Men," and indicated those who stood around.

Football turned to the men and in the common dialect, he informed them of this. There was silence for a moment, while Football's words sank in, then out of the crowd, a single voice called out, "Ya tsayer!"

"What do they say, Football?"

"They say, massah, that you are de deliverer from evil!"

John sensed that it was useless to try to convince him of his innocence in the deeds, so he remained silent. The cheering broke out again and continued for a few moments, then a chant broke out, semi-musical, and continued for some time before they fell into silence again, and repeated the shouts previously made. They were all powerless to stop this so they allowed it to continue until, slowly, the mass started to disperse.

Eventually Klaus managed to engage in conversation with John and above the clamour, he made himself heard. "They refused to go to work until they had addressed you. You are certainly honoured!"

"Perhaps, but you know, Klaus, as well as I do that it was not me who killed the Leopard Men."

"Yes. But you try telling them that!"

As some of the men passed by him, they hesitated and gave him a salute as they came level with him. Some were in the form of a raised arm others were a semi-military type of salute to all of which John responded. There was no mistaking their intent.

"I suppose we will have to put up with this for a while, Klaus?"

"Yah! I think so. Perhaps it will diminish."

However, for the following three weeks or so, John was continually hailed when ever he came into contact with the workers. Even the local villagers and men out hunting, returning from the bush, would stop on the roadside and hail him as he passed by.

He arrived home one evening, just a day following the greetings, and found a large bowl of goats milk on the doorstep.

"Where did this come from, Eb?" he called out.

Eb emerged from the veranda and looked at it then without hesitation he said, "It is from de village downstream. They wish to thank you for the freeing from de Leopard Men, massah."

"Well, we don't need it, shall we give it away?"

Nat and Eb cast glances at each other, then said, "Is not right massah! You must not do this! It will be considered an insult if you do."

"Yes. You're right of course, Eb. All right, bring it indoors."

"Yes massah!" said Eb, now smiling, and he bent low to pick it up and carried it into the kitchen.

As he did so Nat spoke. "If you had sent that back, massah, then that would bring back de curse of de Leopard Men again to de village."

"Really?"

"Yes, massah. This I knows."

"All right, Nat, I wouldn't want to do that to them."

"No suh! You shoah don'!"

John smiled to himself as he crossed to the writing desk and sat down to write the daily report. As he sat at the desk he could hear singing wafting up from the valley floor and, getting up from his seat, he went out onto the veranda and listened

"Who is that singing?" he asked. Nat appeared and listened for a moment.

"Is de people in de village down de river, massah, they are singing while they is at work. I have not heard this for some years now. Is good sign!"

"Is that so?"

"Yes, massah! They will sing now for many days. You will see."

Sure enough, the singing continued as Nat had stated, and went on for almost two weeks, before it gradually petered out.

The euphoria eventually diminished and all returned to normal, although the local people still greeted him as they passed on the road and saluted him wherever he went. The news of this event, however, had spread far and wide, even as far as Lagos itself and to other places also. The local Berger encampment sent messages of congratulation to him also. He thought the fuss was all over, in toto, but he was mistaken.

An unexpected visit from Hendry J. from Lagos who had driven up to the site himself and arrived unannounced at John's house early one evening. "Ah! The all conquering hero!" he called out, as he strode through the doorway.

Nat scurried off into the kitchen and quickly rustled up some food for the massah and Eb took his bags up to the spare room and laid out his things for him.

John was surprised at the visit and said so as he got up from the chair and welcomed him.

"Well, I've been meaning to come for a few days now, John. This Leopard Man business has got everyone talking, my phone never stops ringing! Oh, And before you say it, yes, I know where it is now!"

John smiled at this, recalling the hunt the phone incident.

"Not only that, John. Now I have two phones!"

"Two?"

"Yes, and I know where both of them are as well! How's that for efficiency, eh?"

"Well, Hendry, I'm impressed!"

"Enough said," he commented, "and how about a drink, then, John?"

John waved to the cabinet as if to say help yourself, but Hendry J. was already at it, rummaging about in the bottles and quickly poured them a drink each. Returning to the seats that had been pulled out for them by Eb, they sat down and Hendry J. spoke.

"You have certainly stolen the limelight. Tell me, how did you do it?"

"Well, that's it Hendry, I didn't."

"No?" he queried, raising his eyebrows. Then looking John straight in the eye, he said, "Who then?"

"Well," John said, "it's a long story, but I'll make it as short as I can. "I've been getting all the praise for it, but it was really a combined effort, a group of the workers and our team as well. I'm afraid I took no active part in it, but the men themselves got rid of the Leopard Men. Everyone seems to have forgotten that and have heaped all the praise on me and that's how it got out, I imagine. However, I have had to take the honours myself, but it's all wrong really."

"I see! But don't be surprised if you get a visit from the *Lagos Weekly*, they'll be here, sure as eggs are eggs! They don't miss a trick! In fact, I'm surprised that you haven't had a visit from them already."

"Heaven forbid!"

"Yes, well, enough of that! How's the job going these days?"

"Oh! Just fine, ahead of schedule, as usual. The odd problem here and there but only minor ones, on the whole I'm very pleased."

"Good! That's what I like to hear! Have you any interim reports I can go through while I'm here?"

"Yes! Do you want them now?"

"No! Tomorrow will do, John, I'll pass them on to the client later this week."

"Certainly," John replied. "How long are you staying for, then?"

"Oh, well! I need a break, so how about a few days? Does that suit you?"

"Whatever, Hendry! Stay as long as you like."

"Don't tempt me, I could get used to this life up here quite easily."

They continued their conversation for a long time, with the regular replenishment of the glasses to accompany them into the night.

The following day John left Hendry J. to the reports, and went off to the site. The day passed with boring routine and nothing to distract him at all from his duties. He arrived back at the house at six in the evening to find two dusty, short-wheel-based Land Rovers parked outside his door. Entering the doorway, he called for Eb.

"Yes, massah?"

"Visitors, Eb?" he queried.

"Yes, massah! Is de mens from de newspapers!"

"Damn! How many Eb?"

"Foah, massah!"

"Christ! Well, I suppose I'd better see them then. Where are they?"

"Dey with Massah Hendry now, boss."

"Okay, thanks Eb."

"Yes, massah," he replied and returned to whatever he was doing when John arrived.

John entered the study and on seeing him, the four reporters stood up and bid him welcome. The traditional round of handshakes then took place, and eventually they all managed to sit down after a further bout of bowing and smiling had passed. The lead reporter, one of them said, was John Namibwe who had his three staff members here with him and he introduced them, Dick Agerie, David John Kakwunda and finally, Samual John Abaki. John thought to himself, try remembering that lot! They asked numerous questions and bid John go over the night's activities again for their benefit, and while he did so the others wrote furiously, noting down every little detail. Then there followed the other questions which took some time to get through, but finally they seemed to be satisfied with what they had and then the lead reporter produced a modern camera from his bag at his feet and politely asked for a photograph of John. He acceded, and it was taken.

"When does this go to print, then?" John asked.

"I is goin' to put you on de front page, mistah!" he replied, beaming widely.

"Well! That'll be nice," he said to them.

"More like you'll end up on the back page," commented Hendry, in a low voice, "next to the sex adverts!"

John suppressed a smile. "Will you stay for dinner with us?" asked John.

"No, massah! Thank you, but we has to go quick quick, to catch de presses!"

"Ah, yes of course!" John replied.

They all go up and the reporters took their leave. The round of handshakes was repeated, and finally they filed out through the doorway and entered their vehicles. They set off downhill, waving to John as they went and John returned indoors.

"I'm glad they didn't stay really!" John commented, as he walked into the room. "I don't think I could have stood another round of questions."

"They wouldn't have stayed long anyway, John, any excuse to go and visit a relatives hut would be the temptation, I should imagine."

"Just as well then, eh?" and calling out to Eb he shouted, "When's food up, Eb?"

"Jus' comin' massah!" was the reply.

"Good! I could eat a scabby horse. What's on the menu tonight, Eb?"

His head appeared round the kitchen door and he replied, "Got de meat stew! Fresh vegetables, sweet potato with fried rice," and, smiling, he added, "Nat, he do special for you. De apple pie with de yellow glue!"

"Yellow glue? What's that, Eb?"

Eb's head disappeared into the kitchen, then reappeared again a few seconds later.

"Is de yellow glue you likes, massah! Is yellow sticky stuff. You wait an' see. You will like!"

John frowned at this description, and realising that he was not going to get a more accurate one, he called out, "Okay! Make sure there's plenty of it! I is verrah hungry man! Maybe I eats two scabby horses! You ask Nat if he has any of dem in de kitchen!"

"Yes, massah!" was the faint response.

A few seconds later they heard Eb's voice clearly ordering Nat to get with the action, and to make sure that there was plenty of food, and that it was to be cooked perfectly for de Massah John.

"Okay! Okay!" Nat replied in a high voice, "You old goat! You thinks I not knows how to cook? I was cooking when you was still at yo' mammy's breast!" he replied in a threatening tone.

John and Hendry J. burst out laughing at this exchange, which continued in the depths of the kitchen for some time. True to Nat's word the meal was perfectly cooked and presented. As they were finishing up Nat came to the kitchen door, still with a wooden spoon in his hand, and asked if the meal was all right for de massahs. Looking up John said, "Just perfect, Nat."

Nat looked relieved.

"Why? Is there someting wrong with my reply?"

A strange expression crept over Nat's face. "I is goin' to kill 'im!" he shouted.

"Kill who, Nat?"

"Dat Ebenezer! Dat snake in de grass! He tell me you say de meal is rubbish!"

John and Hendry J. grinned widely as Nat's face got redder and redder, and quickly Nat and the accompanying spoon disappeared from sight into the kitchen.

"Wheah is you, Ebenezer? I is goin' to kill you foh suah! I is goin' to make de soup with you! I is goin' to pluck out yoh eyes! An' den boil yoh brains, dat is if yous gots any! Wheah is you? Come out!" There then followed the sound of a cupboard door banging as Nat hunted high and low for Ebenezer. He, however, was standing outside the kitchen window killing himself laughing, as he watched the antics of Nat as he crept around the kitchen holding the spoon as if it were a club. Eventually Nat spotted him and proceeded to chase him. He grabbed a sweeping brush and Ebenezer displayed a remarkable turn of speed and ran around the house outside with Nat in hot pursuit. Eb ducked and weaved and Nat's swipes all missed their target. "I is goin' to gets you, you ol' goat! I is going to tie you to de ground and pour de bee honey ovah you and den leaves yo' for de ants!"

John and Hendry J. viewed this with great amusement and left the two of them still chasing about, while they went out on to the veranda and sat at the table with a long cool drink each. However, even there they could still hear Nat's remarks about Ebenezer's status in life, and what he was going to do to him when he caught him.

The night wore on, and Hendry J. went over John's report with him to ensure that they were in agreement as to its contents and spent the rest of the evening in social chatter.

The following day, Hendry went walkabout with John, Klaus and Fred, and visited just about everything he could find. By the time that he had finished this he had a very concise picture of the situation. He was impressed with what he had seen and said so. He rounded off the tour by noting down a few statistics in John's office, and then decided to call it a day.

Marcel, who usually lived life at a sedate pace, had been busy of late. An unusual warm air stream had been in evidence for some days now and it seemed as if it was draped across the valley, particularly in their immediate area. This had brought with it an unexpected plague of mosquitoes. Malaria was a common disease in Africa, but most of the population had developed an immunity to it, including the workers.

Numerous minor outbreaks had occurred and a number of men on different shifts were affected. Marcel had been going through his stock of syringes faster than he could count and had ordered more. Also, the local villages were affected and he spent part of his time there, aiding them in the fight against it. So today, he was absent, and John and Hendry J. had been left to converse with each other.

At last Nathaniel and Ebenezer had buried the hatchet, so to speak, but it had provided an amusing interlude in the day to day routine of the running of the house. Hendry left the next morning and made a detour on the way back so that he could look up an old friend of his some thirty miles along the road to Lagos. The height of the dam had increased of late, section three of the upper wall towering high above them. At the top of it where men were working, they appeared only as dots from below. The thickness of this part was over a hundred feet, and many men had been reallocated to this part of the construction phase to ensure that it went ahead smoothly. It was designed so that when the load of water was applied to the dam, the forces would be transferred to the lower thicker part. Scaffolding had been erected on the overhanging sections and a few of the workers had employed their own methods of suspending themselves on a single rope while carrying out the pinning of steel plates on the face. This was frowned upon, but a blind eye was turned to it by the supervisors. All was going well when suddenly, the rope on which one of the workers was suspended gave way without warning, and the man plummeted quickly down the face to his death, his body bouncing off the surface as it rocketed to the bottom. Down below the klaxon blared its strident note and all stopped work immediately. The man's broken, bruised and damaged body was recovered and lay at the base covered in a mixture of blood and dust.

"Better get Marcel down here," said Klaus.

"He's not here, he's away at the village!"

"Ah so! I forgot that, well it won't matter now he's dead, for sure."

"Better put him in a truck and take him up to the hospital, though," said Rock, so they turfed the body into the back of a transit truck and off it went.

Klaus reached for his radio. "Chief to Football!" he called.

Football answered.

"My office right away, and bring the supervisor!"

"Yes, boss!" Football replied.

Shortly afterwards in Klaus's office, the three stood in silence for a moment.

"Right then, Football! An explanation."

Football turned to the man and spoke to him in his own dialect. "He say, massah, dat de men on de rope has been happening long time now!"

Klaus glared at him for a moment before commenting, "We don't put up scaffolding, Football, to look pretty! It is there to be used! Tell this man that."

Football conveyed the message, the man understood but remained silent, any comment being useless.

"Tell him I don't want to see any more men hung on ropes over the face! If I do then I will throw him down the face if it happens again on his shift."

Football added weight to the words and the man looked frightened for a moment, then nodded silently.

"All right, Football! Return to work." The two of them left and went down town.

Later in the day Marcel returned and on hearing of the accident, he went straight to the morgue and examined the body. Almost every bone in his body was broken, he noted, that being consistent with the height he had fallen from. John went over to see him.

"What's to be done then, Marcel?"

"Nothing, mon ami! We just bury him, that's all there is left to do"

"I'll get a truck organised, Marcel, we'll return him to his village. I'll send Football and a couple of men with him."

"Okay, John, I'll make out a certificate of death for you as well."

John nodded and left. As he crossed the compound he met up with Klaus.

"Well, Klaus, what have we, then, on unofficial practices?"

"Yah, I know what the problem is, I have told the supervisor, and I will speak with the others as well. We just have to hope that it doesn't happen again." Marcel came across with the death certificate neatly typed out and handed it to John.

"How's the malaria doing, Marcel?"

"Much better now, John, I think I have it under control. No-one has died yet, so that is a good sign in itself! One or two of the older people in Fake were in a bad way, but they are improving now and a couple of babies were poorly, but since I've given them the injections they are out of danger. The medicine man was not too happy though, his chicken feathers and the magic dust he threw at the victims had no effect whatsoever."

John nodded in understanding of the situation. One had to be careful with these medicine men, they held sway over a number of villages downstream.

"Yes!" added Marcel, "they are very suspicious of the Baturi's medicine!"

"Did you have any trouble with the witch doctor?" John asked.

"No! But he hung around and watched me like a hawk does a mouse. I could feet his eyes upon me as I worked."

"So you think they would have died without the injections, then?" asked John.

"Certainement! But maybe they will thank us in their own way later, eh?"

John nodded, and went off down town.

Next day the wagon bearing the body of the man left for his village to the north, Football taking with him the man's pay to date to hand over to his family.

John went down town again and Klaus remained up top, saying that he would call him on the radio if needed. John ascended the series of walkways and zigzagged his way upwards. It took the wind out of him as he climbed and it was some time before he reached the top. He stopped frequently to inspect the work, then continued to where the pinning of the plates was in progress. This was a different shift on duty now from the one that had lost the man, and although all looked well he felt that there was something about the plates that was not quite right. He looked again at them but could spot nothing and dismissed it from his mind. Later that evening as he sat on his veranda he went over this in his mind.

Next day he climbed up the face again and examined them through his binoculars.

Two days later, Football returned and called in at John's office to say that the family of the dead man was very happy with the return of the body, and thanked the massah for the pay.

"Okay, Football, that will be all for now, then. Take a break before you go back to work."

"Thank you, massah! See you tomorrow then! Same time, same place!" and he grinned as he left the office.

Chapter Nine

A surprise visitor some weeks later turned out to be Phil. John thought that he would probably never meet up with him again, but here he was young and bright and full of the joys of spring. The vehicle had pulled up outside John's office and he had looked up from his desk as it had an unfamiliar sound to it, different from that of his own type.

"Well! This is a surprise, Phil! What are you doing here?"

"Well, I am on my way south to meet a bishop at Ilorin so I decided that on my way, I would divert slightly and call in and see you, that is if I could locate you."

"Well, you obviously succeeded. But was it hard to find me?"

"No, not at all! You see the Leopard Men news told me that you had a hand in it so it did not take much asking to be directed to this place."

"Oh, that! I thought that it had all died out now, apparently not so, eh?"

"Well, tell me about it then, John. I need to know first hand, it will help in our mission out here."

"Yes, you may be right there, well all right, then!"

He related the tale, not leaving out any detail, and when he had finished Phil gave a low whistle, and commented, "Gee! That's some tale! The bishop will be glad of the news from the first hand source. You see we have many problems with this black magic stuff here. We are trying to get rid of the old superstitions, handed down from generation to generation, it helps in wooing the tribes away from the magic over to a more Christian outlook. Now that I personally know the deliverer!"

"Who is that?" asked John.

"Why you! That's what you are known as! Didn't you know?"

"No! I didn't!"

"Well! That's what they say of you."

"How's the priest that met you at the airport? The frosty one?"

"I don't know, really, after I left you at the airport, I went up country and never saw him again. As far as I know he's still around but as to where, I could not say."

"Well, it'll be some hours yet until I'm finished here, so I suggest you go on down to the house and I'll radio ahead and have the servants be prepared so that you can get settled in."

"Okay, John, see you later on, then."

Phil and his driver went off downhill, leaving John in a lighter frame of mind.

In the evening, John asked Klaus, Fred and Matthew down to the house and between them they had a very entertaining time. Next morning Phil left on his journey to see the Bishop, and promised to call in again on the way back up.

There followed a couple of weeks of relative calm, with some revealing conversations between John, Nat and Eb. The two were a mine of information and John's education was now enhanced. Most amusing of all were the riddles that they spoke of. Eb said to Nat, "Tusa ba a lama maaa," meaning 'Breaking wind won't bring a dormant fire to life'.

John thought that most amusing, and Nat responded, "Witagida biyu magunin gobara", 'two homes provide protection against fire'.

Not to be outdone, Eb responded with, "Abokin sarki, sarki ne", 'a chief's friend becomes a Chief', in other words his friend has the advantages of being a chief, that seemed to John to be logical. Some of them made sense but others did not. One of them, relating to a pair of trousers, stuck in John's mind, "hunya daya ta rubu biyu", meaning 'a single path divides in two', in other words a pair of trousers. One night, as they sat on the veranda drinking dawa file, or corn wine, tasteless but quite potent, they heard loud screaming.

"What's that!" said John, sitting upright in his chair.

"No worry boss, is de Kuraya, is what you calls de hyena."

"I didn't know that there were any of them in this country."

"Yes, there are many," and he opened his hand and counted on his fingers, "dey is all around out in de bush, you not sees them, but dey are der!" And he cast his eyes about as he spoke.

Nat was sitting reading a letter as John sat listening to the sounds of the night and the jungle in front of him.

"Who is the letter from?" asked John.

"Is from de cousin," commented Nat.

Looking at the writing, John said, "Looks like it is Arabic."

"Yes boss, is Adjami."

"What's that?"

"Is, how you say?" and he thought for a moment, "is a dialect of Arab tribe, from de north, in de desert, neah Chad."

"Can you read this then?"

"Yes, boss, I read it! I is de clevah man, you see!" and he smiled at Eb as he said it.

"Yes Nat, I'm sure that you are."

Nat grinned in the light, revealing his white teeth.

"Where does he live then?"

"He in de north, his name is Digo, in de place called Gombe, which is near to Cameroon, this side of de Vogel mountain."

John was now even more educated by this. His geographical knowledge of Nigeria was scant, to say the least. Nigeria was a land of mixed races and cultures, and some strange customs also.

As he sat thinking, he said to Eb, "How many races in de workers, then?"

Eb thought for a moment before replying, "Oh, many, massah!"

"How many then?"

"De man you calls Football, he know, is many cross breeds."

"Yes, I suppose so."

Eb looked skywards, then said, "Well, der is de..." and he started to count them off on the fingers of his hand. "You has got de main ones, de Yoruba, Hausa, Fulani, den der is de Nupes, de Gwari, Ebos, Okpoto, Nok, Berbers, Kanuri, Urhobo, and den close to dem der is de Jerki." He continued to look skywards as if the names were written there. "De intelligent ones, de Ebos," and he smiled as he said it, "den de Ijaws, Jukon, Okpoto, I say dem already I think, also de Ibibos," and he searched the sky again for more names. "De Borgawa from Dahomey, de Ekoi, de Efiks, who is known as de brass peoples, and also de Hametics."

"Why are they called the brass peoples, then, Eb?"

"Is long time ago in de old days, they trade in de river at de place called Bonny, and in Calabar, de name they gets from de people who has de brass pans," and he cupped his hands to demonstrate what they were," dey use dem foh de palm oil and salt, you understand?" he asked looking at John.

"Yes, I do!"

"Then we has de Cross River people from Cameroon, all mixed races, so you sees we has de many peoples heah."

"What about the slaves that were sent to America, then?"

"Ah!" he said, "my mother's mother told me of them. They is caught by de Portuguese and de French, Dutchmen and de Spanish men as well."

"Where did they get the slaves from?"

"In de bush! But most of dem is from Lagos area, but others dey come from de Niger state and in Benin, Kwara. De most though, dey is caught in Calabar and dey is kept in de barracoons in Lagos at Victoria Island befoah dey is sent to de America. De place called Badagari is also de big prison foh de slaves, and de name of Lagos then was Lago de Curamo, de Portugueses name of it and it become de big place where all slaves go. Deah dey sent de slaves foah three hundred yeahs, then they is not manys left and de Emir of Kontagora, who is de biggest slave trader, he very bad man, sell thousands of de mens foah de slave."

"Yes, I've read about them, Eb."

"Not many left, as I say, so dey interbreed and so now we has many peoples again. Me, I is Hausa, all my family is Hausa too, and this," and he turned to Nat and clipped his ear, "he is of de Fulani, he cow man!" and he grinned as he said it. Nat smiled at the comment. "But his people, dey live in Hausa land foah de long time now, and dey is de converted ones."

"I is not converted!" said Nat.

"Yes you is, you told me that!"

"You old goat! I is still de Fulani! Maybe I speak de Hausa but I still is Fulani!"

"Okay," replied Eb "you is still de Felani then!" and pursed his lips as he said it, "anyway, you is still my friend even if you is converted and you makes de rotten soup."

At this Nat jumped up, picked up a nearby calabash and proceeded to hit Eb over the head with it while Eb, now laughing, tried to protect himself with his hands. Nat stopped and said, "You wait! I is goin' to put de worms on yoh soup. This week de big fat ones, then I shows you how smart I is!"

"All right," said John, "let's have another beer! Anything to calm Nat down."

The construction of the new highway, a twin dual carriageway the same as had been built in numerous areas of Nigeria, was now closer at hand. Julius Berger's massive force of men pushed onwards relentlessly, carving a path through the jungle at a tremendous rate and the approach road that led to the top of the dam was by now only two miles away.

There were now more frequent visits between the two construction teams and a strong camaraderie had sprung up between them. Initially, a few friendly football matches had been organised, which went down well with the workers, but this was closely followed by house parties, barbecues and various other events. John ensured that all took part in them and life took on a new meaning for many of them. The Berger men were of mixed nationality, being Spanish, Dutch, Italian, French and Indian as well as many Africans and some men from as far away as Mexico and South America. All in all, John had not seen a happier bunch for a long time. The following months brought rapid progress and everything was well ahead of schedule.

John sat poring over the sets of figures in front of him, and commented to Klaus, "This is too good to be true."

"Yah! We are performing well."

John, pencil in mouth, commented, "Something has to go wrong some time, it's too perfect."

"You worry too much, my friend," was the reply.

"Well, if anything is going to happen, I'd sooner have it happen now."

It was now March and the Harmattan had crept in from the northern deserts, and the suspended dust had all but drowned out the sun by day and a foggy panorama existed all around. Visibility was reduced to almost zero and consequently the work had slowed because of this. Still, they were well ahead of schedule so John was not too worried about it. A few days later, John was out on one of his frequent site visits when one of the shift supervisors wandered past.

"Where's Football today?" he asked.

"I not know, massah, not see him dis morning."

That's odd, thought John to himself, as Football was not the type of man to be missing from his work. He reached for his radio and called upon it, "Kingpin to Chief."

"Yah?"

"Have you seen Football today?"

"No, not seeing," answered Klaus.

"Me neither!" answered Boxer.

"Roger."

"Dave here, do you want him?"

"Yes."

"Okay, I'll send Joshua down to look for him"

"Roger."

Joshua, however, returning an hour later, had drawn a blank. All day long John made enquiries but no-one had seen him, not even the men on shift or anyone else for that matter. He discussed it with Marcel, Fred and Klaus, but they were all at a loss as to where he was.

"I'll drive over to the Berger camp," said Fred, "he may have gone over there."

"Not without telling someone," added Dave, then added a comment, "I smell a rat!"

"What makes you say that?" asked John.

"Oh, I don't know. Just a sort of feeling I have, that's all."

As Fred left, John called to him, "Let me know if you come across him, won't you?"

"Sure," replied Fred as he climbed aboard his Land Rover and set off on the dusty track for the Berger camp.

"I'll call you on the radio!" he shouted over his shoulder as he went.

Two and a half hours had gone by, and John meanwhile had gone down to his house and waited there.

Fred did call and the radio burst into life, "Flintstone to Kingpin!"

"Yes, Flintstone, go ahead."

"Well, he's been here all right. But that was yesterday evening apparently. He left about midnight to return to our camp."

"On the normal path?"

"Wait one," was the answer.

A period of silence followed, then the radio spoke again, "They say that he took the bush path and he should have been back with us about an hour later."

"Okay, Fred, you'd better come back over then."

"Roger, on my way."

John thought for a moment, then the radio spoke again. "Bringing back a crate of our favourite beer!" the voice said.

John flicked the transmit button in acknowledgement and switched his radio to standby, went into the kitchen and made himself a cup of coffee.

Later in the day he discussed it with Eb and Nat. They were of the opinion that it was indeed strange for Football to disappear without trace as he was so well known in the area.

"Verrah strange," Nathaniel commented.

The sound of a horn blowing at the door interrupted their conversation, and Fred entered through the doorways.

"I looked for him on the way back but there's no sign of him anywhere." John looked at him but did not comment. Fred continued, "He was over visiting a friend of his who comes from the same village and he stayed for a few hours, then left, saying that he would see his friend again the following night."

"Do we have a channel that is on the same frequency as the Berger one?"

"Yes, if you go over to channel six, you can call them direct."

"Good," said John.

"They are only about four miles away as the crow flies, so you should get them easily enough."

John walked over to his radio and changed the channel switch to position six. "I'll give them a call later, Fred."

"Right then," Fred answered, "I'm off then, back to my house. I've dropped some of the beer off at the accommodation block as well, and I'll get Dave to get a load of it tomorrow as we're out of it completely."

"Okay, Fred, thanks," replied John.

Fred waved as he went out of the door and the sound of the engine revving as he disappeared from sight uphill confirmed his departure.

Ebenezer raised his eyebrows and looked at Nat, who did likewise and neither passed any comment.

After dinner John read for a while then crossed over to the radio and called the Berger camp. "Berger from Consolidated."

There was a brief pause, before the answer came back. "Hello Consolidated! Pieter speaking in the admin office, can we help you?"

"Hi, Pieter, John here."

"Ah! The chief! Okay, go ahead Chief!"

John smiled to himself at the comment. "Have you seen our man, Football, over there anywhere?"

"No, not that I know of but leave it with me and I'll ask around."

"Okay, then, Pieter, you do that please."

"Certainly, will call you back later."

Half of an hour had passed, then the radio broke the silence. "Berger to The Chief."

"Yes, Pieter, John here, go ahead."

"No sign of your man here, Chief, not tonight anyway. The guard on the gate has not seen him come or go and he says he has not been back since he left last night."

"Not at all?"

"No sir, they were expecting him to come but it has now gone past ten-thirty. If he comes I will call you right away, will that be all right?"

"Yes, Pieter, thanks anyway."

"Ciao, then, Chief!" was the reply and the radio lapsed into silence.

During the night, however, there was no call from Pieter or anyone else. Before work commenced the next day, John had Klaus and Dave call in by his house.

"There's been no sign of Football at all, so I think we'd better investigate this, eh?"

"Yah," said Klaus.

"Right, then. Let's go and look for him, better get one of Football's friends who he normally goes visiting with to the Berger camp, and we'll try and trace the route he may have taken."

Dave went off down town and shortly afterwards he returned with the man. Klaus got a few other of the trackers as well, notably the ones that were adept at tracking, and they all climbed into a long-wheel-based Land Rover and set off for the Berger encampment. Dave remained behind, saying that he would listen out on the Berger channel for any messages. On the way downhill, Klaus remembered that a man called Ife, had been recently to the camp with Football and he detoured into the accommodation blocks and sought him out. He was sleeping off night shift but Klaus shook him by the shoulder and woke him saying, "Ife! We need your help to look for Football."

Ife looked surprised for a moment, then slowly climbed out of bed and struggled to don a pair of faded trousers, having great difficulty in doing so because of his erection which diminished as he came fully awake and he succeeded in getting them on. He placed his sandals on his callused feet, and grabbing a faded pink shirt, he threw it over his shoulders leaving it gaping open at the front. The Land Rover set off, they bumped along the track and headed up towards the Berger compound.

The wagon was crowded now and Klaus shifted his rump over on to the petrol tank and made himself as comfortable as was possible for that particular seat.

Turning to the people that were in the truck, five in number, he said, "You all know the path that Football takes from the Berger camp?"

"Yes, massah!" they said, almost in unison.

"Good!" he said, and turned back towards the front of the vehicle as they bumped along.

A voice from behind said, "You not worry boss, we finds him!"

John acknowledged the comment as they rounded the last bend and came within sight of the gates to the Berger compound. The guard on the gate flagged them down as they approached and, seeing John was in the front, the guard recognised him and waved the vehicle through, pointing out the admin office and directing them towards it. They drove over to the door and pulled up at the steps. Klaus and John got out and entered the building, while the rest of the men remained sitting in the back of the Land Rover. They asked for Pieter and he appeared from behind a filing cabinet and came towards them, hand outstretched.

"Good morning, John and Klaus! Come in and sit down." They did that while Pieter went over to the fridge and extracted two cold cokes, and passed them over to them, "So! You are still looking for your man, Football, eh?"

"Yes, he seems to have disappeared."

"Yes, strange," Pieter commented.

"Do you know who he came to see here?" John asked.

"No, but it will not take long to find out," and waving them to follow him, he set off along the corridor. They went into an office marked 'Labour' and Pieter asked for the man that Football had come to see. The man behind the desk looked down a long list of names, and coming to the required one, he picked up his radio and called for the man to come to the office.

"He will be here in about two minutes," Pieter said.

A dust encrusted worker appeared at the door and said in a guttural accent, "You want me?"

"Yes," replied Pieter, "you know, Bombay, where Football went, when he left you?"

John shook hands with the man, and said, "Can you show us where he went?"

Bombay beckoned them outside and they followed, moving along the side of the huts he stopped and pointed out a path that led down to the valley.

"He went that way," and he nodded with his head in the direction.

"Is that the shortest way down to the valley?" asked John.

"Yes," Bombay Joe replied.

"All right then, Bombay, thank you," and he turned to Klaus and said, "Get the men, Klaus, and we'll search the area."

Klaus returned in a few moments with the men, and without further ado they commenced to make their way along the path that led downwards. The men went ahead, the trackers, Ife and Bombay, while Klaus and John brought up the rear.

They proceeded slowly, the three trackers bending low as they examined the path as they went along. Soon the path split into three, and they each took a route. But after a few moments, two of them returned, saying that the paths had petered out. Now they all concentrated on the remaining one which was very narrow and faint. As they went along, Bombay stopped, and said, "This is not the one!"

"No?" queried Ife.

"No! Is longest way, see!" and he pointed the path out as it went on. The trackers studied the route for a moment, then agreed with Bombay, and they commenced to look around in the bushes nearby, their heads about two feet off the ground. Ife and Bombay then located the track, the other men fell in with them and they proceeded slowly along it, indicating now and then a change of direction. They had now covered about half a mile, all continuously downhill, when the man at the front, one of the trackers, held up his hand and signalled them to halt. They did so, and John called out,

"What is it?"

The man at the front waited until all of them had drawn level with him, then said, "See heah! Two or three men join de path from de bush," and he pointed. All eyes followed his outstretched arm, and agreed on the statement.

"Dey goes dis way," Ife said, and they all moved onwards slowly, still downwards. The tall, grey face of the dam was now clearly visible set back behind a screen of trees through which they could see its features. From the point where they stood, they could see down into the valley and out over the nearest village far below, from which wood smoke drifted up in an almost straight line to the sky. Only the sounds of the birds could be heard as they continued on, descending as they advanced and then the trackers stopped again, peering at the ground.

"One set of footprints, heah!" they said, and indicated with a stick, then moved on and a few paces further on they stopped again, indicating another set. John and Klaus accepted what they said, although to them, they could not see anything of any footprints.

"Trail lost," the men at the front called out and stopped. The men backtracked about ten yards or so, then called, "Goes on here," and resumed their slow advance. They then turned off at an angle and entered the bush, then stopped again. "Trail gone again, massah."

They located it again, then just as abruptly, they stopped.

"What is it?" asked Klaus coming up to the front of the group.

"Heah," the tracker said, "Deh is a struggle. See, de groun' is broken," and he pointed down at his feet.

John peered down where the man was indicating but could not determine anything. "Are you sure?" he asked.

"Yes, massah, I'se sure! Heah maybe a fight or struggle, de ground is tell me this!" and he pointed off into the bushes and over to a clump of trees. They all looked at each other ominously.

"I don't like the sound of this!" said John.

"Me neither," said Klaus.

They proceeded more slowly, the trackers stopping frequently and stepping lightly as if they were walking on glass. They stopped again. "Moah struggles," the lead man called out. Now they all stood still, and Ife indicated in agreement that they should fan out from here onwards. The trackers stopped again a few paces further up and called back that now there was only the tracks of three men. They backtracked again and stopped. Now Ife and Bombay and the trackers stood discussing the ground around them, and John and Klaus waited patiently for the outcome. They were talking in their local dialect so Klaus waited patiently for the translation.

"Dey say, massahs, dat heah, deh is foah mens, den further on, der is three mens," and he held up his fingers to indicate the numbers.

"So where is the fourth man, then, Ife?"

Ife shrugged his shoulders, then waved his stick around in a circle. "Is somewheah here!" he stated.

Now the trackers each took a sector and began to examine the ground very closely, their noses almost touching it at times. Twenty minutes had passed, and Klaus asked if they'd found anything else.

"No massahs, nuthin'."

They all stood looking at each other, obviously now deep in thought, then Bombay wandered off into some low scrub and poked around in it. Then his voice was heard, urgently shouting on them to come over. It took a few seconds to locate where his voice was coming from, and when they had located it, they all rushed over into the bushes.

"Here!" shouted Bombay again, his head now just visible in the tall grasses. They came around a clump of rocks at the side of which stood a short tree, Bombay stood in front of it pointing upwards so they all craned their necks upwards. Suspended on a rope upside down, hung the body of Football. He was dead obviously, his throat cut from ear to ear, the blood covered his face and it had congealed there. A constant stream of ants wound its way up and down his body, criss-crossing each other on the rope as they conveyed their source of food, and by now they had begun to gather pieces of flesh from his face. They poured in and out of his mouth and nose.

John stood transfixed, as with the rest of them. They could not believe what their eyes told them.

"How long has he been here, Ife, do you think?"

Ife looked up to the corpse and then said, "Difficult to say, massah, maybe half a day, maybe more, not many ants, but I thinks he dead befoah dat."

Bombay prodded the body with a stick and it spun around slowly, rigor mortis had already set in.

"We should have brought Marcel along," said John to Klaus.

"Who did this then, Ife?" asked Klaus.

Bombay walked over to the swinging body and commented, "Maybe robbers!"

"The Leopard Men, perhaps?" asked John.

"No! They not kill men like this," replied Ife.

"He didn't carry any money that I know of," said Klaus.

"No matter, massah, de robbers kill anyways if you has de money or not."

"Well, we'd better cut him down, then," said John, and they set about this task which was complicated to say the least. After Bombay and Ife had scaled the tree they cut the rope and the body fell to the ground with a loud thump, dispersing the ants in an instant. The trackers cut a carrying pole from the tree branches and soon they had suspended the body like a piece of caught game and, taking an end each, they set off back up the hill to the Berger camp.

They climbed on to the top of the hill, the head of the dead body hanging down, the ants still there as it swung gently from side to side while they proceeded. The path followed the zigzag route they had come on, and Klaus and John followed on at the rear.

"Well! What do we do now then, Klaus?"

"I don't know, John, he was the best man we had! Yah?"

"Yes, is there anyone we can replace him with?"

Klaus thought for a moment, then said, "Yah, there is one man, not as good as Football, but almost. Speaks most of the dialects, he is the supervisor on the third shift, I will see him later today. Leave it to me, John."

"As you wish, Klaus, but let me know as soon as you have made your decision."

"What do we do about this murder, then?"

"I don't know. We will have to see what we can find out."

They fell then, into silence, each preoccupied with their own thoughts as they continued the climb upward to the point where they had first found the path that led downwards. They arrived at the Berger buildings and instantly workers stopped as they passed by and a large crowd quickly gathered around. They put the pole on the ground and the crowd closed in to gawp at the sight. While John and Klaus went inside, those remaining outside then broke into animated conversation as they speculated on what had happened. The news spread like wildfire and soon everyone in the camp had assembled in front of the office to gape at the spectacle before them. Pieter was visibly shocked, as were all the other members of the Berger management.

"Were did you find him?" asked Pieter.

"Halfway down the hill, hung upside down from a tree."

After a period of time, the crowd began to disperse and they loaded Football's body into the back of the Land Rover and the men climbed aboard. John thanked Pieter for his help and they drove off through the gates and made their way back to their own camp. John reached over for the radio and called on it.

"Chief to Doc, come in Doc!"

The answer came back in a few seconds, "Doc, here, go ahead."

"I've got Football here, Doc, he'll need your attention."

"Is he injured, John?"

"Worse, he's dead!"

There was a lull before Doc answered, then he replied, "Dead?"

"Yes, Doc. Throat cut."

"All right then, John, bring him straight to me."

"Okay, Doc, see you in about twenty minutes or so."

They drove along the dusty track and down the hill at a steady speed. No-one spoke as they drove along, and as they reached the accommodation huts they slowed to a halt as Ife and the trackers climbed down from the rear of the vehicle. John thanked them for their help and they responded with a silent wave of the arm. They then continued on up the hill and soon reached the compound where Marcel stood waiting at the door of the clinic. As they pulled up, Marcel came down the steps and looked in the back of the truck at the body.

"Okay, let's get him into the clinic, then!" Between Marcel and Klaus they managed to carry the body, with much difficulty, up the steps and laid it out on the examination table. Marcel looked closely at the jagged edge of the neck, then placed a sheet over the top of him and went into the office.

"I'll start soon, shouldn't be too long. Just a routine task, John."

"I could do with a drink," said John, sitting down heavily in Marcel's chair in his office.

"Me too," added Klaus, sitting opposite him.

Marcel went through to his official medicine cabinet, opened it and extracted a bottle of brandy. "Kept for emergency purposes only," he said, and passed it over to the two of them.

"You're not going to do a post mortem, are you Marcel? I've seen enough blood for one day!"

"In answer to your earlier question, John, I'm not going to do a full post mortem, just a customary check over, that's all. I'll leave the two of you to your brandy," and he went off through to the clinic. John and Klaus busied themselves with the refreshing drink and awaited the return of Marcel. He returned, washed his hands and sat at his desk and commenced to write up the report on the body.

"Well! He was healthy enough, our Mr Football, pity he had to die. I rather liked him, one of the more intelligent ones, he could have gone far! As to his death, well, his throat was cut, and he bled to death, and you should know that the cut was right through the vocal cords, so who ever did it made sure that he could not tell. Any idea who did it?"

"No," replied John, "could have been anyone, the general consensus is that it was robbers but I don't believe that for a minute."

Turning to Klaus, John said, "Remember, Klaus, I said to you a few days ago that everything was going too smoothly?"

"Yes! I remember."

The remainder of the day went by quietly, Marcel filed his report, washed the body and tidied it up a bit. Klaus arranged transport to take the body back to Football's village for burial the following day. As a mark of respect, work was ceased early that day and the night shift was stood down.

John left for the house about three in the afternoon and upon his arrival there found Nat and Eb awaiting him as he pulled up at the door.

"Very sorry, massah," they chorused as he entered. "Very sorry."

"Yes, me too, me too!"

"He was de good man for de workers, dey do everything he say, you not find another one like him, massah, for a long time."

"Yes, Eb, you're right there!"

Next day, Ife volunteered to take the body to the village along with some of the others. It was a solemn occasion, the workers lined the sides of the road as the vehicle passed by and all raised their arms in salute as the body passed them by. The vehicle disappeared round the bend in the road and all was silent.

Work was resumed but there was little enthusiasm for it, most of the men making only a token effort. It was understandable, thought Klaus to himself, so he was not worried about it in the least. Two weeks had now passed since the event and even over at the Berger camps they still talked about it. There they had erected a new security fence and had taken other security measures as well in case of any repetition of the event. By the time that a few more weeks had gone by, work had recovered to its normal standard and pace and life returned to normal again.

John was busy in his office when he heard a vehicle pull up at the front and the door slammed. Half expecting Dave to step through the doorway, he was surprised to see Pieter from Julius Berger stepping through the doorway.

"Hello, Pieter. This is a surprise," he said, getting up from his chair. "What brings you over this way?"

"Well, we were surveying the line for the road on this side so, being as I was close at hand, I thought I'd come in and see how you are all doing. Have you got over the loss of your friend yet?"

"Well, more or less, it's the workers that miss him most, he was our key man, you see."

"Yes, I quite understand."

John got up and made two cups of coffee and handed one of the them across the table to Pieter.

"I have some information for you, I thought you might be interested in it, John."

"Oh, yes? What sort of information is that, then?"

"Over in Bin Yauri at the old police station, they have just locked up two petty criminals and two others as well.

"So?"

"Apparently, they caught them in the course of robbing a supermarket, there."

"And why would that interest me, Pieter?"

"Because," said Pieter, "they found this in their possession," and he reached down into his briefcase and handed over Football's radio.

"Yours, I believe?"

John turned it over in his hand, looked at the channel card and confirmed that the frequencies were the same as the ones they used. John looked at Pieter for an explanation.

"The police inspector thought it was one of ours, as when he switched it on he could hear our people on it." John recalled that channel six was the same as the Berger camp, and consequently he was immediately interested.

"I thought that might help, John. Maybe they are the ones that put paid to your Mr Football!"

"Yes! It certainly looks as if they had something to do with it, Pieter."

"Perhaps, there is very little evidence against them, of course, but I thought you should know anyway."

They continued talking for while, then Pieter took his leave, and John thanked him for the radio and the information. That night, John informed Klaus of the event, and he was pleased to hear of it. "Maybe then, they will get the information out of them?"

"I doubt it, Klaus, they only usually hold them for a couple of days, and if no-one presses any charges, then they just release them. After all, they can't afford to keep them in goal on suspicion only!"

"There's ways of finding out, though," said Klaus.

"How do mean, Klaus? Torture?" asked John.

"Perhaps, been known to happen before. Still, at least we got the radio back. That's something to be grateful for."

"Well! See you tomorrow then, John," and he went off to his own house. Klaus, however, had his mind ticking over after hearing this new information, and he had already decided to deal out some retribution to these robbers. His devious mind had laid a plan and he set about devising a method of gaining access to the prisoners. So, on a planned visit to pick up some provisions for Dave, he had volunteered to drive the truck, making the excuse that he needed a break from the daily routine. No-one queried this and he set off for the collection point, which was only some twenty miles from Bin Yauri on the main road. He picked up the supplies, and then took a detour northwards.

Arriving there, he found the police station located in a back street. A decadent building, crumbling in places, with neither electricity or water, but easily identifiable by the old, dark blue Land Rovers parked indiscriminately at its entrance. On the pretence of asking directions, he gained the confidence of the young officer who sat at the end of the corridor leading to the cells. After engaging him in conversation for a while, he hinted that he could get him some crates of beer at a very cheap price. As bribery and corruption were rife throughout the country, it was a simple matter to obtain acceptance of the offer. He asked as to when he could bring it round, stating that it would have to be at night and there would be no questions asked. Casting a glance over his shoulder the young officer lowered his voice and stated a time. Klaus agreed to it and set his plans accordingly.

He had already set aside four crates of beer from the stocks ready for the occasion. Feeling satisfied with these arrangements he drove quickly back to the site, making the excuse that an accident on the road had delayed his return owing to the traffic being held up, a regular occurrence on most of the Nigerian roads.

On the appointed evening he loaded up the wagon saying that he was off over to the Berger camp for the evening and it would be late before he was back. On the way downhill he stopped off at the accommodation in the darkness and picked up six of the workers who were willing to avenge the death of Football. They drove off. It was a clear night with little traffic on the roads, most people being too scared to travel in the dark because of robberies and muggings on the roads. They approached Bin Yauri, the traffic in the town was light for this time of night, most of the activity being around the street corner salesmen, peddlers, and the odd corn-on-the-cob stands at the roadside. Turning off into the side road they approached the police station, it was in total darkness and was more or less deserted apart from the few police on duty and the prisoners in the cells. As they drove up to the gates, a guard appeared. Klaus asked for the police officer by name and after a short delay, the man appeared and looked out through the fence. He signalled to the guard to open the gate and they drove in. He stopped and got out and in the dark proceeded to unload the crates.

He sat down with the officer and when he had seen the crates, the meagre payment was made, and to ensure that they were completely taken in by the ruse, he added another two crates for nothing. This pleased them enormously and he added yet another crate for the guards as a sweetener. The guards removed this to the side of the building and disappeared into the darkness to drink their fill unseen. Returning to the officer, Klaus sat down beside him and started to drink the beer with him. After about an hour he could see that the man was starting to become affected by the alcohol, so he plied him with more and continued their conversation. As the man became drowsy, Klaus went down to the end of the corridor to confirm that the prisoners were still in their cells.

After one more can of beer the officer slowly fell asleep, his speech slurred. Klaus looked at his watch and noted that it was ten-thirty, just about right. Confirming that the man was asleep, he moved silently over to the door and out into the darkness. He tapped on the side of the Land Rover, and the men inside filed silently out of it and into the building unseen. Klaus reached up for the keys to the cells and silently lifted the bunch from their hook on the wall. They were old and large, being a relic from Victorian days. One of the men looked outside to see how the guards were doing, and after a cursory glance he confirmed that they were engrossed on their drinking round the back of the building. The drunk officer sat slumped in his chair, a can of beer still held loosely in his hand, as they filed silently past him and down the darkened corridor to the cells. They stopped at the cell door and Klaus peered in through the observation slit in the door at eye level, and noted that the prisoners were asleep. Inserting the key in the lock as silently as he could, he turned it slowly and was pleased to find that the lock had been well oiled. He looked again through the slit, the men were still asleep. They swung the door open and entered, all of them moving silently inwards. Their machetes glinted in the faint light and quickly they were swung, severing the heads of all three of them from their bodies, and adding a few indiscriminate hacks for good measure. The blood welled up and out of the necks of the victims and poured out on to the floor. It had taken them all of twelve seconds to dispatch the men, and as silently as they had entered they closed the cell door and locked it, retraced their steps and filed past the now snoring guards, out into the darkness and climbed into the Land Rover. At a communal tap just inside the gate, they stopped and washed their machetes and the blood from their feet. One of them held the gate open while the vehicle moved quietly through it and closed the gate again. The street was deserted and they drove down it for about twenty yards before they came upon any pedestrians, who in any event, paid no attention to them at all. They drove off towards the main road and made good time back to the site. Klaus dropped the men off and drove up to his house, pulled up at the door, and whistling to himself he entered the house and went to bed satisfied with his night's work. Football's death had been avenged!

It was about a week later that John heard of the death of the prisoners from Nat who had heard the gossip in one of the villages. News like this flew like the wind on occasions, but this time it had been slower in trickling through. A general feeling of satisfaction was felt as all thought that the men had been responsible for Football's death. John passed no comment on hearing the news but suspected nothing as to any involvement of his men in the event. He mentioned it to Klaus the following day but the only comment that he made was, "Maybe the gods have wreaked vengeance and retribution, then."

The incident faded quickly from their thoughts and all applied themselves to the job. The supervisor chosen to replace Football was David Ignatius Okade, and it was agreed that the radio call sign of Football would remain to avoid any confusion but that he would be addressed by his first name anyway. He was small and wiry but with a loud voice, he had been the popular choice of the men as he had an eye for detail and was well-liked.

On his way back north, Phil had called in but only stopped for an hour or so before departing, again. He related the tale of the massacre at the police station, as he had heard of it from another policeman further away but made no connection with the killing of Football Boot.

Chapter Ten

The days were now clearer, the Harmattan having passed, and the site was busier than ever. The new road had now been laid up to the east side of the valley and a daily flow of vehicles passed by as they transferred materials for the final resurfacing of it. Over on the west side giant earth movers started to carve up the red soil in preparation for the foundation. Men from the Berger camp had now moved closer to the dam site and a sizeable workforce now worked close to John's office. This was only about two miles from the road to the Consolidated site, and whereas John had enjoyed relative peace and quiet before, he now had to put up with a constant stream of vehicles passing by for most the working day. Thankfully, in the evening the work slackened off and peace returned. John was now up earlier in the morning as there were quite a number of things that the two companies had to liaise upon. Julius Berger's men, however, were at work as soon as it was light and did not stop until it was dark, that being their secret of success. Everything they built was done correctly first time and there was never any need for work to be redone on any count.

The new boss of the workers, David, proved to be very popular and John had noted that he went about things in a different way from that of Football, but he did seem to have more of the ear of the men and any problem that occurred he had it sorted out in record time. A good choice, thought John to himself.

At the work face, the men still toiled daily in the heat, sweating and brushing the flies from their faces as they worked. Most of them had developed an immunity to the common disease of glaucoma, caused by flies infecting the eyeball, usually resulting in early blindness. Marcel had treated many of the men but there was little he could do as most of the cases had resulted from infection when they were children. Young children were not taught to brush the flies from their faces, a fact that was still noticeable in the villages that Marcel visited.

The radio spoke, it was David.

"Yes, David, go ahead."

"Big dust cloud coming up the valley, boss."

"Okay, thanks, David."

Dave and John moved out into the open from the culvert where they had been standing and looked out over the river. Sure enough a huge cloud of dust hung suspended in the air.

"What's that then, Fred?" he asked.

"Don't know, John, looks odd though."

"Earthquake?" suggested John.

"No, we don't get earthquakes in this region!"

"I was only joking, Fred," John replied. "Give Klaus a call. He's up top somewhere."

"Flintstone to Chief, you up there?"

"Yahwohl!" replied Klaus, "what do you want, Fred?"

"Klaus, have a look down the valley, will you, there's a big cloud of dust. Can you see it?"

"Not from here, I'll move over a bit."

The radio channel fell silent for a few moments, then activated again. "Chief to Fred! I can see it now! Looks like something is pushing the cloud forwards slowly."

John looked up at the sky and said, "There's no wind, though."

Fred looked again at the cloud.

"I'll get one of the trackers," said John and sent for the man.

He arrived, hotfoot, saying, "Yus massah, what you want?"

John indicated the cloud of dust and said, "What is that?"

The man looked at it for a moment, then bent down and put his ear to the ground and listened intently. Then, he sat up smiling.

"What is it then?"

The man started to laugh, then turned to John and said, "It is de cattle, massah, but many of them, maybe about a thousand, I think."

"A thousand?" said John.

"Yes, massah! Maybe more!"

"Thanks," he said, and the man went off back along the walkway to where he had been working.

"Must be a big herd then, Fred! See how high the dust is?"

Fred looked at the cloud, then said, "I didn't know there were any big herds these days, mostly they are only about four or five hundred or so."

"Well," said John, "if it's only cows, then we have nothing to worry about," and so saying they returned to their work.

Some three hours later, the herd had moved closer and were approaching the bend in the river just before the accommodation.

Very soon after this the alarm klaxon sounded, the strident notes echoing off the walls of the valley and the face of the dam.

Fred looked at John, and almost instantly they chorused, "The cattle!" They ran over to the nearest vehicle and drove off down to the accommodation as fast as they could, cutting across the low scrub and the dried up river bed. As they arrived at the site they came across the men who were off shift, and who had gathered there at the side of the site.

"What is it?" shouted John, springing down from the driving seat of the vehicle.

Some of the men were laughing as he asked the question, one of them stepped out from the crowd and pointed with his hand and said, "It is de cows, boss! Dey is in de accommodation."

"What?" he said. "You mean in the accommodation itself?"

"Yes, suh! Manys of dem, you go see!" and he smiled as he said it.

Fred looked over at John, and said, "This I've got to see."

They went over to the huts but had to stop before they got there. Sure enough, as the man had said, the cattle were everywhere! In the huts, around them, in the sleeping huts, in the cookhouse and munching away quite happily at anything that took their fancy. The ground was now devoid of grass or scrub and some of the men were attempting to divert the animals but it was a useless task trying to divert the flood of beasts before them. John looked around for the lead herdsman but he could not see him, which was unusual as there was usually one at the front with the leading animal. After a busy ten minutes or so, they had managed to steer the head of the herd away to their right after forcing their way through to the nearest herdsman. He in turn, quickly diverted the mass to a tree-lined area and away from the huts.

Meanwhile, John and Fred went over to view the damage. It looked like a tornado had struck. The buildings had been flattened by the weight of the beasts pushing onwards, timbers had split in two, roofs collapsed and all around the ground had been trampled flat and the vegetation denuded, even the branches of the trees had not escaped the voracious appetite of the cattle. An older herdsman ran over to the animals, whacking them on the rump with his stick, he doubled his efforts and made his way over towards a boy of about seventeen, who apparently had been allocated to lead the herd but for some unknown reason, he had fallen back and was oblivious to the destruction wreaked ahead of him.

A string of obscenities was heard pouring out of the mouth of the older man, and he then proceeded to lay into the youth with his stick who backed away as fast as he could in retreat. He started to run but the older man was fleet of foot and chased him for some distance, accurately raining more blows upon the unfortunate youth. Eventually the youth escaped by ducking in between the cattle where he had adequate shelter, although the old man still cursed and swore at him. The man edged his way over through the cows to John and Fred, and coming up to them, he said, "Sorry, massahs! We will pay for de damage."

John immediately thought of shouting at the man, but realised it was a genuine mistake and reconciled himself with the fact that the sleeping huts and the other buildings were in a state anyway and were in need of replacement. He decided, there and then, to rebuild the huts so he accepted the man's offer with a rueful smile. Later, it was agreed that the payment could be in the form of cattle and after a little haggling, they agreed on twenty cows which, to the herdsman, was a minute fraction of the total number of beasts there. It did, of course, provide some welcome fresh meat for the cook, so all in all, it satisfied everyone. Finally they parted on friendly terms and John had some cartons of cigarettes brought down from Fred's store and these were dished out to the herdsmen. The herd took a further hour to pass by, and crossed the road and made their way up the hillside through the bush, the cloud of dust following them suspended in the air. With the consumption of all that grew, they could now see clearly down the valley, the only thing remaining was the tall, more wiry trees.

Nathaniel and Ebenezer were out quickly after the herd had passed by and so were the local villagers, collecting the large amount of fresh dung that had been dropped along the way. Eb dug it into the soil in the patch where he grew the vegetables and corn, not being one to miss an opportunity like that.

Dave had also become extremely busy, giving nails, wood and all the other commodities that went with the building of wooden structures, and an army of volunteers became available.

Two weeks had now passed since the cattle event, by now the new buildings were taking shape, and many more were added shortly afterwards. There had been built a mess hall, sleeping accommodation, a kitchen, extra storage huts and a building for showering. All in all, it was a useful exercise.

"A blessing in disguise," commented Dave to John, as they surveyed the new layout of the buildings.

"Yes, but what a way to achieve it!" commented Klaus.

The event became the talking point for some time to come and those in the Berger encampment thought the whole thing uproariously funny. Every time cows were sighted from then onwards, the men shouted, "Alarm, alarm, de bush cows come!" A long period of time passed by before the episode was forgotten.

Lately, there had been a delay in the delivery of some of the regular materials used which Dave replenished to keep the stocks up, and he had sent Joshua out to chase things up a bit, but to no avail. In the end Dave saw Klaus about it and asked him to 'chivvy it up', a phrase that Klaus was not familiar with and Dave had to explain it in detail to him. Klaus got the message and said that he'd be certain of getting satisfaction, just leave it to him. In due course, the problems were solved and Dave mentioned this to John one day who did not attach any real importance to the fact, only adding that, "As long as we get the supplies when we need them, that's all that matters. Obviously Klaus has quite a few contacts in influential places."

Nevertheless, some time later, on a Saturday morning, Joshua was going through the invoices and accounts as he regularly did, and interrupted Dave as he was counting up a set of figures.

"Come, look see, massah, these sheets not right."

Dave stopped, and came over to where Joshua sat. "All right, Joshua, let me have a look at them." After a few minutes, Dave looked up and said, "Yes, you're right, there's quite a difference here, but leave this to me Joshua, I'll check it out."

"Yes, massah, you check, I not make a mistake!"

Dave crossed over to the cupboard and withdrew the box of invoices that they kept and started to pair them off. Most of them tallied, but others did not and he separated them from the bunch. He noted dates and the deliveries, and made a few notes. A total of five stuck out like sore thumbs and he sat and thought about this for a while. All of them were ones that Klaus had 'chased up', and he went over to the box where the regular requisitions were kept. He scrutinised each in turn and separated the ones with unusual quantities and sat down to peruse them. A few of them were for alcohol and were repetitive. He placed them in an envelope, and put them at the rear of the filing cabinet. He was immediately suspicious but resolved to keep an eye on it and to keep an open mind on the subject.

The following day, Klaus had gone out on a tour of inspection and three hours had passed by, according to Marcel who had seen him leave.

"I wonder where he is then," commented John, when he heard about it. He called Klaus on the radio but only silence greeted him.

"That's odd," he said, "he's not answering his radio. I'd better go and see if I can find him." He drove off downstream picking up David, the supervisor as he went. "Where did he go to, David?"

"He go up top, massah."

"Right then. We'll cross over and go up the road."

They proceeded to the winding track which rose up the side of the valley in alternative left and right hand turns, each turn increasing the elevation above the valley floor. Reaching the top, they stopped and looked around. They saw no sign of Klaus and after about five minutes they went on along the road. Now, they were closer to the edge and from here they could see down directly on to the dam. They stopped again and looked around for any sign of Klaus, but there was none. John and David got out and walked around, then climbed back into the Land Rover again.

Suddenly David called out, "Ovah deah, massah!"

John slowed down to look but saw nothing. "Where?" he asked.

"Deah!" David replied, pointing downhill into the bush. John followed the line of his outstretched arm but still could not see what David had seen.

"You must have good eyesight," he commented, "I can't see anything."

"Down deah!" replied David in an exasperated tone of voice, "by de big tree."

Just visible and no more, was the rear of Klaus's Land Rover, perched at a crazy angle. Assuming that he must have had an accident, they both leapt outwards as the vehicle came to a halt and descended the steep incline to the vehicle. Klaus was slumped over the wheel and David on reaching him, held up his head to look at him.

He was unconscious but, as far as they could tell, did not seem to be injured in any way.

"Can you smell anything, David?" asked John.

He looked, then sniffed, then said, "Whisky, Massah?"

"Yes, looks like he's drunk!"

John climbed into the back of the Land Rover and found an empty bottle lying on the floor. It was whisky all right. John frowned and went back to the front of the vehicle and looked at it. It was not damaged in any way but he shook his head in dismay. They hoisted Klaus out of the seat and carried him up the hill with some effort, and loaded him into the back.

"I gets de mechanic with de breakdown truck, boss, to get de wagon."

They descended to the valley floor and up the other side and continued on to the compound and drove straight to Marcel's clinic.

"Customer for you!" shouted John as they pulled up outside the clinic door.

"But that's Klaus," said Marcel casting a quick glance at him.

"Yes, Marcel, you're right, and he's drunk or seems to be, but I'll let you be the judge of that!"

They lifted the dead weight of Klaus up and carried him to the doorway, and after a struggle they placed him on the examination table.

Marcel had a quick look at him, and inspected his eyes. "Not much I can do for him. He's drunk all right, we'll just have to wait until he comes round." Then he added "I'll give you a call when he comes to, John.

"Thanks, Marcel," and John and David went off down the steps.

"You take my vehicle David, I'll get it later on."

"Okay, boss!" said David, and climbed in and drove off through the gears. It was a full fifteen hours later before Klaus came to, and after Marcel had given him the once over, he allowed him to return to his house. John called in to see him, where he was propped up in a chair, looking washed out.

"Well then, Klaus! What have you got to say for yourself?"

"I had a whisky or two," he replied.

"I'll say! More like a bottle or two! For Christ's sake, Klaus! And you were driving as well! Do you know where we found you?"

and without waiting for an answer, he continued, "right at the edge of the side above the dam! You could have been killed!"

Klaus said nothing, but looked down at the floor.

"Well then, how long have you been drinking this whisky?"

Klaus raised his hand in a futile gesture.

"Ages then?" said John. "Well, I'm going to ask Marcel to give you the works and if I find that you are an alcoholic, then I'll have to suspend you from your work, is that understood?"

"Yah, yah, I know. I'll be all right by tomorrow, you'll see."

"I'll believe that when I see it!" commented John, and without any further conversation on the subject, he left. John called up Marcel on the radio.

"Hello, John, what can I do for you?"

"Coming over to see you, Marcel, be there in a minute."

"Roger."

John wound his way up to the compound, stopped at the steps to the clinic and leapt out of the Land Rover. He went up the steps and pushed the door open.

"Come in," said Marcel, "what was it you wanted?" He passed a cup of coffee, already poured, over to John, and lifting his own his eyes met John's. Before John had the chance to speak, Marcel said, "It's Klaus, isn't it?"

"Yes! I'm sorry if I seem a bit short but I'm absolutely fuming! How can a man like that with a responsible position, drive about drunk? It beats me."

Marcel shrugged his shoulders noncommittally.

"Probably an alcoholic, I shouldn't wonder," said John.

"C'est possible, John," was the reply.

"Worth a test, then?" asked John, taking another sip of his coffee.

"If you like, I can run some tests to find out, but it would take a few days to analyse the samples, John."

"Yes, well, I really need to know one way or the other, Marcel, so can I ask you to do that and we'll take it from there?"

"Oui! Certainly, I'll get that seen to right away, then."

John drank up the remainder of his coffee and walked over to his office, shaking his head as he went.

The next day he called in upon Fred, who was busy studying a chart at his desk. "You know most of Klaus's work routine, don't you?"

"Yes, most of it. I go around with him regularly, why do you ask?"

"You've heard about what happened the other day, then?"

"Difficult not to, John."

"Has he been drinking whisky for a while, then?"

"I don't really know, John, but I suspect so. I know that he drinks it in his house quite a lot and goes through a bottle an evening easily."

John nodded, then said, "Just as I suspected!" and tapped the table with his fingers in thought. "Well, I've decided to release him from duty while Marcel checks him out so I'm asking you to take over his duties in the meantime."

"Okay, John, I think that I can manage that all right," then asked, "you mean from now?"

"Yes, and remember that David needs some extra men for the transfer of that work for the next level, so you'd better keep a close eye on that, Fred."

After he had left Fred, John thought about this decision for a moment, then on reflection he decided that it was the correct thing to do. The question remained as to what to do about Klaus, but he decided to await the outcome of Marcel's tests.

Needless to say, the news had flown like the wind and when John was in Dave's office, Dave said to him, "I heard about Klaus. Not surprising, really!"

"Why is that then, Dave?" he asked.

"Oh, just a suspicion I had, that's all."

"Why is that then?"

Dave crossed over to the filing cabinet and pulled out the drawer and the invoices that he had placed in there earlier.

"What's that, Dave?" John asked.

"Joshua was doing the books the other day and he came up with some figures that did not tie up with the transactions," and he handed them over to John. As John looked at them, Dave explained, "They're all ones that were delayed deliveries for one reason or another, that is to say that the delivery was late but was quickly sorted out once Klaus got his hands on it."

"So?"

"Well, you'll note that they were for the purchase of some boxes of whisky."

John inspected them more closely now. "But these are quite old, Dave," he commented.

"Yes, but look at the number of cases of whisky on each one."

John read them again.

Dave continued, as John read the invoices, "In order to go through that amount of whisky in that period of time you'd have to be going some, John, eh?"

John remained reading then looking up, he said, "Yes, I see what you mean."

Silence fell upon them for a moment.

"Do you think, then, Dave, that he was actually drinking all of this, or perhaps using it to trade for something else, perhaps?"

"I don't know, John, but my guess is that it could be both really. Sounds feasible, eh?"

"Can I hang on to these?" asked John.

"By all means, John, just let me have them back when you've finished with them." John stood up to go, but before he could reach the door, Dave said to him, "By the way, there's something else you need to know about!"

"Oh, yes? What's that then?"

"How much morphine does Doc use?"

"I don't know, I'm not a medical man. Why do you ask?"

"Well, John," said Dave, and crossed to another cabinet and withdrew a book from it, "This is the booking out book, as we call it. That is when anyone wants an item from the store or from stock anywhere else, they draw it out and sign for it at the time."

"Seems a reasonable system then, Dave. Is there a problem with it, then?"

"Well, I have noticed lately that Klaus has been withdrawing cases of morphine for Marcel for the clinic at various times."

"But Marcel would draw these himself, would he not?"

"Exactly!"

"Go on."

"That's what I thought but see here," and he came around the side of the table and pointed to a few entries on the pages. It read, 'Morphine, 1 case, 72 Ampoules'.

"Who issued it, then?"

"Joshua, but quite correctly I might add."

"Yes, well, what's the problem?"

Dave directed his eyes to three more occurrences where the same amount was withdrawn supposedly for Marcel but for which Klaus had signed. John looked up at Dave, but did not pass a comment.

"So, John, we could have here, and I stress could have, an alcoholic and a drug taker, no?"

"Or maybe a dealer," said John quietly. Dave raised his eyebrows in response. "And I thought that I had enough problems on my hands for now!"

"Well, perhaps it is not a problem but it warrants an explanation, eh?"

"Yes."

He got up from the desk, then turning to Dave, he said, "Is there any chance that I can get safely out of the door this time?"

Dave smiled and replied, "Yes, John, I think you've enough to contend with there."

Deciding that he had had enough for that day, he went off down to his house and on arrival called on Eb to make him a strong cup of coffee.

Eb brought it through, and said, "De massah have a hard day then?"

"Yes, Eb, a hard day indeed." John sat down in the chair on the veranda and ran his fingers through his hair. "What a day!" and then went inside and extracted some report forms from his desk.

"Bring me another coffee, Eb!" he called out.

"Another one, massah?" Eb asked.

"Yes, and put a whisky in it!"

Eb looked puzzled but shrugged his shoulders and went off into the kitchen to do as he was bid. He returned with it and placed it down in front of John saying, "You be careful, boss. You gets drunk."

John smiled at him, put the cup up to his mouth and downed it in two gulps.

"Yes, de massah have de hard day all right," said Eb, and looking at the empty cup he said, "You wants another?"

"No, Eb, that will do fine."

Eb looked at him with raised eyebrows and went back into the house. John started to write and he had written four pages before he was able to put his pen down. It certainly made interesting reading, it was not a pretty tale and he wondered what Hendry J. would make of it. Ah well, that is life, he thought as he got up from the chair and went inside, at least he was blameless, he thought.

Next day, he called on Marcel, early.

"Good morning," he called out as John stepped through the door.

"Morning, Marcel! It's question time again."

"Yes? Well, what is it then?"

"How much morphine do you use, Marcel?"

"Oh, some. More recently, but not that much really. It varies from time to time."

"How many ampoules, then?"

Marcel thought for a moment then said, "Perhaps ten ampoules a month, that's all. Why do you ask?"

"Did you ask Klaus to collect some cases for you from Dave's store?"

"No."

"Never?"

"Non."

"Are you sure?"

"Mais oui, if I need it I go myself. Why, is there a problem with it?"

"Yes."

Marcel looked surprised, then said, "Klaus tell you I ask him to get the morphine?" and he looked up from his desk.

"No Marcel, it was Dave."

"But I do not understand, John, you are talking the double dutch, non?"

John explained about the issue of the cases.

Marcel sat for a moment thinking, then said, "But Dave knows that I only go to him for the morphine. That has always been the arrangement, he told me so when I first arrived here."

"Good, Marcel, I just wanted to hear your side of the story. By the way, have you given Klaus the works yet?"

"Oui, I will have the results ready for you this afternoon."

"Will they be, er, interesting?"

"Certainly! But I will go through them with you."

John shuddered to think what was going to be revealed and was tempted to ask there and then, but decided to wait and see what Marcel had come up with.

He went out of the door and over to his office. He went next to Klaus's office where Fred was busy.

"Everything going all right, Fred?"

"Yes, no problems, or as Klaus would say, Alles in ordnung!"

"Yes, quite!"

John left and went down town, visiting the workings, taking a keen interest in all that was going on. He then went down to the accommodation huts, and he asked the men how they were.

"Verrah good, massah," was the common reply from most of the men.

"That good, eh?"

"Yus massah, dis ones, dey not get eaten by bush cows!" and the man grinned. John looked at his watch, it was almost eleven in the morning, so he went up to the clinic again.

"You ready yet, Marcel?"

"No, about one more hour John, I'll give you a call on the radio."

"All right, thanks," and he left again. He was eager to find out whatever it was that Marcel had discovered but he restrained himself again and went back to the office. At midday, Marcel crossed over to John's office and entered.

"What have you got then, Marcel?" asked John trying not to look interested.

"Well, I have brought you the news that you have been dying to know, John."

"Okay. Let's have it, Marcel!"

"He is in a bad way. I'm afraid the blood tests show that he is definitely an alcoholic, and he has damaged liver and kidneys. He must have been taking this whisky for a long time. His reactions are slower, and when I examined his eyes they told me that he is not in, what you would call, a good physical shape."

"Yes, but on his last medical he was fit, was he not?"

"Oui, mais, this one is a very detailed one. And I can see that he is not well, John."

"Is he fit for his job, then?"

"Non! C'est pas possible! He must go away for, how you say, recuperation, for a long time. I think that will be the best for him."

"Well, that's just what I thought you were going to say, Marcel."

"I have seen another man like this before, John, but he is dead now!"

"Okay then, Marcel, I'll get on to Hendry J. I'll have him sent back to Lagos."

"Yes, it would be the best, John. That's all I can say."

"Okay then, let me have a copy of your report as soon as you can, Marcel."

"Mais certainement, John," and he left to do that.

John picked up the key for his vehicle and left to go down to Klaus's house. As he drove there, he thought about what he was going to say to him. By the time he arrived, he had decided. He entered and the servant, Albert, pointed into the lounge where Klaus was seated.

"Well, how are you today, Klaus?"

"I feel better today, recovered you see."

"Good! You know why I've come, then?

"Yes, you don't have to tell me, I already know!"

"Well, that makes it easier, Klaus. I'll send you down to Lagos tomorrow. Hendry J. knows that you are coming and Marcel tells me that a colleague of his will see you the day after to make sure that you get the proper treatment."

"Yah! I understand."

"It was good while it lasted, Klaus, but you should have told me about this earlier then I might have been able to help you. At the end of it you will be a better man, that I can assure you. I'm only sorry to lose you but I've asked Fred to take your place, do you agree with that?"

"Yah, he will do the job well, he knows it."

John decided that he had said enough and shook Klaus warmly by the hand and left. He had wanted to say a number of things to Klaus, but somehow they didn't seem appropriate at the time. A great pity, he thought, to lose such a good man in this manner.

Instead of going back to his office he called in by the storage compound and saw Dave deep in the bowels of the shed, hidden behind some packing crates and on hearing his name being called, he emerged. "I have done the deed, as they say. In fact it was rather embarrassing."

"If it's any consolation, I would have felt the same, John."

"You're going for supplies today, aren't you?"

"Yes, do you want me to call Hendry J. when I'm down?"

"Yes, just tell him that he'll be arriving at some time during the day but nearer to the evening, I think depending upon the traffic on the roads."

"Okay, I'll do that."

"By the way, I asked Marcel about those ampoules and it looks as if Klaus was using them to trade for whisky."

"Maybe just as well that he is going, then, John?"

"Aye, maybe you're right there."

They parted, Dave continued his stock check, and John drove back up the winding road to the compound. As he drove along his attention was alerted by a wave from an old man from the local village. A wizened character with spindle-shank legs supporting a thin scraggy body above them. His shirt hung on the narrow shoulders and an old battered hat with a torn but sweat-stained brim rested on his head, raked back, reminding John of the way that some cowboys out west, wore them. His hair was close cropped and grey and he smiled a toothless smile as he drew level with John. He pulled up alongside the man and came to a gentle halt. The man approached, in one hand holding a stick on which was suspended two black bats, both dead, their feet tied together.

"Hello, mastah, you want bat?" and his mouth remained open as he finished speaking, a black hole, and the words could be read in his eyes. John cast a glance over the bats, big ones, six or seven inches long with huge wingspans. The man opened one of them out for John to examine it. John noted the wingspan of it. He declined the offer. Who would want to eat those things, he thought to himself.

"No, thank you," he replied smiling.

The old man, totally unperturbed by the rebuff, held them higher, and said, "Make good soup, mastah!"

"I suppose they will," he responded, and as he said that, his attention was drawn to the old rifle that the man had on his back. It hung on a home-made sling of woven grass, showing an intricate pattern stained heavily with constant use.

"Can I have a look at your gun?" John asked.

The man unslung it from his shoulder without a word and passed it over to John. Then he said, "Verrah old, yes?"

"Yes, very old," agreed John as he turned it over in his hands.

"Work good, good shot, long time," the man said.

John could see that it was really ancient, and looked like a relic from the war or even before it, he thought. The barrel was very long and the priming rod was tied on to it with a piece of hide. He looked at the chamber, it was of a very old flintlock type, but with a well shaped grip, much worn by long usage.

"Where did you get it from?" asked John.

"Grandfather gun," the man replied, "Shoot many men, yes?"

"I'm sure it did," replied John, then added, "well, I must be off," and started the engine of the Land Rover, handing the gun back.

"See you, mastah!" called the hunter, and raised his hand to the side of his head in a type of military salute, accompanied by the toothless smile. John waved to him and smiled himself as he drove off. Even in the midst of troubles, he thought, there is always something simple around to bring you back to earth. He continued on upwards, went to his office and sat down to write the long report to Hendry J.

Klaus had been gone three weeks and no-one spoke much about the event. Now the focus was on the new roads carved out of the jungle further uphill from the compound. Palm trees were felled and the red ochre dust sloughed aside by the huge earthmovers and a wide swathe was cut through the undergrowth. A seemingly never-ending stream of vehicles went back and forth, and the steel supports for the approaches to the dam top were installed. Social life with the Berger people took on an even greater meaning, and frequent liaison between them now became a daily occurrence. Asphalt was now ferried in from the store where it was held after being transported up from the mine at the Zuma rock near Suleja.

Klaus's journey down to Lagos was not without incident, however, as on the way they had been attacked by armed robbers on the highway, both Klaus and the driver had been injured but not seriously. John went down to the local Nitel post and, after a long wait, he got through on a scratchy sounding circuit to Hendry J., and waiting for the noise level on the line to diminish, they were able to converse.

"Hendry J., hello!"

"I can just hear you, John! Terrible line!"

"Yes, and this is one of Nitel's better lines as well!"

"What happened on the way down then, with Klaus?"

"Well, they stopped to refuel and they must have got dirty fuel, you know how it is in this country? And they had to stop to clean out the fuel filter. By that time it had got dark, and on the expressway just north of Lagos, they have had a lot of robberies in that area recently."

"Yes."

"It was the old deception trick used by the robbers all over Nigeria. They organise themselves into three groups, the first to signal that a car is approaching. They hide in the elephant grass at the side of the road and when the second group get the signal, they throw out a black bag with bricks in it on to the road. And as there are no lights on the expressway the driver cannot see it. He drives over it and bursts a tyre and then has to pull over to change the wheel. When they do that, the third group waits until they've almost finished then they rush out from the cover of the grass and rob the people of whatever they have. They're usually armed, that is to say maybe one of them has a gun but with no ammunition, the others have clubs or home-made ones made out of metal with nails welded on the sides. Klaus was knocked to the ground and received a nasty wound to the head and the driver suffered bruising but all the robbers got was a suitcase full of clothes and nothing else."

"What are they usually after then, Hendry?"

"Oh, dollars usually, but that's about their limit and jewellery and that sort of thing."

"Were they all right, then?"

"Yes, apart from torn clothes and being covered in blood they seemed okay, but I sent Klaus along to the embassy clinic just in case and they put a few stitches in his head, for good measure."

"Has he recovered from it, then?"

"Yes, he was all right about two hours later."

"Well, I'm sorry to hear that. Did you get the report, Hendry?"

"Yes, no problem. I've already put the wheels in motion but the doctor here will probably send him back to his own country for the full treatment."

"Good."

"I don't think that we will see him again John, at least not working for Consolidated."

"Yes, I realise that, such a waste really."

"Yes, I agree."

"I've nominated Fred to replace Klaus, and he handles things well, so I'm happy for the moment."

"I'll officially inform the company then, and leave to it them, John."

"Right, then Hendry, that's it for now. Let me know if you're coming up at any time."

"It won't be for a while, John, as you know I have all this work to do, and you know what my desk is like?"

John's mind went back to the unruly mess of paperwork, and the hidden ringing telephone and he smiled to himself.

"Yes, I know how busy you are, Hendry. All right then, see you some time."

"Yes. 'Bye," and the line went noisy again.

John paid the clerk, and went back to the camp and the site. He met with Fred and discussed the next phase of the work and then called it a day. He went down to his residence, had his evening meal and sat out on the veranda in the now cooler air, gazing out over the valley below. Tomorrow is another day he mused and watched the bats flitting in and out of the trees in the shadows by the roadside.